OUR FA
INDIAN STORIES

KHUSHWANT SINGH
NEELAM KUMAR

JAICO PUBLISHING HOUSE
Ahmedabad Bangalore Bhopal Chennai
Delhi Hyderabad Kolkata Lucknow Mumbai

Published by Jaico Publishing House
A-2 Jash Chambers, 7-A Sir Phirozshah Mehta Road
Fort, Mumbai - 400 001
jaicopub@jaicobooks.com
www.jaicobooks.com

OUR FAVOURITE INDIAN STORIES
ISBN 81-7224-978-0

First Jaico Impression: 2002
Tenth Jaico Impression: 2010

Printed by
Kumar Offset Printers
381, F.I.E. Patparganj Ind. Area, Delhi-92.

Acknowledgements

An anthology of this range and sweep could not have taken shape without help from various sources. We are grateful to:

Sahitya Akademi, Delhi for the following stories: *The Bed of Arrows* — by Gopinath Mohanty (Oriya); *Death of an Indian* — by Kishori Charan Das (Oriya); *Enlightenment* by Yashpal (Hindi); *Cannibal* — by Vijai Dan Detha (Rajasthani); *The Wan Moon* — by Gangadhar Gadgil (Marathi); *The Vulture* — by Manoj Kumar Goswami (Assamese); *The Bride's Pyjamas* — by Akhtar Mohi-ud-din (Kashmiri); *Housewife* — by Ismat Chugtai (Urdu); *The Farm* — by Chaman Arora (Dogri); *The Dislodged Brick* — by Om Goswami (Dogri); *On the Boat* — by P. Padmaraju (Telugu).

- **Visva-Bharati University** for *Cabulliwallah* by Rabindra Nath Tagore
- **Ms Kamala Suraiya** for the Foreword
- **Mr R.K. Gharai of Sahitya Akademi, Kolkata** for his exemplary help which brought this project to fruition.
- **Ms Neerja Mattoo** for the Kashmiri stories
- **All India Urdu Progressive Writers' Association** for *Housewife* by Ismat Chugtai.
- **Individual authors and translators**
- **Friends,** who made this literary dream possible.

❑❑❑

Foreword

About three years ago the New Yorker commissioned Salman Rushdie to write a special piece on Indian Literature. It was a foolish gesture. It was like requesting one of the tourists thronging the beaches of India to write on Harappan civilization. The result was calamitous. He obviously was not familiar with any Indian language other than English and knew even less of the literature each produced. A literary analyst must know the sensibilities from which emanated the peerless fiction and poetry read and loved by the natives of the country through the centuries.

Indian fiction has robust roots. Myth and reality, like the warp and woof together, construct the rich tapestry of our literature. In translation each story suffers a colour change. A sea change, infact. A reconstructive mode of translation is required but the authors, in distrust, seldom permit anyone to take liberties with their writings for effecting minor alterations or tidying up the phrases, however shoddy or tardy the originals appear in a word to word translation. Poets are effective translators if given the freedom to delete the clumsy passages but they would rather write their own verses than translate. Perhaps the Sahitya Akademi of Delhi can try to lure them into the translation arena by offering liberal grants.

In my formative years I had the good fortune to live in Calcutta which was definitely the axis of the cultural world. Bankim,

Sarat Babu and Tagore influenced us, the young hopefuls. The Bengali touch, like old lace enriched the silk of our writings. Then there was the mammoth shadow of Kalidas falling on each of us, Kalidas whose classic Shakuntala cast a spell on Goethe whose Faust employed the narrator and the chorus before the beginning of the play.

Yes, it is with pride that I write today of Indian literatures that do not seem to wilt despite being ignored by the pundits of Anglo India.

Kamala Suraiya
August 12, 2001

❑❑❑

The Story Behind the Stories

This anthology is a virtual canvas of human emotions. Its pages throb with everything primal to human nature: fear, angst, joy, love, lust and longing. It is my conviction that the map of India — from Kashmir to Kanyakumari lies stamped across the length and breadth of the Indian heart. The emotions that vibrate within each of these stories prove this point. Within the pages of this anthology, the reader may catch a flickering gleam of that intangible quality which has surpassed the boundaries of region, time, space and history. The reader may also catch a fleeting glimpse of some of the majestic highs and dramatic lows that have shaped the Indian character over the centuries.

The inspiration behind this anthology has been the concern that some of the best short stories of India have remained imprisoned within their geographic and linguistic boundaries, flowering and withering away unnoticed. In the absence of translation they have been deprived from reaching a wider audience. What a waste of beautiful thoughts and ideas! How can one talk of understanding India or being Indian without understanding the motivations that drive our countrymen and women spread over distant regions of the country? Can one truly understand the whole without understanding the part?

In my bid to redress part of this problem, over a period of five years, I visited various National Libraries, Sahitya Akademis and bookstores across the country to come up with literary gems. During the course of my search I wrote countless letters, met and interacted with dozens of writers and translators — seeking advice, getting acquainted, pursuing addresses, requesting copyright permissions. The sheer magnificence of my discoveries left me humbled.

I have been fortunate to have shared a special relationship with Mr Khushwant Singh. It all began in the Spring of 1996 when I was asked to introduce him in Jamshedpur at a Rotary District Conference. At first I was hesitant about undertaking such a daunting task. Then, I decided to make use of the opportunity in full measure by telling Mr Singh a few home truths publicly — particularly about women's reaction to his outrageous descriptions of members of their species. There was much laughter from the audience when I described him as a one-man institution pounder as well as a one-man shock therapist. I also described him as a man who had swept through Indian society like a powerful blizzard, bent on changing hypocritical attitudes, taking taboo topics out of Indian closets, giving them a through dusting and painstakingly polishing them up for public viewing. By the end of my speech, I suspected I had overdone the malice bit a little. I waited with bated breath as he walked up to where I was standing on stage. I quite expected him to show his displeasure by reprimanding me. Instead, to my horror, he kissed me on the cheek publicly! I was more embarrassed when the local Press covered the incident in a colourful manner the next morning.

Later, in his popular column, *With Malice Towards One and All* he described me as the fourth Neelam in his life and the act as a gesture of warmth to show his appreciation. He praised my poem *Separation,* which I had written after the death of my husband. My poem was read across the length and breadth of the country. Long lost school friends who responded to my anguished cry of *'With your going away, they have taken the bangles from my arms...'* sought me out. The sheer reach of his column overwhelmed me.

From then on, a warm friendship flowered between us. Mr Singh has been described as stingy, lecherous, malicious, flirtatious. Those who know him closely as I do, have stumbled on to the fact that he is none of these. In fact it is he who has revelled in feeding the gossip mills about this image of himself as *'Not A Nice Man To Know.'* At 80 plus, he is without doubt, India's youngest man and has a fun-filled attitude towards life, which keeps him so. I remember how much he laughed his famous belly laugh when I wrote an article in *The Times of India* about how this tough man has no qualms about taking up cudgels with religious fanatics and pompous politicians but turns into a lamb the moment his wife commands him to follow his strict bed-time hour — 9.p.m.! He is actually as fun loving as a child and hides a soft heart beneath the tough exterior.

This is how I came to requesting my very special friend, savant and confidante, Mr Khushwant Singh to utilise the six decades of his rich experience in literature to select his favourite short stories. That proved to be a very difficult task. What lifts a story from the level of ordinary to extraordinary, to finally become engraved in the mind as a *favourite*? Sometimes it is a childhood association or a fond memory of youth. Many times one just does not know why, but one simply likes a particular story.

The Urdu and Punjabi sections did not prove to be difficult. Mr Khushwant Singh is an authority in these fields. He has been generous enough to include his own translations in this anthology. Making selections from other regional languages — those neither he nor I can read or write, proved to be an intimidating task. We went by the opinions of experts and literature lovers of that particular language.

We are certain the reader will keep in mind that comparing fairly unknown writers to all-time greats such as Munshi Premchand or Gurudev Rabindranath Tagore may not be fair. As is bound to happen, many ideas may have been lost in the translation, despite our best attempts. We appeal to the reader to look beyond these into the story's essence. In some regions, short story writing is still a fledgling craft. We were compelled to include these as being representative of the language. The craft itself merited no special attention; the spark of promise in it did. Such stories have been included in the hope that they will provide a window to the distinctive culture of that region. This is why many stories have a 'regional flavour' about them.

With an ancient history of 5,000 years, India has been the cradle of fascinating folklore, mythical tales and magical fables. Ancient writings of the land: the Upanishads, Panchatantra, Hitopdesh and Jataka tales bear testimony to this. Over the years, India's rich oral tradition has gradually crystallised into the formal short story as we know it today.

The passage of centuries has seen India develop into a social structure with fascinating customs. The Indian consciousness down the decades has recorded all: the wonder, the anguish, the joy, the frustration, the pain and the pride of being born an Indian. Right through the grand sweep of time, the Indian imagination has remained alive to diverse stimuli and has expressed these emotions in creative outpourings. Besides national and geographic influences, each region's writings have been shaped by local influences too. Today's global Indian has aromas of all these flavours in his personality.

From Kashmir to Kanyakumari, writers have spoken in myriad tongues which are as local as they are national — as insular as they are global. This is what makes India's regional writing so powerful.

Ms. Neelam Kumar
August, 2001

❑❑❑

CONTENTS

Dogri

Konkani

English

❑❑❑

Our Writers

Hindi

PREMCHAND

Premchand (1880-1936) was the greatest novelist and short story writer in Hindi. He was the author of *Sahitya ka Uddeshya* (criticism); *Kuchh Vichar* (essays); *Rangabhumi, Sevasadan, Nirmala, Kayakalpa, Premashram, Ghaban* and *Godan* (novels) as well as several collections of short stories.

YASHPAL

Yashpal (1903-1976) was a prominent writer in Hindi. Has published fourteen collections of short stories, nine novels, three volumes of reminiscences and four volumes of socio-political satirical essays. His works have been translated into many languages.

NIRMAL VERMA

Nirmal Verma (1929—) was born in Simla and lives in Delhi. From 1959 to 1968, he lived in Czechoslovakia where he translated a number of Czech works into Hindi. For a brief while he was a member of the Communist Party of India, but resigned in protest against its support for dictatorships. He has so far published five novels, eight collections of short stories, three travelogues, six collections of essays and three plays. Many of his works have been translated into English, German and French. His awards include *Sahitya Akademi* (1985*); Moortidevi Award* (1997) and the *Jnanpith Award* (2000).

RAJENDRA AWASTHI

A prominent political journalist, poet, author and fiction writer, Dr. Rajendra Awasthi has pioneered new trends in post-independence Hindi fiction writing. He has more than 60 fictional works to his credit and has received numerous awards including the *National Citizens' Award* (1990); the *Sahitya Bhushan and Bharat Bhasha Bhushan* Awards.

He first joined The Times of India group publication — *Sarika* as its editor (1960-64); left Bombay for Delhi and joined the Hindustan Times Group in 1964, continuing as editor of all periodicals. He is currently editor of *Kadambini.* He holds positions in several prestigious bodies.

USHA MAHAJAN

Usha Mahajan (1948—) represents the New Short story style in Hindi. A prolific writer, she is also a freelance journalist. Important among her works are *Savitri Ne Kaha* (story collection); *Samay Ke Sakshi* (interviews with journalists); *Chatur Charvaha* (childrens' stories); *Utho Annapurna Saath Chalen* (research) as well as translations of several books by Khushwant Singh.

Bengali

RABINDRA NATH TAGORE

A master of the short story *genre,* Tagore was Bengal's leading writer and poet. He continues to hold sway over readers' hearts even after so many years of his death. Tagore's writings have a firm narrative thread and delight young and old alike. In all his writings, Tagore had a remarkable capacity to empathise with people in different situations. His writings reflect a great deal of psychological and creative insight.

MAHASWETA DEVI

Mahasweta Devi (1926 —) is a progressive Bengali novelist and short story writer. She is the author of over 50 publications and has won several awards including the *Sahitya Akademi Award* in 1979 for her novel *Aranyer Adhikar.* She has taught English in a Calcutta College and works among the tribals for their welfare and for creating new social awareness among them. She now lives in Calcutta. There is a deep influence of the Naxalite movement on her works. She has also been the recipient of *Jnanpath Literary Award* and the *Magsaysay Award.* Her book has been made into a Hindi movie called *Hazaar Chaurasi ki Ma.*

Urdu

SAADAT HASAN MANTO

Manto (1912-1955) is widely regarded as one of the best Urdu writers. In a literary and journalistic career spanning more than two decades, he wrote over 200 stories apart from plays, film scripts, novels and essays. *Toba Tek Singh Mozail* and *Mummy* are some of his powerful stories. He lived in Amritsar, Bombay and Lahore.

ISMAT CHUGTAI

Ismat Chugtai was a leading short story writer in Urdu. Known for her bold writing, Ismat Chugtai is regarded as a gifted woman writer. Her collections of short stories include: *Chotein, Chhui Mui, Kaliyan Shaitan.* She has also written novels like *Ziddi.*

Punjabi

AJEET COUR

Born in 1934, Ajeet Cour is one of the better known Punjabi writers. Some of her important collections of short stories are *Gulbano, Mahik Di Maut, But Shikan, Saviyan* and *Churiyan.* And among her novelletes are *Postmortem, Dhup Wala Sheher, Khana Badosh* and *Kachche Ranga de Sheher.* She is the recipient of *Punjabi Academy Award* (1984) and *Sahitya Akademi Award* (1986) for *Khana Badosh.*

KHWAJA AHMED ABBAS

Khwaja Ahmed Abbas (1914-1989) was a journalist, novelist and film producer-director of international repute. A writer with leftist leanings, Abbas published over 40 books in Urdu including *Diya Jale Sari Raat* (novel), *Main Kaun Hun, Ek Ladki* and *Zafran Ke Phul* —all collections of short stories. His other important works include *When Night Falls, Face to Face with Khrushchev,* a 2-part biography of Mrs Indira Gandhi — *Indira Gandhi: Return of the Red Rose* and its sequel *That Woman.*

Oriya

GOPINATH MOHANTY

Gopinath Mohanty was a celebrated Oriyạ novelist and short story writer. He received the *Jnanpith Award* in 1964 for his novel *Matir Matala.* He lived mostly in Koraput district, the tribal area of Orissa. His novels bear testimony to his knowledge of tribal life.

KISHORI CHARAN DAS

Born in 1924, Kishori Charan Das is a renowned short story writer in Oriya and English. His *Thakur Ghara* received the Sahitya Akademi Award in 1976. A former employee of the Indian Audit and Accounts Service, he has travelled extensively on various foreign assignments, the experience of which enriches his stories. A prolific writer, Kishori Charan Das has authored several collections of short stories, novels, essays, poems, abridgements and translations. He represented India at the International Writers' Week at Adelaide in February 1980 and later, toured Australia under the Indo-Australian Cultural Exchange programme.

Gujarati

DINKAR JOSHI

Born in 1937 at Bhavnagar in Gujarat, Dinkar Joshi is a prominent Gujarati novelist, short story writer, essayist and columnist. He is a scholar on the Hindu epics — the *Mahabharat* and the *Ramayan*. His novel *Prakash-no-Padcchayo*, based on Gandhiji's family life has been adapted into a play in different languages including English. His works have been translated into Hindi, Marathi, Telugu, Malayalam and Tamil. Five *State Sahitya Akademi Awards* have been conferred upon him.

KUNDANIKA KAPADIA

A popular Gujarati writer, Kundanika Kapadia was born in Saurashtra, worked as a free lance writer, edited magazines and, quitting Mumbai (where she lived most of her life) in 1987 has now shifted to a small village in South Gujarat where she and her husband poet Makarand Dave have established a Centre named Nandigram Trust, dedicated to spiritual development and service to Adivasi people living around the Centre. Ms Kapadia has written three novels, short story collections and books, including translations from English and Bengali. One of her novels, *Saat Paglaan Aakashma* won five awards, including one from *Sahitya Akademi*, Delhi. This novel, translated into many Indian languages, has the English title *Seven Steps in the Sky*. She has also won other awards from literary bodies.

Rajasthani

VIJAI DAN DETHAA

Vijai Dan Dethaa was born in 1926. He is popularly known among his readers as 'Vijji'. He is a well known Rajasthani writer and recipient of the *Sahitya Akademi Award*. He has also published several works in Hindi. He is currently associated with the Rupayan Sansthan, Borunda.

Sindhi

GOBIND PANJABI

Panjabi was a leading Sindhi writer. He belonged to the Progressive school of writers. His writings depict the painful experience of being uprooted from one's homeland and related problems. Along with his contemporaries, Panjabi took up the cause of Sindhi language and literature. He wrote feelingly about the life of the common man and gave expression to his sorrows. Writing prolifically after the Partition, Gobind Panjabi was one of the pioneer publishers of a literary magazine of the early forties — *Nai Duniya*.

NARAIN BHARATI

A prominent Sindhi writer, Dr Bharati wrote in the post-independence years between 1947 and 1948. His collection of short stories is titled *Zindagi-a-jo-Babu* (A Chapter of Life). He has done pioneering work in the area of preserving Sindhi folk literature. He has painstakingly recorded customs, traditions, myths, legends, lullabies, wedding songs etc. of an ancient and rich culture which has a vast variety of folk literature. He has done so in a series of eight volumes which include *Sindhi Lok Kala* (Sindhi Folk Art); *Sindhi Lok Kahaniyan* (Sindhi Folk Stories) and *Sindhuri thi Gave* (Sind is Singing).

Marathi

GANGADHAR GADGIL

Born in 1923, this Marathi short story writer, novelist, playwright and critic has more than fifty literary works to his credit. Gangadhar Gadgil has been thrice awarded State Awards for his books *Talavatale Chandane, Ore Unha,* and *Sat Samundra Palikade.*

GAURI DESHPANDE

Born in 1942, Gauri Deshpande has emerged as a popular writer in Marathi. She has written 16 novels, several collections of short stories and essays in Marathi. She has also published collections of her poems and short stories in English, besides six volumes of translations from Marathi into English. Sixteen State Prizes in various categories have been bestowed on her. Her translation of sixteen volumes of Sir Richard Burton's *Arabian Nights* is considered a landmark event in Marathi publishing history. Her work has been translated into all major languages, including German and Norwegian.

Assamese

MANOJ KUMAR GOSWAMI

Born in 1962 at Nagaon, Assam, Manoj Kumar Goswami has published seven collections of short stories, one novel and a travelogue. He has worked in two dailies, *Natun Dainik* and *Ajir Batori* and is currently the Executive Editor of *Amar Asom.* In 1994, he was awarded the *Katha* prize for his short story *Samiran Barua Ähi Ache* and the *Sanskriti Award* in 1996. He is also active in the electronic media.

Kashmiri

AKHTAR MOHI-UD-DIN

Akhtar Mohi-ud-din (1928—2001) was a distinguished Kashmiri author. He made a significant contribution to the enrichment of modern Kashmiri literature. His volume of short stories, *Sat Sangar* received the *Sahitya Akademi Award* in 1958. He is the author of *Dod Dag* which is considered the first novel written and published in Kashmiri.

ABDUL GANI BEG ATHAR

Abdul Gani Athar (1943-....) is a teacher in the Jammu and Kashmir Education Department. He has written poems, short stories and plays in Kashmiri. A collection of his short stories in Kashmiri was published some time back. His work has also appeared in *Sheeraza* (Jammu and Kashmir Academy of Art, Culture and Languages).

Malayalam

KAMALA SURAIYA

Born in Malabar in 1934, Madhavi Kutti assumed her pen name Kamala Das which brought her fame. Her English poems and Malayalam stories became famous the world over. Kamala Das has been honoured with prestigious awards. Her mother is an acknowledged poet. While non-Malayalis know her as a writer of fiction, she is better known in Kerala as a poet.

THAKAZHI SIVASANKARAN PILLAI

Thakazhi Sivasankaran Pillai is the doyen of Malayalam writers. He has received a dozen literary awards and honorary doctorates. Some of these are: *Kerala Sahitya Akademi Award; Central Sahitya Akademi Award; Vayalar Award; Soviet Land Award; Jnanpith Award; Padma Bhushan* and an honorary doctorate conferred upon him by Kerala University. His stories are more the work of an artist rather than a medium for conveying messages.

Kannada

CHADURANGA

Chaduranga, a scion of the royal family has authored such outstanding novels as *Vaisaka, Sarvamangala* and *Uyyala. Savatha Mana* is among his prominent short stories. His novel *Vaisaka* won him the *Sahitya Akademi Award.* He is regarded as one of the forerunners of the *Pragatishila* movement, considered the embodiment of progressive thinking in the Fifties.

DEVANOOR MAHADEVA

Devanoor Mahadeva is a prominent writer of Kannada. His real name is Subramanya Raja Urs. His writing career began in the

Navya phase. He has been described as a modern, universal writer. Despite his progressive thinking, he differs from the writers of the *Pragatishila* phase as he does not raise loud slogans. His collection of short stories titled *Dayavanooru* is considered a milestone in Kannada literature. His novellete *Kusumabale* won him the *Sahitya Akademi Award*.

Telugu

P. PADMARAJU

P. Padmaraju (1915-1983) was a distinguished short story writer and dramatist in Telugu. His short story *The Cyclone* was awarded second prize in the World Competition conducted by the *New York Herald Tribune* in 1952. Two of his important works are *Padmaraju Kathalu* and *Kooli Janam.*

MALATI CHENDUR

Malati Chendur has over forty-five years of writing experience behind her. She is one of the leading names in progressive Telugu writing. Her dimunitive frame houses a forceful personality. She uses this to the maximum effect to speak up against the current degradation in society. Among the many honours she has won are *Bharatiya Bhasha Parishad Award* and *Central Sahitya Akademi Award.*

Tamil

INDIRA PARTHASARTHY

Born in 1930 in the town of Kumbakonam, Ranganathan *nee* Indira Parthasarathy obtained his M.A. degree from Annamalai University and Ph.D from Delhi University.

Dr Parthasarathy has worked as a teacher and researcher in Delhi, Poland and Canada. He has been commended by Warsaw University for his contribution to the field of Dravidian research.

Indira Parthasarthy has won laurels in various forms of literature such as the novel, short story and drama. Prominent among the awards he has won are *Central Sahitya Akademi Award; Tamil Nadu Government Award*; and *Kasturi Srinivasan Award.*

PRAPANCHAN

Prapanchan was born and brought up in Pondicherry. Vaidyalingam, as he was earlier called, went to Karandai College where he won the title 'Pulavar' or Pandit. He spent his early years in a French Colony. Yet, rather than being deeply affected by French literature, he was affected by 'Surya Mariyathai Iyakkam', the Self Respect Movement against Brahmin domination.

He has worked as a teacher of Tamil, journalist and sub-editor. His writings have been appreciated for their richness and quality and have been translated into English, French, Swedish and German, besides into various Indian languages. He has won several coveted awards which include *Central Sahitya Akademi Award; Bharatiya Bhasha Parishad Award; Kasturi Rangammal Award* and the prestigious *Illakkiya Chinthanai Award.*

Dogri

CHAMAN ARORA

Born in 1945, Chaman Arora is one of the most promising Dogri short story writers today. He has published two collections of short stories *Lohe Diyan Phingran* and *Kandhan Te Qile* and has contributed to an anthology of short stories by upcoming short story writers titled *Sach Te Sach.* He has also co-authored a play with Lalit Mangotra titled *Jeene Di Qaid.*

OM GOSWAMI

Born in 1948, Om Goswami is one of the most distinguished and popular Dogri short story writers. He also writes in Hindi. He has to his credit four collections of short stories in Dogri and three in Hindi. Arora has been awarded by the Sahitya Akademi for his Dogri collection *Sunne Di Chidi.* Until recently, he was the editor of Dogri publications of J & K Academy of Art, Culture and Languages. He has also contributed to children's literature, published a collection of plays and is currently editor of a quarterly children's magazine and chief editor of the Dogri Dictionary Project.

Konkani

CHANDRAKANT KENI

Editor of the Marathi Daily *Rashtramat* since its inception in 1963, Chandrakant Keni (born in 1934) writes short stories in Konkani, Marathi and Hindi. The first editor of *Sunaparant,* the first ever Konkani daily and Chairman of the Goa Editors' Guild, Keni has also been the recipient of the *National Award for Journalism* (1995). Notable among the honours received by him have been the *Sahitya Akademi Award* (1989); *Dr. TMA Pai Foundation Literary Award* (1990); *Goa State Literary Awards* on three occasions and the *Goa State Cultural Award* (1997). A champion of the Konkani language, Chandrakant Keni has been closely associated with the freedom struggle of the territory from Portuguese colonialism.

EDWIN JOSEPH FRANCIS D'SOUZA

Edwin D'Souza has written 27 novels and more than one hundred short stories to date. He has conducted several Konkani literary camps, seminars and panel discussions. He has also presented several papers on Konkani literature at prestigious forums. Some of his noteworthy literary awards have been from: *Konkani Bhasha Mandal* (1973,1993); *Karnataka Konkani Sahitya Akademi* (1995-1997; 1997-1998); *Dr. TMA Pai Foundation, Manipal* (1992) and *Konkani Literature Award* (1998). He has been President of the 11th All India Konkani Sahitya Sammelan and Konkani Writers' Forum, Karnataka. Editor of *Amar Konkani*, D'Souza is currently faculty at the Institute of Konkani, St Aloysius College, Mangalore.

English

KHUSHWANT SINGH

Khushwant Singh was born in Hadali, Punjab. He was educated at Government College, Lahore and at King's College and the Inner Temple in London. He practised at the Lahore High Court for several years before joining the Indian Ministry of External Affairs in 1947. He began a distinguished career as a journalist with All India Radio in 1951. Since then he has been founder editor of *Yojna* (1951-1953), editor of the *Illustrated Weekly of India* (1979-1980), chief editor of *New Delhi* (1979-1980), and editor of the *Hindustan Times* (1980-1983). Today he is India's best-known columnist and journalist.

Khushwant Singh has had an extremely successful career as a writer. Among his works are the award winning *Train to Pakistan, Delhi, Religion of the Sikhs, Guru Gobind Singh – the Saviour, My Bleeding Punjab, Punjab's Tragic Story, Need for a New Religion in India and other essays, Indira Gandhi Returns, and A History of the Sikhs, vol. I and vol. II*. Khushwant Singh has written more than 72 books till date. His latest novel, *The Company of Women* was published in 1999, and his autobiography, *Truth, Love and a Little Malice* is now in the news.

Khushwant Singh was Member of Parliament from 1980 to 1986. Among other honours he was awarded the *Padma Bhushan* in 1974 by the President of India (he returned the decoration in 1984 in protest against the Union Government's siege of the Golden Temple, Amritsar).

MULK RAJ ANAND

Mulk Raj Anand (1905—) is one of the most distinguished and front-ranking Indo-Anglican writers. Educated at Punjab and London Universities, he held the Tagore Chair in the Department of Comparitive Literature at the Punjab University, Chandigarh. He was Chairman of the Lalit Kala Academy and edited *Marg*, a reputed arts quarterly for quite some time. *Untouchable, Coolie* (both novels), *Death of a Hero* (novel), *Private Life of an Indian Prince, Seven Summers* (novel), *Lament on the Death of Master of Arts, Persian Painting* (essays) and *The Story of India* are some of his famous works.

ATUL CHANDRA

A journalist by profession, Atul Chandra (1953——) started his career in 1976. A promising short story writer, Chandra holds a Masters degree in Economics. He has worked with *National Herald, The Pioneer* and *Hindustan Times*. Currently he is Deputy Resident Editor of *The Times of India*, Lucknow.

SHOY LALL

Shaildharee Lall (1926-1975) was born in Bhagalpur and educated in Doon School. He started writing in the early 50s. He was a Farming Correspondent for *The Statesman*. Having been cured of TB in Switzerland, he returned to India and devoted his time to writing and building the house at Tikratoli — an architectural delight he writes so fondly about. The house is still as breathtakingly lovely, if not lovelier today. His wife Nilika who still lives there has ensured that.

NEELAM KUMAR

Neelam Kumar's early childhood was spent in the erstwhile USSR where her parents, Mr O.N. Panchalar and Mrs Urmila Panchalar were posted. When they joined H.E.C. Ranchi and later, Bokaro Steel Plant, Neelam moved to India.

After completing her schooling from St. Xavier's School, Bokaro Steel City, she obtained an English Hons. degree followed by a Bachelor of Education and post graduation in Public Relations & Advertising. She then won a scholarship which took her to the United States. She obtained her Masters degree in Journalism from the University of Arizona, Tucson, USA. Her thesis, *The American Perception of India as Reflected in the Top 5 US Newspapers* won accolades.

In 1982, she joined Steel Authority of India Ltd. at Bokaro Steel Plant as the Editor of the house magazine. She is currently Chief of Communications at SAIL's R&D Centre (RDCIS) at Ranchi.

❑❑❑

HINDI

The Resignation

Premchand

An office Clerk is a dumb creature. Glare at a labourer and he will glower back at you. Speak rudely to a Coolie and he will throw the load off his head and walk away. Reprimand a beggar and he will stare angrily at you and turn away. Even a donkey, if mistreated, will kick back. But the poor Clerk! Scold him, abuse him, kick him and he will not so much as frown. He has more control over himself than a saint. He is the picture of contentment, tolerance and obedience, the epitome of the noblest of human qualities.

Even ruins have their better days of glory. On the night of Diwali, they are lighted up. During monsoons, they have green moss on them. They reflect the changing moods of Nature. The poor Clerk never changes. His pale face never lights up with a smile. The rains do not bring relief to his dry as dust existence.

Lala Fatehchand was one such clerk. It is said that a man's name affects his fortunes. This was proved wrong in the case of Lala Fatehchand. His name meant *Winner.* But it would not be an exaggeration to call him Haarchand (*Loser*). A failure in office, a failure among friends, he had faced only setbacks and disappointments.

Fatehchand had no sons; only three daughters. He had no brothers, only two sisters-in-law. He had very little money but a heart full of gold. He was kindness and tolerance personified. Cheated by many, he had not one true friend with whom he could share confidences. He was in poor health. At the age of thirty-two, he had salt and pepper hair. His eyesight was poor; so was his digestion. His complexion was pale, his cheeks sunken. His back was bent and heart empty of courage. He would go to office at nine and return home at six. He did not have the heart to go out in the evening. He had no knowledge of what was happening in the outside world. His entire life revolved around his office. He constantly worried about losing his job. He was concerned neither with religion, not with the poor. He had no interest in arts, literature, stage, the cinema or in sports. He could not remember when he had last played cards.

2.

It was winter. There were a few clouds in the sky. When Fatehchand returned home from work, lights had already come on. He never spoke to anyone after office hours. He would simply lie down and remain silent for fifteen-twenty minutes before he opened his mouth. Only then would he speak. That evening he was lying down quietly as usual when somebody called out to him. When his youngest daughter went out to inquire who it was, she learnt that it was the office Messenger. Sharda was scrubbing utensils to prepare the evening meal.

She said — 'Ask him what he wants. He has just come home from office. Is he needed there again?'

The Messenger said — 'Saheb has asked him to come over immediately. There is some urgent work.'

Fatehchand broke his silence. He raised his head and asked — 'What is it?'

'Nothing,' replied Sharda. 'Only the office peon.'

Fatehchand— 'The office peon! Has Saheb called for me?'

'That's what he says. What kind of Saheb do you have? He's always sending for you. You have just come home. Why does he want you to see him again? Tell him you won't go. Can he do anything worse than take your job away?'

Fatehchand said — 'Let me find out why he wants to see me. I had cleared my desk before I left. I'll be back soon.'

Sharda — 'Please have something to eat before you go. Once you start talking with the peon, you will forget everything.'

She brought out some snacks. Fatehchand looked at the plate and asked— 'Have you given the girls something to eat?'

'Yes, yes,' replied Sharda impatiently. 'You eat!'

Just then his youngest daughter came up. Sharda looked at her and said angrily— 'Why are you standing on my head? Go outside and play!'

'Why do you scold her?' asked Fatehchand. 'Come here Chunni, take some snacks.'

Chunni looked at her mother in fear and ran out.

Fatehchand protested— 'Why have you made the poor thing run away?'

Sharda shot back— 'How much is there in this plate? If you had given it to her, wouldn't the other two girls have wanted their share?'

Meanwhile, the peon shouted from outside — 'I am getting late.'

Sharda — 'Why don't you tell him that you will not go at this hour?'

'How can I? My job is at stake,' replied Fatehchand.

'Does that mean that you will give your life for your job? Have you seen your face in a mirror? You look as if you have been ill for six months.'

Fatehchand tossed a few bits into his mouth, gulped down a glass of water and ran out. The *paan*, which Sharda was making for him, remained uneaten.

The peon said — '*Babu Jee!* You've taken a long time. Come along quickly now or he will rebuke you soundly.'

Fatehchand replied — 'Whether he scolds me or shouts at me, I can walk only as fast as I can. He's in his bungalow, isn't he?'

'Why should he be at the office at this hour? He is an Emperor, not a nobody!'

The peon was used to walking fast. Babu Fatehchand was not. After some time he started panting. He kept on lifting his feet one after another until his thighs started paining. Then, his legs refused to cooperate. He was bathed in sweat and his head started reeling. Butterflies seemed to fly before his eyes.

The peon shouted — 'Keep walking, Babu!'

Fatehchand replied— 'You go ahead. I'll follow.'

He sat down on the kerb with his head between his hands and tried to catch his breath. The peon went ahead.

Fatehchand became frightened. What if the devil went and told the Saheb something?

He pulled himself up and started walking again. He managed to reach the Saheb's bungalow. Saheb was pacing up and down in his verandah.

On catching sight of the peon he shouted — 'What took you so long?'

The peon replied — '*Huzoor!* What could I do? The Babu was taking his time. I've come running all the way.'

'What did Babu say?'

In the meantime, Fatehchand ducked under the boundary wire, saluted to the Saheb and stood before him with his head bent low.

'Where were you all this time?' demanded the Saheb angrily.

'Sir, I returned from office only just now. I set off as soon as the peon called out to me.'

'You are lying. I've been standing here for an hour,' said the Saheb.

'Sir, I do not lie. I can't walk very fast. I left my house as soon as the peon called me.'

'Shut up, you swine! I have been waiting for an hour. Catch your ears!' roared the Saheb.

'*Huzoor*, I have worked for you for ten years. I have never...'

'Shut up! I order you to hold your ears!'

'But what have I done?'

'*Chaprasi*! Hold this swine's ears or I'll flog you as well.'

'Sir, I have come here to work, not to get beaten up. I am a respectable person. You can keep your job, Sir! I am willing to take any punishment you mete out to me, but I cannot attack another's honour.'

The Saheb could not control his anger any further. He ran to get his walking stick. Seeing the Saheb's mood, the peon quietly slipped away. Fatehchand remained standing. Not finding the peon there, the Saheb caught Fatehchand by the ears and shook him.

'How dare you disobey me? Go to the office at once and fetch the file.'

Fatehchand asked humbly 'Sir, which file should I bring?'

'File-File what else? Are you deaf? Can't you hear? I'm asking for the file.'

Summoning up courage, Fatehchand spoke up — 'Which file do you require?'

'The file I am asking for. Bring the same file. Bring it at once!'

Fatehchand did not have the courage to ask anything more. The Saheb was very short-tempered. He was also drunk. If he hit him with his cane he would not be able to do anything. He quietly left for the office.

'Go fast-Run!' Saheb shouted.

'Sir, I am unable to run.'

'Oh, you have become very lazy. I shall teach you how to run.' The Saheb gave him a violent push. 'Run! You will not run even now?'

The Saheb went off to fetch his cane. Fatehchand realised he was in for a beating. But under these circumstances, his fate was only to get beaten up. He scuttled away and quickly came out of the gate on to the road.

3.

Fatehchand did not go to office the next day. What could he have gone for? Saheb had not even told him the name of the file he wanted. Perhaps he had forgotten it in his drunken state. He set off to his house with slow steps—as if the insult had put chains on his feet. Agreed, when compared to Saheb he was weaker physically. Besides, he had nothing in his hands then with which he could have defended himself. But he could have answered back! After all, he did have shoes on his feet. Could he not have flung them at him? Perhaps he would have been awarded simple imprisonment for one or two months. Perhaps he would have had to pay a fine of two to four hundred rupees. But his family would have been ruined. Who in the whole world would look after his wife and children? If he had enough money to look after his family he would not have tolerated such an insult.

Fatehchand rued his physical weakness as never before. Had he paid attention to his health, had he been exercising, had he known how to wield a stick, the devil would not have dared to pull his ears. He would have kicked him back. He should have at least carried a knife. He could have slapped him a few times. He should have worried about jail and other complications later.

The more he went ahead, the more he fumed at his own cowardice. What worse could have happened to him if he had slapped the Saheb? Perhaps Saheb's cooks and bearers would have jumped on him and given him a beating. At least it would have been clear to Saheb that he could not insult an innocent man without reason. After all, if he was to die today, there would be no one to look after his children. If he died tomorrow, they would face the same fate, so why not today?

The thought filled his heart with fervour. He retraced his steps, determined to avenge his humiliation. At the same time he thought—after all, whatever had to happen had happened. Who knew if Saheb was still in the bungalow or had left for the Club? At that moment, he felt overcome with the thought of Sharda's helplessness. The image of his children becoming fatherless deterred him. He turned back and headed for home.

4.

As soon as he got home, Sharda asked — 'Why had he called you? Why did you talk so long?'

Fatehchand lay down on his charpoy and replied — 'He was drunk. The devil abused me and insulted me. He kept on repeatedly asking me why I had taken so long? The rascal ordered the peon to catch hold of my ears.'

Sharda spoke angrily — 'Why did you not give the swine a shoe-beating?'

'The peon was very decent. He spoke out— Sir, I cannot do this. I have not taken up the job to insult good people. He saluted him and walked away.'

'That was very brave of him. Why did you not take the Saheb to task?'

'Of course I did,' replied Fatehchand. 'He got his stick — I took off my shoes. He hit me with his stick. I hit back with my shoes.'

'Well done! You put him in his place.'

'He was stunned.'

'You did well. You should have given him a sound thrashing. If I had been in your place, I would have killed him.'

'I beat him; now I will have to pay the price. Let's see what happens. My job, ofcourse, will go. Perhaps I'll have to go to prison too.'

'Why should you go to prison? Is there no justice? Why did he abuse you? Why did he beat you with a stick?'

'Who will listen to me when he speaks? Even the court will side with him.'

'Let it happen. But you'll see. You'll see, after this, no Saheb will dare to abuse any Clerk. You should have hit him the moment he opened his mouth.'

'He would have certainly shot me dead.'

'We would have taken care of that.'

'How? What would have become of all of you?'

'Whatever God would have willed. Honour is man's greatest possession. It is stupid to raise your family at the cost of self-respect. At least you have come back after beating up that devil. I am proud of you. Had you come back after being beaten, I would have hated the sight of your face. Even if I did not put it in words, my respect for you would have gone. Now, whatever befalls us I shall accept gladly. Hey, where are you going? Listen, listen. Where are you off to?'

As if possessed, Fatehchand walked out of the house. Sharda kept calling out to him. He hastened towards the Saheb's bungalow— not cowering in fear, but proudly holding his head high. His face reflected firm resolve, his legs were no longer weak. His appearance had undergone a dramatic change. In place of a humble, pale office Clerk with an emaciated body, he had become a young man with courage and determination. Fatehchand first went to a friend's house to borrow a stick. Then, he headed for the Saheb's bungalow.

5.

It was nine p.m. Saheb was having his dinner. Fatehchand did not wait for him to finish. As soon as the bearer left the room, Fatehchand slipped in through the wooden partition. The house was a-glitter with lights. On the floor was a carpet, the like of which Fatehchand had never seen.

The Saheb looked up angrily and shouted, 'How did you get in? Get out at once!'

'You asked me to get the file. That's what I've brought. Finish your dinner, then I'll show it to you. Take your time eating. This could be your last meal, so eat well.'

The Saheb was struck dumb. There was fear in his eyes. He trembled. He realised that the clerk had come prepared to kill or be killed.

It was a new Fatehchand he had to deal with. He weighed the pros and cons of taking on his clerk, 'I understand. You are angry. Have I said anything to upset you?'

Fatehchand drew himself up and replied— 'Just half an hour back you had taken me by my ears and had abused me soundly. Have you already forgotten?'

'I caught you by your ears? Ha-ha-ha-ha! What sort of a joke is this? Am I mad?'

'Am I lying? The peon was a witness. Your servants were also watching.'

'When did it happen?'

'Just half an hour back. You had sent for me and when I came you caught my ears without any reason and hit me.'

'*Babu Jee,* I was a little high. The bearer had given me too much to drink. I don't remember what happened.'

'If in your drunken state you had shot me, I would have died. Is everything excusable when you are drunk? I too am drunk now. Listen to my decision. Hold your ears and promise that hereafter you will never behave badly with any innocent person. If you don't, I shall box your ears! Do you understand? Don't move! If you so much as get up from your chair I'll use my stick. Don't blame me if your skull breaks. Just do as I say. Hold your ears!'

Saheb pretended to laugh it off, 'Well, *Babu Jee,* you do know how to take a joke. If I said anything wrong, I apologise.'

'Not good enough. Just hold your ears,' ordered Fatehchand, twirling his stick as he spoke.

Saheb could not take more. He jumped up, hoping to snatch the stick from Fatehchand's hands. But Fatehchand was alert. The moment Saheb got up from the table, he dealt a solid blow on his head. The Saheb staggered. He held his head in his hands and said — 'I shall sack you.'

'I don't give a damn. I will not leave without making you hold your ears and promise never again to treat a good man so nastily.'

Fatehchand lifted his stick again. The Saheb feared that the second blow might crack open his skull. Placing his hand on his ears he said — 'Are you happy now?'

'Say that you will never abuse anyone again.'

'Never again, I promise.'

'Alright. I shall leave now. I'm resigning from today. In my resignation letter I shall state that I resigned because you called me names.'

'Why are you resigning? I am not dismissing you.'

'I will not work under a wicked man like you.'

Fatehchand came out of the Saheb's bungalow and walked towards his home in a leisurely manner. He had tasted the pleasure of true victory. He had never felt happier. This was the first triumph of his life.

Translated by **Ms. Neelam Kumar**

Enlightenment

Yashpal

Sage Deerghalom had kept himself away from temptations of earthly bonds. Only once, just for a brief period, had he been drawn into family life and it was then that his wife had given birth to a daughter.

Self-enlightenment had followed and he had then taken up residence in a hermitage on the banks of the river Narmada. For him, salvation lay in self-denial. His wife and daughter lived in a hut nearby. Deeply devoted to her husband, his wife too avoided earthly entanglements and prayed that the light of her master's wisdom would help her attain salvation.

The sage had guided his daughter Siddhi, towards the path of self-denial. Brought up amidst Nature in their forest retreat, the girl had remained pure. In keeping with the rules of the hermitage, she sought to only perfect her soul.

Living in perfect chastity, Siddhi had stepped into her twenty-sixth year. Her long tresses had never been decorated with ornaments. The only ornaments that adorned her locks were the moss and the sand, which clung to her when she bathed in the Narmada.

On her forehead shone the trident—Lord Siva's holy symbol. Her maturing breasts, which she considered to be an inconvenient load to the body, would be gathered up in a plantain bark which she would knot up at the back. Below the waist she covered herself with deerskin.

In tune with her father's teachings, she considered the urges of the body to be evil and suppressed these ruthlessly as enemies of the soul. Her pleasure lay in harnessing the ego and putting a rein on unruly passions through spiritual exercises. Joy was the absence of desire; renunciation the purpose of life.

Sage Deerghaloma's hermitage by the river Narmada was surrounded by mountains and was situated in a secluded spot of the forest. Yet, even far-off monasteries—those by the rivers Godavari, Ganga, Yamuna and on the Himalayas, echoed with the glory of his spiritual attainments. For him, ritual was only a means to seclusion. He taught that the soul that seeped itself in worldliness became worn out; consequently, it suffered the endless cycle of birth, death and rebirth. The only way out was freedom from human bonds in which lay salvation and joy. The aim of life was the pursuit of such joy.

A learned and renowned interpreter of the Vedas, the Sage was constantly surrounded by devotees who came to him in search of knowledge and salvation. Kings and sages from far-off places came to listen to his discourses on detachment. During the rainy season, many wandering ascetics would camp in his hermitage. One of these was Needak.

Ascetic Needak had attained enlightenment early. He had taken to asceticism soon after reaching puberty. Through devotion to the Supreme Being, he had realised the futility of sensory pleasures. Through detachment and meditation he had as much access to the supernatural as to this world. Some of his yogic immersions lasted as long as ten to fifteen days at a stretch. It was rumoured that once, while he had been immersed in deep meditation a lark had built its nest *(need)* in his long hair. This is how he had got his name — Needak, or the one with the nest in his hair. Since then, word had spread about his power of meditation.

Sage Deerghaloma was happy to welcome ascetic Needak to his hermitage. He prayed that through his supreme wisdom the ascetic would be able to dispel the ignorance of the pleasure-seeking mind.

The hermitage was filled with the fragrance of aromatic roots, herbs and offerings made to the sacrificial holy fire. To this was added the scent of wild flowers wafting in the breeze. Sages and disciples had gathered under the big banyan tree to listen to ascetic Needak's sermon. A few elderly nuns and the girl Siddhi were also seated on one side.

Coloured rice had been scattered on the ground to welcome the sages. The hermitage deer frisked and frolicked about. Melodious tunes from the birds on the trees wafted about in the air. Indifferent to these distractions, learned sages engrossed themselves in listening to Needak's discourse on eternal bliss.

A long flowing beard covered Needak's face. Adorning his forehead was the sign of the trident, drawn out with the earth of the Narmada. Eyes bright with knowledge, he radiated self-confidence. The sacred thread across his broad, hairy chest tapered down to his narrow waist. Below the waist he was covered with a rough fabric. Seated thus in the yogic posture of *Padmasan,* the lotus position, he spoke on for hours.

'Logic is a perversion of the mind. Human needs and desires dictate one's reasoning; hence, directly or indirectly, they start advocating the cause of temptation. Knowledge of the Eternal Being can be attained only through inner perception, which transcends all other human faculties. Logic too is dependent on such perception. An air bubble is ephemeral,' he explained. 'Though it skims the surface, it is only a part of the mass of water. So is life merely a bubble on the ocean of the Supreme Being. A bubble such as this cannot be real. The eternal reality is *Brahman*. The cause of material consciousness is desire. Desire creates the bubble of life through this airy consciousness; and the bubble creates the ego and resultant suffering.'

'The soul is but a fragment of the Supreme Being' he continued. 'It is a manifestation of its playful aspect. Sensory perception—pain as well as pleasure, is an illusion. When the bubble created by the air of material consciousness disappears into the water, the soul reunites with the Supreme Being. In this lies eternal joy and salvation.

Everlasting pleasure is to be found in the rejection of ephemeral pleasure and in the pursuit of life everlasting. The path to vanquish desire is through meditation. Through meditation the barrier of material existence can be overcome and assimilation of the soul with God achieved. The body is the prison of the soul. To give attention to the body is to strengthen the prison. Those with wisdom should shun the needs of the body as this leads only to illusions. To rise above bodily needs is to find the way to salvation.'

Ascetic Needak glanced at his audience to observe the effects of his sermon. Some devotees sat with their eyes closed as if in an effort to assimilate this knowledge. Some gazed at him intently. He looked to his left. Nuns of the hermitage sat at his side. Their bodies were spent and shorn of youth. Devoid of any hope of physical pleasure, their eager eyes stared at the ascetic from the caves of their decaying forms, as if to absorb as much of the sermon as possible by way of some consolation. Their backs were bent. Their dried-up breasts hung uselessly down to their knees. Like mango peels which have been sucked up and then discarded, their bodies appeared to be monuments to the seeming meaninglessness of human life.

The girl Siddhi was sitting with the elderly nuns. Rigours of asceticism had lent brightness to her glowing youth. She looked like a sunflower blossoming out of common manure. Her long hair was tied up in a tight knot on top of her head. Her softly curving eyelashes were closed. Her youthful bosom was gathered up in a plantain bark, which she had tied at her back with a string. She sat, spine erect, in the yogic posture of meditation. Her shapely arms carried the holy signs of the morning's ablutions.

Ascetic Needak could not help noticing her presence. He said, 'The most opportune time for renunciation and meditation is youth. One should realise that attachment is misleading and it is renunciation that leads to supreme happiness. To realise this one does not have to wait for the onset of old age... In old age the physical senses, losing their vitality, become incapable of experiencing even the bare pleasures of life. In such a state how can they contain the subtle knowledge which leads to salvation?' He glanced at the frail wrecks of the nuns' bodies.

The confidence of youth surged through Needak's powerful frame. 'The time when the body radiates vigour is the time for battling with desire, for pursuing knowledge and self-mortification.' His gaze now wandered to Siddhi's bosom which was heaving with her deep breathing.

When the sermon ended at noon the sages dispersed for their frugal midday meal. Lost in thought, Needak walked by the riverside and settled down on a rock. Pangs of hunger reminded him that it was time to eat. He ignored this bodily need. Asceticism meant rigorous discipline of the body and control of its demands. The girl Siddhi was a living example of such self-control. Instantly, the ascetic reminded himself that it was not proper to let thoughts of the hermit-girl enter his mind.

Looking at the turbulent flow of the river he fell into a reverie. He looked at the fish playing about in the clear water and began to think about how carnal desires—the root cause of man's suffering could be conquered. Yet his thoughts kept returning to the vision of the hermit-girl in the posture of meditation. The erect spine, the forehead, nose, chin, the confluence of the breasts, the navel hidden in the folds of the stomach — all in one line.

Needak had seen women earlier. But he had passed by the simply clad nuns of the forests as well as the finely clad sinful women of the towns in detachment. Not once had he spared a thought for them. But the image of Siddhi continued to disturb him. Why, he asked himself, had she closed her eyes, when everyone else, including the other nuns had looked straight at him? Was she listening to him with unusual attentiveness? Or was it because she did not wish to look at him? Why did she not wish to see him? Was she afraid of him? But why? His thoughts began to torture him.

The frivolities of the fish distracted him. 'Those fish........' he muttered. A screech pierced the expanse of sky above the high rocks by the Narmada banks. Two kites were engrossed in love play. One, with wings outspread perched on the edge of a precipice while the other hovered above it under the sun. Here was need and deep animal compulsion. A kind of magnetism seemed to prompt the kites towards each other. Their cries filled the sky. Needak became agitated. With single-minded concentration he sought an answer to the riddle. 'What was it in the nature of those kites that was disturbing them? Could they not control their instincts? Why were they not afraid of the bondage of life and death? Why did their souls not aspire for final release, for Mukti?'

He answered his own questions, 'Because of ignorance and illusion these birds do not see pain.' But the answer put his thoughts in a turmoil. 'What is the cause of an animal's ignorance and illusion? Desire.... appetites? If so, then such desires and appetites must be part of its body and soul. If this were a part of God's design, how could it work against God's will? Is not man's nature a manifestation of God?'

Once again the ascetic's eyes turned to the fluttering wings and the cries of the birds on the peaks. The two were now lost in the processes of procreation. Needak felt an unfamiliar urge stir through his veins. The moment, however, was lost in a haze of confusion. Why was his mind so crowded with arguments and doubts? Could one look for happiness through self-denial? Drawing a deep breath he whispered to himself, 'Is the struggle for life opposed to the laws of life?'

The sun had dipped towards the West. It was the moment when Nature appeared to be flowing naturally towards its consummation. A sound in the river attracted Needak's attention. His gaze fell on a deer skin and an ablution bowl kept on the banks. Whose was it?

He stood transfixed at what he saw. Siddhi, the young nun was standing shoulder deep in water. In the gradually gathering dusk she dipped herself in the river again and again. Her movements agitated Needak's pulse as much as they did Narmada's water. He looked on, spellbound.

At last she waded through the river towards the bank. Needak looked unblinkingly at the gradually emerging figure. His breathing became hard. Strange feelings rose from his heart into his throat.

Apparently secure in this secluded spot, Siddhi stripped off her wet garments. Carefully, she wound the deerskin around her middle, and covered her breasts with the plantain bark. Then she filled her bowl with water and, making an obeisance to the sun, which was now concealed behind multicoloured clouds, she proceeded towards the hermitage.

A sudden movement made Siddhi look in his direction. Coming towards her with long strides was ascetic Needak. She greeted him with bowed head but her body trembled with apprehension.

She awaited the ascetic's command. Needak's gaze was upon her embarrassed figure. After a while he spoke in a trembling voice,

'Nun, what is the goal of life?'

'Life's goal is salvation from life's bondage,' she answered.

Looking at her intently he questioned, 'Is life's goal its own destruction? What is life, Sister?'

Eyes lowered, she said, 'According to the seers, life is a bondage of pain.'

Needak went on, 'Life is a bondage of pain and the same life has as its goal freedom from itself? Nun, forget what is said. Consider this. Does the life-giving Brahma, the creative life force, create life only to end it? Does it will its own destruction? Such an argument appears illogical!'

Pausing a little, Siddhi replied, 'This topic has never arisen in our Maharishi's discourses. How would the Enlightened One explain it?'

Ignoring her question Needak pursued, 'Which is life's deepest pain, Sister?'

Siddhi's answer was brief, 'Death.'

A faint smile appeared on Needak's lips. Siddhi looked away at the Narmada.

Needak exclaimed, 'Death! Nun, in life's progress death is inevitable. It is foolishness to fear death. Death is not the end of life; it is only the end of one link in life's chain. To continue life is life's main goal. To doubt this goal, to oppose this goal, to fear unhappiness and look for ways to end it - is that life's purpose? Nun, desire is life; love is life; life's demands are natural. Has life never beckoned you towards it?'

Siddhi answered tremblingly, 'O source of light, my penance and meditation are incomplete. My soul has not yet received the light.'

'Nun, I'm not thinking of the light that is arrived at with eyes closed. I'm thinking of the wisdom one gathers from the experience of life!'

Her voice faltered, 'I do not follow the Enlightened One's words correctly. Please enlighten me about life!'

Taking a deep breath Needak answered, 'Narmada's flow is Narmada's life. If you try to reverse its course the result will be unnatural. If this river, imagining its flow to be painful were to oppose it, what sort of salvation could it expect?'

Siddhi bowed down and pleaded with folded hands. 'Enlightened One, my soul is weak and full of ignorance.'

Needak replied, 'Nun, do you take the love of life itself as weakness? By calling life lust and appetite and pitting all of life's energy against it — you are only trying to forget what life really is all about.'

Siddhi remained unaware of Needak's fast pulse. What she could sense, however, was a sudden change in his tone. The ascetic who had given his morning discourse in a calm, majestic voice and the one who now spoke in a trembling, hoarse voice appeared to be two different persons. Meeting him in solitude, where she could well have expected to feel a certain hesitation only caused a strange sweetness to enter her soul. Looking down on the ground she said, 'Would the Enlightened One initiate me into Wisdom?'

'Wisdom!' Needak exclaimed and took a deep breath. His gaze fell once again on the peaks where the pair of kites was still busy creating new life. Their love play reached a climax and they broke away from each other, their cries echoing in the gathering dusk. The waters of the Narmada reverberated with the sound. 'Look - that way...' cried Needak, pointing upwards.

Siddhi looked up. She had watched such love transactions earlier. On all such occasions she had turned her eyes away and by controlling her mind and senses had striven to save her spirit from corruption. In the presence of the youthful ascetic, however, her body felt a sudden anguished restlessness. She lowered her eyes, her face reddening.

Needak's breathing became faster; his nerves were taut like the strings of a *sitar*. The nun's body pulled him like a magnet. He restrained himself with difficulty as he looked at the lowered eyes of the blushing girl. Coming a step nearer to her he whispered in a trembling voice, 'Is this corruption and sin? Is life the result of sin and corruption?'

Tremblingly, the nun answered, 'Lord, such conduct, according to the sages, is due to the ignorance of the soul; to be in lust is to stray from the true path of salvation. They say that life is an illusion and a mirage.'

Coming a step still closer to the nun, Needak said, 'Is this suffering, nun? Do you really believe that this pair of kites is crying because of the fear of life and death? Does it appear to them as mere illusion? Are they not involved with their entire being in the joyous task of creating life?'

'Is this life a delusion, nun?' He flung the words again at the silent figure of Siddhi. 'To deny the joy that one can get out of one's senses and to take the consequent happiness as pain--Is this right? Is it the truth? Are we really supporting Brahma by believing that all his Creation is a mirage and an illusion? Are we not taking truth as falsehood and falsehood as truth?'

Siddhi remained silent.

Pointing with his little finger, Needak exclaimed, 'Nun, do you not harbour in your heart the surge of this life-force? Don't you too feel this struggle, this assertion of life?'

The nun lifted her half-closed eyes for a moment, 'O Enlightened Master, your words are true. I'm a weak soul; I have not yet been able to master my senses completely!'

Needak put his hand on Siddhi's shoulder. He felt her body tremble. Supporting her with one arm, he tilted her chin up with the other and whispered, 'Is the touch of my harsh body painful to you, Siddhi?'

Leaning towards his body, Siddhi muttered in a broken voice, 'No, it is an unknown quantity, quite unfamiliar, quite...something dear, very dear....' Her voice became hoarser. The knot of her hair was now resting on Needak's broad chest. His lips touched her wet, sandy hair. Startled, Siddhi straightened herself and gasped, 'O Enlightened One, the darkness of ignorance overpowers me; please show me the light.'

'The light of knowledge!' His voice grew in power. 'Sharpen your senses; the way to wisdom is through sensibility. To repress and crush human nature is ignorance.' Feeling weak, Siddhi placed both her arms and her weight upon Needak's shoulders.

Making a double pair of footprints, they proceeded towards a deserted part of Narmada. The cool rays of the stars, piercing through the monsoon clouds seemed to express satisfaction at this earthly transaction; Nature seemed to be conspiring with the creation of life.

It rained in torrents the next morning. But the sages and inmates of the hermitage, who stuck to their rules without fail, gathered as usual beneath the giant banyan tree for meditation and sermons. The fragrant smoke from the holy fire, moved by the breeze, seemed to have become entangled amidst the trees and become strangely motionless.

The absence of Needak and Siddhi from the previous evening had become a cause of concern for all the hermits.

23

In his discourse that morning, Sage Deerghaloma pointed out, 'Lust is man's greatest foe. In the flames of lust, man's knowledge is reduced to ashes.'

At daybreak, in one of Narmada's caves, Needak stretched himself languidly, still drowsy with sleep. The movement woke Siddhi. Even before he could open his eyes, she covered her body with a deerskin. Looking outside the cave she exclaimed, 'The *Brahma-Muhurta* must have been on for quite sometime!'

'Yes,' Needak answered, 'the time for immersion in the *samadhi* has passed.'

Drawing Siddhi to himself, he held her by the nape of her neck, 'Tell me the truth. You have tried to be forgetful of the self for so many years. For so long, you have tried to forget the world through *samadhi*. But, truthfully, have you ever been as content, as self-forgetful as on this night?'

And he smiled into her sleepy eyes.

Once again, self-abandon took possession of Siddhi, 'Arya, you speak the truth!'

Translated by **Keshav Malik**
Edited and condensed by **Ms. Neelam Kumar**

Under Cover of Darkness

Nirmal Verma

Bano had to cut across three goat-paths to reach our house. 'Any news?' She always fired the question at me immediately on entering the room. I was sorely tempted to lie to her and say, 'Yes, there is. It's all settled. We'll be leaving for Delhi soon.' But I refrained from doing so. Bano was too shrewd not to see through my lies. Instead, I lay silently, with my eyes closed.

As usual, she came over and felt my forehead. When her touch was cold, I knew that my fever had not gone down. But when it was warm I felt elated. Eagerly opening my eyes I would ask, 'Bano, don't you thing I am getting better?'

Looking disappointed, she would reply hopefully, 'But your temperature is bound to shoot up in the evening!'

She was unhappy whenever my temperature came down. She knew that as long as my fever lasted I could not leave her and would stay put in Simla. Sometimes when I heard her footsteps, I quickly applied a wet towel to my forehead.

'Feel my forehead.' I would reach for her hand and brush it against my brow.

'Cold, is it?' Without a word, Bano would start looking out of the window.

Outside, one could see the forests enveloped in a blue haze, and lofty mountains, range upon range. When the curtain fluttered in the breeze, the room was drenched with a dream-like fragrance, wafted from afar.

'Beyond those mountains, lies Delhi. You know that, of course,' I said.

Bano nodded. She had no interest in Delhi, had never been to that city. Her father's office remained in Simla all the year round. I pitied her.

'I have been to our house,' she said changing the subject.

The mention of "our house," which on other days swept me off my feet, today held no interest for me.

'Bano, you can keep my share of plums,' I said, without opening my eyes.

'Who would care to eat your rotten plums?' Bano said, peeved. 'Take them along when you go to Delhi — your precious cargo of rotten plums!' She went into the verandah.

It made me angry. But when one is ill, one cannot work himself up to a high pitch of anger. In illness, all feelings peter out without reaching the crescendo of passion. If one cries, no tears come — only the eyelids flutter. If one feels exhilarated, the heart does not beat faster — only the lips tremble.

The house, which Bano had referred to as "our house", was said to be haunted and lay deserted all the year. They said an English woman had committed suicide in this house. We would store our treasure trove of raw plums and apricots in one of the bathrooms. It was a closely guarded secret and no one was aware of our secret.

Bano kept swinging in the verandah for a long time. As the swing went up, her *salwar* puffed out like a balloon. The rhythmic creaking of the swing acted like a soporific; I dozed off and dreamt. I always remembered the dreams I had in the afternoons. I dreamed that the *chaprasi* had come from the office to fetch father's lunch. He laughed and told us that we would soon move down to Delhi. Then I saw Bano throwing apricots out of the window of the haunted house. Far away in the hills, I could see the English woman who had committed suicide, leaning out of the window of the Kalka-Simla train. With outstretched hands she grabbed at the apricots which Bano was casting to the winds.

When I woke up, Bano had been gone a long time.

In the evening when mother brought in the tea I asked her if the *chaprasi* had come in the afternoon.

'Yes, he did. Why?'

'Did he tell you anything?'

'No, nothing. What's the matter with you?'

I kept silent. Propping myself up against the pillow, I sipped my tea.

After some time mother took my temperature and immediately after, jerked down the column of mercury. Previously, I used to insist upon knowing my temperature. But she was reluctant to tell the truth and I stopped asking. I tried to guess it by watching the expression on her face. Sometimes when I became grave she would say, 'Now get well, and then we shall leave for Delhi.' She said it in a casual manner, as if it was entirely up to me to get well or remain ill; as if I was keeping ill out of sheer obstinacy and that I had to be cajoled into getting well. This would put me in a temper, and turning on my side I would lie facing the window. For a long time she would not realize that I was angry, till I stiffened my legs, clenched my fists, grit my teeth and started breathing heavily.

Mother, who had all this while been looking out of the window then get alarmed. She would look at me intently, sigh and sit down on the bed by my side. I sensed at once that she had seen through my game, though she never gave me that impression. Taking out a bar of Cadbury's chocolate from the almirah, she would place it under my pillow. 'Don't tell your father about it,' she would warn me, running her fingers through my hair. But the very next moment she would forget me; she would be miles away, lost in her own would of thoughts. I knew this from the way her fingers became inert. The piece of chocolate she had given me was not so much to put me in good humour as to keep me out of her way — so that she could again burrow into her shell, undisturbed. I would look at her face without her being aware of it. The shadowy lines would be gone, and her face would be a blank emptiness. Her eyes would glow with an inner fire and seem to be misted over with a thin film. I wanted to delude myself with the pleasant thought that she was thinking of my illness, but in my heart of hearts I knew that her thoughts had nothing to do with me.

I gently put my hand on hers. She started, as if my touch had dragged her back from some remote recesses of the mind. She looked hard at me and then kissed me on the lips. I wiped my mouth with my sleeve. She smiled.

'Child, may I ask you one thing?'

'Yes?'

'If I go away, will you take it amiss?' She looked at me without blinking her eyes.

'Will father go with you?'

'No.'

'Then?' I was puzzled.

She started laughing and lay down by my side.

I put my cheek against hers. Mother was very beautiful and everybody was afraid of her. Sometimes I wondered what was that something about her, which kept every one on his toes. I was also afraid of her—especially of her eyes, when she looked at me closely.

A long time back I had once accompanied Father to his friend's house. Our path lay along a ravine and as we climbed up we stopped for a while in the forest grove to regain our breaths. The silence of the grove felt eerie.

Now when I looked at mother's eyes I was reminded of that dark forest grove.

Mother's arms were white and smooth as marble. I was shy about touching them. She parted her hair in the middle, sweeping it back tightly, which made her forehead still more prominent.

Her ears were small, almost doll-like, and remained hidden under her hair. When she lay by my side I pulled them out from underneath her hair and I would be suddenly reminded of what Bano had once told me about people with small ears having short lives. I shivered to think of it but I never told mother. I imagined that when she lay dying I would tell her she was dying before her time because of her ears.

Sometimes I had a feeling that she was not particularly worried over my illness; that perhaps there were times she even forgot I was ill. I also knew that mother was not eager to go to Delhi. Once I had heard her saying so to uncle Biren and I wondered why.

For the past few months, mother and father had been sleeping in separate rooms. This seemed odd to me. But then there were many mysteries I did not try to delve into; I simply relegated them to the back of my mind.

Mother's room was at the other end of the gallery and her two windows overlooked mine. Sometimes she could be seen at a window, her bunch of hair, like molten gold in the sun. I knew she was sitting by the window, reading.

She had many books, scattered all over the place — on the sofa, by the pillow, under the bedstead. Perhaps she slept very little. Often I saw the light burning in her room till late in the night.

Once I opened one of her books. On the flyleaf I saw uncle Biren's name inscribed in spidery characters in blue ink. It fascinated me. Later I saw his name on many more books which lay scattered about in her room.

This reminded me of uncle Biren's small cottage which I had visited with mother. One room was full of books and there was a stepladder, which he used for taking down books from the shelves. The walls of another room were covered with oddly framed paintings before which I would pause for hours. Father told me that uncle Biren had purchased these paintings in Europe before the War. My feelings for uncle Biren were a mixture of wonder and pity. How could he bring himself to live in this lonely cottage all by himself, the year through, winter and summer?

Among Father's friends uncle Biren had a distinct place of his own. It was only he whom father invited to take tea in my room — others he received in the drawing room. When uncle Biren came I was not packed off at bedtime. I was allowed to stay on while they sat talking for long hours. Those were pleasant evenings.

One evening, when uncle Biren called on us, he was so funnily dressed that for a moment I did not recognise him. Long boots which came up to his knees, a *khaki* knap-sack slung over one shoulder and a camera over the other, a *sola* hat, and quaintest of all, a goatee, which did not suit his face. His pockets bulged with books.

He came to my bed and shook hands with me. Uncle Biren was always like that. He always greeted me as one greets a normal, healthy person. And he never wasted his breath in inquiring after my health.

Mother sat beside us, busy knitting. She cast a fleeting glance at Biren and lowered her head. Uncle Biren told us that he was bound for Kufri. He would stay the night in the Rest House and return the following evening. 'I am told the watchman of the Rest House has been living in Kufri for the last thirty years,' uncle Biren said. 'He must know a lot about Kufri.'

A faint smile spread on mother's face. 'You have been at this game for more years?

'Oh, so you don't believe me. Then you must look at my Notes.' Uncle Biren's blue eyes lit up. Somehow any mention of his book, *A History of Simla*, always made mother smile.

'Sometimes I come across valuable scraps of information while collecting material for my book,' uncle Biren said.

'What kind of information, uncle?' I asked.

I always showed keen interest in uncle's book. It buoyed up his spirits.

'Once I chanced upon an old photograph,' uncle Biren said. 'An Englishman must have taken it.'

'A photograph of...?' mother asked, looking up from her knitting.

'Of a crowd at a race course. Most of the faces were indistinct. But one face, a girl's had come out clearly. She was standing by the pavillion, an umbrella in her hand. Everyone's eyes were glued to the running horses but hers seemed to be held by something behind her. A rather incongruous note. Her looking back like this…'

Uncle Biren suddenly stopped. The knitting lay quiet in mother's hands.

'The caption under the photograph read: *Annandale, Simla — 1903*. Fifty years ago. And she was still looking back, umbrella in hand.'

Uncle Biren laughed — as if at his own whimsey. Mother looked up at him, her eyes icy. Sometimes I wondered why uncle Biren indulged in such meaningless talks.

'At times I feel it is much easier to write about men than about cities,' uncle Biren said. 'I've assembled a huge mass of notes, old photographs, travelogues on Simla, but I doubt I will ever succeed in writing my book.'

'Why?' mother asked.

'Because... because every city is so much absorbed in itself. It does not let you pry into its secrets easily.' Uncle Biren got up. He touched my forehead.

'I met the doctor while coming down,' he said bending over me. 'He said you will be fit enough to walk about in a few days' time.'

'Will you just sit up?' he said, taking the camera from his shoulder. 'I'll take your photograph. Let's see how you look.'

After taking my photograph he picked up his walking stick, ready to leave.

'When will you come again?' mother asked, looking him straight in the eye for the first time.

'Perhaps tomorrow evening — I'll drop in for a minute.' When uncle looked at mother, his eyes would become dazzled and he would turn his face away.

'Uncle Biren...' I said shyly.

'Yes, child?'

'I'll take a photograph.'

He smiled and handed me the camera.

I looked at mother.

'No, no, not mine, son,' she said, her words tumbling over each other.

'You will not be alone. Uncle Biren will also be there.'

Uncle Biren turned pale and cast a fleeting look at mother. She rose form her chair without any more fuss, saying to me, 'You are very willful.'

'Uncle Biren, you stand by the railing — in the sun. And mother, you stand to the right.'

I climbed out of the bed and stood leaning against the wall. My head reeled. But the photograph was a great success. I have it with me to this day...

I did not know when darkness crept into the room. Uncle Biren had been gone a long time. Only mother was there, reclining in a chair by my side — silent and motionless. I did not ask for the light. I like the feeling of darkness slowly invading a room.

Suddenly the memory of one particular evening flitted across my mind. This was much before I fell ill. Mother had taken me to uncle Biren's house.

Uncle Biren was taken aback on seeing us. He let us in at the wicket gate, looking flustered.

'Pono, you here?' It was the first time I had heard uncle Biren addressing mother by her name. Coming from his lips, her name rang strangely. Mother started laughing. I don't know why, but I did not like the way she laughed. I felt cramped and a vague numbness spread over my heart.

'We came out for a stroll,' said mother. 'We thought we might as well say hello to you.' It was the first time I had heard mother lying.

For a fleeting second uncle Biren's blue eyes clouded over with doubt; then he held my finger and led us into his cottage.

I saw his library for the first time. He showed me photographs of the mountain peaks of Simla, its valleys and waterfalls. He had collected these for his projected book. A lamp with a light green shade rested on the table by the side of a heap of books. He brought out two slabs of chocolate from somewhere. I was not prepared for this sleight of hand, and he laughed at my discomfiture.

'I have laid by quite a stock of chocolates,' he said. 'It comes in handy during winter when I'm snowed in.' I looked at uncle Biren. How different he was from Father! He had none of that oppressive grimness and tenseness which I associated with Father. There was an intangible tenderness about uncle Biren. Above his trim beard, the soft eloquence of his eyes seemed to shed the coarseness from everything they ranged over.

'Have you ever seen a snow-capped peak from close range?' he asked me. I shook my head.

'The snow looks blue,' he said. 'I took a coloured photograph...' He went into the adjoining room. Idly, I thumbed through his albums which were lying on a table. Each photograph represented a view of Simla: Glenn, Jakhu, Chetwick Falls. I easily recognised each of those spots. Uncle had not shown up and I began to feel bored. I picked up another album, a small one, which was lying at the corner of a bookshelf. I turned the first page, and a known face stared at me. It was a picture of mother.

Had mother ever been like this? My heart missed a beat. It was the same broad forehead, but with the small red mark which mother now does not put on. Two locks of hair fell over her shoulders. She was wearing a full sleeved sweater and her small ears were hidden under her hair — the same as now. Looking at her expression, I had a sudden feeling that face had nothing to do with me or with father. It was mother, but I could not see my mother in her.

Hearing uncle Biren's footsteps, I guiltily put away the album.

When we came out onto the lawn the shadows of the evening had begun to fall. Wrapped in a shawl, mother was sitting on a stone bench. Uncle Biren sat down on the grass near mother's feet. 'Where were you all this while?' She tenderly pulled me to her. I looked searchingly into her face. The same eyes, mouth and forehead. Separately, they were nothing special; together the total impression was different in a way I could not define. Perhaps it was an expression which annihilated distance and yet never came closer.

'What's the matter, son?' Mother ran her fingers through my tangled hair. I shrank into myself and looked away.

Mother did not pay any further attention to me. We sat quietly, lost in our own thoughts. Since our coming, uncle Biren had not talked with Mother. It seemed strange, but its meaning was lost on me.

A blue haze had descended upon the lawn. Among the distant hills, lights shone like glow-worms. The outlines of the hills having been blurred by darkness, the sky seemed to nestle closer to the earth.

While I was ill, I often recalled this evening, although nothing unusual had happened to distinguish it from other evenings. Uncle Biren accompanied us some distance and when mother assured him that we would manage all right on our own, he had turned back. Mother was not there. I retraced my steps, peering into the darkness, my heart beating faster.

At the turn of the road, I found mother leaning over the railing, the end of her *sari* fluttering in the breeze. She was looking below at uncle Biren's cottage. In the evening it looked lonely and deserted. A pale streak of light from the library window lay across the lawn.

For a while we stood silent and then mother resumed her walk. Her gait was so slow that she seemed to be walking in her sleep. When she came up to me, for a long time she stared at me with helpless eyes. Then she drew me close and put her cold, dry lips to my mouth.

After some days I felt the taste of illness begin to leave my mouth and life seemed to surge back slowly into my limbs. I had the windows opened, and the curtains drawn so that I could bathe in the soft furry warmth of the sunlight.

One morning I came out onto the verandah. A little away from me auntie was busy hanging out her washing on the wooden railing. Stealthily, I crept past her and stepped into the balcony at the back of father's room. The doors and windows of the room at the other end were barred and no curtains were hanging in them. When mother used to go away to her aunt's, Father would lock up her room, carry all his things upstairs into the study and spend his nights there.

The balcony looked forlorn. In front of me in the walled compound of the school, I could see small boys, satchels in hand, standing four in a row, reciting their prayers in a nasal sing-song: *'God's name comes to my lips with the fervour of a keen desire ...'* Unable to stand their shrill lacerating voices any more, I looked beyond, over the haunted house across the ravine, and then along the serpentine path which lost itself behind the compound of Bano's house. Fetching Father's old discarded walking stick, at the end of which I had tied a red piece of cloth I waved it above my head. This was a favourite game with Bano and me. She saw me and waved back. Then she pointed me to her mother, who also waved. Embarrassed, I threw away the stick and ran inside.

Before I could enter my room, a servant came to tell me that Father wanted to see me. A wave of joy surged through me. It was rare for Father to invite me to his room. Hastily, I bit my nails to make sure that they were clean; Father always looked at my nails the first thing.

Father's room had a distinct individuality compounded of the smell of cigarsmoke, an oppressive stillness, subdued lighting which did not change with night or day and, above it all a sour medicinal odour that hung pervasively, like a layer of thinly spun colour.

'What were you doing outside?' I knew Father's moods. There was no anger in his voice.

'I was looking for Bano.' I fumbled and became silent.

'Father!'

Father looked up.

'I am well now. The fever has left me.'

Father placed my hands one upon the other and held them in his big hairy hands. 'You must rest in bed a few days more,' he said.

'Father, when are we going to Delhi?' It was a question I always asked whenever I met him.

Father removed his cigar from his mouth, and studied the wallpaper, as if trying to read something there.

'Son, are you sometimes afraid?'

'Afraid? Afraid of what?' I asked.

Father's eyes turned to me. 'I mean, now that your mother is away.'

'But she'll be back soon.' I hoped that Father would affirm my statement; but he just looked on expressionlessly and then said

'Yes' in a feeble voice as if speaking to himself.

'Son!'

'Yes, Father?'

'Would you like to meet your mother?' His voice sounded hard and his question strange and devoid of meaning. I wanted to say 'Yes' but when I looked at him I sensed that he wanted me to reply differently, to deliberately lie to him.

I shook my head. He looked at me, surprised, and removed my hands from his lap.

He got up from the chair and went to the window.

As I watched him I felt sympathy well up in my heart for him. My relations with Mother were not hedged with complexity. I did not feel tense and withdrawn with her, as I did with Father. She would agree to all my demands without ado. Yet she failed to win my sympathy, whereas, even though I was afraid of Father and could not make demands on him or open my heart to him, he touched a chord in my heart. Separating Mother and us lay some intangible reality.

Father looked quite forlorn. The stillness that reigned in his room seemed to permeate the whole house. Without Mother every room looked empty and desolate.

Mother had left for her aunt's place without seeing me. I had happened to wake up in the middle of the night before she went.

My room was dark. In the breeze the window curtain flew up and kept fluttering over my pillow. For some time a doubt hovered in my mind; everything in the room seemed to have shifted from its proper place. The window on my left had quietly moved down to the middle of the wall. The door had slipped two yards to the right. The door was ajar, and from Father's room showed a thin mercurial column of light so slender and fragile that a touch would have slivered it to bits. Suddenly, flapping like a black birdwing, the door stood open for a second, then slowly closed. As it closed, a beam of light streaked across the floor and climbed the opposite wall. I heard someone breathing heavily behind the door and I thought it was Mother come to fasten the latch. But no one came. I heard voices, now coming from afar—indistinct, wordless sounds, then so close it was as if someone were whispering into my ear.

'No, you won't go in.' It was Father's voice.

A thin cry, like a bright sliver of glass pierced the heart of darkness. What was wrong with Mother? Why did she shriek in this strange manner?

'Let go my hand!' she cried.

'Pono, I won't allow you to go in.'

'Who are you to stop me? Aren't you ashamed of yourself?'

'Pono, don't shout, he's sleeping.'

'I won't shout. Let me go in.'

'No, no, not now.'

'Do you think I am mad? Do you think I'll tell him...?'

'Pono, go to your room. You are not in your senses.'

Before Father could say more, the curtain parted and my bed was flooded with light. I saw two marble-like arms spread against the curtain and a shadowy figure with two hungry, distraught eyes. Thin, long fingers clutched the curtain, trembling violently, and a nosepiece shone like a star above quivering lips. I glimpsed the phantasmagoric sight in the fleeting instant before the curtain was pulled across the door. Then there were only muffled groans.

After this, I could not believe my ears. I could only hear slow continuous laughter behind the curtain. No, it could not be Mother. I had never before heard her laughing like that. I could neither hear nor see anything more. My mind went blank and I felt that the darkness had gathered itself into something tangible, something foul and ragged that coiled and twisted before my eyes.

I was lying on the terrace one afternoon during my convalescence. No one was taking any notice of me and I had my way with everything. Father did not drop into my room in the evenings and I had not seen uncle Biren for a long time. If any one was sorry about my recovery it was Bano. Had I remained ill the chances of our going to Delhi would have receded.

Behind the terrace there were two low hills, pointing towards the sky like a pair of scissors. Between them a forest range stretched far into the distance. When the train bound for Kalka passed through it, a column of smoke drifted above the trees toward the sky.

'Bano, we'll be leaving for Delhi soon,' I told Bano who was busy picking apricots from the terrace. The apron of her skirt was filled with apricots. She knelt and her booty spilt on the ground.

'Here, eat this,' she said picking up a ripe yellow apricot. 'It's nice.'

I shook my head. Father had forbidden me to eat apricots.

'Its ripe, it will do you no harm,' she said and, without waiting for my answer popped it into her mouth. She turned the apricot in her cheek and said that if it was turned often enough the saliva made the fruit juicier.

'So it is settled that you are going to Delhi,' she said sucking noisily at the apricot.

'Yes, as soon as mother returns.'

'Where has your mother gone?'

'To her aunt's place.'

'Are you sure?' Bano looked at me mysteriously.

'What's the matter, Bano?' I asked, puzzled.

'Nothing. Just asking.' She pressed the apricot between her lips and added, 'I won't tell you. Mother has warned me not to.'

I felt angry but smiled, feigning indifference. When I was angry I tried to hide my feelings behind a smile so that no one would think me an ill-tempered fool.

The hills behind the terrace were grey under the low clouds and their thin elongated shadows flitted across them from the east.

'Is Delhi beyond those mountains?' Bano asked me.

'Delhi is in the plains,' I replied. 'One has to climb over those hills to reach Delhi.'

Bano looked at me skeptically. 'But below us is Annandale Race Course, and beyond that the ravine. Is Delhi in the ravine?'

Without trying to satisfy her curiosity I turned my back on her.

Near the terrace was the pavillion and behind it the guestroom of the haunted house. Bano threw the apricot stones into the guestroom and stood leaning against the wall.

All of Simla was hushed in the afternoon; only the sound of falling apricots punctuated the silence. Bano beckoned me to her. The glass of one of the guesthouse doors was broken. She peeped through the hole and invited me to join her.

The room was empty, its wallpaper faded. It was full of stale air and cobwebs. In the middle of the floor there was a small circle of light, which seemed to change from white to faded yellow and back again. In the darkness the spot of light looked eerie.

'That English woman must have lived in this room,' Bano whispered.

'And she must have died in this room,' I added, and a shiver ran down my spine. I saw a face gradually emerging on the peeled off plaster of the wall — its mouth gaped, its lustreless eyes seeming to mock me, and I heard laughter. It must have been the face of the woman who had taken her own life here, years ago... her laughter reminded me of mother's laughter that night.

'Bano, did your mother tell you something about my mother?'

'How does that concern you?'

The doors of the deserted house rattled in the wind.

'Bano, when I was ill, sometimes I had strange feelings. I felt I was also like Mother — that there was something common between us, something which no one likes. I saw an apparition wrapped in snow, whose hands were white as marble and it remained dangling in the air. An apparition which, coming from behind suddenly bottled me up — and then I fell apart from my own self. Yes, from my own being, Bano!'

Bano shook like a leaf and her eyes grew wide with fear.

We were all packed and ready to leave. Labels of *'Simla-Delhi'* had been pasted on all the boxes, bags and bedrolls, with Father's name in bold letters below. The servants and peons from Father's office ran all over the place, busy with the arrangements. The house bustled with activity.

Mother was in her room upstairs, doing nothing. Father had asked me not to go to her. Perhaps she was not well. I had not met her since she had returned from her aunt's place. She had arrived in the night when I was asleep.

Having nothing to do, I knocked about the house till I felt suffocated with boredom. Keeping out of everyone's way I escaped from the house.

Descending the footpath I started along the ravine, picking pine cones till both my pockets were stuffed with them. On the distant hills the late sunlight still lingered, too tired to merge into darkness.

I had come a long way from home and when I started walking back, I suddenly spotted uncle Biren's tiny cottage down below, cosily ensconced amidst a cluster of trees. I remembered that particular evening when I had come to the cottage with Mother. Since the time Mother had gone to stay with her aunt, uncle Biren had stopped calling on us. Once I had asked Father about uncle Biren. But his expression had become so hard that I dared not pursue the subject.

I walked down to the cottage. In the western sun, the sloping roof had become a glowing red. The wicket gate was open. I tip-toed on to the lawn. The wind sighing through the grass added to the sense of desolation. At the edge of the lawn I could see the stone bench on which Mother had sat.

I gently knocked at the door, 'Uncle Biren, uncle.' My voice went ringing through that lonely, mute cottage. I felt it was not my own voice, but an unfamiliar one, which chased my own.

'Come in. The door is unlocked.'

I went in. The dim light of the table lamp fell on the book and the papers which lay in disorder on the table. Uncle Biren asked me to sit on his bed and pulled up his easy chair beside me.

'Have you walked alone, this long distance?' He took my hand in his and smiled.

Suddenly his eyes fell upon my bulging pocket and I went red in the face.

'What have you in those pockets of yours?' he asked me. 'Pine cones?'

I nodded.

'What will you do with them?'

'They are for the train.'

'For the train?' Biren uncle's face had become a question mark.

'Yes, we are leaving for Delhi tonight, uncle.'

He looked at me without blinking. Then he got up and without taking further notice of me started gazing out of the window. A suffocating silence filled the room. I felt he had already known about our going away. When he turned from the window his blue eyes shone.

'You remember the photograph you took that day?' he asked me. 'Its ready. Would you like to see it?'

He took out an envelope from the almirah and handed it to me. 'You are quite an expert,' he said. 'The photograph has come out very well.'

I looked at the photograph. The event, which I had consigned to the limbo returned vividly.

Against a hazy backdrop of mountains, I saw uncle Biren standing close to the railing of the balcony, his arm unknowingly touching mother's *sari*. And mother... she stood with half-closed eyes, her lips parted, as though she was on the point of uttering something, and had then abruptly checked herself.

I kept looking at the photograph for a time.

Then I was reminded of the train journey which I had to make. I climbed off the bed.

'Well, uncle...' I was too overwhelmed to unburden my thoughts.

Uncle Biren came close to me. He touched my hair and gently kissed me on the forehead — the same way Mother had kissed me that night.

We came out.

'May I see you home?' he asked me.

I shook my head. I knew the way. For a while we stood silent in the verandah.

'Son...!' Startled, I looked at him.

'Your mother once wanted a book. I forgot about it...' He hesitated.

'Please give it to me. I'll take it with me.'

Handing me the book I thought he wanted to say something, but could not.

The cottage was left behind. I made my way back along the deserted road. When I neared home, I stopped under a lamp post and examined the book.

The envelope containing the photograph was lying within its pages.

The book was very old. Even today I can vividly recall its yellow and brittle pages—*'Flauberts' Letters to George Sand.'* Those days I was not familiar with the names of Flaubert or George Sand. Years after when I read the book, Mother was no more and uncle Biren had long since left the country and settled in Italy.

But that day the book had no significance for me. For a long time I stood under the lamp post, holding the book and looking at the room upstairs.

The window of Mother's room was closed, but a sepulchral light shone through.

That was our last evening in Simla.

Translated by **Jai Ratan**

Like A Pigeon

Rajendra Awasthi

He could not sleep the whole night. He wondered why he kept on turning on his sides. Other passengers in that small railway compartment were fast asleep, almost unconscious. After all there was none among them for whom he should have to keep his eyes open. Entering the compartment, he had casually glanced at his fellow-passengers, and then had turned to read the newspaper of the day. But he knew very well that his attempt at reading was just a way to pass time.

Outside the window, the forest looked as though it had come to a standstill. At first it seemed that there was nothing at all in the darkness. Only the train whistling in the stillness and chaotic sounds like vessels clanging. If one sees friction produced on the surface of the iron rail one can see sparks, and the sound seems to signify blows rattling the Past. All night the compartment swayed like a windmill. He remembered every sound...the sound of the speeding train as well as the static stations.

The route was not new to him, or the train, or the accompanying sounds and the floods stretching outside. But when the Past suddenly starts knocking at the door of the Present, the person experiencing those moments suddenly trembles with unlooked-for possibilities. As he read the names of the stations in the faint light of the dusk, he felt a strong jolt. It was as though someone had suddenly called out to him, '*Arre*, do you recognise her?'

'No, mother, who is she?'

'Look closely. Of all the persons, you can't recognise her?'

He had then looked carefully at the bashful cheeks, the downcast eyes, the imitation pearls on the nose, the lips parted slightly and a marigold flower fixed in the well-oiled hair. He saw earrings in the shape of half moons and a straight central parting, tinted vermillion. From somewhere, he heard the sound of a child crying and her heavy, deep breathing telling so many untold stories.

He felt as though hot steam had jolted him from behind and was running down his neck

'Ma, you're talking in riddles.'

Mother became angry: 'What! You've forgotten everyone after going to Delhi? She's Ramrati, yes, Ramrati!'

It seemed as if a voice from the Past had wafted in and called out — 'Ramrati!'

The voice whirled round the Fort of Madan Mahal and struck its walls. The echo created a disturbance in every corner of nis heart: 'Now, you shouldn't hold me by my plait like that. Supposing I start screaming?'

'So what?'

'Go away! Are you going to play hide and seek with me or...?'

And then a loud voice came floating: 'Sunita has been caught! Come out, everybody. She will be blindfolded!'

'We shall come here and hide again.'

'Why, pray? I won't come here again,' he had said.

Nevertheless, he had kept going back to the same corner of Madan Mahal Fort where Time stood gazing at the deep trenches. He remembered catching worms that formed lac on the *palash* trees behind the mangos and custard-apples that had grown at random. He remembered singing the tune of the mildly blowing breeze, and the fear emanating from the grave-yard where the spirits lay buried with the sinking sun.

During one such hide-and-seek game, he had clipped Ramrati's plait with a pair of scissors. What else could he do if no one believed in what he said? Then the visits had stopped. There had been quarrels and feuds. Inspite of those, at every lonely turn of the road, there was teasing and sticking out of one's tongue at the other!

What a long time back it had all been! How on earth could he recognize Ramrati? And when he did recognize her afresh, there had been her complaints and reproaches to deal with. *He had become such a big officer! He couldn't even get a new wig for her. There was no dearth of saris in Delhi. And one gets chappals in so many colours! Fashions change every day. He could have got something for her—something currently in fashion. Couldn't he take her to Madan Mahal dressed in that fashion?*

'No...' it was a helpless situation for both of them.

He remembered the continuous stream of visitors to their house and then Father calling out, 'Do see who has come. When you were young, you used to be in his house the whole day. Now you don't come even when we call you. You must touch his feet.'

How could he convince his father that he had travelled far from the Past? Even as a child, he had found it irksome. Now he just could not lower his head before anyone. What else does a man have except his dignity and self-respect? How often does one have to lower everything day and night?

It's a mockery too that all of them still considered him to be an ordinary man. They praised him and admired him, but clearly they had something else on their minds. It was not difficult to read their faces. Their looks concealed their complaints. He had noticed a similar look in his father's eyes. Father had always wanted to build a mansion in the ancestral backdrop so that the neighbours would be left staggered in amazement. During each visit home he would be shown a new blueprint of the dream house. Father had always expected him to deposit a pile of currency notes with him so that the blueprint on paper could be turned into a reality. He had already borrowed a thousand rupees and passed them on to his father. At that moment Father had quietly taken the money, but he had overheard him remarking to his mother in the evening, 'See, didn't I say he has plenty of money? He earns quite a lot — only he doesn't want to give it to us....'

'Why won't he give it? For whom is it meant, after all?'

'Not for us,' father had said emphatically. 'What can you do with a thousand rupees? For him it's just some dirt off his hand. He saves that much money every month!'

He had heard that by mere accident and was stunned. He had regretted that he had ever borrowed the money at all. What a complicated situation it was! There was trouble if he did not give money, and when he did, the wonderful compliments! His mind protested.

But however much he may have revolted against him, Father's importance could not be denied. The day Father died, he was overwhelmed with sorrow and grief. He had not even been able to see him before his death. That was painful enough and then, the pain of seeing his body reduced to ashes! How frequently he had broken down while carrying his ashes to the Ganges. What he was carrying in his hands was stark reality. That is the fate of man, he had thought, and yet the things he does before reaching that point! The line of transition when the Past is turned into history — that alone is the range of his identity. He felt like shouting at the ashes of his father, 'You did build your house. Then why didn't you carry it away with you?'

He could not imagine that the burden of Father's death could be just an everyday occurrence to others. He could not bear the priests on their bicycles pursuing him as he carried his father's ashes, bundled in a red cloth, to the banks of the Ganges.

'They stick to you like dogs stick to dead flesh,' he thought.

But he deliberately forced himself to smile and say, 'Don't follow us. We are just going to the riverbank for a quiet walk.'

He had heard the reply, 'Why are you telling a lie, *Babu*? Sorrow is writ large on your face... *Arre*, we shall perform all the rites and only charge a nominal fee. Oh, yes! Where do you come from?'

And then a whole list of names, known and unknown, meaningless talk and arguments that hurt. Ultimately, irritated, he was compelled to agree, 'Very well, man, do perform the rites.'

Looking at his sorrowful face the priest resorted to his usual tricks. For the priest his sorrow was a mere joke. He had not been able to spend even a few quiet moments with his father who was dead.

He had not even been able to tell him, 'You wanted to pile up things to show off to society, which waited only to see the fun of your death! Society only aims at satisfying its own greed. All those people are in no different from dogs who always come back with their tails between their legs, even after having been repeatedly kicked.'

But no.... if his father could not understand that in his lifetime, how would he understand it after his death? How often had he felt like scattering his father's ashes in the air just there and going back! All the compromises he had avoided making all along, he now had to make at the funeral of his father. He still had that pain in his heart. He had done everything—made rice-balls, recited *mantras,* held the sacrificial grass in his hand, handled the newly-worn sacred thread as though he had been wearing it all his life, even faithfully lowered his head before the priest, mumbling the entire list of his ancestors. He had enacted exactly the same drama played by the bride and bridegroom at the time of their marriage to buy each other's bodies. At the end of the whole farce came the moment of making payment to the priest. You would think that the entire scenario had been arranged just for that!

The sun had started peeping out like the light emerging from a corner of a theatre. He saw that the compartment was no longer quiet. His three fellow passengers were up and about. They seemed to be addressing themselves. One asked about the station that had just passed, and another looked at the railway timetable to find out about the next station. The whole of their outside world seemed enclosed in the railway compartment. Morning held the smell of stagnant water. He opened the window, looked out and was kissed by a whiff of fresh air. The racing trees seemed to jump like hares.

He had even forgotten his destination. His fellow passengers were exchanging notes about the rest of the journey. Though there, he was really not there. For how long his sister had been complaining! He had not visited his city after his father's death. The ceremony for his father's death anniversary had been performed by his brother. In between, six or seven monsoons had come and gone. His sister was keen to tie *raakhi* around his wrist. Every time he wrote a letter, wet with tears — she reminded him of his father. Would she have behaved like a stranger if his father had been alive? Actually nobody bothered about him. He had seven nephews and nieces and, though all remembered him, nobody knew what their uncle was doing. His sister only remembered that when she was a child, she used to get a rupee for tying *raakhis*. Now...?

Tears came to his eyes. How brother and sister had quarrelled as children! How the sister used to drink away the brother's share of milk and then add water to it! And how she used to be beaten up when discovered! Only then was it that she had come to realize the difference between being a boy and a girl. She had to wash her brother's shirts every day and if she didn't do that, he would catch hold of her by her hair and beat her up. But there was always peace between them when mother was not at home.

When their period of peace extended a little longer, the two of them would play 'house-house' in the balcony. The sister would become the wife of the brother and then both of them would enact all the scenes from the world of reality with a touch of drama. They imitated everything — starting with the quarrels between their parents and ending with a display of all that symbolizes love. They would also have a rag-doll. Everything was so life-like, yet now so meaningless! That's what infuriated him. Marriage, love—everything was so complicated! They devoured life like vultures, till one was reduced to ashes and was tied up in a bundle.

Verily, like travelling by train, he had left all those halts behind. His sister's face remained fixed before his eyes. Her face appeared to him like a mushroom grown in a pot, with seven new offshoots sprouting, and the taller mushroom gazing at those sprouts with pride. They would all welcome him on his arrival. At the same time, there would be only one thought in everybody's mind, 'Brother has become a big officer; uncle has a machine to print currency notes; his terelene bush shirt is stitched just to fit us; his trousers too, fit us perfectly. Why should uncle have three fountain pens? Brother is funny because he keeps his suitcase locked. *Arre*, does one keep things locked up in one's own house? Chiffon tie-and-dye *saris* are very much in vogue these days. Brother must have surely brought at least one such *sari* for us. After all, doesn't he have to make up for not one but five or six *raakhi* presents?'

He sensed how his brother-in-law, with his air of detachment talked in a hushed tone. He was vocal about the fact that, since he belonged to the same clan, he should not have severed his ties and chosen for himself a separate path. And having done so, he was now duty-bound to make amends.

He got up suddenly, opened his attaché case, brought out a copy of the railway timetable and started flipping through its pages. As he turned the pages, he forgot what he had wanted to see. He glanced at them one by one. He felt that his companions' eyes were glued to those pages. He surveyed those eyes in one go. Shekhar's eyes sprang up from his files. Shekhar had now become a schoolteacher. Hari was an overseer. Deshmukh was a police sub-inspector. Savita... He wanted to observe more closely, but could not make out anything. It seemed that only the expression of her eyes was absorbed by the timetable printed on newsprint. He tried very hard but couldn't find Savita anywhere. Remembering her, his thoughts flew to himself. Was he something apart from those memories? Perhaps not... Then, why had he decided to appear for his I.A.S.? Who had provoked him to do that? All of a sudden, he had become the Director of a very big department. After all, why? How?

A flood of worries surrounded him as it were. Everything happens according to tradition. Whoever allowed a flower of modernity to bloom in the jungle of tradition?

The moving train had slowed down. Perhaps it was nearing a station. He put the timetable on the seat upside down and his eyes started roving in the compartment. There were two passengers on the opposite seat. One of them was reading the morning paper and the other was gazing at him. He encountered that gaze. The other passenger at once lowered his eyes and looked away.

He looked out through the window. The train's motion had slowed down further. Outside, in the dried up fields stood the stalks of harvested crops. The earth had cracks here and there, and resembled the face of a very aged man. Bunches of red flowers hung from the *palaash* trees growing close to the railway line. He had loved these flowers right from his childhood. They burnt like phosphorous and emitted a freshness to the dry, bare jungle. As a child he would pluck those flowers and bring them home to play *Holi* with the colour extracted from them. Subsequently, these flowers changed to look like flattened petals in the shape of a rupee coin. In those days the flowers served as money in their make-believe world. And it was then that he had come to recognize the value of money. As he looked in front him, he suddenly went back several years in the Past. He was not destined to remain there, however. The third passenger asked conversationally, as he wiped his face with a towel, 'Are we nearing a station, Sir?'

He felt the question was addressed only to him. He sat up erect and said, 'Yes, Sir, it's Narsinghpur.'

'How long does the train stop here?'

'Isn't there a big station a little further?'

'Another hour or so, and we shall reach Jabalpur,' another passenger interrupted.

'The train stops there for a long time. What do you want to do?'

Nothing. I'll just get down and walk a bit. I'll have some tea and...'

He continued in an utterly carefree manner like one on a holiday.

He paced up and down the compartment. 'I'm a military man. If I sit long in the same place, my body becomes stiff and numb.'

The man, who had been reading the newspaper a little while ago remarked as though throwing a challenge, 'I'm getting down at Jabalpur.'

He suddenly felt disturbed on hearing the reply. At the mention of the city, he began to stare down at the floor of the compartment with blank eyes.

'I've heard about the marble-rocks there. Is it a lovely place?'

The army man seemed to be a very jolly fellow. But he did not consider it proper to join in the discussion. He continued to stare at the dirty floor of the compartment. A man becomes alert at the mention of the city of his birth. He feels as though somebody has called him by his first name amidst a jungle full of people. Now that name was like a dream. Everyone had started referring to him as *Tiwari Saheb*, and his first name Sharad seemed to have got lost somewhere in the years. How much time had he spent in those very marble-rocks at *Bheda Ghat*. And what satisfaction he used to feel whenever he looked at the Mithuna images in the temple of *Chaunsath Jogini*! And how often he had enjoyed eating *daal-baati* outside that temple! He had spent several nights there with a campfire and, in his idle moments, memories of those days would start floating around him. That was because a man who is used to living in the Past is never able to live in the Present.

He heaved a sigh. What a great mockery that rather than living in the Present, man removes himself from the moment of the Present! But how could one live in the Present? Suddenly he felt that all the passengers getting off at Jabalpur knew him well. They would surely announce it to everyone that Sharad *Saheb* had proceeded straight to Allahabad without getting off at Jabalpur. What would happen then?

How that Champu would curse him! Champu, that is, Seth Ratan Lal Jain, who now owned a bookshop. He had once written to him, 'You are in the capital of the country and are a big officer. Get a licence for me so that I can set up some factory.' He had not bothered to even reply to the letter because he had no such inclination. When he had been studying for his M.A., he had gone to take some books on credit from Champu's shop. Champu had given him the books but with an indirect hint that his business was selling books, not running a library. He knew that Champu was not wrong. But at the time, he had been in no position to buy any books either.

He could see Champu's face clearly before him — cheerful and glowing with the faint radiance of the warmth of money. When he had been performing his father's funeral rites under a *peepal* tree, Champu had said, 'Sharad *Bhai*, what your father did not do for you sake! You must definitely give a gold ring to the priest!'

He was furious. In truth, Father had left him only fit to be a mere ordinary clerk. Soon after passing the matriculation examination he had had to take tuitions here and there so that he would not have to ask Father for money to finance his studies. But he had merely stared at Champu, given away the gold ring to the priest and clenched his teeth. After that he had fed three hundred persons all day, from morning till evening, and in the whole process, had got a stiff waist. He was made to do everything he had never wanted to.

Suddenly, he felt darkness spreading before him. When he closed his eyes, he was surrounded by voices. They were not clear, but they were definitely the voices of his relatives. His uncle had a habit of reproaching him. And his aunt always took away money from his pocket. His maternal aunt invariably rifled through everything he had and took away by force any clothes she thought would be useful to her husband. And then the biggest question of them all, 'They say, you earn a lot under the table over there?'

'Is it something one asks?' his uncle would add promptly. '*Arre*, our nephew is a big officer, yes, an officer! All the wealthy businessmen hover around him like moths round a flame and give bundles of notes concealed in baskets of fruit. When they come with those baskets in their cars, our nephew treats them with contempt and asks them to leave the baskets behind. They quietly fold their hands and go away.'

His uncle said it as though he himself had been receiving that extra income. That is what made him so furious when he heard those words. The truth was he had never accepted a bribe nor made any underhand deal. That's exactly why he was held in respect. He felt like an innocent person being teased and branded a thief per force. He knew his uncle's words only had one meaning, and it all centred around money.

He felt as though he had been caught like Abhimanyu in an entangled maze of questions. He did not even remember that he was travelling by train; nor did not hear the voices at the stations that were being left behind; nor the sound of the iron striking like a hammer. Everything moved before him in layers. From licence, to clothes, to money — let those who wanted them, deprive him of them. By hinting that everything had come to him easily, it had become their legitimate right to have them. What a crime it is to turn something precious and hard-earned into something useless and meaningless! He felt all those deals for which he had fought since his childhood, mocking him.

He felt a jolt. The train had come to a sudden halt, breaking his stupor. There was some commotion in the compartment. Had there been an accident? Had someone pulled the chain?

'What's happened *Bhai*?'

'Don't know!'

'We seem to be nearing some big city.'

Then he looked out. The train had come to a halt near the signal. He knew that signal very well. Even the lifeless railway bogies to its right and left were not unfamiliar to him. But the open blue sky above them seemed to pass unwelcome comments as it were. Under the sky, the sprawling city on both sides of the railway lines began forcibly drawing him out. How could he go beyond that city? His mind was in a turmoil. He felt a hollow wind swirling inside his whole body. He looked at the passengers in front of him.

Then he closed his eyes like a pigeon closes its eyes on seeing a cat. For sometime, he remained in the same position. With his eyes closed, he stretched himself straight on the berth and covered himself with a sheet, cutting himself off from his fellow passengers. Then he turned on his side, showing them his back and covered his face with his hands. He was like an ostrich hiding its neck at the first indication of a storm in a desert.

Breaking Point

Usha Mahajan

In the afternoons this corner of the restaurant was usually empty. By the evening the place filled up and it was futile coming there without a prior reservation in the hope of finding a place. That evening it appeared as if the whole of Calcutta had turned up for tea. Right from the elevators upto the entrance there was a queue waiting for tables and greedily eyeing those inside.

'I hope you haven't been waiting for too long!' he said as he sat down on the sofa and stretched his left leg to get his handkerchief out of his trouser pocket. 'There was heavy traffic all along the route. See, how I am sweating! And its winter time.'

Madhukar wiped the beads of perspiration off his forehead. She fixed her gaze on him. He did not sound as if he was lying; he had a childlike innocence about him. She wanted to take the end of her *sari* and mop the pearls of sweat from his body.

'Why are you looking at me in this way?' he asked tenderly. He noticed her twisting the ends of her sari between her fingers. Gently he took her hand. The storm of emotions gathering within her found an outlet. Before she could check herself, the words burst out of her mouth, 'Madhukar, do you love me?'

He was taken aback almost as if his hand had touched a live wire or an icy blast of wind had blown into the easy corner of the restaurant and chilled the atmosphere. He suddenly let go her hand and sank back into his seat. 'The waiter is coming to take our order,' he replied and tried to look very business-like.

Madhukar's reluctance to answer a direct question made her very unsure of herself. How could she have been so brash as to expose herself so shamelessly before him. She felt as if a tidal wave of disillusionment had suddenly swept her off her feet and cast her on the hard rocks of reality. She realised she had blundered and felt sorry for herself. Married couples who have lived together for many years do not ever dare to ask each other such questions. What right had she to do so on the strength of just a few meetings?

What did she have to bring up the question of love in their relationship? He was doing everything he could for her. He took her out for lunches and dinners to the most expensive joints in the city. And the countless little things he was always doing for her! Despite all that every time they met she looked into his eyes to find an answer to just one question.

Madhukar glanced at his wristwatch and said, 'Neera, I forgot about an appointment I made for four o'clock to see a patient in Ballygunge. It slipped out of my mind. Let's go; we'll come here another evening.' And without waiting for an answer, he got up and announced, 'I will drop you on the way.'

She followed him out of the restaurant feeling smaller and smaller till she felt being reduced to a midget.

'Don't worry about me. It will make you go out of your way. I'll get home on my own,' she said trying hard to smile.

She spent the night thinking about him. She knew she should not see any more of Madhukar; but she also knew she would not be able to keep up her resolve. The more she tried to put him out of her mind, the stronger became her desire to win over Madhukar's heart. The next evening when Madhukar dropped in on the excuse of seeing her sick husband, she felt she had got a second lease of life. He brought him a bouquet of flowers; she knew that it was really meant for her because they were her favourite gladioli. He knew she kept them in her vase till the last blossom had withered away.

As she was leaving, he touched her lightly on her shoulders and murmured, 'Sorry about last evening.'

Neera could not make out what he was apologising about. For not having replied to her question or not having given her tea?

However, she felt there must be something abiding in their relationship to make him come to see her.

Maybe soon the time would come when she could put him the same question and he would answer 'Yes.'

All said and done, what else is it that keeps humans alive except hope! It was the same with her husband. He had been badly injured in a traffic accident but had hung on to life in the hope that he would be his old self again.

She remembered how lying in bed in the hospital, he had said, 'Neera, I don't think I will be of any use to you any longer. Would you like to be freed of me?'

She had broken down. She had run her trembling fingers across the face of the man who had been her life's support but was now lying disabled and helpless. She reassured him, 'Don't ever say such things again. I'll never leave you. I wish God had inflicted this injury on me rather than on you.'

Time takes its toll of everything. It not only ages the face and the body but the head and the heart as well. Time makes people forget their own words, forget the solemnity of vows made. When rains fall, withered trees begin to sprout fresh leaves. The scorching sun of mid summer turns the same green woodland into a barren desert. There was time when she had waited anxiously all day for the evening when her husband would be back home. And now that he was home all day long, she felt that there was nothing left in the world for her to look forward to.

How could she ever forget what Madhukar had done for her! When her world had become pitch-dark without a glimmer of hope anywhere, he had taken her out into the light. He had assuaged the pain that she had inflicted upon herself through self-torture. She had become a living corpse; he had breathed life back into her.

'Look upon me as a friend. Tell me all that you have on your mind. Grief shared is a burden lightened,' Madhukar had said to solace her.

Alas! If only anguish in the heart could be lessened by opening it out to others! Inner sorrow is an unending, wordless tale which only the truly concerned can comprehend.

At the time she felt that no one could read her mind better than Madhukar. She started adorning her days and nights with the pearls of dreams surrounding him. In her desert she saw a mirage of sparkling, life-giving water. Never before in her life had she felt closer to anyone as she felt to Madhukar.

The last five years had not been without meaning for them. They had gone a long way together. He set the pace, holding her hand in a tight grasp to help her keep up with him. His name was now listed amongst the most successful doctors in the city. He never had any problem with money; now he had plenty to squander. He could not bear to see Neera living in a miserable, dilapidated tenement in Tollygunj. He bought her a spacious apartment in Calcutta's upper class south district and made special arrangements for her husband's treatment. The same Madhukar who had shied away on hearing the word 'love' had showered her with affection. He had also seen how devoted Neera was to him. She catered to every little whim that took his fancy; in his hands she was like a puppet dancing to his tune. All this was concrete proof, if anywhere needed, that in his happiness she found fulfillment.

There was only one problem. Her seven-year-old son, Anjul, had taken a dislike to 'Uncle' Madhukar. 'Mama, you should not leave papa alone and go out with uncle,' he had often grumbled. It was Madhukar who had suggested that Anjul be put in a boarding school in Darjeeling. It would make a man out of him. His own son was in the same boarding school. Her heart swelled with pride at his concern with her problems. He looked upon her son as if he was his own child. Why else would he want to give him the same opportunities as he was providing his own son? How she had cried when time came for Anjul to leave home. She had steeled her heart and agreed to Madhukar's proposal because she believed that it would be best for her son to stay away from her.

Receiving favours can become such a burden that there comes a time when one is better off freed of them. However, her husband had fallen in line with all that had happened. But the burden of favours received was borne by her. It had become a habit. But even with her the load was becoming too heavy for her shoulders. She felt like throwing it off and casting it into a gutter. Thereafter, she could not care what slights and kicks she got from the passers-by. Perhaps it was this kind of fate that her husband had wanted to save her from.

That day had been really dreadful. Madhukar had dropped her home. The lift was out of order. She ran out of breath climbing the long flights of stairs. She had barely turned the key to let herself in when she heard him call, 'Neera, come here.' It had been ages since he had called by her name; most of the time it was 'anyone there?' An unknown fear gripped her heart. He was a helpless paralytic - what could he possibly do to her? Even so, she could not muster up courage to face him. She came upto the door of his room and noticed a strange gleam of resignation in his eyes. 'Come to me, Neera.' The voice was full of life. She went and sat down on the corner of his bed. He picked up his son's photograph from the side-table and began to stare at it. 'Neera, will you agree to do what I ask of you?' Before she could reply he said, 'Get Anjul to come back home. Let him stay with you.' Then after a pause he said in a flat monotone, 'Neera, why don't you marry Madhukar? He loves you. You can forget all about me.'

She felt the earth slip away from under her feet. She did not dare to raise her eyes to meet his. 'I'll get your paper,' she said and went to the kitchen.

Marry? What on earth for? Is marriage the ultimate of all man-women relationships? Is marriage all that holds them together? If there is more to it, what is it? Despite being married, Madhukar had come to her to steal a few moments of happiness. Was the bright vermilion she wore in the parting of her hair just a symbol of her belonging to her disabled husband? What was it that Madhukar had not done for her? He came to see her because he preferred her company to that of his wife. Would not asking for more amount to asking for too much? An admission of pettiness and greed? Of wanting to displace his wife and children to make room for herself? Shame on her! How could she ever think of doing such a thing! Admittedly she had often dreamt of appearing openly in society with Madhukar's hand in hers; but dreaming it was and no more. Wasn't she paying the price for being 'the other woman'? Another name for love is sacrifice.

She heard the sound of something crashing and the splintering of glass. Perhaps Anjul's framed photograph had fallen down. She took the platter of food and hurried to her husband's bedside. Her hands began to shake. Anjul's picture was lying on the floor; her husband's left arm was dangling by the bed; a deathly pallor had spread over his face; his lifeless eyes carried an accusation of guilt. Was it for this that he had summoned her to his bedside? Something inside her snapped and opened a flood-gate of pent-up emotions. She stood rooted to the ground like one found guilty of a crime. She felt as if she had cut a limb of her own body and thrown it away.

The neighbours heard her screams and came running in. She could not recall how she passed that night. She tried to send word to Madhukar. There was not a trace of him. Her neighbours helped her to arrange all the details of the funeral.

For the first time it occurred to her how secure she had felt with that helpless, invalid husband of hers. How could she bear to live alone now? If only Madhukar had come over, taken her in his arms and said, 'Neera, what makes you think you have been left alone? I will always be with you. You are not a widow; I am your protector and your husband.'

She got up and faced the mirror. Her eyes were swollen with crying and wailing. Her hair was dishevelled; the *bindi* mark was spattered across her forehead. She refused to wipe it off. For the last many years, she had put it there to please Madhukar. She took a little vermillion powder from her box and with a trembling finger put the *bindi* mark where it always had been.

She could no longer control herself. With fear in her heart she rang up Madhukar's home. She had never dared to do this before. It was Madhukar's wife who picked up the receiver.

'This is Neera calling. Can I speak to Madhukar? It's very urgent.'

After a pause a very acid voice replied, 'Aren't you satisfied with all that you have grabbed? Or do you now want to break into my home as well? For God's sake leave me alone.' The receiver was put down.

A storm of anger welled up in her mind. Surely she had a claim on everything connected with Madhukar. From the time they had got to know each other, she had hung on every breath he took. If his wife had been so conscious of safeguarding her 'wife's rights', why wasn't she able to keep him tied down with bonds of love? For the first time Neera realised the existence of Madhukar's wife and sensed her own helplessness. The question of status suddenly arose in her mind.

The next evening Madhukar came to see her. She wanted to run up to him, put her head against his broad chest and cry her heart out till she had shed all her tears. Why she remained rooted to the spot she did not know; nor why Madhukar had that uncertain look in his eyes. It seemed as if he wanted to say something but could not find the exact words.

Ultimately, Neera broke the silence, 'Where were you?'

'I was out of town. I had to leave suddenly. I would have come over as soon as I was back. But you rang up for me at home— I don't know why. My wife was very upset and created a scene. To avoid it getting worse I kept away yesterday.'

'He could not come because ....'

Something very tender preserved with care and patience over the years had suddenly snapped. The web of illusions that she had spun out of the threads of hope had come apart. Was this the moment of truth for which she had waited so long and for which she had defied all social conventions and given herself body and soul to Madhukar?

A heavy silence descended on the room; a pall of gloom darker than when her husband had died, enveloped her. Tears welled up in her eyes and fell on her wrists. She turned her face towards the window. The sun was about to set. In the dim light of the heavily curtained room, Madhukar was unable to see another sun setting in Neera's tear-sodden eyes and another hearse wading through them.

She drew one end of her *sari* and rubbed the *bindi* off her forehead, smashed her bangles against the arms of the chair and was convulsed with hysterical sobbing. Madhukar could not make out what had come over her. Between the splintered glass of bangles were drops of blood. Madhukar tried to comfort her. 'Neera, take a hold on yourself. Things will soon take a turn for the better. See you have cut your wrists.' He ran and got out his first-aid kit.

She cried and cried till she could cry no more. Madhukar sat by her for a long time trying to make out what had happened to her. As he left he said, 'Neera, take a little rest. You are not yourself today. I'll look again tomorrow.'

She had a blank look in her wide open eyes. She did not turn round to see him leave.

He came the next day. He knocked at her door many times. All he could hear was the sound of sobbing. The door did not open. He turned back, grumbling to himself, 'She is still mourning her dead husband. Perhaps she loved him.'

Translated by **Khushwant Singh**

BENGALI

Cabuliwallah

Rabindra Nath Tagore

My five years' old daughter Mini cannot live without chattering. I really believe that in all her life she has not wasted a minute in silence. Her mother is often vexed at this, and would stop her prattle, but I would not. To see Mini quiet is unnatural, and I cannot bear it long. And so my own talk with her is always lively.

One morning, for instance, when I was in the midst of the seventeenth chapter of my new novel, my little Mini stole into the room, and putting her hand into mine, said: 'Father! Ramdayal the door-keeper calls a crow a krow! He doesn't know anything, does he?'

Before I could explain to her the difference of language in this world, she was embarked on the full tide of another subject. 'What do you think, Father? Bhola says there is an elephant in the clouds, blowing water out of his trunk, and that's why it rains!'

And then, darting off anew, while I sat still making ready some reply to this last saying: 'Father! what relation is Mother to you?'

'My dear little sister in the law!' I murmured involuntarily to myself, but with a grave face contrived to answer: 'Go and play with Bhola, Muni! I am busy!'

The window of my room overlooks the road. The child had seated herself at my feet near my table, and was playing softly, drumming on her knees. I was hard at work on my seventeenth chapter, where Protap Singh, the hero, had just caught Kanchanlata, the heroine, in his arms, and was about to escape her by the third-storey window of the castle, when all of a sudden Mini left her play, and ran to the window, crying: 'A Cabuliwalla! A Cabuliwallah!' Sure enough in the street below was a Cabuliwallah, passing slowly along. He wore the loose soiled clothing of his people, with a tall turban; there was a bag on his back, and he carried boxes of grapes in his hand.

I cannot tell what were my daughter's feelings at the sight of this man, but she began to call him loudly. 'Ah!' I thought, 'he will come in, and my seventeenth chapter will never be finished!' At which exact moment the Cabuliwallah turned, and looked up at the child. When she saw this, overcome by terror, she fled to her mother's protection, and disappeared. She had a blind belief that inside the bag, which the big man carried, there were perhaps two or three other children like herself. The pedlar meanwhile entered my doorway, and greeted me with a smiling face.

So precarious was the position of my hero and my heroine, that my first impulse was to stop and buy something, since the man had been called. I made some small purchases, and a conversation began about Abdurrahman, the Russians, the English and the Frontier Policy.

As he was about to leave, he asked: 'And where is the little girl, sir?'

And I, thinking that Mini must get rid of her false fear, had her brought out.

She stood by my chair, and looked at the Cabuliwallah and his bag. He offered her nuts and raisins, but she would not be tempted, and only clung the closer to me, with all her doubts increased.

This was their first meeting.

One morning, however, not many days later, as I was leaving the house, I was startled to find Mini, seated on a bench near the door, laughing and talking, with the great Cabuliwallah at her feet. In all her life, it appeared, my small daughter had never found so patient a listener, save her father. And already the corner of her little *sari* was stuffed with almonds and raisins, the gift of her visitor. 'Why did you give her those?' I said, and taking out an eight-anna bit, I handed it to him. The man accepted the money without demur, and slipped it into his pocket.

Alas, on my return an hour later, I found the unfortunate coin had made twice its own worth of trouble! For the Cabuliwallah had given it to Mini, and her mother catching sight of the bright round object, had pounced on the child with: 'Where did you get that eight-anna bit?'

'The Cabuliwallah gave it me,' said Mini cheerfully.

'The Cabuliwallah gave it you!' cried her mother much shocked. 'O Mini! how could you take it from him?'

I, entering at the moment, saved her from impending disaster, and proceeded to make my own inquiries.

It was not the first or second time, I found, that the two had met. The Cabuliwallah had overcome the child's first terror by a judicious bribery of nuts and almonds, and the two were now great friends.

They had many quaint jokes, which afforded them much amusement. Seated in front of him, looking down on his gigantic frame in all her tiny dignity, Mini would ripple her face with laughter, and begin: 'O Cabuliwallah! Cabuliwallah! what have you got in your bag?'

And he would reply, in the nasal accents of the mountaineer: 'An Elephant!' Not much cause for merriment, perhaps; but how they both enjoyed the witticism! And for me, this child's talk with a grown-up man had always in it something strangely fascinating.

Then the Cabuliwallah, not to be behindhand, would take his turn: 'Well, little one, and when are you going to the father-in-law's house?

Now most small Bengali maidens have heard long ago about the father-in-law's house; but we, being a little new-fangled, had kept these things from our child, and Mini at this question must have been a trifle bewildered. But she would not show it, and with ready tact replied: 'Are you going there?'

Amongst men of the Cabuliwallah's class, however, it is well known that the words *father-in-law's house* have a double meaning. It is a euphemism for *jail*, the place where we are well cared for; at no expense to ourselves. In this sense would the sturdy pedlar take my daughter's question. 'Ah,' he would say, shaking his fist at an invisible policeman, 'I will thrash my father-in-law!' Hearing this, and picturing the poor discomfited relative, Mini would go off into peals of laughter, in which her formidable friend would join.

These were autumn mornings, the very time of year when kings of old went forth to conquest; and I, never stirring from my little corner in Calcutta, would let my mind wander over the whole world. At the very name of another country, my heart would go out to it, and at the sight of a foreigner in the streets, I would fall to weaving a network of dreams — the mountains, the glens, and the forests of his distant home, with his cottage in its setting, and the free and independent life of far-away wilds. Perhaps the scenes of travel conjure themselves up before me, and pass and repass in my imagination all the more vividly, because I lead such a vegetable existence that a call to travel would fall upon me like a thunderbolt. In the presence of this Cabuliwallah I was immediately transported to the foot of arid mountain peaks, with narrow little defiles twisting in and out amongst their towering heights. I could see the string of camels bearing the merchandise, and the company of turbanned merchants carrying some of their queer old firearms, and some of their spears, journeying downward towards the plains. I could see — But at some such point Mini's mother would intervene, imploring me to 'beware of that man.'

Mini's mother is unfortunately a very timid lady. Whenever she hears a noise in the street, or sees people coming towards the house, she always jumps to the conclusion that they are either thieves, or drunkards, or snakes, or tigers, or malaria or cockroaches, or caterpillars, or an English sailor. Even after all these years of experience, she is not able to overcome her terror. So she was full of doubts about the Cabuliwallah, and used to beg me to keep a watchful eye on him.

I tried to laugh her fear gently away, but then she would turn around on me seriously, and ask me solemn questions, Were children never kidnapped?

Was it, then, not true that there was slavery in Cabul?

Was it so very absurd that this big man should be able to carry off a tiny child?

I urged that, though not impossible, it was highly improbable. But this was not enough, and her dread persisted. As it was indefinite, however, it did not seem right to forbid the man the house, and the intimacy went on unchecked.

Once a year in the middle of January Rahmun, the Cabuliwallah, was in the habit of returning to his country, and as the time approached he would be very busy, going from house to house collecting his debts. This year, however, he could always find time to come and see Mini. It would have seemed to an outsider that there was some conspiracy between the two, for when he could not come in the morning, he would appear in the evening.

Even to me it was a little startling now and then, in the corner of a dark room, suddenly to surprise this tall, loose-garmented, much bebagged man; but when Mini would run in smiling, with her 'O Cabuliwallah! Cabuliwallah! and the two friends, so far apart in age, would subside into their old laughter and their old jokes, I felt reassured.

One morning, a few days before he had made up his mind to go, I was correcting my proof sheets in my study. It was chilly weather. Through the window the rays of the sun touched my feet, and the slight warmth was very welcome. It was almost eight o'clock, and the early pedestrians were returning home with their heads covered. All at once I heard an uproar in the street, and, looking out, saw Rahmun being led away bound between two policemen, and behind them a crowd of curious boys. There were blood-stains on the clothes of the Cabuliwallah, and one of the policemen carried a knife. Hurrying out, I stopped them, and inquired what it all meant. Partly from one, partly from another, I gathered that a certain neighbour had owed the pedlar something for a Rampuri shawl, but had falsely denied having bought it, and that in the course of the quarrel Rahmun had stuck him. Now in the heat of his excitement, the prisoner began calling his enemy all sorts of names, when suddenly in a verandah of my house appeared my little Mini, with her usual exclamation: 'O Cabuliwallah, Cabuliwallah! Rahmun's face lighted up as he turned to her. He had no bag under his arm to-day, so she could not discuss the elephant with him. She at once therefore proceeded to the next question: 'Are you going to the father-in-law's house?' Rahmun laughed and said: 'Just where I am going, little one!' Then seeing that the reply did not assure the child, he held up his fettered hands. 'Ah,' he said, 'I would have thrashed that old father-in-law, but my hands are bound!'

On a charge of murderous assault, Rahmun was sentenced to some years' imprisonment.

Time passed away, and he was not remembered. The accustomed work in the accustomed place was ours, and the thought of the once free mountainer spending his years in prison seldom or never occurred to us. Even my light-hearted Mini, I am ashamed to say, forgot her old friend. New companions filled her life. As she grew older, she spent more of her time with girls. So much time indeed did she spend with them that she came no more, as she used to do, to her father's room. I was scarcely on speaking terms with her.

Years had passed away. It was once more autumn and we had made arrangements for our Mini's marriage. It was to take place during the Puja Holidays. With Durga returning to Kailas, the light of our home also was to depart to her husband's house, and leave her father's in the shadow.

The morning was bright. After the rains, there was a sense of ablution in the air, and the sun-rays looked like pure gold. So bright were they that they gave a beautiful radiance even to the sordid brick walls of our Calcutta lanes. Since early dawn today the wedding-pipes had been sounding, and at each beat my own heart throbbed. The wail of the tune, Bhairavi, seemed to intensify my pain at the approaching separation. My Mini was to be married tonight.

From early morning noise and bustle had pervaded the house. In the courtyard the canopy had to be slung on its bamboo poles; the chandeliers with their tinkling sound must be hung in each room and verandah. There was no end of hurry and excitement. I was sitting in my study, looking through the accounts, when someone entered, saluting respectfully, and stood before me. It was Rahmun the Cabuliwallah. At first I did not recognise him. He had no bag, nor the long hair, nor the same vigour that he used to have. But he smiled, and I knew him again.

'When did you come, Rahmun?' I asked him.

'Last evening,' he said, 'I was released from jail.'

The words struck harsh upon my ears. I had never before talked with one who had wounded his fellow, and my heart shrank within itself when I realised this, for I felt that the day would have been better-omened had he not turned up.

'There are ceremonies going on,' I said, 'and I am busy. Could you perhaps come another day?'

At once he turned to go; but as he reached the door he hesitated, and said: 'May I not see the little one, sir, for a moment?' It was his belief that Mini was still the same. He had pictured her running to him as she used to, calling 'O Cabuliwallah! Cabuliwallah!' He had imagined too that they would laugh and talk together, just as of old. In fact, in memory of former days he had brought, carefully wrapped up in paper, a few almonds and raisins and grapes, obtained somehow from a countryman, for his own little fund was dispersed.

I said again: 'There is a ceremony in the house, and you will not be able to see anyone today'.

The man's face fell. He looked wistfully at me for a moment, said 'good morning,' and went out.

I felt a little sorry, and would have called him back, but I found he was returning of his own accord. He came close up to me holding out his offerings, and said: 'I brought these few things, sir, for the little one. Will you give them to her?'

I took them and was going to pay him, but he caught my hand and said: 'You are very kind, sir! Keep me in your recollection. Do not offer me money! - You have a little girl: I too have one like her in my own home. I think of her, and bring fruits to your child - not to make a profit for myself.'

Saying this, he put his hand inside his big loose robe, and brought out a small and dirty piece of paper. With great care he unfolded this, and smoothed it out with both hands on my table. It bore the impression of a little hand. Not a photograph. Not a drawing. The impression of an ink-smeared hand laid flat on the paper. This touch of his own little daughter had been always on his heart, as he had come year after year to Calcutta to sell his wares in the streets.

Tears came to my eyes. I forgot that he was a poor Cabuli fruit-seller, while I was—. But no, what was I more than he? He also was a father.

That impression of the hand of his little Parbati in her distant mountain home reminded me of my own little Mini.

I sent for Mini immediately from the inner apartment. Many difficulties were raised, but I would not listen. Clad in the red silk of her wedding-day, with the sandal paste on her forehead, and adorned as a young bride, Mini came, and stood bashfully before me.

The Cabuliwallah looked a little staggered at the apparition. He could not revive their old friendship. At last he smiled and said: 'Little one, are you going to your father-in-law's house?'

But Mini now understood the meaning of the word 'father-in-law,' and she could not reply to him as of old. She flushed up at the question, and stood before him with her bride-like face turned down.

I remembered the day when the Cabuliwallah and my Mini had first met, and I felt sad. When she had gone, Rahmun heaved a deep sigh, and sat down on the floor. The idea had suddenly come to him that his daughter too must have grown in this long time, and that he would have to make friends with her anew. Assuredly he would not find her as he used to know her. And besides, what might have happened to her in these eight years?

The marriage-pipes sounded, and the mild autumn sun streamed round us. But Rahmun sat in the little Calcutta lane, and saw before him the barren mountains of Afghanistan.

I took out a bank-note and gave it to him, saying: 'Go back to your own daughter, Rahmun, in your own country, and may the happiness of your meeting bring good fortune to my child!'

Having made this present, I had to curtail some of the festivities. I could not have the electric lights I had intended, nor the military band, and the ladies of the house were despondent at it. But to me the wedding-feast was all the brighter for the thought that in a distant land a long-lost father met again with his only child.

Draupadi

Mahasweta Devi

NAME: DOPDI MEJHEN, age twenty-seven, husband Dulna Majhi (deceased), domieile Cherakhan, Bankahjarh, information whether dead or alive and/or assistance in arrest, one hundred rupees....

An exchange between two medallioned *uniforms.*

FIRST MEDALLION: What's this. A tribal called Dopdi? The list of names I brought has nothing like it! How can anyone have an unlisted name?

SECOND: Draupadi Mejhen, Born the year her mother threshed rice at Surja Sahu (killed)'s Bakuli. Surja Sahu's wife gave her the name.

FIRST: These officers like nothing better than to write as much as they can in English. What's all this stuff about her?

SECOND: *Most notorious* female. *Long wanted in many.....*

Dossier. Dulna and Dopdi worked at harvests, *rotating* between Birbhum, Burdwan, Murshidabad, and Bankura. In 1971, in the famous *Operation* Bakuli, when three villages were *cordonned* off and *machine gunned,* they too lay on the ground, faking dead. In fact, they were the main culprits. Murdering Surja Sahu and his son, occupying upper-caste wells and tubewells during the drought, not surrendering those three young men to the police. In all this they were the chief instigators. In the morning, at the time of the body count, the couple could not be found. The blood-sugar level of Captain Arjan Singh, the *architect* of Bakuli, rose at once and proved yet again that diabetes can be a result of anxiety and depression. Diabetes has twelve husbands — among them anxiety.

Dulna and Dopdi went underground for a long time in a *Nean-*

derthal darkness. The Special Forces, attempting to pierce that dark by an armed search, compelled quite a few Santals in the various districts of West Bengal to meet their Maker against their will. By the Indian Constitution, all human beings, regardless of caste or creed, are sacred. Still, accidents like this do happen. Two sorts of reasons: (1) the underground couple's skill in self-concealment; (2) not merely the Santals but all tribals of the Austro-Asiatic Munda tribes appear the same to the Special Forces.

In fact, all around the ill-famed forest of Jharkhani, which is under the jurisdiction of the police station at Bankrajharh (in this India of ours, even a worm is under a certain police station), even the southeast and southwest corners, one comes across hair-raising details in the eyewitness records put together on the people who are suspected of attacking police stations, stealing guns (since the snatchers are not invariably well educated, they sometimes say 'give up your *chambers'* rather than give up your gun), killing grain brokers, landlords, moneylenders, law officers, and bureaucrats. A black-skinned couple ululated like police *sirens* before the episode. They sang jubiliantly in a savage tongue, incomprehensible even to the Santals. Such as:

Samaray hijulenako mar goekope

and,

Hendre rambra keche keche
Pundi rambra keche keche

This proves conclusively that they are the cause of Captain Arjan Singh's diabetes.

Government procedure being as incomprehensible as the Male Principle in Sankhya philosophy or Antonioni's early films, it was Arjan Singh who was sent once again on *Operation Forest* Jharkhani. Learning from Intelligence that the above-mentioned ululating and dancing couple was the escaped corpses, Arjan Singh fell for a bit into a *zombie* like state and finally acquired so irrational a dread of black-skinned people that whenever he saw a black person in a ball-bag, he swooned, saying 'they're killing me,' and drank and passed a lot of water. Neither uniform nor Scriptures could relieve that depression. At long last, under the shadow of a *premature and forced retirement,* it was possible to present him at the desk of Mr Senanayak, the elderly Bengali specialist in combat and extreme-Left politics.

Senanayak knows the activities and capacities of the opposition better than they themselves do. First, therefore, he presents an encomium on the military genius of the Sikhs. Then he explains further: is it only the opposition that should find power at the end of the barrel of gun? Arjan Singh's power also explodes out of the *male organ* of a gun. Without a gun event the 'five Ks[1] come to nothing in this day and age. These speeches he delivers to all and sundry. As a result, the fighting forces regain their confidence in the *Army Handbook.* It is not a book for everyone. It says that the most despicable and repulsive style of fighting is guerrilla warfare with primitive weapons. Annihilation at sight of any and all practitioners of such warfare is the sacred duty of every soldier. Dopdi and Dulna belong to the *category* of such fighters, for they too kill by means of hatchet and scythe, bow and arrow, etc. In fact, their fighting power is greater than the gentlemen's. Not all gentlemen become experts in the explosion of 'chambers'; they think the power will come out on its own if the gun is held. But since Dulna and Dopdi are illiterate, their kind have practised the use of weapons generation after generation.

I should mention here that, although the other side make little of him, Senanayak is not to be trifled with. Whatever his *practice,* in *theory* he respects the opposition. Respects them because they could be neither understood nor demolished if they were treated with the attitude, 'it's nothing but a bit of impertinent game playing with guns.' *In order to destroy the enemy, become one.* Thus he understood them by (*theoretically*) becoming one of them He hopes to write on all this in the future. He has also decided that in his written work he will demolish the gentlemen and *highlight* the message of the harvest workers. These mental processes might seem complicated, but actually he is a simple man and is as pleased as his third great-uncle after a meal of turtle meat. In fact, he knows that, as in the old popular song, turn by turn the world will change. And in every world he must have the credentials to survive with honour. If necessary he will show the future to what extent he alone understands the matter in its proper perspective. He knows very well that what he is doing today the future will forget, but he also knows that if he can change colour from world to world, he can represent the particular world in question. Today he is getting rid of the young by means of *'apprehension and elimination,'* but he knows people will soon forget the memory and lesson of blood. And at the same time, he, like Shakespeare, believes in delivering the world's *legacy* into youth's hands. He is Prospero as well.

At any rate, information is received that many young men and women, *batch by batch* and on jeeps, have attacked police station after police station, terrified and elated the region, and disappeared into the forest of Jharkhani. Since after escaping from Bakuli, Dopdi and Dulna have worked at the house of virtually every landowner, they can efficiently inform the killers about their targets and announce proudly that they too are soldiers, *rank and file.* Finally the impenetrable forest of Jharkhani is surrounded by real soldiers, the *army* enters and splits the battlefield. Soldiers in hiding guard the falls and springs that are the only source of drinking water; they are still guarding, still looking. On one such search, army informant Dukhiram Gharari saw a young Santal man lying on his stomach on a flat stone, dipping his face to drink water. The soldiers shot him as he lay. As the .303 threw him off spread-eagled and brought a bloody foam to his mouth, he roared 'Ma — ho' and then went limp. They realized later that it was the redoubtable Dulna Majhi.

What does 'Ma-ho' mean? Is this a violent slogan in the tribal language? Even after much thought, the Department of Defence could not be sure. Two tribal specialist types are flown in from Calcutta, and they sweat over the dictionaries put together by worthies such as Hoffman-Jeffer and Golden-Palmer. Finally the omniscient Senanayak summons Chamru, the water carrier of the *camp*. He giggles when he sees the two specialists, scratches his ear with his 'bidi', and says, the Santals of Maldah did say that when they began fighting at the time of King Gandhi! It's a battle cry. Who said 'Ma-ho' here? Did someone come from Maldah?

The problem is thus solved. Then, leaving Dulna's body on the stone, the soldiers climb the trees in green camouflage. They embrace the leafy boughs like so many great god Pans and wait as the large red ants bite their private parts. To see if anyone comes to take away the body. This is the hunter's way, not the soldier's. But Senanayak knows that these brutes cannot be dispatched by the approved method. So he asks his men to draw the prey with a corpse as bait. All will come clear, he says. I have almost deciphered Dopdi's song.

The soldiers get going at his command. But no one comes to claim Dulna's corpse. At night the soldiers shoot at a scuffle and, descending, discover that they have killed two hedgehogs copulating on dry leaves. Improvidently enough, the soldiers' jungle scout Dukhiram gets a knife in the neck before he can claim the reward for Dulna's capture. Bearing Dulna's corpse, the soldiers suffer shooting pains as the ants, interrupted in their feast, begin to bite them. When Senanayak hears that no one has come to take the corpse, he slaps his *anti-Fascist paperback* copy of *The Deputy* and shouts, '*What?* Immediately one of the tribal specialists runs in with a joy as naked and transparent as Archimedes' and says, 'Get up, *sir!* I have discovered the meaning of that 'hende rambra' stuff. It's Mundari *language.*

Thus the search for Dopdi continues. In the forest *belt* of Jharkhani, the *Operation* continues — will continue. It is a carbuncle on the government's backside. Not to be cured by the tested ointment, not to burst with the appropriate herb. In the first phase the fugitives, ignorant of the forest's topography, are caught easily, and by the law of confrontation they are shot at the taxpayer's expense. By the law of confrontation, their eyeballs, intestines, stomachs, hearts, genitals, and so on become the food of fox, vulture, hyena, wildcat, ant and worm, and the untouchables go off happily to sell their bare skeletons.

They do not allow themselves to be captured in open combat in the next phase. Now it seems that they have found a trustworthy courier. Ten to one it's Dopdi. Dopdi loved Dulna more than her blood. No doubt it is she who is saving the fugitives now.

'They' is also a *hypothesis.*

Why?

How many went *originally?*

The answer is silence. About that there are many tales, many books in press. Best not to believe everything.

How many killed in six years confrontation?

The answer is silence.

Why after confrontations are the skeletons discovered with arms broken or severed? Could armless men have fought? Why do the collarbones shake, why are legs and ribs crushed?

Two kinds of answer. Silence. Hurt rebuke in the eye. Shame on you! Why bring this up? What will be will be...

How many left in the forest? The answer is silence.

A *legion?* Is it *justifiable* to maintain a large battalion in that wild area at the taxpayers' expense?

Answer: *Objection.* 'Wild area' is incorrect. The battalion is provided with supervised nutrition, arrangements to worship according to religion, opportunity to listen to 'Bibidha Bharati[2] and to see Sanjeev Kumar and the Lord Krishna fact-to-face in the movie *This is Life?* No. The area is not wild.

How many are left?

The answer is silence.

How many are left? Is there anyone *at all?*

The answer is long.

Item: *Well, action* still goes on. Moneylenders, land lords, grain brokers, anonymous brothel keepers, ex-informants are still terrified. The hungry and naked are still defiant and irrepressible. In some *pockets* the harvest workers are getting a *better wage.* Villages sympathetic to the fugitives are still silent and hostile. These events cause one to think....

Where in the picture does Dopdi Mejhen fit?

She must have connections with the fugitives. The cause for fear is elsewhere. The ones who remain have lived a long time in the primitive world of the forest. They keep company with the poor harvest workers and the tribals. They must have forgotten book learning. Perhaps they are *orienting* their book learning to the soil they live on and learning new combat and survival techniques. One can shoot and get rid of the ones whose only recourse is extrinsic book learning and sincere intrinsic enthusiasm. Those who are working practically will not be exterminated so easily.

Therefore *Operation* Jharkhani *Forest* cannot stop. Reason: the words of warning in the *Army Handbook.*

2.

Catch Dopdi Mejhen. She will lead us to the others.

Dopdi was proceeding slowly, with some rice knotted into her belt. Mushai Tudu's wife had cooked her some. She does so occasionally. When the rice is cold, Dopdi knots it into her waist cloth and walks slowly. As she walked, she picked out and killed the lice in her hair. If she had some *kerosene,* she'd rub it into her scalp and get rid of her lice. Then she could wash her hair with baking soda. But the bastards put traps at every bend of the falls. If they smell *kerosene* in the water, they will follow the scent.

Dopdi!

She doesn't respond. She never responds when she hears her own name. She has seen in the Panchayat 3 office just today the notice for the reward in her name. Mushai Tudu's wife had said, 'What are you looking at?

Who is Dopdi Mejhen! Money if you give her up!'

'How much?

'Two hundred!'

Oh God!

Mushai's wife said outside the office. 'A lot of preparation this time. A — ll new policemen.'

Hm.

Don't come again.

Why?

Mushai's wife looked down. Tudu says that Sahib has come again. If they catch you, the village, our huts.....

They'll burn again.

Yes. And about Dukhiram.

The Sahib knows?

Shomai and Budhna betrayed us.

Where are they?

Ran away by train.

Dopdi thought of something. Then said, Go home. I don't know what will happen, if they catch me don't know me.

Can't you run away?

No. Tell me, how many times can I run away?

What will they do if they catch me? They will *kounter* me. Let them.

Mushai's wife said, We have nowhere else to go.

Dopdi said softly, I won't tell anyone's name.

Dopdi knows, has learned by hearing so often and so long, how one can come to terms with torture. If mind and body give way under torture, Dopdi will bite off her tongue. That boy did it. They kountered him. When they kounter you, your hands are tied behind you. All your bones are crushed, your sex is a terrible wound. *Killed by police in an encounter....unknown male...age twenty-two...*

As she walked thinking these thoughts, Dopdi heard someone calling, Dopdi!

She didn't respond. She doesn't respond if called by her own name. Here her name is Upi Mejhen. But who calls?

Spines of suspicion are always furled in her mind. Hearing 'Dopdi' they stiffen like a hedgehog's. Walking, she *unrolls the film* of known faces in her mind. Who? No Shomra, Shomra is on the run. Shomai and Budhna are also on the run, for other reasons. Not Golok, he is in Bakuli. Is it someone from Bakuli? After Bakuli, her and Dulna's names were Upi Mejhen, Matang Majhi. Here no one but Mushai and his wife know their real names. Among the young gentlemen, not all of the previous *batches* knew.

That was a troubled time. Dopdi is confused when she thinks about it. *Operation* Bakuli in Bakuli. Surja Sahu arranged with Biddibabu to dig two tubewells and three wells within the compound of his two houses. No water anywhere, drought in Birbhum. Unlimited water at Surja Sahu's house, as clear as a crow's eye.

Get your water with canal tax, everything is burning.

What's my profit in increasing cultivation with tax money?

Everything's on fire.

Get out of here. I don't accept your Panchayat nonsense. Increase cultivation with water. You want half the paddy for sharecropping. Everyone is happy with free paddy. Then give me paddy at home, give me money, I've learned my lesson trying to do you good.

What good did you do?

Have I not given water to the village?

You've given it to your kin Bhagunal.

Don't you get water?

No. The untouchables don't get water.

The quarrel began there. In the drought, human patience catches easily. Satish and Jugal from the village and that young gentleman, was Rana his name? said a landowning moneylender won't give a thing, put him down.

Surja Sahu's house was surrounded at night. Surja Sahu had brought out his gun. Surja was tied up with cow rope. His whitish eyeballs turned and turned, he was incontinent again and again. Dulna had said, I'll have the first blow, brothers, My great-grandfather took a bit of paddy from him, and I still give him free labour to repay that debt.

Dopdi had said, His mouth watered when he looked at me. I'll put out his eyes.

Surja Sahu. Then a *telegraphic message* from Shiuri. *Special train. Army.* The *jeep* didn't come up to Bakuli. *March-march-march.* The *Crunch-crunch-crunch* of gravel under hobnailed boots, *Cordon up: Commands* on the *mike.* Jugal Mandal, Satish Mandal, Rana *alias* Prabir *alias* Dipak, Dulna Majhi-Dopdi Mejhen *surrender surrender surrender. No surrender surrender. Mow-mow-mow down the village.* Putt-putt-putt-putt — *cordite* in the air — putt-putt — *round the clock* — putt-putt. *Flame thrower.* Bakuli is burning. *More men and women, children...fire —fire. Close canal approach. Over-over-over* by nightfall. Dopdi and Dulna had crawled on their stomachs to safety.

They could not have reached Paltakuri after Bakuli. Bhupati and Tapa took them. Then it was decided that Dopdi and Dulna would work around the Jharkhani *belt.* Dulna had explained to Dopdi, Dear this is best! We won't get family and children this way.But who knows? Landowner and moneylender and policemen might one day be wiped out!

Who called her from the back today?

Dopdi kept walking. Villages and fields, bush and rock — *Public Works Department* markers — sound of running steps in back. Only one person running. Jharkhani Forest still about two miles away. Now she thinks of nothing but entering the forest. She must let them know that the *police* have set up *notices* for her again. Must tell them that that bastard Sahib has appeared again. Must change *hideouts.* Also, the *plan* to do to Lakkhi Bera and Naran Bera what they did to Surja Sahu on account of the trouble over paying the field hands in Sandara must be cancelled. Shomai and Budhna knew everything. There was the *urgency* of great danger under Dopdi's ribs. Now she thought there was no shame as a Santal in Shomai and Budhna's treachery. Dopdi's blood was the pure unadulterated black blood of Champabhumi.[4] From Champa to Bakuli the rise and set of a million moons. The blood could have been contaminated; Dopdi felt proud of her forefathers. They stood guard over their women's blood in black armour. Shomai and Budhna are half-breeds. The fruits of war. Contributions to Radhabhumi by the American soldiers stationed at Shiandange. Otherwise crow would eat crow's flesh before Santal would betray Santal.

Footsteps at her back. The steps keep a distance. Rice in her belt, tobacco leaves tucked at her waist. Arijit, Malini, Shamu, Mantu — none of them smokes or even drinks tea. Tobacco leaves and limestone powder. Best medicine for scorpion bite. Nothing must be given away.

Dopdi turned left. This way is the *camp.* Two miles. This is not the way to the forest. But Dopdi will not enter the forest with a cop at her back.

I swear by my life. By my life Dulna, by my life. Nothing must be told.

The footsteps turn left. Dopdi touches her waist. In her palm the comfort of a half-moon. A baby scythe. The smiths at Jharkhani are fine artisans. Such an edge we'll put on it Upi, a hundred Dukhirams — Thank God Dopdi is not a gentleman. Actually, perhaps they have understood scythe, hatchet, and knife best. They do their work in silence. The lights of the *camp* at a distance. Why is Dopdi going this way? Stop a bit, it turns again. Huh! I can tell where I am if I wander all night with my eyes shut. I won't go in the forest, I won't lose him that way. I won't outrun him. You fucking jackal[5] of a cop, deadly afraid of death, you can't run around in the forest, I'd run you out of breath, throw you in a ditch, and finish you off.

Not a word must be said. Dopdi has seen the new *camp,* she has sat in the *bus station*, passed the time of day, smoked a 'bidi' and found out how many *police convoys* had arrived, how many *radio vans* Squash four, onions seven, peppers fifty, a straightforward account. This information cannot now be passed on. They will understand Dopdi Mejhen has been kountered. Then they'll run. Arijit's voice. If anyone is caught, the others must catch the *timing* and *change* their *hideout.* If *Comrade* Dopdi arrives late, we will not remain. There will be a sign of where we've gone. No *comrade*[6] will let the others be destroyed for her own sake.

Arijit's voice. The gurgle of water. The direction of the next *hideout* will be indicated by the tip of the wooden arrowhead under the stone.

Dopdi likes and understands this. Dulna died, but, let me tell you, he didn't lose anyone else's life. Because this was not in our heads to begin with, one was kountered for the other's trouble. Now a much harsher rule, easy and clear. Dopdi returns — good; doesn't return — *bad. Change hideout.* The clue will be such that the opposition won't see it, won't understand even if they do.

Footsteps at her back. Dopdi turns again. These three and a half miles of land and rocky ground are the best way to enter the forest. Dopdi has left that way behind. A little level ground ahead. Then rocks again. The *army* could not have struck *camp* on such rocky terrain. This area is quiet enough. It's like a maze, every hump looks like every other. That's fine. Dopdi will lead the cop to the burning 'ghat' Patitpaban of Saranda had been sacrificed in the name of Kali of the Burning Ghats.

Apprehend!

A lump of rock stands up. Another. Yet another. The elder Senanayak was at once triumphant and despondent. *If you want to destroy the enemy, become one.* He had done so. As long as six years ago he could anticipate their every move. He still can. Therefore he is elated. Since he has kept up with the literature, he has read *First Blood* and seen approval of his thought and work.

Dopdi couldn't trick him, he is unhappy about that. Two sorts of reasons. Six years ago he published an article about information storage in brain cells. He demonstrated in that piece that he supported this struggle from the point of view of the field hands. Dopdi is a field hand. *Veteran fighter. Search and destroy* Dopdi Mejhen is about to be *apprehended.* Will be *destroyed.* Regret.

Halt.

Dopdi stops short. The steps behind come around to the front. Under Dopdi's ribs the *canal* dam breaks. No hope. Surja Sahu's brother Rotoni Sahu. The two lumps of rock come forward. Shomai and Budhna. They had not escaped by train.

Arijit's voice. Just as you must know when you've won, you must also acknowledge defeat and start the activities of the next *stage.*

Now Dopdi spreads her arms, raises her face to the sky, turns toward the forest, and ululates with the force of her entire being. Once, twice, three times. At the third burst the birds in the trees at the outskirts of the forest awake and flap their wings. The echo of the call travels far.

3.

Draupadi Mejhen was apprehended at 6:53 p.m. It took an hour to get to *camp*. Questioning took another hour exactly. No one touched her, and she was allowed to sit on a canvas camp stool. At 8:57 Senanayak's dinner hour approached, and saying, 'Make her. Do *the needful'*, he disappeared.

Then a billion moons pass. A billion lunar years. Opening her eyes after a million light years, Draupadi, strangely enough, sees sky and moon. Slowly the bloodied nailheads shift from her brain. Trying to move, she feels her arms and legs still tied to four posts. Something sticky under her ass and waist. Her own blood. Only the gag has been removed. Incredible thirst. In case she says 'water' she catches her lower lip in her teeth. She senses that her vagina is bleeding. How many came to make her?

Shaming her, a tear trickles out of the corner of her eye. In the muddy moonlight she lowers her lightless eye, sees her breasts, and understand that, indeed, she's made up right. Her breasts are bitten raw, the nipples torn. How many? Four-five-six-seven — then Draupadi had passed out.

She turns her eyes and sees something white. Her own cloth? Nothing else. Suddenly she hopes against hope. Perhaps they have abandoned her. For the foxes to devour. But she hears the scrape of feet. She turns her head, the guard leans on his bayonet and leers at her. Draupadi closes her eyes. She doesn't have to wait long. Again the process of making her begins. Goes on. The moon vomits a bit of light and goes to sleep. Only the dark remains. A compelled spread-eagled still body. Active *pistons* of flesh rise and fall, rise and fall over it.

Then morning comes.

Then Draupadi Mejhen is brought to the tent and thrown on the straw. Her piece of cloth is thrown over her body.

Then, after *breakfast,* after reading the newspaper and sending the radio message 'Draupadi Mejhen apprehended,' etc., Draupadi Mejhen is ordered brought in.

Suddenly there is trouble.

Draupadi sits up as soon as she hears 'Move!' and asks, Where do you want me to go?

To the Burra Sahib's tent.

Where is the tent?

Over there.

Draupadi fixes her red eyes on the tent. Says, Come, I'll go.

The guard pushes the water pot forward.

Draupadi stands up. She pours the water down on the ground. Tears her piece of cloth with her teeth.

Seeing such strange behaviour, the guard says, She's gone crazy, and runs for orders. He can lead the prisoner out but doesn't know what to do if the prisoner behaves incomprehensibly. So he goes to ask his superior.

The commotion is as if the alarm had sounded in a prison. Senanayak walks out surprised and sees Draupadi, naked, walking toward him in the bright sunlight with her head high. The nervous guards trail behind.

What is this? He is about to cry, but stops.

Draupadi stands before him, naked. Thigh and pubic hair matted with dry blood. Two breasts, two wounds.

What is this? He is about to bark.

Draupadi comes closer. Stands with her hand on her hip, laughs and says, The object of your search, Dopdi Mejhen. You asked them to make me up, don't you want to see how they made me?

Where are her clothes?

Won't put them on, *sir*. Tearing them.

Draupadi's black body comes even closer. Draupadi shakes with an indomitable laughter that Senanayak simply cannot understand. Her ravaged lips bleed as she begins laughing. Draupadi wipes the blood on her palm and says in a voice that is as terrifying, sky splitting, and sharp as her ululation, What's the use of clothes? You can strip me, but how can you clothe me again? Are you a man?

She looks around and chooses the front of Senanayak's white bush shirt to spit a bloody gob at and says,There isn't a man here that I should be ashamed. I will not let you put my cloth on me. What more can you do? Come on, *kounter* me – come on, *kounter* me –?

Draupadi pushes Senanayak with her two mangled breasts, and for the first time Senanayak is afraid to stand before an unarmed target, terribly afraid.

1981

Translated by **Gayatri Chakravarty Spivak**

Notes:

I am grateful to Soumya Chakravarti for his help in solving occasional problems of English synonyms and archival research.

1. The 'five Ks' are *Kes* ('unshorn hair'); *kachh* ('drawers down to the knee'); *Karha* ('iron bangle'); *kirpan* ('dagger'); *kanga* ('comb'); to be worn by every Sikh, hence a mark of identity.

2 'Bibidha Bharati' is a popular radio program, on which listeners can hear music of their choice. The Hindi film industry is prolific in producing pulp movies for consumption in India and in all parts of the world where there is an Indian, Pakistani, and West Indian labour force. Many of the films are adaptations from the epics. Sanjeev Kumar is an idol-

ized actor. Since it was Krishna who rescued Draupadi from her predicament in the epic, and, in the film the soldiers watch, Sanjeev Kumar encounters Krishna, there might be a touch of textual irony here.

3. Panchayat is a supposedly elected body of village self-government.

4. 'Champabhumi' and 'Radhabhumi' are archaic names for certain areas of Bengal. 'Bhumi' is simply 'land.' All of Bengal is thus 'Bangabhumi.'

5. The jackal following the tiger is a common image.

6. Modern Bengali does not distinguish between 'her' and 'his'. The 'her' in the sentence beginning 'No *comrade* will.....' can therefore be considered an interpretation.

7. A sari conjures up the long many-pleated piece of cloth, complete with blouse and underclothes, that 'proper' Indian women wear. Dopdi wears a much-abbreviated version, without blouse or underclothes. It is referred to simply as 'the cloth.'

❑❑❑

URDU

Exchange of Lunatics

Saadat Hasan Manto

A couple of years or so after the partition of the sub-continent, the governments of Pakistan and India felt that just as they had exchanged their hardened criminals, they should exchange their lunatics. In other words, Muslims in the lunatic asylums of India should be sent across to Pakistan; and mad Hindus and Sikhs in Pakistan asylums be handed over to India.

Whether or not this was a sane decision, we will never know. But people in knowledgeable circles say that there were many conferences at the highest level between bureaucrats of the two countries before the final agreement was signed and a date fixed for the exchange.

The news of the impending exchange created a novel situation in the Lahore lunatic asylum. A Muslim patient who was a regular reader of the Zamindar was asked by a friend, '*Maulvi Sahib,* what is this thing they call Pakistan?' After much thought he replied, 'It's place in India where they manufacture razor blades.' A Sikh lunatic asked another, '*Sardarji,* why are we being sent to India? We cannot speak their language.' The *Sardarji* smiled and replied 'I know the lingo of the Hindustanis.' He illustrated his linguistic prowess by reciting a doggerel.

'Hindustanis are full of shaitani

They strut about like bantam cocks.'

One morning a mad Mussulman yelled the slogan 'Pakistan *Zindabad'* with such vigour that he slipped on the floor and knocked himself senseless.

Some inmates of the asylum were not really insane. They were murderers whose relative had been able to have them certified and thus saved from the hangman's noose. These people had vague notions of why India had been divided and what was Pakistan. But even they knew very little of the complete truth. The papers were not very informative and the guards were so stupid that it was difficult to make any sense of what they said. All one could gather from their talk was that there was a man of the name of Mohammed Ali Jinnah who was also known as the *Qaid-i-Azam.* And that this Mohammed Ali Jinnah alias *Qaid-i-Azam* had made a separate country for the Mussulmans which he called Pakistan.

No one knew where this Pakistan was or how far it extended. This was the chief reason why inmates who were not totally insane were in a worse dilemma than those utterly mad: they did not know whether they were in India or Pakistan. If they were in India, where exactly was Pakistan? If they were in Pakistan how was it that the very same place had till recently been known as India?

A poor Muslim inmate got so baffled with the talk about India and Pakistan, Pakistan and India, that he got madder than before. One day while he was sweeping the floor he was suddenly overcome by an insane impulse. He threw away his brush and clambered up a tree. And for two hours he orated from the branch of this tree on Indo-Pakistan problems. When the guards tried to get him down, he climbed up still higher. When they threatened him he replied, 'I do not wish to live either in India or Pakistan; I want to stay where I am, on top of this tree.'

After a while the fit of lunacy abated and the man was persuaded to come down. As soon as he was on the ground he began to embrace his Hindu and Sikh friends and shed bitter tears. He was overcome by the thought that they would leave him and go away to India.

Another Muslim inmate had a Master of Science degree in radio-engineering and considered himself a cut above the others. He used to spend his days strolling in a secluded corner of the garden. Suddenly a change came over him. He took off all his clothes and handed them over to the head-constable.

He resumed the peripatations without a stitch of clothing on his person.

And there was yet another lunatic, a fat Mussulman who had been a leader of the Muslim League in Chiniot. He was given to bathing fifteen to sixteen times during the day. He suddenly gave it up altogether.

The name of this fat Mussulman was Mohammed Ali. But one day he proclaimed from his cell that he was Mohammed Ali Jinnah. Not to be outdone, his cell-mate who was Sikh proclaimed himself to be Master Tara Singh. The two began to abuse each other. They were declared 'dangerous' and put in separate cages.

There was a young Hindu lawyer from Lahore. He was said to have become unhinged when his lady-love jilted him. When he heard that Amritsar had gone to India, he was very depressed: his sweet-heart lived in Amritsar. Although the girl had spurned his affection, he did not forget her even in his lunacy. He spent his time cursing all leaders, Hindu as well as Muslim, because they had split India into two, and made his beloved an Indian and him a Pakistani.

When the talk of exchanging lunatics was in the air, other inmates consoled the Hindu lawyer with the hope that he would soon be sent to India — the country where his sweetheart lived. But the lawyer refused to be reassured. He did not want to leave Lahore because he was convinced that he would not be able to set up legal practice in Amritsar.

There were a couple of Anglo-Indians in the European ward. They were very saddened to learn that the English had liberated India and returned home. They met secretly to deliberate on problems of their future status in the asylum: would the asylum continue to have a separate ward for Europeans? Would they be served breakfast as before? Would they be deprived of toast and be forced to eat chappaties?

Then there was a Sikh who had been in the asylum for fifteen years. And in the fifteen years he said little besides the following sentence: *"O pardi, good good di, anekas di, bedhyana de, moong di dal of di lantern".*

The Sikh never slept either at night or in the day. The warders said that they had not known him to blink his eyes in fifteen years. He did not as much as lie down. Only on rare occasions he leant against the wall to rest. His legs were swollen down to the ankles.

Whenever there was talk of India and Pakistan, or the exchange of lunatics, this Sikh would become very attentive. If anyone invited him to express his views, he would answer with great solemnity, '*O, pardi, good good di, anekas di, bedhyana di, moong di dal of the Pakistan government.*'

Some time later he changed the end of his litany from 'of the Pakistan Government' to 'of the Toba Tek Singh government'.

He began to question his fellow inmates whether the village of Toba Singh was in India or Pakistan. No one knew the answer. Those who tried, got tied up in knots when explaining how Sialkot was at first in India and was now in Pakistan. How could one guarantee that a similar fate would not befall Lahore and from being Pakistani today it would not become Indian tomorrow? For that matter how could one be sure that the whole of India would not become a part of Pakistan? All said and done who could put his hand on his heart and say with conviction that there was no danger of both India and Pakistan vanishing from the face of the globe one day!

The Sikh had lost most of his long hair. Since he seldom took a bath, the hair of the head had matted and joined with his beard. This gave the Sikh a very fierce look. But he was a harmless fellow. In the fifteen years he had been in the asylum, he had never been known to argue or quarrel with anyone. All that the older inmates knew about him was that he owned land in village Toba Tek Singh and was a prosperous farmer. When he lost his mind, his relatives had brought him to the asylum in iron fetters. Once in the month, some relatives came to Lahore to find out how he was faring. With the eruption of Indo-Pakistan troubles their visits had ceased.

The Sikh's name was Bishen Singh but everyone called him Toba Tek Singh. Bishen Singh had no concept of time — neither of days, nor weeks, nor of months. He had no idea how long he had been in the lunatic asylum. But when his relatives and friends came to see him, he knew that a month must have gone by. He would inform the head warder that 'Miss Interview' was due to visit him. He would wash himself with great care; he would soap his body and oil his long hair and beard before combing them. He would dress up before he went to meet his visitors. If they asked him any questions, he either remained silent or answered, *"O, pardi, anekas di, bedhyana di, moong di dal of the lantern."*

Bishen Singh had a daughter who had grown into a full bosomed lass of fifteen. But he showed no comprehension about his child. The girl wept bitterly whenever she met her father.

When talk of India and Pakistan came up, Bishen Singh began to question other lunatics about the location of Toba Tek Singh. No one could give him a satisfactory answer. His irritation mounted day by day. And now even 'Miss Interview' did not come to see him. There was a time when something had told him that his relatives were due. Now that inner voice had been silenced. And he was more anxious than ever to meet his relatives and find out whether Toba Tek Singh was in India or Pakistan. But no relatives came. Bishen Singh turned to other sources of information.

There was a lunatic in the asylum who believed he was God. Bishen Singh asked him whether Toba Tek Singh was in India or Pakistan. As was his wont God adopted a grave mien and replied "We have not yet issued our orders on the subject".

Bishen Singh got the same answer many times. He pleaded with 'God' to issue instructions so that the matter could be settled once and for all. His pleadings were in vain; 'God' had many pressing matters awaiting 'His' orders. Bishen Singh's patience ran out and one day he let 'God' have a bit of his mind *"O, pardi, good good di, anekas di, bedhyana di, moong di dal of wahi-i-guru ji ka khalsa and wahi-i-guru di fateh! Jo boley so nihal, sat sri akal!"*

This was meant to put 'God' in his place as God only of the Mussalmans. Surely if He had been God of the Sikhs, He would have heard the pleadings of a Sikh!

A few days before the day fixed for the exchange of lunatics, a Muslim from Toba Tek Singh came to visit Bishen Singh. This man had never been to the asylum before. When Bishen Singh saw him he turned away. The warders stopped him: 'He's come to see you; he's your friend, Fazal Din,' they said.

Bishen Singh gazed at Fazal Din and began to mumble. Fazal Din put his hand on Bishen Singh's shoulder. 'I have been intending to see you for the last many days but could never find the time. All your family have safely crossed over to India. I did the best I could for them. Your daughter, Roop Kaur...'

Fazal Din continued somewhat haltingly 'Yes... she too is well. She went along with the rest.'

Bishen Singh stood where he was without saying a word. Fazal Din started again. 'They asked me to keep in touch with you. I am told that you are to leave for India. Convey my salaams to brother Balbir Singh and to brother Wadhawa Singh...and also to sister Amrit Kaur...tell brother Balbir Singh that Fazal Din is well and happy. Both the grey buffaloes that they left behind have calved — one is a male, the other a female... the female died six days later. And if there is anything I can do for them, I am always willing. I have brought you a little sweet corn.'

Bishen Singh took the bag of sweet corn and handed it over to a warder. He asked Fazal Din, 'Where is Toba Tek Singh?'

Fazal Din looked somewhat puzzled and replied, 'Where could it be? It's in the same place where it always was.'

Bishen Singh asked again: 'In Pakistan or India?'

'No, not in India; it's in Pakistan' replied Fazal Din.

Bishen Singh turned away mumbling *'O, pardi, good good di, anekas di, bedhyana di, moong di dal of the Pakistan and Hindustan of dur phittey moonh.'*

Arrangements of the exchange of lunatics were completed. Lists with names of lunatics of either side had been exchanged and information sent to people concerned. The date was fixed.

It was a bitterly cold morning. Bus loads of Sikh and Hindu lunatics left the Lahore asylum under heavy police escort. At the border at Wagah, the Superintendents of the two countries met and settled the details of the operation.

Getting lunatics out of the buses and handing over custody to officers of the other side proved to be a very difficult task. Some refused to come off the bus; those that came out were difficult to control; a few broke loose and had to be recaptured. Those that were naked had to be clothed. No sooner were the clothes put on them than they tore them off their bodies. Some came out with vile abuse, others began to sing at the top of their voices. Some squabbled; others cried or roared with laughter. They created such a racket that one could not hear a word. The female lunatics added to the noise. And all this in the bitterest of cold when people's teeth chattered like the scales of rattle snakes.

Most of the lunatics resisted the exchange because they could not understand why they were being uprooted form one place and flung into another. Those of a gloomier disposition were yelling slogans, 'Live Pakistan' or 'Death to Pakistan.' Some lost their tempers and were prevented from coming to blows in the very nick of time.

At last came the turn of Bishen Singh. The Indian officer began to enter his name in the register. Bishen Singh asked him, 'Where is Toba Tek Singh? In India or Pakistan?'

'In Pakistan.'

That was all that Bishen Singh wanted to know. He turned and ran back to Pakistan. Pakistani soldiers apprehended him and tried to push him back towards India. Bishen Singh refused to budge. 'Toba Tek Singh is on this side.' He cried , and began to yell at the top of his voice *'O, pardi, good good di, anekas di, bedhyana di, moong di of Toba Tek Singh and Pakistan.'*. They did their best to soothe him, to explain to him that Toba Tek Singh must have left for India; and that if any of that name was found in Pakistan he would be dispatched to India at once. Bishen Singh refused to be persuaded. They tried to use force. Bishen Singh planted himself on the dividing line and dug his swollen feet into the ground with such firmness that no one could move him.

They let him be. He was soft in the head. There was no point using force; he would come round of his own — yes. They left him standing where he was and resumed the exchange of other lunatics.

Shortly before sunrise, a wierd cry rose from Bishen Singh's throat. The man who had spent all the nights and days of the last fifteen years standing on his feet, now sprawled on the ground, face down. The barbed wire fence marked the territory of Pakistan. In the no man's land between the two barbed-wire fences lay the body of Bishen Singh of village Toba Tek Singh.

Translated by **Khushwant Singh**

Housewife

Ismat Chughtai

The day Mirza's new maid ambled into his house, there was a sensation in the neighbourhood. The sweeper, who normally avoided work, stayed on and scrubbed the floor with great vigour. The milkman, notorious for adulterating his ware, brought milk clogged with cream.

Who could have named her Lajo — the coy one? Bashfulness was unknown to Lajo. No one knew who begot her and abandoned her on the streets to a lonely, weeping, childhood. Begging and starving, she reached an age when she could snatch a living for herself. Youth etched her body into bewitching curves and this became her only asset. The street initiated her into the mysteries of life.

She never haggled. If it was not a cash-down proposition, it would be sex on credit. If the lover had no means, she would even give of herself free.

'Aren't you ashamed of yourself?' people asked.

'I am!' Lajo would blush brazenly.

'You'll regret it some day.'

'I couldn't care less!'

How could she? With a face that was innocence itself, dark eyes, evenly set teeth, a mellow complexion and a gait so swinging, so provocative?

Mirza was a bachelor. Flattening and baking *chapatis* daily had flattened out his existence. He owned a small grocery shop which he pompously called "General Store." The shop did not give Mirza any leisure even to go to his home town and get married.

Mirza's friend Bakhshi had picked up Lajo at a bus stop. Bakhshi's wife was nine moths pregnant and they needed a maid. Later, when Lajo was not required, Bakhshi deposited her at Mirza's. Instead of squandering away at brothels, he thought, why not let Mirza enjoy a free dish?

'God forbid. I won't have a tart in the house!' said Mirza warily. 'Take her back!'

But Lajo had already made herself at home. With her skirt hiked up like a diaper, broom in hand, she was sweeping Mirza's house in dead earnest. When Bakhshi informed her of Mirza's refusal, it fell on deaf ears. She ordered him to arrange the pans on the kitchen shelf and went out to fetch water. 'If you wish, I'll take you back home,' Bakhshi said.

'Out with you! Are you my husband to take me back to my mother's? Go! I'll tackle the Mian myself!'

Bakhshi's departure left Mirza helpless. He ran out and took refuge in the mosque. He was not prepared to incur this extra expenditure. Moreover, she was bound to pilfer and cheat. What a mess Bakhshi had got him into!

But on returning home he held his breath. As though his late mother, Bi Amma, was back! The house was sparkling.

'Shall I serve dinner, Mian?' Lajo asked and disappeared into the kitchen.

Spinach and potato curry, *moong ki dal* fried with onion and garlic — just the way Ammaji used to cook!

'How did you manage all this?' Mirza asked, baffled.

'Borrowed from the *bania.*'

'Look, I'll pay your return fare. I just cannot afford a servant.'

'Who wants to be paid?'

'But...'

'Is the food hot?' Lajo asked, slipping a fresh *chapati* into his plate.

'Not the food but I am certainly hot from top to toe!' Mirza wanted to shout as he went into his room to sleep.

'No, Mian, I am here for good!' Lajo threatened when he brought up the question again the next morning.

'But..'

'Didn't you like the food?'

'It's not that...'

'Don't I scrub and clean well?'

'It's not that....'

'Then what is it?' Lajo flared up.

She had fallen in love, not with Mirza, but with the house. Bakhshi, the bastard, had once rented a room for her. Its previous occupant had been Nandi — a buffalo. The buffalo was dead and gone to hell but had left behind his stench and Bakhshi did not treat her well either. Now here she was, the unrivalled mistress of Mirza's house. Mirza was uncomplicated. He would sneak in, softly and quietly, and eat whatever was served.

Mirza, for his part, checked the accounts a few times and was satisfied that Lajo did not cheat.

At times she went across to Ramu's grandmother for a tete-a-tete. Ramu was Mirza's dissipated teenaged help in the store. He fell for Lajo the minute he saw her. It was he who told her of Mirza's frequent visits to the singing girls.

This hurt Lajo. After all, what was she for? Wherever employed, she had served well in every capacity. And here a full chaste week had passed! She had never felt so unwanted before. Several offers came her way but she was Mirza's maid. She rejected one and all, lest Mirza should become a laughing-stock. And here was Mirza—an iceberg, or so he appeared. Lajo could not see the volcanoes erupting within him. He kept away from home deliberately.

Lajo's name was on every lip — today she slapped the milkman, yesterday she had aimed a dung-cake full in the face of the *bania* and so on. The schoolmaster insisted on educating her. The *Mullaji* of the mosque burst into prayers in Arabic, beseeching God to ward off impending danger!

Mirza came home annoyed. Lajo had just had her bath. Strands of wet hair clung to her shoulders. Blowing into the kitchen fire had flushed her cheeks and filled her eyes with water. She ground her teeth at Mian's untimely entry.

Mirza almost toppled over! After a silent, uneasy meal, he picked up his walking-stick, went out and sat in the mosque. But he could not relax. Ceaseless thoughts of home made him restless. Unable to hold out any longer, he got back and found Lajo on the threshold, quarrelling with a man. The man disappeared the moment he saw Mirza.

'Who was that?' Mirza's tone was that of a suspicious husband!

'Raghava!'

'Raghava?' Mirza had been buying milk from him for years and yet did not know his name.

'Shall I prepare the *hookah, Mian?*' Lajo changed the subject.

'No! What was that man up to?'

'Was asking me how much milk he should bring from now on.'

'What did you say?'

'I said: May God hasten your funeral! Bring the usual measure.'

'Then?' Mirza was furious.

'Then I said: Bastard, go, feed the extra milk to your mother and sister!'

'The scoundrel! Don't let him set foot here again! I will myself fetch milk on the way home from the store.'

That night, after dinner, Mirza put on a starched, freshly laundered *Kurta,* stuck a scented piece of cottonwool in his ear, picked up his walking and walked out.

Jealousy wrung Lajo's heart. She cursed the singing-girl and sat dumbfounded. Was Mirza really indifferent to her? 'How could that be?' she wondered.

The singing-girl was haggling with a customer. This upset Mirza. He turned away and made for the Lala's shop. There, he cursed inflation, rising prices, national politics...and returned home at midnight, spent and irritated. He drank a lot of cold water but the fire in him continued to blaze.

A part of Lajo's smooth golden leg was visible from the open door. A careless turn in sleep tinkled her anklets. Mirza drained another glass of water and bundled up on his cot, cursing everything under the moon.

Ceaseless tossing in bed reduced his body to a blister. Litres of cold water bloated his stomach. The roundness of the leg behind the door was irresistible. Unknown fears strangled him. But the devil egged him on. From his bed to the kitchen, he had walked so many miles but now he couldn't move a step.

Then an innocent idea crossed his mind. Were Lajo's leg not so exposed, he wouldn't be so uncomfortable...Gradually, this idea took strength and so did Mirza. What if she woke up? Yet he had to take the risk — for the sake of his own safety.

He left his slippers under the cot, held his breath and tiptoed across, gingerly lifted the hem of the skirt and pulled it down slowly. He stood a while indecisively and turned away.

With one quick move, Lajo grabbed him. Mirza was speechless. He struggled, pleaded, but Lajo wouldn't let him go!

When he encountered Lajo the next morning, she blushed like a bride! Lajo, the victor, went about her chores boldly, humming a *kajri*. Not a shadow of the night's happening flickered in her eyes. When Mirza sat down to breakfast, she sat on the doorstep, as usual, fanning the flies away.

That afternoon, when she brought his lunch to the shop he noticed a new lilt in her gait. Whenever Lajo came to the shop, people would stop by and enquire about the price of groceries. She sold in a short while what Mirza couldn't during the entire day!

Mirza began to improve in his looks. People knew the reason and sizzled with envy. Mirza, in turn, grew nervous and ill at ease. The more Lajo looked after him, the more he was enamoured of her and the more afraid he was of the neighbours. She was utterly brazen. When she fetched his lunch, the entire bazaar throbbed with her presence.

'Don't bring lunch any more!' he told her one day.

'Why not?' Lajo's face fell. Staying home all by herself bored her. The bazaar was an interesting break.

Having stopped her from coming, many doubts assailed Mirza. He dropped in at odd hours to spy on her and she would insist on rewarding him fully for his attentions!

The day he caught her at a game of *kabaddi* with street urchins, his anger knew no bounds. Her skirt was billowing in the wind. The boys were engrossed in the skirt. Mirza passed by, holding his head high with affected indifference. His discomfiture amused the onlookers.

Mirza had grown fond of Lajo. The very idea of separation drove him crazy. He was unable to concentrate on his shop. He feared that some day she might desert him.

'Mian, why not marry her?' Miran Mian suggested.

'God forbid!' he shouted. How could he form so sacred a relationship with a slut?

But that very evening, when he didn't find her at home, Mirza felt lost. The confounded Lala had been long on the wait. He had offered her a bungalow! Miran Mian, a friend from all accounts, had himself made a proposition to Lajo on the sly.

Mirza was losing hope when suddenly Lajo appeared. She had just gone across to Ramu's grandmother!

That day Mirza made up his mind to take Lajo for a wife even at the cost of his family's pride and prestige.

'But why, Mian?' Lajo asked, surprised at his proposal.

'Why not? Want to have a fling elsewhere?' he asked crossly.

'Why should I have a fling?'

'That Raoji is offering you a bungalow.'

'I wouldn't spit on his bungalow!'

But the need for marriage completely escaped her. She was and would be his for life. A master like him was not easy to come by. Lajo knew what a gem Mirza was. All her previous masters inevitably ended up as her lovers. They would first have their fill, then beat her up and kick her out. Mirza had always been tender and loving. He had bought her a few clothes and a pair of gold bangles. No one in seven generations of Lajo's family had ever worn ornaments of pure gold.

When Mirza spoke of his plan to Ramu's grandmother, she too was surprised.

'Mian, why tie a bell around your neck?' she asked. 'Is the slut making a fuss? A sound thrashing will set her right. Where beating up can do, why think of marriage?'

But Mirza was obsessed with the idea.

'You there, are you hesitating on account of the difference in religion?' Ramu's grandmother asked Lajo.

'No, I've always regarded him as my husband.'

Lajo looked upon even a passing lover as a passing husband and served him well. Riches were never showered upon her, yet she gave of herself fully — body and soul. Mirza was an exception, of course. Only Lajo knew the pleasure of the give-and-take game with him. Compared to him the others were pigs.

Also, marriage was for virgins. How did she qualify to be a bride? She begged and pleaded, but Mirza was bent upon entering into a legal contract of the *nikah.*

That day, after the evening prayer, *nikah* was solemnised. Young girls of the neighbourhood sang wedding songs. Mirza entertained his friends. Lajo, renamed Kaneez Fatima, became wife of Mirza Irfan Ali Beg.

Mirza imposed a ban on *lehngas* and prescribed *churidar pyjamas.* Lajo, however, was used to open space between her legs. This new imposition was a big irritant. She could never get used to it. One day, at the first opportunity, she took off the pyjamas and was about to get into the *lehnga,* when Mirza turned up. In her confusion, she forgot to hold the skirt around her waist and dropped it to the floor.

'The devil take you!' Mirza thundered a Quranic curse. He hurriedly threw a bedsheet over her.

Lajo could not understand his annoyance and the grandiloquent oration that followed. Where had she erred? This very act had taken Mirza's breath away so many times in the past. Now he was so upset. He picked up the *lehnga* and actually fed it to the fire.

Mirza left, leaving Lajo shocked and uncomprehending. Discarding the sheet, she examined her body. Maybe some repulsive skin disease had erupted overnight.

When bathing under the tap in the open, she kept wiping her tears. Mithwa, son of the mason, climbed the terrace daily on the pretext of flying kites and watched her. She was so sad today she neither stuck out her thumb nor hurled a slipper at him. She wrapped the sheet around and went indoors.

With a heavy heart she got into the long trousers — as long as the devil's intestines. To add to her misery the cummerbund got lost inside the waistband. She shouted for help. Jullu, the neighbour's daughter, appeared and the tape was located. 'Which sadist could have adapted this rifle case for a feminine dress?' Lajo wondered.

Later, when Mirza returned home, the tape played truant once again. Lajo tried desparately to catch it with her fingers. Mirza found her nervousness endearing. After a combined concentrated chase, the tape was found.

But a ticklish problem popped up for Mirza. What used to be intoxicating coquetry in Lajo now turned to brazenness in his wife. The indecent ways of a flirt are unbecoming to respectable women. Lajo failed to be the bride of his dream — one who would blush at his amorous advances, be annoyed at his persistence and feign indifference to his attention. Lajo was a mere pavement slab.

Checking her at every step, Mirza curbed her excesses and tamed the wild in her — or so he thought. Also, he was no longer impatient to get back home in the evenings. Like all husbands, he spent more time with friends to avoid being labelled henpecked.

To make up for his frequent absences, he suggested engaging a maid. Lajo was furious. She knew of Mian's renewed visits to the singing-girls. She also knew that every man of the neighbourhood went there. But, in her own home, she would not tolerate another woman! Let anybody step into her kitchen and tinker with her glistening vessels, Lajo would tear her to bits! She would share Mirza with another woman but certainly would not share her home.

Mirza seemed to have installed Lajo in his house and forgotten all about her. For weeks he spoke only in monosyllables. When she was his mistress, all men had their eyes on her. Now that she had gained respectability, she became "mother, sister and daughter". No one cast even a stray glance at the jute curtain — except the faithful Mithwa. He still flew kites on the roof, although only when Mirza was away and Lajo was bathing in the courtyard.

One night Mirza stayed away, celebrating Dussehra with friends. He came home the next morning, had a quick wash and went off to the shop. Lajo was annoyed. It was then, while bathing, that she looked up at the terrace. Or maybe that day Mithwa's stares pierced her wet body like so many spears.

Suddenly his kite snapped. The broken cord brushed sharply against Lajo's body. Lajo was startled. She got up quickly and ran into the room, absent-minded or deliberately forgetting to wrap the towel around her.

From then on, Mithwa was always found hanging around Mirza's house. Whenever Lajo wanted something from the market, she would draw the jute curtain aside and shout 'Mithwa, don't stay put like a dunghill! Get us a few *kachoris.*'

If Mithwa did not appear on the terrace during her bath, she rattled the bucket loud enough to wake a corpse in its grave. The love, of which she had given so lavishly all her life, was now Mithwa's for the asking. If Mirza did not turn up for a meal, she would never waste the food but feed someone poor and needy. Who was needier than Mithwa?

Mirza was convinced that, chained to wedlock, Lajo had become a genuine housewife. Had he not seen for himself, he would never have believed it. Seeing him on the doorstep so unexpectedly, she laughed uproariously. She could not, even in her wildest dreams, imagine that Mirza would be offended!

But Mithwa knew. Clutching his *dhoti* firmly with one hand, he bolted and stopped for breath only after he had crossed three villages! Mirza flogged Lajo so much that, had she been made of softer stuff, she would have breathed her last.

The news that Mirza had caught his wife with Mithwa spread throughout the village. People came in large numbers to watch the fun and were sorely disappointed to know that Mithwa, the hero, had fled and that the wife lay dismantled. Ramu's grandmother arrived and took her away.

One would think a flogging like that would turn Lajo against the very idea of Mirza. Far from it! Beating helped achieve what marriage could not. The bond was stronger. The minute she came to, Lajo enquired after Mirza. All her masters inevitably ended up as lovers. After giving her a sound thrashing, the question of pay was set aside. She slogged free and was beaten from time to time. But Mirza had always been good. Other masters had even "loaned" her to friends but Mirza regarded her as his own. Everyone advised her to run away and save her skin but she did not budge.

How was Mirza to face the world? He was no way but to kill her in order to save his honour. Miran Mian held him back. 'Why must you stick your head in the noose for a bitch? Divorce the whore and forget her!'

Mirza divorced Lajo immediately and sent 32 rupees of dower, *mahr,* her clothes and other belongings over to Ramu's grandmother.

When Lajo heard of the divorce, she heaved a sigh of relief. *Nikah* had proved unlucky. All mishaps had been due to that.

'Is Mian still angry?' she asked Ramu's grandmother.

'Shan't set eyes on you. Wants you to get lost! Drop dead!'

The news of Mirza's divorce rocked the village. Lala sent out a feeler: 'The bungalow is ready!'

'Dump your mother in it!' Lajo retorted.

After a fortnight in bed, Lajo was up on her feet again. The beating seemed to have spring-cleaned her and left her more glowing than ever. When buying *pan* or *kachori,* she took the whole bazaar by storm.

Mirza died a thousand deaths. Once he spotted her at the *bania's* arguing over something. The *bania* drooled. Mirza left, avoiding notice.

'You are crazy, Mian! Why care for what she does? You have divorced her, haven't you?' Miran Main asked.

'She has been my wife.'

'If you want the truth, she was never your wife!'

'What about the *nikah*?'

'Thoroughly illegal!'

'How?'

'It was never valid. No one knows who begot her. And, I suppose, *nikah* with a bastard is not valid,' Miran Mian passed the verdict.

'So the *nikah* never came into effect?' Mirza asked.

'Never!' confirmed Miran Mian.

'And I never lost face either? My family's reputation is involved.'

Mirza felt immensely relieved. 'But what about the divorce?' he asked, worried.

'My dear Mian, no *nikah,* no divorce!'

'So the thirty-two rupees were wasted!' Mirza said sorrowfully.

In no time, news travelled all over the neighbourhood that Mirza was never married to his "wife", that the *nikah* and divorce had both been unlawful.

When Lajo heard the news she danced with joy. The night that was her marriage and divorce was over. What made her happy was the fact that Mian had not lost face, after all. She had genuinely grieved that he had lost his honour because of her. 'What a boon it is to be a bastard,' she thought. God forbid, were she a legitimate child...Even the idea of such a possibility made her shudder.

Lajo was feeling suffocated at Ramu's grandmother's. Thought of house kept her worried. Mian could not have had it swept or dusted for fear of theft. The place must be in a mess.

One day Mirza was on his way to the shop when Lajo waylaid him.

'Mian, shall I resume duty from tomorrow?'

'Damn,' said Mirza and walked away briskly. 'But I'll not have a maid sooner or later,' he thought. 'maybe this wretch if none other.'

Lajo did not wait for Mirza to make up his mind. She jumped into the house from the roof, tied up her *lehnga* and set to work.

That evening, on his return, Mirza held his breath. It was the late Bi Amma come back! The house was sparkling clean. A smell of incense filled the air. The pitcher was filled with water and over that was placed a well-scrubbed bowl.

Mirza's heart went heavy with nostalgia. He ate the roast mutton and *parathas* in hushed silence. As usual Lajo sat on the door-step fanning the flies away.

At night, when she spread jute curtains on the kitchen floor and went to sleep, Mirza once again had a severe bout of thirst. He tossed and turned, listening to the provocative tinkle of her anklets. It clutched at his heart, as also a feeling of guilt. He felt he had been very unfair to her and had grossly underestimated the poor creature. A deep sense of regret overtook him. He lay cursing himself.

Then with a sudden 'Damn it all,' he got up, ran across and collected the housewife from the mat.

Translated by **Fatima Ali**

PUNJABI

Happy New Year

Ajeet Cour

After years of hammering away on typewriters, Kapoor's fate came to be linked with that of the Hon'ble Minister of the Central Government. Overnight his status was elevated from plain and simple Kapoor to Kapoor *Sahib:* Personal Assistant to the H.M. (Honourable Minister). In those few hours his chest expanded visibly by a couple of inches. When he strutted down the office corridors his breast puffed out like that of a crested bantam cock, it seemed as if corridors were not broad enough for him. Peons, who usually sat on their stools chewing betel leaf or nodding with sleep would spring to attention and salute him as he passed.

The metamorphosis took place a few days before the year was to end. In the long years that Kapoor had been a clerk he had never as much as thought of such trifles as New Year's Eve or New Year's day. It had never occurred to him that the year which had been young a little while ago had aged and would soon give up the ghost. The thirty-firsts of December were no different from the thirtieths or thirty firsts of other months: days of penniless penury. The firsts of January were like the firsts of all other months when he received his months's salary, paid off his debtors, fulfilled his childrens' oft-postponed demands for new exercise books, new textbooks, new pairs of socks to replace the old riddled with holes, school uniforms, pencils, etc. It was a strange mixture of sensations: an imperious feeling of governing other peoples' destinies as well as a diminution of stature which came with the realisation that before half the day was over more than half his salary would be eaten up.

After Kapoor had been transformed into Kapoor *Sahib,* his life style changed. How the transformation came about was very simple.

A businessman to be more exact, an industrialist who had done business with this Minister, arrived at the Ministerial residence armed with a New Year's gift. The date 31st of December. Time : 8 a.m. Mr Kapoor was ensconced in a room in the outer verandah and seated in the chair of the Personal Assistant to the Hon'able Minister.

The Minister took one look at the Parcel and remarked: 'Sorry, I have given up drink. You must know what the Prime Minister's views on the subject are. PM has ordered...'

The industrialist muttered an oath. Of course, only inside himself, but one which had reference to the Minister's relations with his own mother. He also felt apprehensive that the bugger might be trying to slip out of his grasp. However, he bared his entire denture in a broad smile and replied: 'Not at all, Sir. I'll bring something else tomorrow or the day after. But this is New Year's Eve and I mustn't leave without an offering for you.' He opened his briefcase, took out a diary and placed it on the table before the Minister. It was a miserable little specimen printed in the government press. However, in its pages was a wad of other papers also bearing the imprint of the Government of India. The Minister opened the diary, felt the thickness of the wad of notes and remarked: 'You needn't have taken this trouble: it wasn't really necessary for you to put yourself out in this way.'

'No trouble at all, sir' sniggered the industrialist. 'This is only to buy sweets for the children.'

It can be established that as a person rises in the world, his children's appetite for sweets and candies increases. The "candy box" in the diary was worth more than a confectioner's shop crammed with goodies.

The Minister gave a wan smile baring two-and-a-half of his dentures and quietly slipped the diary in the drawer of his table.

The industrialist sighed with relief. It had been a touch-and-go affair. As he stepped out of the Minister's office he handed the parcel he had brought for the Minister to Kapoor. The Personal

Assistant to the Minister had also to be kept happy. All this happened so quickly that Kapoor was neither able to protest nor as much as utter a word of thanks. It was the first time in his life that someone had considered him worthy of a gift of any kind.

He was somewhat ill at ease but the industrialist's voice as he left with a triumphant smile was most reassuring: 'It's a small gift for the New Year.' Kapoor's hands shook as he put the bottle in a drawer of his table. He felt hot all over his body.

Vashisht, the typist, shared the room with Kapoor. He had been the Minister's typist and had sat in the same corner for many years. On the very first day that Kapoor came to occupy his new chair, Vashisht had introduced himself with a reassuring smile: 'Do not worry sir, I will show you all the ropes. Ministers come to go; their jobs are not permanent. But your humble servant had been confirmed in his post and is quite familiar with the goings on that take place in this room. I will not let any trouble come near you.'

Vashisht sensed Kapoor's discomfiture and casually walked up to him as he took a leaf of betel out of a wrap of paper. 'Congratulation Kapoor Sahib. The first gift is like the ceremony of removing the nose-ring of a bride. You must entertain your humble servants and thus ensure the grace of God. We will always pray for your health.'

Kapoor was novice at the game. He realised he could not drink an entire bottle of Scotch all by himself and was relieved to have someone share it with him: 'Sure! Sure!' he replied.

'Fine! This evening we'll welcome the New Year in your home as all the *burra sahibs* do in big hotels. Singing and embracing each others' wives at the midnight hour. Can I also invite Gupta on your behalf?' Gupta was the second typist. He sat in another room which he shared with the two other clerks. Gupta was incharge of receiving and sorting out the mail; the other was responsible for the despatch.

'Sure!' replied Kapoor expansively.

Kapoor came home a little earlier than usual carrying the bottle of Scotch in his attache case. He was not prepared for the tongue-lashing his wife gave him. 'Did you have to bring this destroyer of families in our own home? And drink the evil stuff in the presence of children! New Year? What the hell is this New Year? Today is the thirty-first and there is neither a vegetable nor a scrap of biscuit nor anything else to eat in the house. I am ashamed of asking the grocer for another loan. Only yesterday I told him I would not be buying anything more this month and asked him to make out our bill so that I could clear his account by the first. We already owe him hundred and eighty-three rupees. If we took another loan your guests will eat it up. They will go back merrily to their homes but what will we live on? You want us to eat at the free kitchen in the gurdwara all of the next month? New Year indeed! These fads are for the idle rich, people who frequent five-star hotels. We have barely enough to fill our bellies and never a paisa to spare. Only I know how I count every paisa to spread it out over thirty days!'

What was poor Kapoor to do? If you put your head in the jaws of a crocodile you cannot hope to escape without a scratch! He tried to explain in his softest tone: 'My good woman! This New Year is an English festival exactly like our *Baisakhi* or *Diwali*.' But the good woman was beyond reasoning and refused to understand.

Exactly at quarter to eight the two men arrived accompanied by their wives and their brood of children. The women and children went into the inner room. Normally, children could be expected to create an uproar, but being clerks' offsprings they clung to their mother's aprons and whimpered like little pups. In any case it was a very cold evening, and their mother could not get rid of them by ordering them to go out to play.

In the sitting-room the men were gathered around the bottle of Scotch. With it they nibbled salted peanuts. Inside, their women folk compared the prices of potatoes.

'In any event Kapoor *Sahib* owed us a feast for his promotion,' remarked Vashisht. Kapoor expanded like an inflated balloon. However, he pulled a long face and replied, 'What kind of promotion, *yaar!* Promotion is when there is an increase in one's salary. All I have got is increase of work. I used to get to the office at 10.30 in the morning and leave at 4.30 in the evening. Now I have to report at the Minister's residence at 7.45 and stay upto 8 or 9. I don't have to tell you all this.'

'To hell with the work, Mr. Kapoor! Your sphere of influence has increased, your status risen to new heights!' remarked Gupta. 'Lots of things happen to people who occupy your chair. You recall that fellow called Sood? Narinder Sood was his full name. He used to sit in the same chair. It must have been about eight years ago when a licence applied for by a Bombay firm got stuck somewhere in the files of the Ministry. The firm's chaps had been going round and round for weeks but the Minister was like a duck which would not let a drop of water stay on its back. Utterly defeated, these Bombay Johnnies came to Sood's house and fell at his feet. This Sood fellow performed such jugglery that before the months was over, the licence was cleared. It was entirely Sood's handiwork. The Bombay people worked out that each visit to Delhi cost them five to six thousand rupees. So why not employ Sood to do the work for them? They persuaded him to resign his job and made him their Resident Executive Director in Delhi. They gave him an air-conditioned office and a spacious apartment. Now Mr. Sood and his pretty private secretary travel in a chauffeur-driven car. They make the rounds of different offices handing out invitation cards for dinner. He dines out every night with officials at swanky hotels like the Oberoi, the Taj or the Maurya. Every month lakhs of rupees pass through his hands; everyday he wears a new suit made of imported textiles.' Vashisht narrated the story of Sood's achievements as though they were blood-brothers.

'And *banda parwar* (protector of the poor) you must know that every currency note has a little glue stuck to it. As they are passed along from hand to hand some get stuck to one hand, some to another. You are a man of the world, you must know all this,' said Gupta.

Kapoor's third eye was beginning to catch a glimmer of light.

'My good friend, all I know is one basic fact. These eighty-four lakh species of lives that our holy books talk of are in fact one that of a clerk. A clerk goes through all the incarnations: cat, dog, scorpion, turtle, jackal, pig, and everything else. And just as a person goes through the eighty-four lakhs of incarnations before he takes birth as a human to rule the world, so once in a mellenia a clerk is fortunate enough to be appointed personal assistant to minister.' Vashisht was well-versed in the holy texts.

'That may well be so,' conceded Kapoor with a half hearted laugh, 'but there is no escaping from the fact that the work-load becomes much heavier. Your sister-in-law (my wife) has been going at me for the last ten days.'

'She is not sparing you!' sniggered Gupta.

'Why don't you put some sense in her head? Tell the good lady that by the grace of the chair you occupy all the four horizons will soon light up. Then she will cook *halva* full of dry fruits and glasses of milk laced with almonds before she sends you to your office,' Vashisht roared happily.

'This bottle of Scotch is the first ritual — the sort of gift you give a bride when she first unveils her face,' added Gupta.

The two men treated Kapoor like a neophyte about to have its ears pierced before he is accepted by a Guru as his disciple. 'When my wife looked at this bottle, it seemed all hell would break loose,' said the new convert Kapoor.

Vashisht interrupted him by pleading in a mewling voice. 'Please, please explain all this to our *bhabi.* Put some divine wisdom into her head.'

Gupta added his voice in support. 'Tell her how everyone in the Customs Service is eager to be posted at Palam of Sant Cruz airport and get all sorts of influential people to speak for him. Ev-

Every traffic constable, every sales tax officer does his level best to be posted in the Chandni Chowk, Sadar or Chawri Bazar. How many shoes do they have to polish with butter before they get these postings? What is more, these big hospitals, when a doctor is put in charge of the wing reserved for V.I.Ps his colleagues are burnt up with envy. Such posts do not go abegging. The work load is undoubtedly doubled. But just think: the bigger the head, the bigger the headache.'

'Now take the case of the Prime Minister,' said Vashisht. 'the poor thing works 18 to 19 hours everyday. During the elections the PM runs from one village to another. What booby prizes does the PM get for all this trouble?'

'Quite right! All these Ministers and leaders of political parties do not run around for the heck of it. Time will come when your wife will be singing and dancing with joy. She will take your big head in her lap and kiss away all its aches,' said Vashisht laughing.

The bottle was nearly empty. The peanuts had been nibbled away. Gupta glanced at his watch. 'Friends, it is nearly 9.30. Let us have something to eat. We will not get any buses after 10.30. And we are not ministers who can order our cars....' Kapoor got up and went inside. A little later Kapoor's children trooped in carrying bowls full of lentils cooked in onion and potato curry. The three men ate in the outer room; their wives and children in the room inside. Kapoor's wife was busy baking chappaties; her children ran around the two rooms serving them hot to the guests. By 10.15 the guests departed.

Kapoor felt like a criminal. He started making the beds in the rooms. He could hear his wife grumbling away as she rinsed the cooking pots and plates. 'New Year indeed! To hell with such festivals in this biting cold. They may suit white people. We have our own *Diwali* and Baisakhi, both in fair seasons. *Only* Lohri is in winter and people light bonfires to warm themselves. And I have to rinse all this garbage with icy cold water. To hell with this New Year.'

At long last the lights were switched off. The children were fast asleep. But Kapoor's wife went on nagging and grumbling. After a while she said: 'This New Year be damned! Why doesn't it fall on the 2nd of January? By then you will have drawn your salary.'

Kapoor kept silent.

His wife's voice flitted about in the dark like a bat going round and round the room. And then found a perch on some wall.

At the hour of midnight when lights in all the five-star hotels were dimmed so that men could embrace and kiss other men's wives and burst into singing *'auld lang syne'* to usher in the New Year, the Kapoors were fast asleep with their backs to each other.

Translated by **Khushwant Singh**

The Death of Shaikh Burhanuddin

Khwaja Ahmed Abbas

My name is Shaikh Burhanuddin.

When violence and murder became the order of the day in Delhi and the blood of Muslims flowed in the streets, I cursed my fate for having a Sikh for a neighbour. Far from expecting him to come to my rescue in times of trouble, as a good neighbour should, I could not tell when he would thrust his *kirpan* into my belly. The truth is that till then I used to find the Sikhs somewhat laughable. But I also disliked them and was somewhat scared of them.

My hatred for the Sikhs began on the day when I first set my eyes on one. I could not have been more than six years old when I saw a Sikh sitting out in the sun combing his long hair. 'Look!' I yelled with revulsion, 'a woman with a long beard!' As I got older this dislike developed into hatred for the entire race.

It was a custom amongst old women of our household to heap all afflictions on our enemies. Thus for example if a child got pneumonia or broke its leg, they would say 'a long time ago a Sikh, (or an Englishman), got pneumonia; or a long time ago a Sikh, (or an Englishman), broke his leg.' When I was older I discovered that this referred to the year 1857 when the Sikh princes helped the *ferringhee*—foreigner — to defeat the Hindus and Muslims in the war of independence. I do not wish to propound a historical thesis but to explain the obsession, the suspicion and hatred which I bore towards the English and the Sikhs. I was more frightened of the English than of the Sikhs.

When I was ten years old, I happened to be travelling from Delhi to Aligarh. I used to travel third class, or at the most in the intermediate class. That day I said to myself, 'Let me for once travel second class and see what it feels like.' I bought my ticket and I found an empty second class compartment. I jumped on the well-sprung seats; I went into the bathroom and leapt up to see my face in the mirror; I switched on all the fans. I played with the light switches. There were only a couple of minutes for the train to leave when four red-faced "tommies" burst into the compartment, mouthing obscenities: everything was either "bloody" or "damn". I had one look at them and my desire to travel second class vanished.

I picked up my suitcase and ran out. I only stopped for breath when I got into a third class compartment crammed with natives. But as luck would have it it was full of Sikhs — their beards hanging down to their navels and dressed in nothing more than their underpants. I could not escape from them: but I kept my distance.

Although I feared the white man more than the Sikhs, I felt that he was more civilised: he wore the same kind of clothes as I. I also wanted to be able to say "damn", "bloody fool" — the way he did. And like him I wanted to belong to the ruling class. The Englishman ate his food with forks and knives, I also wanted to learn to eat with forks and knives so that natives would look upon me as advanced and as civilised as the whiteman.

My Sikh-phobia was a different kind. I had contempt for the Sikh. I was amazed at the stupidity of men who imitated women and grew their hair long. I must confess I did not like my hair cut too short; despite my father's instructions to the contrary, I did not allow the barber to clip off more than a little when I went to him on Fridays. I grew a mop of hair so that when I played hockey or football it would blow about in the breeze like those of English sportsmen. My father often asked me 'Why do you let your hair grow like a woman's?' My father had primitive ideas and I took no notice of his views. If he had had his way he would have had all heads razored bald, and stuck artificial beards on people's chins...That reminds me that the second reason for hating the Sikhs was their beards which made them look like savages.

There are beards and beards. There was my father's beard, neatly trimmed in the French style; or my uncle's which went into a sharp point under his chin. But what could you do with a beard to which no scissor was ever applied and which was allowed to grow like a wild bush — fed with a compost of oil, curd and goodness knows what! And, after it had grown a few feet, combed like hair on a woman's head: My grandfather also had a very long beard which he combed...but then my grandfather was my grandfather and a Sikh is just a Sikh.

After I had passed my matriculation examination I was sent to the Muslim University at Aligarh. We boys who came from Delhi, or the United Provinces, looked down upon boys from the Punjab; they were crude rustics who did not know how to converse, how to behave at table, or to deport themselves in polite company. All they could do was drink large tumblers of buttermilk. Delicacies such as vermicelli with essence of *kewra* sprinkled on it, or the aroma of Lipton's tea was alien to them. Their language was unsophisticated to the extreme, whenever they spoke to each other it seemed as if they were quarreling. It was full of *"ussi, tussi, saadey, twhaadey"*, — Heaven forbid" I kept my distance from the Punjabis.

But the warden of our hostel, (God forgive him), gave me a Punjabi as a room mate. When I realised that there was no escape, I decided to make the best of a bad bargain and be civil to the chap. After a few days we became quite friendly. This man was called Ghulam Rasul and he was from Rawalpindi. He was full of amusing anecdotes and was a good companion.

You might well ask how Mr Ghulam Rasul gate-crashed into a story about the Sikhs. It is through these anecdotes that I got to know the racial characteristics, the habits and customs of this strange community. According to Ghulam Rasul the chief characteristics of the Sikhs were the following:

All Sikhs were stupid and idiotic. At noon-time they lost their senses altogether. There were many instances to prove this. For example, one day at 12 o' clock noon, a Sikh was cycling along

Hall Bazaar in Amritsar when a constable, also a Sikh, stopped him and demanded, 'Where is your light?' The cyclist replied nervously, '*Jemadar sahib,* I lit it when I left my home; it must have gone our just now.' The constable threatened to run him in. A passer-by, yet another Sikh with a long white beard intervened 'Brothers, there is no point in quarrelling over little things. If the light has gone out it can be lit again.'

Ghulam Rasul knew hundreds of anecdotes of this kind. When he told them in his Punjabi accent his audience was left helpless with laughter. One really enjoyed them best in Punjabi because the strange and incomprehensible behaviour of the uncouth Sikh was best told in his rustic lingo.

The Sikh were not only stupid but incredibly filthy as well. Ghulam Rasul, who had know hundreds of them, told us how they never shaved their heads. And whereas we Muslims washed our hair thoroughly at least every Friday, the Sikhs who made a public exhibition of bathing in their under-pants, poured all kinds of filth, like curd into their hair. I rub lime-juice and glycerine in my scalp. Although the glycerine is white and thick like curd, it is an altogether different thing — made by a well-known firm of perfumers of Europe. My glycerine came in a lovely bottle whereas the Sikh's curd came from the shop of a dirty sweetmeat seller.

I would not have concerned myself with the manner of living of these people except that they were so haughty and ill-bred as to consider themselves as good warriors as the Muslims. It is know over the world that one Muslim can get the better of ten Hindus or Sikhs. But these Sikhs would not accept the superiority of the Muslim and would strut about like bantam cocks twirling their moustaches and stroking their beards. Ghulam Rasul used to say that one day we Muslims would teach the Sikhs a lesson that they would never forget.

Years went by.

I left college. I ceased to be a student and became a clerk; then a head clerk. I left Aligarh and came to live in New Delhi.

I was allotted government quarters. I got married. I had children.

The quarters next to mine were occupied by a Sikh who had been displaced from Rawalpindi. Despite the passage of years, I remembered what Ghulam Rasul had told me. As Ghulam Rasul had prophesied, the Sikhs had been taught a bitter lesson in humility at least, in the district of Rawalpindi. The Muslims had virtually wiped them out. The Sikhs boasted that they were great heroes; they flaunted their long *kirpans.* But they could not withstand the brave Muslims. The Sikhs' beards were forcibly shaved. They were circumcised. They were converted to Islam. The Hindu press, as was its custom, vilified the Muslims. It reported that the Muslims had murdered Sikh women and children. This was wholly contrary to Islamic tradition. No Muslim warrior was ever known to raise his hand against a woman or a child. The pictures of the corpses of women and children published in Hindu newspapers were obviously faked. I wouldn't have put it beyond the Sikh to murder their own women and children in order to vilify the Muslims.

The Muslims were also accused of abducting Hindu and Sikh women. The truth of the matter is that such was the impact of the heroism of Muslims on the minds of Hindu and Sikh girls that they fell in love with young Muslims and insisted on going with them. These noble-minded young men had no option but to give them shelter and thus bring them to the true path of Islam. The bubble of Sikh bravery was burst. It did not matter how their leaders threatened the Muslims with their *kirpans,* the sight of the Sikhs who had fled from Rawalpindi filled my heart with pride in the greatness of Islam.

The Sikh who was my neighbour was about sixty years old. His beard had gone completely grey. Although he had barely escaped from the jaws of death, he was always laughing, displaying his teeth in the most vulgar fashion. It was evident that he was quite stupid. In the beginning he tried to draw me into his net by professions of friendship. Whenever I passed him he insisted on talking to me. I do not remember what kind of Sikh festival it was, when he sent me some sweet butter. My wife promptly gave it away to the sweepress. I did my best to have as little to do with him as I could. I snubbed him whenever I could. I knew that if I spoke a few words to him, he would be hard to shake off. Civil talk would encourage him to become familiar. It was known to me that Sikhs drew their sustenance from foul language. Why should I soil my lips by associating with such people!

One Sunday afternoon I was telling my wife of some anecdotes about the stupidity of the Sikhs. To prove my point, exactly at 12 o'clock, I sent my servant across to my Sikh neighbour to ask him the time. He sent back the reply 'two minutes after 12.' I remarked to my wife 'You see, they are scared of even mentioning 12 o'clock!' We both had a hearty laugh. After this, many a time when I wanted to make an ass of my Sikh neighbour, I would ask him 'Well, *Sardarji* has it struck twelve?' The shameless creature would grin, baring all his teeth and answer, 'Sir, for us it is always striking twelve.' He would roar with laughter as if it were a great joke.

I was concerned about the safety of my children. One could never trust a Sikh. And this man had fled from Rawalpindi. He was sure to have a grudge against Muslims and to be on the look-out for an opportunity to avenge himself. I had told my wife never to allow the children to go near the Sikh's quarters. But children are children. After a few days I saw my children playing with the Sikh's little girl, Mohini, and his other grandchildren. This child, who was barely ten years old, was really as beautiful as her name indicated; she was fair and beautifully formed. These wretches have beautiful women. I recall Ghulam Rasul telling me that if all the Sikh men were to leave their women behind and clear out of the Punjab, there would be no need for Muslims to go to paradise in search of houris.

The truth about the Sikhs was soon evident. After the thrashing in Rawalpindi, they fled like cowards to East Punjab. Here they found the Muslims weak and unprepared. So they began to kill them. Hundreds of thousands of Muslims were martyred; the blood of the faithful ran in streams. Thousands of women were stripped naked and made to parade through the streets. When Sikhs, fleeing from Western Punjab, came in large numbers to Delhi, it was evident that there would be trouble in the capital. I could not leave for Pakistan immediately. Consequently I sent away my wife and children by air, with my elder brother, and entrusted my own fate to God. I could not send much luggage by air. I booked an entire railway wagon to take my furniture and belongings. But on the day I was to load the wagon I got information that trains bound for Pakistan were being attacked by Sikh bands. Consequently my luggage stayed in my quarters in Delhi.

On the 15th of August, India celebrated its independence. What interest could I have in the independence of India! I spent the day lying in bed reading *Dawn* and the *Pakistan Times*. Both the papers had strong word to say about the manner in which India had gained its freedom and proved conclusively how the Hindus and the British had conspired to destroy the Muslims. It was only our leader, the great Mohammed Ali Jinnah, who was able to thwart their evil designs and win Pakistan for the Muslims. The English had knuckled under because of Hindu and Sikh pressure and handed over Amritsar to India. Amritsar, as the world knows, is a purely Muslim city. Its famous Golden Mosque — or am I mixing it up with the Golden Temple! — yes of course, the Golden Mosque is in Delhi. And in Delhi besides the Golden Mosque there are the Jamma Masjid, the Red Fort, the mausolea of Nizamuddin and Emperor Humayun, the tomb and school of Safdar Jang — just everything worthwhile bears imprints of Islamic rule. Even so this Delhi (which should really be called after its Muslim builder Shahjahan as Shahjahanabad) was to suffer the indignity of having the flag of Hindu imperialism unfurled on its ramparts.

My heart seemed rent asunder. I could have shed tears of blood. My cup of sorrow was full to the brim when I realised that Delhi, which was once the footstool of the Muslim Empire, the centre of Islamic culture and civilisation, had been snatched out of our hands. Instead we were to have the desert wastes of Western Punjab, Sindh and Baluchistan inhabited by an uncouth and uncultured people. We were to go to a land where people do not know how to talk in civilised Urdu; where men wear baggy *salwars* like their women folk, where they eat thick bread four pounds in weight instead of the delicate wafers we eat at home!

I steeled myself. I would have to make this sacrifice for my great leader, Jinnah, and for my new country, Pakistan. Nevertheless the thought of having to leave Delhi was most depressing.

When I emerged from my room in the evening, my Sikh neighbour bared his fangs and asked 'Brother, did you not go out to see the celebrations?' I felt like setting fire to his beard.

One morning the news spread of a general massacre in old Delhi. Muslim homes were burnt in Karol Bagh. Muslim shops in Chandini Chowk were looted. This then was a sample of Hindu rule! I said to myself 'New Delhi is really an English city; Lord Mountabatten lives here as well as the Commander-in-Chief. At least in New Delhi no hand will be raised against Muslims'. With this self assurance I started towards my office. I had to settle the business of my provident fund; I had delayed going to Pakistan in order to do so. I had only got as far as Gole Market when I ran into a Hindu colleague in the office. He said 'What on earth are you up to? Go back at once and do not come out of your house. The rioters are killing Muslims in Connaught Circus.'

I hurried back home.

I had barely got to my quarters when I ran into my Sikh neighbour. He began to reassure me. *'Sheikhji,* do not worry! As long as I am alive no one will raise a hand against you.' I said to myself: 'How much fraud is hidden behind this man's beard! He is obviously pleased that the Muslims are being massacred, but expresses sympathy to win my confidence; or is he trying to taunt me?' I was the only Muslim living in the block, perhaps I was the only one on the road.

I did not want these people's kindness or sympathy. I went inside my quarter and said to myself, 'If I have to die, I will kill at least ten or twenty men before they get me'. I went to my room where beneath my bed I kept my double barrelled gun. I had also collected quite a hoard of cartridges.

I searched the house, but could not find the gun.

'What is *huzoor* looking for?' asked my faithful servant, Mohammed.

'What happened to my gun?'

He did not answer. But I could tell from the way he looked that he had either hidden it or stolen it.

'Why don't you answer?' I asked him angrily.

Then he came out with the truth. He had stolen my gun and given it to some of his friends who were collecting arms to defend the Muslims in Daryaganj.

'We have hundreds of guns, several machine guns, ten revolvers and a cannon. We will slaughter these infidels; we will roast them alive.'

'No doubt with my gun you will roast the infidels in Daryaganj, but who will defend me here? I am the only Mussulman amongst these savages. If I am murdered, who will answer for it?'

I persuaded him to steal his way to Daryaganj to bring back my gun and couple of hundred cartridges. When he left I was convinced that I would never see him again. I was all alone. On the mantlepiece was a family photograph. My wife and children stared silently at me. My eyes filled with tears at the thought that I would never see them again. I was comforted with the thought that they were safe in Pakistan. Why had I been tempted by my paltry provident fund and not gone with them? I heard the crowd yelling.

'Sat Sri Akal....'

'Har Har Mahadev...'

The yelling came closer and closer. They were rioters — the bearers of my death warrant. I was like a wounded deer, running hither and thither with the hunters' hounds in full pursuit. There was no escape. The door was made of very thin wood and glass panes. The rioters would smash their way in.

'Sat Sri Akal...'

'Har Har Mahadev...'

They were coming closer and closer; death was coming closer and closer. Suddenly there was a knock at the door. My Sikh neighbour walked in- '*Sheikhji,* come into my quarters at once.' Without a second thought I ran into the Sikh's verandah and hid behind the columns. A shot hit the wall above my head. A truck drew up and about a dozen young men climbed down. Their leader had a list in his hand — "Quarter No.8 — Sheikh Burhanuddin". He read my name and ordered his gang to go ahead. They invaded my quarter and under my very eyes proceeded to destroy my home. My furniture, boxes, pictures, books, druggets and carpets, even the dirty linen was carried into the truck. Robbers! Thugs! Cut-throats!

As for the Sikh, who had pretended to sympathise with me, he was no less a robber than they! He was pleading with the rioters: 'Gentlemen, stop! We have prior claim over our neighbour's property. We must get our share of the loot.' He beckoned to his sons and daughters. All of them gathered to pick up whatever they could lay their hands on. One took my trousers; another a suitcase.

They even grabbed the family photograph. They took the loot to their quarters.

You bloody Sikh! If God grants me life I will settle my score with you. At this moment I cannot even protest. The rioters are armed and only a few yards away from me. If they get to know of my presence....

'Please come in.'

My eyes fell on the unsheathed *kirpan* in the hands of the Sikh. He was inviting me to come in. The bearded monster looked more frightful after he had soiled his hands with my property. There was the glittering blade of his *kirpan* inviting me to my doom. There was no time to argue. The only choice was between the guns of the rioters and the sabre of the Sikh. I decided, rather the *kirpan* of the old man than ten armed gangsters. I went into the room hesitantly, silently.

'Not here, come in further,' I went into the inner room like a goat following a butcher. The glint of the blade of the *kirpan* was almost blinding.

'Here you are, take your things.' said the Sikh.

He and his children put all the stuff they had pretended to loot, in front of me. His old woman said 'Son, I am sorry we were not able to save more.'

I was dumb-founded.

The gangsters had dragged out my steel almirah and were trying to smash it open. 'It would be simpler if we could find the keys,' said someone.

'The keys can only be found in Pakistan. That cowardly son of a filthy Muslim has decamped,' replied another.

Little Mohini answered back: '*Sheikhji* is not a coward. He has not run off to Pakistan.'

'Where is he blackening his face? He is in...' Mohini realised her mistake and stopped in her sentence. Blood mounted in her father's face. He locked me in the inside room, gave his *kirpan* to his son and went out to face the mob.

I do not know what exactly took place outside. I heard the sound of blows; then Mohini crying; then the Sikh yelling full-blooded abuse in Punjabi. And then a shot and the Sikh's cry of pain *hai.*

I heard a truck engine starting up; and then there was a petrified silence.

When I was taken out of my prison my Sikh neighbour was lying on a *charpoy*. Beside him lay a torn and blood stained shirt. His new shirt also was oozing with blood. His son had gone to telephone for the doctor.

'*Sardarji,* what have you done?' I do not know how these words came out of my lips. The world of hate in which I had lived all these years, lay in ruins about me.

'*Sardarji,* why did you do this?' I asked him again.

'Son, I had a debt to pay.'

'What kind of a debt?'

'In Rawalpindi there was a Muslim like you who sacrificed his life to save mine and the honour of my family.'

'What was his name, *Sardarji?*'

'Ghulam Rasul.'

Fate had played a cruel trick on me. The clock on the wall started to strike...1...2...3...4...5...The Sikh turned towards the clock and smiled. He reminded me of my grandfather with his twelve-inch beard. How closely the two resembled each other!

He smiled again. His white beard and long white hair were like a halo, effulgent with a divine light...10...11...12...The clock stopped striking.

I could almost hear him say: 'For us Sikhs, it is always 12 o'clock!'

But the bearded lips, still smiling, were silent. And I knew he was already in some distant world, where the striking of clocks counted for nothing, where violence and mockery were powerless to hurt him.

Translated by **Khushwant Singh**

ORIYA

The Bed of Arrows

Gopinath Mohanty

Back home from work, he emitted a sweet fragrance. Kamala could feel its presence clearly. Turning on her side, she crumpled up in pain. She looked up at his face from the tired bed.

She remembered her decision of not letting him know of her pain or revealing the pallor on her face. Instead, she would smile. Or at least try hard to smile. And yet, why did she hear this weeping inside? It was a happy thought that her days were numbered. It was useless to continue being a burden on him.

Before she could put on a smile, Surababu came near her with a sad face. Pressing her head with his left hand and playing with her dishevelled hair he asked, 'Has the pain increased today? Oh God, what should we do? How long will you carry on in this way?'

Kamala smiled as she said, 'It is the same old pain, what is new about it?'

His face seemed to dry up further before her sharp gaze as he said, 'Yes, why won't you say that? That is your habit, the habit of all women. Never admitting even to yourself what you are going through. You people feel that if you burn yourself out in serving others you will be the first to reach heaven. Isn't that so, Kama?'

Surababu extended his hand to caress her cheeks. But as if in a desperate bid to escape his touch, she withdrew her face, writhing in pain. She felt a stab of pain in the chest and a sudden dizziness as she closed her eyes and floated into emptiness. Half a minute later, she was herself again.

Biting her lower lip she said, 'You have not even changed your clothes. You must be feeling wretched. Do please go and eat something.' She then called out to the servant Indra in a broken voice.

Surababu said, 'I shall go but don't speak so loudly; it will only aggravate your weakness and pain.'

She sighed and closed her eyes. A minute later, as she opened her eyes Surababu was still standing there.

Those few words echoed in her ears, 'What is left of this body?'

The familiar fragrance came back to her. She could see things dissolving—now clear, now hazy before her steady gaze. And now she could see, in the pale wintry light after the rains, the sparkle of the human body — her husband's. His forty-sixth birthday was near at hand and yet he displayed the same inflexibility of body — the wide forehead, the glow of knowledge in the face, the careless tilt of the chin as if to fight and overcome misfortune. And this was her body, only hers. Kamala got gooseflesh.

Her face felt hot; the space around the eyes seemed to burn and, hungrily, she stared at Surababu. She remembered his words of sympathy. But what had she been reduced to! The tiny cloud of suspicion that floated in her consciousness suddenly became a huge screen and there seemed to be an intimation of rain.

She clenched her teeth hard as she spoke, 'What use is an empty wine-cup?'

Surababu was startled and asked, 'Oh, what did you say?'

Kamala smiled in envy and said, 'Nothing. But it is now ages since I have been telling you that I am bedridden. I can do precious little for you and you need care. For God's sake, you...'

To her surprise, she noticed that Surababu did not turn his face away. His eyes did not look misty and there was no anguish at such a proposal. Instead, there was anger in his voice, as he said, 'What is this you are talking about?'

Kamala felt as if she was sinking. Not because of any anger but out of an unknown fear.

She said, 'Are you angry with me? You have just returned after a hard day's work. Why don't you go, change, have a wash and eat something? Why, instead, are you standing here?'

And once again she squeaked, 'Indra, can't you hear me? Babu is standing here.'

Surababu walked away. The breeze retained his fragrance only for a while. Kamala kept thinking, vacantly looking up from her bed. Outside, the shadows lengthened. From her bed, the drumstick plant could be seen clearly. Its leaves had flashed a smile in the sun a little while ago, and now it was slowly becoming a column of darkness. She went back twenty-two long years in memory. Ghana was yet to be born. Manika and Suna had not even been thought of. It was the first year after their marriage.

'You are so fragrant, Kama!'

'Hush…Please go away, mother is in that room and look, someone — may be one of your students, is knocking at the door. You have come back after a hard day's teaching. Are you not hungry?'

All around there was fragrance. Covering her dishevelled hair in the spreading net of his face, she blushed. He remained there, unmoving.

'Would you please go away?'

'Do be quiet. I am listening to the song.'

'What song are you talking about?'

'There is music in the human breast, fragrance in the body; and do you know what there is in the touch?'

'Fire!'

'No you are wrong. The touch has the caress of lotus and sleep.'

'Yes, everything is in your language. You are, after all, a professor of literature!'

'Let us not talk of literature. Literature is not greater than life. It is no substitute for life. I lean on life, I drink life.'

'Are you not ashamed?'

'Shame is only a superficial mask. Why have something you don't believe in?'

Startled, Kamala tried to get up, but in a burst of fire all the nagging pain and the sickness of her body came back. She continued lying down, sulked and could recognise that the fragrance was of an *attar* which was sold in the bazaar. It had been a long time ago. She had forgotten all about toiletry. Forgetting all personal pleasures, all pleasurable habits, she had turned herself into a tough housewife intent on rearing up children. Now they had gone out into the wide world. Manika and Suna had set up their own homes. Ghana was studying forestry at Coimbatore. Once he took up a job, Ghana too would get married even though he was still a child. Then there would be a daughter-in-law in the house. She had sacrificed all her desires and pleasures, deriving pleasure only in giving. Sacrificing and bringing up children.

The softness of her palms had been sacrificed on the altar of domestic chores. Her delicate colouring had faded and there was an increasing loss of hair. Eating had become only a ritual after feeding the family. She would just wear anything and apply just a little bit of coconut oil on her hair. Now, for a year and half, she had lost even that capacity to work and remained immobilised in bed. Many doctors had examined her. She had swallowed too many medicines but no good had come out of them. The same soreness remained in the waist and the feet; the weakness increased and she knew that her body was slowly wasting away. She and *attar*! The fragrance had returned through his body, perhaps only to ease her. He was unusual that way. He never used perfume and often forgot to shave his face, comb his hair or put on appropriate clothes. He was a renowned professor, great in knowledge. Everything appeared nice on him, but surely not *attar*. Then where was that smell from?

How good her husband was, she thought! God had gifted much to her.

Darkness was deepening. Kamala wept—just a few wet drops of tears from hot eyes. Indra brought in the lamp. Kamala asked where he was and was told that Surababu had gone out for a stroll.

'Where to?' she asked.

'He did not tell me.'

'Alright,' she said and kept quiet. *Attar* was available in the market and it was no one's monopoly. The world was full of human beings and if you sought out, you could get someone. No one waited for anyone else. And all the concerns, all the affections - they were there only for a while, something of a lie, really.

Turning over in bed, Kamala lay quietly. More tears welled up. Indra stood by silently. He was used to her tears and now only tried to fathom the nature of her sorrow or pain as he asked, 'What should be the curry for the night?'

'How long do you think I am here that you should keep on asking me this?' Her voice was slurred.

Chewing the tip of his *dhoti*, Indra asked, 'You are crying, sister? Why, won't you get well soon?'

'Let this body go into the hearth-fire. What use is this living except to bear more suffering? And in any case who belongs to whom?' she demanded.

Indra was gone. Kamala felt that at least she had spoken out before someone. She wiped her face. She had declared her wish to die and felt somewhat light now. She kept lying in bed, thinking of death, which would be better than this kind of living. But when would it come? She could not recollect any forgiveness but only a mounting sense of being left out.

Ghana was deeply attached to her but he had his studies, his future. Four months back when she had been very ill, he had not managed to stay for more than four days. His father also insisted that he should not spoil his studies. In fact that was everybody's chorus. And Manika and Suna - belonging to another household, how often could they come? No one should come in fact. Each one, after all, had a world to look after.

The only one who she could call her own had returned from college and had gone out, without even a word to her.

The lights were on. Kamala looked outside as she lay quietly, her mouth half-open as if she had stopped in the midst of saying something and her mind had flown away elsewhere.

She thought she was at the age when the body's desires should end. She had borne him one son and two daughters. Entering her in-laws' house at the age of fifteen, she had put in twenty years of house-management. It had been one long stretch of time in which some had got broken homes, while others had left for the other world. She thought of those days of twenty-one years ago after the birth of Ghana. The hospital, the pain, the operation, the dressing, the unseasonal rain and the bitter cold wind that had made her shiver. The peace-loving professor would be startled at her cry and ask, 'Can't you sleep quietly? You have woken up the baby!' Sometimes, the baby also cried loudly.

Life leans on happiness. It cannot continue with a sense of fear submerging it, she reflected. So sometimes, she had let herself go and in sheer self-defense had ignored the precepts of the *shastras*. The body remained a body, suffered injuries, recovered and only awaited other injuries.

Manika came after Ghana and then came Suna. They were the fruits of happiness, if not of mere sensation.

Even then, she had persuaded herself that the body's desires must end.

So often she would tell her weakling friend Sovana, 'Dear friend, this is only a form of suffering and not happiness. It used to be so wonderful back in our father's home. All that swimming, plucking of flowers, climbing trees, racing to nowhere. Can one ever get back to those carefree days?'

Often she remembered the living shadow of the strong, healthy, disease-free limbs and would hear the seductive whispers from the past.

Often, sighs mingled with waves of philosophy and sought to overpower her.

Her friend understood this. After the birth of her second child she had fallen victim to various ailments of the body and was soon reduced to a frame of bones. Her husband, on the contrary, a Foreman in a plant fabricating steel, looked as strong as Bhima.

She always agreed with Kamala. 'Really, who knows about all the pain inherent in housekeeping and raising children? Where does one lose one's shine, one's strength?'

Kamala would nod quietly. She could never think of Surababu as greedy or cruel. She had the keys and he always brought to her whatever he earned. He had also no expensive habits. He could never be compared to her friends' husbands. She would negate her own words and console her, 'It is all destiny, dear friend.'

Kamala could guess her friend's economic condition from her crumpled clothes, uncombed hair and weak body. But she knew that the *paan*-chewing bony figure was a rebel. Her friend sustained her secret spirit of revolt but yet once again she became pregnant. However, this time she could not live to see the baby's face. Before the doctor's guilty eyes her Foreman husband stood with the baby boy in his arms while the mother lay on the bed like a dirty, cast-out piece of linen.

Kamala had heard about this tragic finale from Surababu. With tears in his eyes, the sympathetic professor had given a graphic picture of the event. Through his elegant words the event had come alive. Kamala had felt the loss inside — not as a writer but as a woman. Her consciousness looking for deliverance had, as it were, met her friend somewhere in the sky. She had a sudden vision of the bony face with a curve of a smile, ridiculing life. Kamala used to pity that. Today, she herself was an object of pity. She felt as if it was her friend who had won. She felt like asking, 'All of us shall depart some day. Why then this unbearable existence?' Her pain boiled over as she remembered details and pieced them together.

That evening, Surababu introduced her to a "new person," Srimati Chandra Midha *alias* Usharani Devi from Siam. He told her that she was a professor in a Ceylonese women's organisation. She had come under an exchange programme for teachers. She taught English but was also at ease with Hindi, Bengali and Tamil. She had spent two months at Puri before her arrival and in this time had become fairly fluent in Oriya.

She was guileless, almost like a child. Surababu added, 'I am now proving to her that her ancestors hailed from Kalinga and hence her knowledge of Oriya has been acquired by past deeds.'

Chandra Midha kept smiling. But there was a suggestion of sharpness in the movement of her arms, which she kept crossing and extending. Surababu said, 'Swagatam,' she said. 'Welcome.' Surababu tried to explain to her not only the meaning but the origin and derivation of words. Chandra Midha winked and tried to compare the words for love in respective languages— English, Hindi, Bengali and Oriya. Kamala laughed. Surababu said nothing.

Kamala asked, 'Devi Chandra Midha, how many children do you have?'

Surababu stared hard at her. Chandra Midha laughed strangely, and the ripples spread all over her face and along the pearls of her teeth inside the oval lips.

She asked Surababu, 'Wachat,' meaning 'What is that?'

Surababu took good care of her reception; Kamala did not struggle to get up again. From the drawing room, their laughter floated in. Kamala understood that Chandra Midha was quite fascinating and her laughter was music. She was the symbol of unembarrassed, strong and free life. It was something to be envied. Kamala has never had either that health or that freedom. From her narrow, tradition-bound bylane, she stared at Chandra Midha's unhampered highway. For the first time, she felt a secret shiver of fear inside. No one explained anything to her, but her woman's mind picked up the meaning from a refined level. That evening, she prayed to God to release her from life.

The meaning of an event depends on one's attitude, and that attitude depends on one's mental condition, which in turn depends on several other situations. She recalled the events he had narrated to her and his analysis of them. She was not illiterate, even though she hailed from an interior rural area. She had studied up to primary school and had read out scriptures to please her mother. For her own pleasure she had also read some novels which prepare one to seek out a partner in life.

Looking back at her past, she now felt that Surababu had never loved her, that he had loved only himself and, in order to let that self-love grow and spread out, he had used her only as a support. From the beginning he had attempted to teach her further, had failed and given up hope. She had been taken out on social rounds only when it was unavoidable. Otherwise he remained lost behind his pile of books.

The selfish meaning of his monologue sometimes came back anew to her, 'If only someone had helped me a bit in my work I would have gone much farther in life. Doing a D.Litt. would not have been that difficult.'

She remembered her cooking, her household worries, looking after children — surely these were of little use for his D. Litt.

However, now that Chandra Midha had come, she could surely help him in his D.Litt.

She was after all a dwarf in knowledge, and what could she have done for him?

Often, he gave his opinion on womenfolk in our society. He felt they were good housewives but no good as life-partners.

'Do you understand, Kama?' he would say. '*Dharma* is not idol worship; it is activity according to one's ideal. If the husband is a doctor and the wife's *dharma* is the kitchen, do you think that makes for a good partnership?'

She also recalled his comments on life and society with literature as the model.

'Look at ethics. Many people ascribe new meaning to it and hide many lies, much false pretence behind it. There is no faith in the heart, but the name of Rama is on the lips. Our womenfolk take pride in their ethics but live in the dark, narrow cubicles of the mind. Trying to be careful, they end up being selfish; sometimes the dullest passes off as liberal-minded. And those who revel in sordid rumours and whose minds run in dark directions put on dazzling vermillion marks on the forehead and a broach with "Husband is the greatest guru" inscribed on it. True ethics does not consist in merely reserving one's body for the husband and storing a lot of garbage inside.'

To all these she had nodded. He must, after all, be right. All that must be in the books which he taught to others. She never questioned or raised any arguments concerning the truth of those theories.

Bisibabu, a senior student, often used to come to consult his "Sir." He was handsome, with thick eyelashes peeping out of his eyeglasses. He was a lovable person— ever smiling, and bright, and one always felt comfortable and happy in his presence. Sometimes, when Bisi was closeted with Surababu she had brought in tea and snacks for them.

But suddenly one day, Surababu had poured venom against him, 'Don't trust that guy. He is a camouflaged devil. Please remember this.'

Since then, she had never even come out when Bisi visited. He had such complaints against many other people. Looking into the past she realised that whenever anyone had tried to come close, Surababu had always spoken against him or her. That was perhaps his way of putting shackles on her feet. Behind his genial temper there lurked a lack of trust. So much about ethics, affection, and housekeeping. To her it all appeared to be an empty staying together, only gilt, edged by ideas. Life had taken a back seat. She would never regain her adolescent days, she thought sadly.

Sometimes she felt like blurting out, 'Sure enough your Chandra Midha has globetrotted, known many people and her mind is not narrow. But she has no husband, no son. She does not depend on anyone for a living. Is she like us that she should be afraid of anyone?'

But she always held back these words. She had never been able to say them. She recalled his anxiety-ridden face, his sleepless nights. Was it not after all only for her? The memory of the spring of yesteryears always put her with her husband on a swing where there was no envy, no meanness, no selfishness, only the scattering of flowers of happiness. Let him be happy, let everyone be happy, let my life's lamp burn out before him.

It was as if her body was dying away slowly from the feet upward. Like an empty vessel the mind resonated even with a slight hurt. She always felt that now the body and the mind had become mutually dependent and both were surrounded and pressed down by time. She had danced uncontrollably, but not the dance of youth, but that of a half-dead leaf trembling precariously on a branch in the cold northern wind. It was a dance bereft of hope and forgiveness. How could she forgive another when she wanted to die, not forgiving even herself? How healthy he was even now! Like a stone with rain lashing on it, he had overcome all life's experiences.

Years had rolled by. Age had increased along with poverty. But he too had gone ahead and enviably, had kept his head high. Even now he would get up in the morning, do his exercises and go a mile for his walk. In the morning the earth and the sky would be open before him to seek out poetry. He also read a lot and even played the *sitar* late into the night. And her own world?

It was one of physical suffering and pain, a burnt-out mind, the routine of somehow crawling to the toilet and back. When she looked out of the window, she saw a hedge of small and big trees, and in the distance, the back of a house. Leaning on them was the curve of the sky, the water towers, the chimney of a sugar mill, the tall trees and the heads of tall buildings. And enclosing them all, the sky. The lonely, empty sky. Would she go there? When? But inside the body the last drop of life force still cried out to live, to see the changing seasons, the familiar crows, house sparrows, the kites, their movements and changing winds. But when the sky looked deep blue and the drumstick tree bent down with flowers, she tended to forget her disease.

She would call out to Indra, 'What beautiful drumstick flowers! Why don't you cook them for Babu? He is so fond of them.' The sound of human voices outside, brought happiness. When it was quiet all around she felt the dewfall on her chest and tears trickled down her eyes. Like a lunatic or a weakling discovering strength in anger or envy, she gathered strength from a hidden sense of being lost or ignored. With an effort, she brought her endless coughing to a stop. It was foolishness to think that the healthy could go on looking after the sick endlessly. That was a deception, a delusion.

So she would tell him now and then, 'I have troubled you a lot. Please get married again.'

And the reply would inevitably be, 'Do keep quiet. Are you crazy? People will only laugh at this.'

It was true that she had lost her head since the coming of this Usharani. He insisted on calling her by that name rather than her original name. Her name came up everyday. He sang her praise in various ways. And lying in her bed Kamala realised that a healthy man looks only at the rising sun. She often repeated to herself that the desires of the flesh were a mistake.

Only the servant and cook Indra anxiously listened to her.

'This is the way of the world, Indra, never trust a man.'

Indra hardly saw the meaning of the statement. He too had a permanent anger against menfolk. He wanted to be born a woman. Sulking, he said, 'You will become alright, sister.'

The two decrepit boats touched each other through inadequate words and then floated along. Kamala derived some peace from her loneliness. But she could not help noticing the changing mood of her husband and realised how he looked brighter everyday. In his face, in his eyes there was the sparkle of new youth, sometimes in charmed silence, sometimes in sudden startles. There was a new symphony in his *sitar*. Sometimes he returned late from college and then went out again for a walk after dark.

In the beginning once or twice he had said, 'I have to go to Chandra Midha to discuss a paper in Comparative Linguistics which I have written.'

Gradually he forgot to even mention her name. He only kept getting delayed "somewhere outside."

Kamala understood that life would always win over death. That day, once again, she noticed that fragrance on him. Once again he was out late in the evening. What was that streak of fire in the sky? She looked up. The round, large moon came up smiling and even the drumstick tree looked like a beauty in its glow. That was her hope, her pitiable desire. Suddenly, on her consciousness she felt huge waves of a tide encircling the horizon. She felt that she had found something. She had now something to say—but the words were leaving her. In any case, of what use were they now? And yet her mouth remained half-open. Surababu returned at half past nine. He too was thinking of life all the way. He felt certain that life and happiness were inseparable. So too were death, misery and narrowness.

Kamala lay face upward, bent towards the moon. The mouth was slightly open in a gesture of not having completed what she had wanted to say.

Translated by **Sitakant Mahapatra**

Death of An Indian

Kishori Charan Das

The weatherman had announced that we were likely to have snowfall towards evening. It was the midday news: one John Douglas had conveyed the news to us along with a recipe for New Frontier nail polish. It was his usual hour that runs as follows: a lady's tender and long fingers unfold on the television screen and accept a liquid poured from above. The nails begin to shine, the owner of the hands stretches them languidly towards a packet of cigarettes and smokes away the exquisite moments of leisure. An appropriate music score provides the background to a caress and its culmination. Then enters John Douglas to tell you smilingly that you too can buy these delights if you use such-and-such product of so and so. The story is over, he introduces himself—my name is John Douglas, your weatherman. Today's weather has taken an interesting turn ... etc. Similarly we got our evening news, courtesy of a firm devoted to the extermination of white ants, and the late news from a firm dedicated to the care of kitchen sinks.

My children danced with joy when they heard the news. Several questions and comments were flung at me, all at once - How is it going to fall? Like sand or pebbles? How can the people walk in the streets? We have to clear the sidewalk in front of our house or else we will be fined hundred dollars, I am telling you ...

There was a spark of eagerness in Latika's eyes too. But she did not confess to it. The spark smothered; she looked upset. She could not stand this foreign cold. There were other reasons too, I guessed. 'It was announced in the papers today that a sale is on at Lansburghs downtown - Ladies' coats going cheap for thirty dollars, and girls' dresses for as little as three dollars. But how do we go out if it snows?'

I wanted to comfort her, and said, 'Well dear, you are thinking of the sale, aren't you? Do not lose heart. There will always be a sale in this country, today, tomorrow and ever after. Today it is Lansburghs, tomorrow it is Sears ... surely you can't miss them all.'

She was not satisfied. And she started all over again, 'Look, it is you who made me leave all my things in India. So when all your Indian ladies have a matching coat for each *sari*, your wife has a miserable one-and-a-half! You can pooh-pooh these sales now, but I know you will have to buy the same stuff at the regular rate of sixty... Go ahead, by all means!'

My first-born joined her mother. She said that her classmate had definite information about the sale of ballpoint pens at thirty cents each at the nearest drug store.

The middle one remembered that her socks were just no good for the American winter. Then of course that she needed gloves for her hands and earmuffs for the ears. How else could she manage the cold blasts on her way to school? Auntie Ray, she said, had assured her that all these things are being offered at cut-rates at a corner store on Fourteenth Street.

Lastly, my little son chimed in, 'Get me a sale daddy! Get me one p-l-e-a-s-e?'

I did succeed, in due course, in bringing them back to the theme of snowfall. Truly, sales are wonderful. But a snowfall is even bigger, more wonderful. A sight not to be seen in the plains of India, to which we belong. Contemplate the scene, if you please. The pure white little darlings coming to us from the high heavens, free of the smog of civilisation. Free of sound and smell, of colour and conflict. They come to us, for a while, to remind us of the eternal values.

It was thus that I held forth on the subject of snowfall. Latika listened to me for sometime and then interrupted, 'But you forget, there is another aspect to it. The body alive is warm, the body dead is cold.So if you ask me ...'

I knew the rest. Snow is the symbol of death and all that perverse prattle. But I did not let her prolong the conversation knowing that she wanted only to tease me.

We waited for the first snowfall of the season in Washington, D.C. We had arrived in the city about two months back to stay for three years as desired by the Government of India. We had till then made no friends among the foreigners. We knew some fellow-Indians in the Embassy, but not too well. Once in a while we came across *sari*-clad women in supermarkets and on side-walks. At once, our eyes gleamed with recognition - there goes an Indian. But the recognised party never seemed to have any irrepressible urge to communicate. Sometimes the painted lips would part a little—but no further.

I had to explain to a despairing Latika, 'Don't you understand? We belong to the same family. Need we say hellos and how-do-you-dos in our own family all the time? It feels good just to see them, to have been made aware of the trials and tribulations that bind us together in this foreign city. For all you know, this lady is also, like us, looking for the rare Mexican chick-peas to have her *Alu chhole*, trying to figure out the English name for *suji*, and is looking for sales that can give her the maximum benefit on her foreign allowance, so she can carry a few things home. Don't you see? She is an Indian. One of us.'

Thus we had no fear of intrusion from any friend or neighbour, as one would have back home on a holiday afternoon. We were left to ourselves, cosy in the warmth of the family, to welcome the advent of snow.

But I had reckoned without the telephone. There was a persistent ring, and a woman's voice asked, 'Will you kindly call Mrs Das?'

It must be one of them, I thought, Mrs Ray or Mrs Kapur—the only two wives who along with their husbands had evinced great interest in our rehabilitation. I could well imagine the course of their conversation. 'When are you buying a car? My husband was telling me that the new Ford Galaxie is a shade better than

Impala .. Have you tried the new blender? ... Started giving trouble? I thought so. Didn't I tell you that you should buy the Osterizer ... So on and so forth. I was not very far wrong. After a ten-minute session on the telephone, Latika summarized to me, 'It was Mrs Kapur. A nice lady. Was enquiring about the welfare of our children, and whether we have decided on the car. Yes, she told me that vacuum cleaners are on sale at Lerners. Quite cheap.'

After a moment's pause she said, 'It seems we are going to have a heavy snowfall this evening, within an hour or so. Mrs Kapur got the news on telephone.'

'Oh yes Daddy, here they tell you about the weather on the telephone. You just have to lift the receiver and it goes on and on. You know the number, don't you?'

'No, and I don't want to'. I snapped. Is there no end to this process of scientific education?

And so the snow came. Within an hour there was a flush of crimson on the grey-white sky. Then I saw grains of silver floating in the air. Could this be the snow? Or is it that the grains of dust have taken the shine off a pale evening? A few were moving towards me. I tried to hold them but could only get the inadequate feeling of dewdrops in my hands. Ah, the sky is bursting with grains and globules! Each one of them is growing bigger and bigger and is showing off like an adolescent. They are playing, running, chasing and falling over each other, weightless with sheer inconsequence. No, I refuse to take you as the real ones!

The real ones came in full regalia, not a moment too soon. By then the snowflakes had left their imprint on the grass and the foliage. They were twinkling, revelling as it were in the fun of evanescence, while the white strands, the white bunches, the white messes were descending on the earth. This is the snowfall indeed! The pervasive passion of the fall took my breath away. Even the feel of Latika crouching over me to have a better view of the snow failed to revive me. I wished I could be there in the centre. I wished I could take my fill of the bounty, cleansing myself of all the pitiful pigmentations of life. I wished, but I wished in vain. The telephone rang.

'Yes?' I asked severely into the mouthpiece.

'Shahni speaking. Sir, I am sorry to disturb you. Rangarao died this evening in Georgetown hospital.'

'Died? Rangarao ... who is Rangarao?'

'Rangarao was an assistant in the Embassy. He was suffering for a long time from some kidney trouble. A young widow and a daughter are the survivors.'

Now I remembered. On an afternoon, a few days back, we had been to a big Departmental Store called Bargain City. There we were treated to a thrilling display of kisses by a doll named Kissy. You just had to press her hands and she would start throwing kisses at you. I was discussing the worth of this contraption at a forfeit of ten dollars when our escort, an Indian gentleman, whispered in my ears, 'Do you see her, that girl in the white *sari*? A sad case. The husband has been very sick for the last three months. His days are numbered. She is managing somehow, poor girl, on a typing job ...'

I had a momentary glimpse of the young woman. She had an angular face with an intense pair of eyes, and was walking fast notwithstanding the giant shopping bag flapping on her sides. She looked like one who was not in the habit of answering casual questions.

Shahni went on to say, 'The funeral takes place tonight at eleven. Quite a number of Indians are expected to attend.'

Shahni was my personal assistant. Well, what did he mean to suggest? That I should attend the funeral at that unearthly hour in a roaring snowfall? But before I could repeat the question to myself, the answer came with a thud ... He was one among us. It would indeed be a shame, a thousand times... I did not allow the self-reproach to proceed further, and told Shahni, 'Yes, I would like to go. Will you take me along?' Shahni obliged me by saying that he would bring round his car at about half-past ten to my place.

I told Latika. She agreed that I should go and added, 'How unfortunate! I do hope the Government will pay for her passage home ... please do not forget your topcoat and hat ... Are ladies supposed to attend funerals over here? I wish I knew ...'

The eldest could not contain herself any longer and asked, 'Who died, Daddy?'

'An Indian.'

They exchanged glances and assumed a solemn air. That did not surprise me. But the solemnity of the four-year-old, the manner of his pressed lips and fluttering eyelids was rather ominous. He had a penchant for awkward questions and I feared that he may come out now with the all-important question ... But what is an Indian?

I had judged him wrong. I was comforted by his continued silence. In fact, the entire family seemed to appreciate the compulsion of silence on an occasion, which was vaguely national and out of their depth.

I went near the window and surveyed the passing scene. I wanted to absorb the snowfall, the best I could, in spite of the odd relevance of the death of an Indian. I saw the cars shrouded in white, moving slowly, bravely. I saw the neon lights brushing off the nagging snow and blinking roguishly at the courageous traveller. I could imagine an exciting evening in the warm haven of cabarets and night clubs. I could imagine the friendly ones asking for another tall glass, another joke, another ... still another... in an unerring response to the gift of the heavens.

I could imagine the intimate ones ask for each other with a rare urgency. And then it came to me that the snowfall invites the living world to quicken the pace of life— while the company lasts. But here I am, an outsider, a snow-struck fool of an Indian, watching the falling objects with primeval wonder!

I cursed myself, and in the process I had an unholy urge to curse Rangarao. He seemed to have committed the death-act on this particular day, in order to spite me. To underscore my sense of deprivation in the new land which I was only beginning to know.

Shahni came after I had had my dinner and smoked three cigarettes in a row. I looked at my watch; it was barely five minutes past the appointed hour. Even so, I mumbled something about his being late and was quick to lead him to his Volkswagon. The children had gone to bed. But Latika was wide-eyed and followed me to the car. She repeated her wish to join me. If only she knew ladies were not out of place at a funeral. I dismissed her with a perfunctory smile.

Shahni was driving slowly. Shahni loves to tune the car radio on to a high pitch. But now I found the radio in merciful repose. It was a deliberate concession, I thought, to the purpose of the journey. He had no qualms, however, about filling the vacuum with an unending commentary on the affairs of the world—such as, 'It seems the snow is not going to be too severe this year. The first snowfall last year was seven inches thick ... Mrs Das wanted to have some good nylon. I think it will be better to import it directly from Hongkong rather than buy it in New York. Houses are going cheap in this area. But .. but ... it is a Negro neighbourhood... This road to the right goes past Banerji's house. A clever fellow - has managed to extend his stay here for another term...'

Perhaps he realized that I was hoping to hear something more appropriate. So he commenced on the topic of Rangarao. 'Rangarao was a very nice man. Used to send fifty dollars every month to his old parents. His wife is equally nice...' He did not have a chance to elaborate as we had by then reached our destination. Shahni pointed at a non-descript flat-roofed structure and said, 'That is the building. Lees' Funeral Home.'

On second thoughts, I approved of the Funeral Home. This is how these homes should be—slight and simple, in deference to the majesty of death.

There were a number of cars parked in front of the building. 'They all belong to Indians,' Shahni told me with conviction. I was overwhelmed by the massive response of my people and exclaimed, 'So many Indians, so many cars!' Shahni assured me, 'Yes sir, almost all the Indians in Washington possess cars.'

He guided me to a room where I put away my hat and overcoat. On my way to the inner hall I met Mr Saxena of the Supply Mission. I smiled and said 'Hello.' But I was surprised that he neither smiled nor spoke.

The inner hall was almost filled to capacity by ladies and gentlemen dressed in dark clothes and seated in straight-backed chairs. There was a hush of expectancy in the air.

I saw a covered object stretched out on a raised platform ahead of us. This must be the body, I thought.

The body of Rangarao. The awareness evoked a sigh. Why did he come to America, this young man? To die on foreign soil? To leave a young woman disconsolate? A child bewildered? I felt several such sighs being merged into each other in a mighty effort to commune and condole. I felt the dark cold night closing in around us, the Indians in Washington, D.C., so that we may be pinpointed to our tragedy. I had the sensation, akin to ecstasy, of being engulfed.

I envied Rangarao. What more could he expect?

Presently there was a rustling of dresses and shuffling of feet. The gentleman to my left spoke in an undertone, 'The Ambassador, himself.'

Yes, the Ambassador was coming forward in slow steps, followed by a couple of senior officials. I spotted Mr Shah, the Second Secretary whom I knew well and I smiled at him. But there was no responsive smile or nod.

I now got the general idea. The Shahs and Saxenas have a better sense of decorum. They do not encourage smiles or any such levity in the Hall of Death.

I was ashamed and fervently hoped that I would not commit such indiscretions again. I sat straight and looked ahead, the same as others, including the Ambassador.

We waited. Suddenly, in the interminable silence, it occurred to me - but where is she? I was not looking for her mere presence in the assembly, but the loud presence of a widow ... the streaming tears, the soiled *sari*, the smeared *kajal*, the anguished cries and the incoherent indictment of gods.

It did not take me long to banish the thought. Mrs Rangarao is undoubtedly here, possibly in the front row. But she is a civilised person and the Lees' Funeral Home is a far cry from the cremation *ghats* of the Ganges. She is not one, no sir, to mar the collective image of our sorrow by her snivellings. I admired the restraint of the young woman and made a note of it to tell Latika.

The minutes went passing by. I looked at my watch; it was past midnight. What are we waiting for? When are the proceedings going to begin? I found that some others also were fidgeting in their seats. The good lady by my side seemed to have gone to sleep. A gentleman nearby was refusing to acknowledge the superiority of Morpheus. He was shaking himself off from his fitful slumber and was looking at me with challenging eyes. One in the front row - perhaps Mr Kulkarni, the First Secretary, would every now and then, with a pained look, travel all the way to the entrance and return. I was convinced that something was going to happen and we had to remain patient.

Then I saw a tall well-built gentleman striding past the entrance. I recognised him, he could be no other than Mr Raghunandan Misra, the repository of Indian culture in Washington, D.C. Maybe he had an official designation of some sort but that was incidental. I had met him casually at a cocktail party and had heard him comment disdainfully on officialdom. I was told that at one time he had been a professor in an Indian University, and it was by sheer mischance that he had strayed into the fold of bureaucrats. Legend went that his father was a famous scholar of Varanasi and Mr Misra was soaked in Sanskrit texts, thanks to his early education. It was even rumoured that he was authorised to perform priestly functions in Hindu marriages abroad. I could not dismiss his reputation as being unfounded. For, I had personally seen him recite, that evening, half-a-dozen Sanskrit *shlokas* from Kalidasa's *Abhigyana-Shakuntalam*, over the course of three cocktails.

With no previous warning Mr Mishra stood by the side of the body and proffered a slight bow. We all stood up, including the Ambassador. Then he began in a sonorous tone, to recite a *shloka* - it was, I believe from the *Bhagavad Gita* - the meaning of which was:

For whenever Right declines and Wrong prevails
Then O Bharata, I come to birth.

Another:

One looks upon This as a marvel;
another speaks of This as such;
another hears thereof as a marvel;
Yet having heard of This none truly
knows This.

Thus it went on for about ten minutes. The relation between one and the other, and their relevance to the funeral ceremony was not quite clear to me. But after all, I thought Mr Mishra was an expert in the field. He knew what was best. Without him the soul of Rangarao would have been cheated of the last rites. The undertaker of Lees' Funeral Home would have had the impression that we do not have any funeral service or that we do not know how to honour the dead.

After the recital, Mr Mishra made another bow and retired. We resumed our seats. Then followed a gentle murmur of release, as that of receding waves. I imagined that there would now be a quick change of scenes and the conclusion was not far off.

Two members of the undertaker's establishment carried the body of Rangarao away from the hall.

The crowd became diffused after the exit of the body. There was a free flow of conversation - you know, the crematorium here is the latest of its kind. The body is burnt, bones and all, in two minutes flat ... Mr Mishra was engaged in a dinner party, that is why... the blasted snow has started again. I wish there were no office tomorrow... Is the Ambassador going to stay till the end? etc. I was following a stream moving towards the crematorium when I found a few people, mostly ladies, huddled in a corner and leaning over someone. I stopped for a while, to see what it was all about.

I heard a brief moan. Brief but substantial. It was like a streak of lightning that barely writes on the sky but writes well. An articulation full of promise, yet destined to die. Yes, it was the voice of the widow. The voice of Mrs Rangarao, who had broken down and betrayed her human weakness at the last moment, in an unforgettable half note of pathos. I started towards her in a mounting surge of sympathy. I watched her nestling against the bosom of the elder sisters, begging forgiveness, as it were, for her bad manners. For once I felt that I was going to cry.

I composed myself and mused on the nature of sympathy. There are moments when the sorrow of a fellow human being creates discomfort but one is tempted to deny it, claiming to some superior wisdom. There are also occasions on which one suffers helplessness in not being able to relieve the distress of the unfortunate fellow. But in this instance my response, despite the unshed tears, was not entirely negative. It appeared to me that Mrs Rangarao had been able to provide the missing piece in a portrait of infinite beauty. She had expressed herself at the right moment and in the right proportion. I wished I could go near her and stroke her tresses gently, the same as that elderly lady was doing. The experience was strangely satisfying.

Mrs Rangarao released herself from her sympathisers and exposed a tear-washed face. The elderly lady stood up and surveyed the scene. She had an aristocratic bearing, rendered more attractive in sadness. It was a familiar presence, seen somewhere in print or in person. While I was trying to recall her identity I saw a group of persons led by the Ambassador entering the hall. The Ambassador approached the lady and they both walked back to the entrance at a measured pace. Then I realised — I should have known earlier that it was the Ambassador's wife.

Shahni was back by my side and announced that the funeral was over. He also invited me to leave immediately in order to avoid the rush.

The snow was dropping listlessly on my way home. But the houses, streets and trees were all covered with snow. Many tall trees, denuded of leaves looked like silvery pillars, whereas the leaves in the small ones had gathered the snow unto themselves in balls of cotton wool. The earth seemed overladen with bounty. After a long spell of silence, I spoke to Shahni, still on the subject of Rangarao, 'When is she leaving for India? She must leave within six months, you know, or else Government will not pay for the passage.'

'Mrs Rangarao will not return to India.'

'What do you mean?'

Shahni did not seem to appreciate the surprise or sharpness in my tone. He took some time to answer. 'She is not going back. We met her downtown recently. She told my wife in quite so many words that if anything happened to her husband, she would adopt this country as her home.'

'But why? Doesn't she have any close relatives in India? For how long can she manage in a foreign country as a typist?'

Shahni could scarcely conceal his exasperation when he said, 'Of course she has her relatives— her parents, in-laws, brothers and sisters. But don't you see, why should she go back? To languish in want and misery in some remote corner in the South? Can they assure her a decent life, a proper education for her child, the minimum modern facilities?'

I did not pursue my enquiry. Mrs Rangarao could surely look

after herself. But I lapsed into a deeper silence till Shahni bade me goodnight.

In the early hours of the morning I had a frightful dream. I dreamt that I was being laid on the snow with due ceremony, but I was crying out.... 'NO! NO!! Please let me have the funeral pyre, the fire, the flame...' The Ambassador's wife was, however, passing her hands ever so gently over my brow and pinning me down to the cold surface. Mrs Rangarao and Latika were standing on both sides of her and smiling at each other in complete accord and understanding.

On waking up I found Latika with the morning newspaper. She gave me the good news... 'Have you seen this? Kanns are offering silver-plated cutlery for only fifty dollars at the Washington Birthday Sale ....'

Translated by the **Author**

GUJARATI

Wings of a Silent Wish

Dinkar Joshi

Ketan looked into the mirror. His hair had greyed. Instantly it brought to his mind the story of King Dasharath of Ayodhya who, having noticed his first grey hair had taken the decision of handing over the reins of his kingdom to Prince Rama and retiring into the woods. It's time for me to renounce certain things too, thought Ketan.

Once again he looked into the mirror, and then at his photograph on the wall. The picture had been clicked when he had just turned twenty. It showed him wearing the black gown of graduation, holding the rolled sheet of his Certificate.

His gaze turned towards the bunch of letters in his hands. Wrapped in a pink handkerchief it represented an unnamed joy. Instantly he stopped himself. The decision had to be taken.

He would destroy the letters for good. It made no sense to preserve them anymore. All they could cause were problems and complications. His eldest daughter had been married off two years back and was living happily with her husband and in-laws. His son would also be getting married in about a year's time. And then, some day, Ketan would suddenly die.

His heart would quietly switch off. This is how it had been in his family. His father had died without warning at the age of 57—his elder brother, at 56. And his uncle had barely got into his 52nd year!. With a start, Ketan reminded himself that he had already turned 50. Soon he would be starting the sixth decade of his life. All the males in his family had left for their heavenly abode when they had been in their fifties. Going by family history, he would soon be gone too... and then.

Then, this bunch of letters would fall into the hands of one of his relatives! The image of Ketan as a good husband, a good father, a good and responsible family member would come shattering down. The thought worried him.

But how could he ever forget Seema who had written all these letters to him? In the beginning of their relationship she had addressed him as *Dear Ketanbhai*.... then progressed into *My dear Ketanbhai*.... and had finally settled into *My dear* only.

They had met each other late in life. Ketan had been married for almost fifteen years. Seema too had completed ten years of married life. But God knows... how? All of a sudden things had burst into the open. It would have been better had it been left unexpressed. But now, such thoughts had no meaning. Everything had been expressed very clearly. It was Ketan who had taken the initiative one evening. He had told her... or rather something within him had forced him to speak out — 'Seema! from the day we met, I have liked you and wanted you. Why is it so? I really do not know, but....'

Seema had put her finger on Ketan's lips and had stopped him from finishing his sentence.

'I have never ever felt that you are away from me Ketan! All these years I have always felt your presence within me...' she had whispered softly.

That was all! Only so much had been expressed. But, within a miniscule span of time, they had come close as never before. For a minute, Ketan thought, what was wrong if his relatives came to know about it after his death? He had not been disloyal to anyone. He had merely given voice to his tender feelings and had accepted hers. It had not progressed into anything more serious.

But the exchange of letters had continued.

Seema had been the first to regain her composure. Perhaps the momentous acceptance must have threatened her sense of security. After all she was a married women, a respectable housewife, the mother of three children, above all, the wife of a husband who held an important position in society. It was true that her heart had merely given vent to feelings - emotions that had remained unsaid for so many years. It was also true that she had expressed those feelings in so many words - but so what? What about her family life? What about the future of her children? What if her husband came to know?

The journey that had begun with *Dear Ketanbhai* had returned to *Dear Ketanbhai...* after having digressed for a while.

Seema had written, 'Dear Ketanbhai. That was one of our moments of weakness. I cannot bear the burden of having expressed my feelings to you. Please do not write to me any more....'

Ketan laughed to himself. He opened the 'kerchief and arranged the letters date-wise. The letters written before the Acceptance had no indications of these feelings. And yet, he had preserved all of them. But then Seema too had preserved Ketan's letters addressed to her.

She herself had confessed 'I have with me even the first letter that you wrote... that very first one...and all subsequent ones also. All of them.'

'Seema, why have you preserved them for so long?' Ketan had asked her on the Day of Acceptance.

'The reason I don't know' Seema had replied. 'If I ask you the same question, what would be your reply?'

Ketan had no answer to that. He knew she didn't either. And yet, both understood.

Many years had passed since that chance confession. Both of them had gone back to living their lives as before, as if nothing had happened. But occasionally they did experience a mysterious restlessness. The bunch of letters would draw their attention to it and hold it there for a while. Ketan would inevitably feel the need to destroy the letters. But on the wings of this thought, another would follow. Had he also not poured out his heart in the letters he had written to Seema? He should get them from her and give hers back. If he destroyed Seema's letters without her knowledge, she would never trust him in future. If she ever asked for those letters any time in future, his reply would not sound truthful to her. The image of an emotional Seema, full of tender feelings for him was just that. An unreal image. The other one of Seema talking about that moment as one of weakness was real. An undeniable reality. The pink 'kerchief preserved both these images of Seema.

But now Ketan had taken the decision. He should once again, possibly for the last time, contact Seema. He should tell her, 'Seema! Come, let us destroy these letters together. The past should be permanently destroyed so that the moment you consider to be your moment of weakness may also be destroyed forever. May it never cast its shadow on our children!'

He had not spoken to Seema over the phone for all these years. Yet he had noted down her number in all the telephone diaries which he changed regularly every two years. He had carefully noted all the changes in her number that had taken place over the years. Her latest number was also there in his diary. With trembling fingers he dialled it. The sweet sound of Seema's voice stroked his ears. It had changed over the years. It was slightly heavier than before, but it was Seema for sure. Hesitating for a moment, he felt like putting down the receiver. He had muttered 'Hello' and had then paused.

'Yes! Go on, Ketanbhai! Why did you pause?' laughed Seema softly.

'You ... you... you recognized my voice?' Ketan stuttered.

'Why not? Pausing thus after saying hello and sounding confused is not new to you. It's an old habit of yours' she teased.

For a moment, Ketan felt ten years younger. But immediately he came back to the present. In a dry tone he explained to her his idea — 'Seema! Let us meet once again for the last time. Let us both destroy those letters.'

Seema remained silent for awhile. Then she agreed. Once this agreement was reached, the decision to meet the following Saturday evening to destroy the letters was made swiftly enough.

It had been a Saturday when he had first met Seema, Ketan remembered with a start. The day when both had expressed their feelings to each other had also been a Saturday. And now, the day of burying their past would also be on a Saturday. Why, why should all this have happened on Saturday evenings only? Ketan decided that it must be the workings of a Power greater than them.

The clock on the wall was ticking as usual. Its rhythmic tick-tock continued as usual. The cyclical journey of the sun, the moon and even the earth continued as before. The date of the calendar changed as usual. Ketan thought... I wish all this would stop so that the coming of Saturday could be delayed. But almost the next instant he thought - how nice it would be if Saturday evening came and passed off quickly. It would be better to get it over with.

Saturday came. His eyes fell on Seema. Even after so many years, she had not changed much. But the imprint of passing years was quite visible on her face. Seema too looked at him intently. Ketan smiled hesitantly. Seema too smiled. But their smiles did not appear natural. Both were aware of this. Each hoped the other would start the conversation.

'You ... you have lost weight!' Finally it was Seema who managed to break the daunting silence.

'Really?' Ketan replied.

'We are meeting today for a specific reason' added Ketan.

'Yes, I know!' Seema sounded nonchalant.

'You have...?'

'What?'

'I mean, the letters that can prove embarrassing to our children?'

'I have brought them.'

'I too have brought them' said Ketan.

The road ahead of them stared blankly at them. Where should they go? Neither of them could decide. Many years back—it seemed ages back now, they had walked aimlessly together...without deciding the direction ahead, until one day, a silent wish had started fluttering its wings in their hearts.

Years later, when they were walking together again, it felt that their magical bird was hopping without legs. Why, even their time together seemed to be hopping forward, as if experiencing strange obstructions in its natural flow.

'These...letters....' Ketan repeated.

'Hmm' Seema nodded.

It was Ketan who finally took the decision. He hailed a taxi. Seema got in quietly.

'Take us to the beach,' Ketan instructed the taxi driver.

As the taxi began to move ahead, Seema looked out of the window.

There was a certain stillness on the beach. A few rocks on the shore separated it from the onslaught of the waves. The place was practically deserted. Ketan began walking towards a rock closest to the waves. Seema quietly followed him. The *pallu* of her saree was fluttering in the sea breeze. Occasionally, it touched Ketan and he would move away, self-consciouly. Seema would gather her *pallu* by her side. But after a while it would start fluttering again. They sat down on a rock. Silence enveloped them.

'So many years have passed, isn't it?' muttered Seema.

'Humm!' Ketan whispered softly, touching the bunch of letters in the pink kerchief. Then he held it forward towards Seema. 'Those years are preserved on these letters. They should be...'

'Why did you stop?' asked Seema looking at him. She opened

her purse, took out a bunch of letters and said softly, 'The past is also alive in these letters.'

Gently, Ketan touched Seema's letters. He noticed that Seema also was stroking the letters with the *pallu* of her *sari*.

'Enough! Now it should not live any more' said Ketan decisively. 'Those letters...'

'What?' asked Seema, sitting up.

'Throw away these letters…my past...into the sea.'

'And what about my past that is with you?'

'I will throw that too.'

Seema stared quietly at the bunch.

'Okay, I think that's the right thing to do!' She paused for a while and said, 'I have a request. Let us both close our eyes and throw these letters into the sea together.'

Ketan did not say anything. He closed his eyes and held out the letter in his hands, towards the sea. Seema too had closed her eyes. A moment passed. Ketan opened his eyes. Seema too opened her eyes. Both had the letters in their hands.

'Seema!' said Ketan with a sigh, 'Please return my letters to me and take back yours.'

'What's on your mind?'

'That you immerse your feelings into the sea yourself. I won't be able to do so.'

Seema looked at him..... A wave of deep sadness swam in her eyes.

'Perhaps I won't be able to either. Take back your letters and throw them into the sea yourself.'

They exchanged their letters. In the process of doing so, their hands touched lightly, awakening old feelings.

Ketan again closed his eyes. When he opened them, Seema was still sitting with her eyes closed. The bunch of letters was still in her hand.

'Seema!'

'Humm'

'We have met here today to bury our past. This is our last meeting. It is getting late now.'

'I know. It was you who called me for this purpose. So why are you delaying?'

'I want to make a request.'

'What?'

'You...'

'You what?'

Ketan remained quiet.

'You were saying something' said Seema, in a bewildered tone, 'Why don't you ever finish what you begin?' She appeared to be unable to face him.

'Very soon we shall be completing 50 years, Seema.'

'We know each other's birth dates very well, Ketan' replied Seema.

Everything around them was quiet except for the sound of the waves lashing futilely at the rocks.

'Take these. Please immerse both bunches into the sea.' Seema held out her bunch towards Ketan.

'I too want to make a request'. Ketan looked deeply at Seema's face and extended his letters towards her.

Seema's lips quivered. Her eyes became moist. Ketan was shaken. He extended his hand towards Seema to take back her letters and closed his eyes. He had taken back the letters that Seema had written to him. But...

How had his letters gone back into Seema's hand? How had the letters got exchanged?

Ketan opened his eyes. Seema was crying silently with her eyes closed.

'Seema,' Ketan whispered, his lips quivering.

Slowly, Seema rested her head on his shoulder. Sighing audibly she said, 'I won't be able to do it.'

Who had said it? Seema or Ketan?

Gently, he put his hand on Seema's shoulder. Seema accepted the support of his hands as if it were the most natural thing on earth.

The silent wish had spread its wings again.

Translated by **Ms. Neelam Kumar**
and **Taral Prakash**

Red Glow of the New Moon

Kundanika Kapadia

She glanced at the sky from the window. She had so arranged her bed that through the window she could have a good view of the *neem* tree in the courtyard. Very often, the boughs of the *neem* tree swung violently in the wind and seemed to be trying to touch the window. Through the gaps between the boughs she could get a glimpse of the blue sky and bits of clouds occasionally floating across the sky. At times a noisy bird would come and perch on the boughs. The bird with a long tail, may be *doodhraj*. Normally that bird lives amidst dense foliage of trees and is not easily seen. But the bird came and sat in such a way as though it had come to visit her.

There was much excitement in the house. Deepankar and Maria were to arrive by the afternoon flight. Deepankar was her youngest son. He had gone to the States seven years ago. He had married an American girl. He had often written to say that he wanted to come home, but had not. But now that the mother was on her deathbed, he was coming with his wife. An American girl. She wondered what she would be like.

She smiled faintly to herself. It was a song by Tagore, rendered into Gujarati by the poet Meghani — *'I wonder what she would have been, my mother. I don't remember in the least.'* In her own time she had pored over Tagore's writing. Tagore and Yeats and Ibsen. On Sundays, she would go with friends to the riverbank or to the forest. They would eat and drink, rest under the trees, sing songs and then they would recite some poems aloud... Tagore's *'I shall not let you go...'* and William Blake's *'To see the world in a grain of sand...'*And *'I will arise and go now.... to see where night and day the waters of the lake pat the bank* — that poem of Yeats they had almost learnt by heart. And the poems of Masefield — *'Give me a pathway and sky overhead... a bonfire* *by the roadside when it's cold... again the dawn and travel once more....'*

She had lived in the midst of beauty in myriad forms. She had found life always worth living. And now the present generation... her elder son and his wife Maya, her middle son and his wife Chhaya... she wondered if they ever read Tagore, Kalidas, Shakespeare? As for Nietzsche and Bergson, they had probably not even heard their names! She had kept her favourite books in the bookcase in her room. Right from *Creative Evolution to Fourth Way, Ekottoarashari* and *Rabindra Veena*..... and the combined anthology of John Donne and Blake... there were many books. But her daughter-in-law had never touched her bookcase. They had shown no curiosity about those books. They read books by Alistair Maclean, James Hadley Chase, Ian Fleming, Gulshan Nanda. 'We are feeling bored" — that was their constant refrain. The word *boredom* constantly figured in their talks. She had not particularly experienced *boredom* in her life. She and her husband very often would go to Lonavala on a full moon night. There was a guesthouse called "The Dream" situated in a quiet spot for tourists who loved beauty. It was a small, single-storeyed house. It had a small room at the top with glass windows from ceiling to the floor. They went there especially to see the full moon rising. On the eastern side was a whole range of hills and the moon rose above them a little late. They would catch the faintest vibration and wait for that vision of light which was so familiar to them and yet always so delightful. Gradually, a reddish glow would be seen behind the hills and then a shining white edge. Automatically, their hands would be linked together in the conviction of being partners in the same experience of joy. Then the moon would come up fast, very fast. It was at that moment that they became somewhat aware of the motion of the earth. If it were convenient, they would stay on for two or three days more. It was much more thrilling to see the moon rising on the first or the second day after the full moon. Everything lay still in the lap of quietness. The sky would look on, holding its breath. There would be no smoke in the air, no sharp rays of lamps in the houses, no vibrations of sound. There would be only a tender, soft stillness full of darkness. Then the moon would rise a little late, watching the hills with a ruddy wonder and gaze at the sleeping earth. And then there would be a shower of brightness. She could feel its physical touch. She would feel drenched in every limb.

Her life had acquired splendour due to hundreds of such experiences of beauty. Sometimes she would sit under the neem tree and recall Rilke's poem. *'We, the wasters of sorrows.. We waste all our sorrows, waiting to be free from pain....'* Her husband would listen to her in silence. She had a flickering glimpse of the secret of coming and going in life. It was possible to accept pain with a serious understanding. It was possible to grasp somewhat, the meaning underlying anguish.

How did these people look at life, she often wondered? But Maya and Chhaya were never free to have any leisurely chat with her. They attended cooking classes and learnt how to make French pudding and Italian pizza. They learnt interior decoration and indulged in Ikebana. They arranged candlelight dinners and learnt hairstyles, and tried different types of coiffures.

But every time they came back home after an outing they would say— 'So bored! We are fagged out. That Prem Nath was utterly boring!'

Their day would start and pass into evening in the bed of an ever-growing boredom. They did talk about revolting against establishment and traditional values. Occasionally some hippies also came as their guests. Still, there was a great void in their lives. The element of joy of slipped through their hands. They lived, but always wondered about the meaning of it all.

And now a new woman was coming to the house. She must be hardly twenty-three or twenty-four. Deepankar had sent the wedding photographs. She was curious. What would the girl Deepankar had chosen be like?

It was of no importance whether or not she respected and loved her. How long was she going to live anyway? Nevertheless, she did have a desire to know that unknown girl from a far off country who was coming as a daughter-in-law of the house. Maya and Chhaya too must be quite curious about her. They must be having some fears, some misgivings. She had overheard them one day as they whispered to each other, 'We will have to make some adjustments.' Fortunately the house was very big and everybody could be accommodated. Even the daughters had come with their children and husbands. They had come to be with their mother in her last moments. But even they had no time. 'Bhabhi, is Tinu's milk warm? Ask the cook to take out some *dal* and vegetables before adding chillies. Avinash has an ulcer in his stomach.' Their behaviour betrayed a kind of impatience. They must be calculating how much leave was still left, wondering if the leave would have to be extended. They must have left their homes in a mess.

Everyone came in to see the mother, one by one. Have you taken your medicine, Ma? Did you sleep well? How did you pass the night? They would adjust the corners of the mosquito net, pull the bedsheet, put fresh flowers by the side of her bed and drive away the children if they came in shouting. They took all possible care of their mother. They prepared a variety of light dishes for her. And they felt satisfied that their nursing was perfect. Only the mother knew where the void existed. But being close to death, she had withdrawn herself from all expectations. All her life she had loved beauty. She had loved life. Now, in the face of death, she would not let it be fragmented. Her favourite author was Henry Fredrick Amiel. Born in Switzerland, he lived in France, and was a professor of aesthetics. He had spent thirty years in solitude and had written journals filling 16,900 pages. Amiel. Bergson, Tagore... she and her husband talked about them as if they were their friends. They had drunk deep from their writings, their lives and their philosophy. And now the moment of death was not far away. The greatest, most delightful moment—the highest experience of life. She wanted to retain the glow of that moment like the full moon or the new moon, with its reddish light so that it would drench her limbs.

A sound made her look at the door. It was Maya, 'Do you want anything. Ma?' She shook her head and smiled. But Maya did not respond with a smile. She had not even noticed her smile. She was absorbed in her own thoughts. She was clever, efficient, smart and selfish. She managed, somehow, to get everything she wanted without bothering about what happened to others. Her husband and her children — these were the limits of her world. Friends, parties, cinema — everything was there. But one did not remember her cherishing deep feelings for anyone or exerting herself for someone.

The middle daughter-in-law Chhaya, was somewhat different. She was cheerful, generous, full of a rugged sense of humour. She was of heavy build, an extrovert and quite insensitive. In the same big house, Maya and Chhaya maintained separate kitchens. There was enough money to go round, and hence there were no particular occasions of conflict. The mother had her own room upstairs. She got her food from both the kitchens by turn. Rarely, very rarely, she too would go down to have her meal with the family. But only when no visitor was present. Quite often they played music downstairs. They also danced to the music of the guitar and organs were played. Maya sang well. Her own daughter Uma also sang beautifully. Their voices, as they sang, reached her room upstairs. Sometimes she enjoyed their singing.

But not once had Uma or Maya come to her and asked, 'Shall I sing a song or a *bhajan* for you, *Ba*?' It would be nice even if one could recite a poem. *'I won't let you go'* — those words full of pride of love in the mouth of a four-year-old girl — she had read that poem to let one go. One goes away, everything goes away with a hooting sound in the deluge of the sea.

Now it was time for her to go. No one had said, *'I won't let you go.'* Maybe they were waiting for her departure. May it be so. There was no craving at heart, no fear.

Or, was it still there?

The boughs of the *neem* tree swinging near the window would be full of white blossoms in the summer months. Like beautiful white almond blossoms mentioned by Albert Camus in his dairy. Perhaps even more beautiful, giving out fragrance all through the night. There was a generation gap, yet God had allowed her last nights to be fragrant somehow.

Suddenly she thought about Maria. Would she like being here? The summer of this place, the heat, the squalor, and people's habits — how would she be able to put up with all that? Would she be aware of the real conditions of this country or would she be lost in an infatuation of love and get disillusioned after her arrival?

Whatever it would be — the curiosity would end in a few hours.

She felt a faint note of music rising in her heart. She hoped the splendour of her last moments would not be shadowed by the conflicts among her sons and daughters and daughter-in-law. Her strength was now almost gone. She could not move her hands and feet. Her voice had become feeble. Only her eyes were sharp. And sharp were her memories.

The flight was a little delayed. Instead of the afternoon, the plane landed at six in the evening. It was seven-thirty by the time they reached home after the Customs formalities were gone through. When Deepankar and Maria entered her room, it was the moment of transition from light to darkness. Deepankar rushed in, his affection surging.

'How are you, *Ba*?' It was sheer love that dripped from his voice.

She was overwhelmed. For a while he sat, almost embracing his mother.

Then he got up as if he had remembered something. 'Maria, this is my mother,' he said. Was there a touch of pride in those words? Or mere illusion? Maria advanced and extended her hand. She held her hand and shook it. She did not say anything, only smiled. Both of them sat by her side. Deepankar quickly told her about many things. He talked about his stay there, his anxiety on receiving the letter about her illness, her present condition. He assured her that she would be better with his arrival. For some time they continued talking of love and anxiety and childhood memories.

'Do you remember, *Ba*? One day when *Bapu* scolded me for coming home in torn clothes? Later, you had given me *sheera* to eat?'

She listened as she lay there. She felt nice.

Then both of them got up to go downstairs. 'Sleep well, Ma! We shall meet in the morning. We shall have tea together,' said Deepankar. Maria also nodded her head. She felt that Maria's eyes were beautiful—full of depth and sensitivity, as if telling her, 'I know what's on your mind.'

Deepankar had said he would see her in the morning. But, left alone, she felt certain that this would be her last night. She suddenly felt extremely worn out. She felt very fatigued. What was the day today? Second day after the full moon. The lovely red moon would rise today, a little late. That was enough. She wanted nothing else. It would be only proper if the end came tonight.

The voices downstairs had stopped. It could not be very late. It must be hardly nine o'clock. Perhaps they were seated at the threshold on the other side. Deepankar must be talking about America. Her daughters and Maya and Chhaya must be eager to know what Deepankar had brought for them. And Maya must be planning how to get the best thing for herself.

There was a whiff of wind and the boughs of the *neem* tree swung. A couple of tiny blossoms were swept into her bed.

Suddenly she felt the door open. Who could have come? The maidservant had already given her the last dose of medicine. Then who could it be?

Somebody came up to her, walking softly. It was Maria. She was astonished beyond words. Why had Maria come?

Maria came and sat by her side, holding her hand. She said nothing for a while. She simply gazed at her and smiled. Then she asked, 'I would like to sit here. May I?'

She nodded but she had not yet ceased to wonder.

For a long time, Maria sat in silence, watching the sky behind the *neem* tree. Then she said gently, 'You have arranged your bed in a nice corner. That tree looks lovely. Now the tree will flower, won't it? A few flowers can be seen already.' Maria spoke in English, slowly. She spoke with an American accent, but she understood everything.

Maria said again, 'I loved that book of Tagore's poem you had sent at the time of our wedding. I have read the poems several times. Some poems are on the tip of my tongue.'

Maria smiled and stroked the mother's hand. 'I loved you for that book. It was wonderful, to love the world with all its people in such a beautiful way...' and then Maria said, 'Do you still remember those poems?'

She nodded her head with joy.

Maria slid a little closer and leaned right above her. 'You look very weak.'

She said nothing.

Maria looked straight into her eyes and stroked her hair. Then bringing her mouth near her ear she whispered softly, 'You… you are not afraid, are you?'

'Afraid of what?'

'Of the unknown...' Maria said gently. 'Afraid of leaving behind all that is familiar and sliding into nothingness. Are you afraid?'

A tidal wave rose in her heart. A wave of joy. That girl had understood her. She longed to know her inner feelings. She was worried about her fear. Perhaps she wanted to dispel that fear.

She wanted to reply. But she was tired after the excitement of that tide of joy. A new relationship had been born in her last moments. A bit late…but a lovely relationship nevertheless. She looked at Maria with love and satisfaction. Suddenly she wondered. People say that a woman who dies while her husband is still alive is *saubhagyawati*. But what do they know about the meaning of good fortune? Here is good fortune. The slow, imperceptible development of a new relationship, a new love in the firmament of the end moments of one's life — that is good fortune. It is the greatest good fortune to be able to die with joy.

The white edge of the moon was seen behind the *neem* tree. Maria switched off the light in the room. It seemed as if the boughs of the tree were covered with countless white flowers. She held Maria's hand and pointed at the moon... Look, she is bidding farewell....

Maria gently passed her hand over her forehead. 'May your journey be peaceful.'

A reddish glow spread on her face.

Translated by **Sarla Jag Mohan**

RAJASTHANI

Cannibal

Vijai Dan Detha

Of all the beings in this world, only the descendants of Adam lack an inherent nature. You may say that a certain person looks like a thorn-apple tree or an acacia, and that another acts like a lion or a python, a vulture, or a donkey. These kinds of observations are as old as the ages. One day a priest of a Goddess Temple was born in the usual manner — a man's organ plus a woman's womb — yet he seemed more the product of a *dhatura*— cactus and a crow.

He was but a child when his parents had grown so tired of his mean-spirited antics that they had sent him off to a far-away temple of the Goddess hoping that She would somehow reform him. But water a cactus with milk and butter everyday and it will still remain just a cactus. A crow can spend years listening to hymns and *bhajans*, and still squawk like a crow. Every being has a certain nature you can see right from birth. This stays with him until death. A donkey can spend his entire life reading from the sacred *Bhagavat-Gita,* and still he will be nothing but a donkey. This Brahmin wasted plenty of sandalwood anointing himself for worship. He chanted his prayer beads. He said prayers to the Goddess, partook of hash, offered smokes of *ganja*. His eyes glowed red as cinders, day and night. He grew a beard up to his belly and let his hair become as matted and twisted as a weaverbird's nest. His teeth were yellow and his lips were thick. He was tall and had a stumpy neck. His entire body was covered with bear-like fur. He looked like the typical ascetic.

As Fate would have it that this boorish Brahmin's wife was kind and patient. He hit her whenever he felt like it, as if wife beating was part of his daily routine. His wife thought it over and decided this was just another hardship she had to bear. When there was no food left to cook, that's when she really started to worry.

It wasn't easy surviving on the meagre daily offerings made to the Goddess of their temple. And, with the Brahmin's nature as it was, faith in the Goddess gradually dwindled. Offerings grew smaller day by day. Even the Goddess began to worry.

One day after dinner, the Brahmin had just smoked some *ganja* and was falling asleep when he jerked up awake.

He said to his wife, 'This Goddess of ours is a cheap slut. No one's going to believe she's anything but a pile of shit! Look at the way she lets me live! Me! Her very own priest! As if I'm good for anything else after hanging around this temple all these years. I might as well go over there and torch it. Let it all go up in flames: me, the Goddess, everything. Ha! Then she'll know who to watch out for. Just wait a few days and see. I'm really going to teach her a lesson.'

'Don't leave me behind like that!' his wife cried out. 'How will I ever survive in this world alone, without husband or Goddess to protect me?'

'Oh, I completely forgot about that. Good thing you reminded me. Let's wait until the next new moon. Then we'll pull our stunt. People will be talking about it for years!'

He lay back down on the edge of the bed when his wife exclaimed, 'This can't be happening! How are you going to fall asleep when you haven't hit me yet?'

Now, in his childhood the Brahmin may have forgotten himself and smiled once or twice, perhaps, but never after that. No word that was even remotely good-natured had ever passed through his lips. But, tonight, when he heard his wife's innocent comment, a faint grin flickered across his lips for the very first time.

'You need a good thrashing to relax at night, huh? You probably think it's cruel of me. You know why I do it, don't you? I only feel like a man when I'm slapping you around. And you're the only one in the world I can flex my muscles to. I suppose if we had children I'd knock them around, too. You know there's nothing better than pummelling the lights out of someone. I don't care how much you miss these bouts of ours, though. I've had enough. From now on, if I lay my hands on anyone, it's going to be to wring that damn Goddess' neck. I'll find myself a hammer and go in there and smash her to pieces. Then I'll light the whole temple on fire with me inside, and die there in peace. Look, if I forget, make sure you remind me. We can't let the next new moon go by.'

It took him a long time to fall asleep that night. And his wife didn't close her eyes once. How had this burden suddenly gotten dumped on her shoulders? Obey her husband and there'd be a disaster. Disobey him, disaster. When had they ever had even a glimmer of happiness in this life? The two had seen nothing but grief. Good thing they didn't have any children. They'd just spend all their time crying over their misery. Troubles churned inside her head until it felt absolutely empty — no more worries, no more sorrow. She looked into the sky. There are more shades of malice, despair, gratification and serenity mixed in the night's dark cloak than even the Creator could name.

Well, time doesn't heed even an apocalypse, so why would it concern itself with this measly Brahmin priest? The cycle of days and nights moved along at their natural pace when finally the new moon day dawned. The Goddess was upset. There was no telling what the crazy priest was capable of. If the worshippers' faith in Her lapsed for a moment, there would be no one left even to remember Her name. The other creatures in the world didn't think of anything besides watching out for their own skins. It wouldn't matter to them if the Lord died today or tomorrow — vultures, crows, jackals and ants would be there feeding on His corpse. If She left her temple, she'd have to go a hundred miles just to find another. There's no relying on these selfish humans! You never knew when their stomachs would growl and everything would change.

The Brahmin's wife thought over her predicament long and hard. In the end she decided that once in her life she might as well do something out of the ordinary. She reminded her husband of his vow the night before the new moon day.

He threw a fit. 'You're reminding me just as I'm falling asleep? Tell me again in the morning and may be I'll remember.'

But the next morning when the Brahmin set off to the temple his wife's mind was on other matters, and she forgot all about his vow. He got angry when he realized this, 'I've told you so many times and still you forget! My faith in you has gone from molasses to cow dung! I'm going to borrow a hammer from someone today, and arrange for the wood and kindling. You come with me after dinner tonight. The whole district will be talking about us tomorrow.'

Meanwhile the Goddess was in a state. She couldn't concentrate on the prayers people were offering. She knew Her Brahmin too well. He could get into one of his moods anytime now and smash Her to pieces. She had to think of a way to appease him.

The sun was setting as he was performing the last evening rites when suddenly the Goddess emerged from her idol. She was adorned so gaily that she sparkled like a thousand lamps. Priceless diamonds and pearls glittered as she walked. When the Brahmin looked up and saw this lone devotee standing beside him, he thought this was his golden opportunity.

He was just about to snatch her jewellery when she spoke: 'Son, I have been testing you these many years. If only you could have waited a little longer, you would have received the very throne of Indra. But you have lost patience prematurely. Nevertheless, I will give you whatever wish you ask for.'

The temple cymbals tumbled from his hands, sending a piercing clang echoing throughout the small temple alcove. The Goddess stood in front of him smiling. He spat contemptuously and asked, 'And what if I had died first?'

She kept smiling and assured him, 'I would never have let that happen. Our devotees receive Our unfailing care. It was simply due to some confusion in the divine realm that your reward has been so long delayed.'

And what if She would disappear just as suddenly as She had appeared? There was no telling with her! A moment later he said, 'Give me all Your jewellery then. Then we'll both get to enjoy a life of leisure.'

She cried out without thinking: 'I'd be lost without My Jewellery!' But She regained her composure quickly and explained, 'Divine jewellery is useless to you people. It would turn to sand at your touch.'

'So why did you tell me to wish for anything I wanted? I asked for what I wanted. And unlike You, I mean what I say when I say it. Well, now at least I know how to get You here when I want You here. Next time I need anything I'll just get myself a hammer. Humph. Anyway, there's no hiding my troubles from you. If you really want to grant me a boon, then just go ahead and give me something. Whatever you want.'

Such bravado! She could scarcely conceal her rage. She knew this worshipper well. He had suffered too much to be easily cowed. A man living a cushy life could never hazard such recklessness. But the Brahmin would get soft, too, as soon as he tasted luxury. Then she wouldn't have to worry. This was the kind of man who'd lop off his nose just to be a portentous sight for others. So She would give him a boon that would please him, yes, but would do more for the people around him. That would make him burn with envy.

She said, 'All these years you have spent worshipping me and your moral fortitude has done nothing but deteriorate. Get rid of that fire burning in your heart. Whenever it flares up, try doing something kind for someone instead.'

Listening to advice about doing something helpful for someone else made him sick. "What kind of lecture is this? I've heard this too many times already. Forget the lecture, just gave me my boon.'

'You are one in a million. One in a million. Actually I am impressed by this impudence of yours. What's the use of all those fawning fools, constantly grovelling and tittering? But you can't even look after your own interest. From now on, I'll look after you.'

'Okay so everything's going to be happy ever after, but why are You taking so long?'

The Goddess was so pleased words couldn't express it. She didn't even mind his insolence. She laughed and said, 'All Children are equal in a mother's eye. Maternal feelings are never lacking, even for the most wicked. Until this day no one has ever received a boon such as the one I'm about to grant you. And, along with you others will profit.'

'Others will profit? By my boon? What could be worse? Me, I've no use for a boon like that.'

'You have spent your entire life enduring one hardship after another. It has made your thinking a little skewed. Getting angry like this doesn't help matters. Go. From now on, anything you ask for will appear before you. But whatever you ask for, others will receive too and double, for twelve and twelve makes twenty-four miles around.'

He started to scream, 'You call that a boon? It's worse than a curse! Compared to this boon of yours, my miserable life is a first-class train ride. Take back your stupid boon and get out of here!'

The Goddess vanished back inside the icon as miraculously as She had come. He began shaking the Icon, but She wouldn't reappear: didn't make a single sound. He stood there for a while completely still. He thought to himself, I'll just go home and talk it over with the wife. What could it hurt? After all these years, finally the Goddess had granted him a boon!

He felt happy as he walked home from the temple. His wife was standing in the doorway. Such long, bounding strides! She had never seen him like this.

She called out, 'What's happened? Why are you so excited?'

'Today I found out that you don't mince words with someone used to kicks.'

Then the Brahmin explained in detail all that had led up to his getting the boon. As she stood listening to him, the Brahmin's wife felt the weight of all those years of suffering and hardship lift from her shoulders. She became ecstatic.

She told him, 'I knew that all the time you spent in prayers would prove worthwhile.'

'Prove worthwhile? What do you mean, the prayers would prove worthwhile? It's been completely worthless! Whatever I get everyone else will get also, only twice as much. You couldn't think of a worse curse! God, has the hash started rotting out your brain?'

'As a woman I have no right to challenge you, but really, what does it matter to us if others have more? We have spent so much of our lives toiling away in such misery; just the thought of it makes my hair stand on end. Let's just try to be happy. Then we'll know. It's up to you now. What's there to worry about? It hasn't been easy staying devoted to a husband like you. Why can't you just grant me just one taste of joy?'

He was not a man born with compassion in his heart. But it must be said that he did not get angry after hearing his wife's nonsense. He scratched his head and said, 'You are right. We should see if it works. The Goddess, after all, may be trying to trick us somehow.'

But what should he ask for first? Suddenly he thought of his broken pipe and empty bowl of *ganja*. He called out, 'Oh Mother Goddess, if this boon is genuine, then give me a new pipe and a big bowl of *ganja*."

The words had scarcely left his lips when the gifts appeared. He stared at them wide-eyed, flabbergasted. If he could get every wish to come true this easily, there would be no end to his joy! Every want of the past would be taken care of. What did he wish for first? Just a pipe and some *ganja*.. But what now? And what if the boon was only meant to be used once, then what would he do? That would be an outrage. And everyone else getting twice as much? What torture! This was the real dilemma. Maybe, if he could just have some of that fresh *ganja* his mind would be come more alert. He tapped the *ganja* into the pipe until it was completely full. His wife brought him an ember to light it with. He was thinking about what to wish for next. He had spent his entire life scrounging. Now what would be the best thing to wish for next? This or that, that or this? His mind felt tangled up in knots. He thought of so many things he wanted to wish for. This was the kind of leisure afforded by a full stomach. A person who goes hungry is not even allowed the luxury of clear thinking. His wife wouldn't stop nagging him. So, to please her he wished for a cannister of flour, a container of salt, a bin full of pepper and spices, and a bundle of firewood. It was odd — one moment he asked for things and the next moment there they were before him.

The couple was astonished. His wife dashed off to light the fire. Why linger now? As happy as he was, he was still bothered. Everyone around him was getting twice as much! Nothing could be worse!

The Brahmin's wife fed her husband and then sat down to eat. There's nothing like the pleasure of a full stomach. It was the first time in the Brahmin's entire life that he had eaten his fill, and it only made him sadder. He went to his wife and said, 'Dear, would you please do me one favour?'

'Have I refused you before that you suddenly have to start asking?'

'Refused and you would have had me to answer to. I'd have paddled you with my shoe so hard you'd have had a bald spot on the top of your head. No, I want you to run out and look in every house to see if they've gotten twice as much as we've gotten.'

'Why should we bother with anyone else? What we have, we have for ourselves. No need now to go around the neighbourhood, begging for a light. And it is all because of you that no one has to worry. You're doing well, and everyone is doing well.'

'Absolutely brainless, and still you go on chattering like you have something to say. I've been putting up with this for a lot longer than I've had to, but today it's too much. If everyone is doing well just because of me, then I might as well die. Don't try to argue with me. Just do as I say.'

And talk about doing well! Wherever she went the Brahmin's wife found the Goddess's words had come true. She spun around the village like an unwound top. And in every house it was the same. People were dumb-founded. Was this some sort of magic or sorcery? Then the Brahmin's wife told them about the boon. At last her husband's penance had been rewarded.

When she came home she found her husband sitting outside with a long face... At the sound of her footsteps, he lifted his head and asked, 'Is it true? Are they getting twice as much as we are?'

When his wife nodded her head, it was as if a cannon had been fired into his ear. He wasn't worried about the people he didn't know, but the thought of the people in his own village getting all those things made him crazy. And not one speck of thanks — the bastards hadn't said a word. Helping ingrates like these should be considered a sin! He reeled around like a mad man and collapsed on his broken cot. His wife started massaging his hands and feet.

After some time she tried to soothe him by saying, 'Why are you getting so upset over nothing? Let the world go up in smoke. What do you care? This shouldn't bother you.'

'How am I supposed to let it all go up in smoke? If I really burned up, I'd be okay.'

'You are part of this world. Keep yourself safe and sound and everything else will fall into place. Take a look in the mirror. You need to be healthy. Instead you grow skinny as a thorny bush right before my eyes. If I had a loaf of raw sugar, a pot of butter, and a kilo of fenugreek I would make you *laddus* to eat tonight, and then feed you some *halwa* besides. If I could bother you for the trouble, it'd be done before you know it. If you want, that is. Just make the wish.'

As soon as he heard the words *laddu* and *halwa* the Brahmin's mouth began to water. He would have to get back his strength first if he wanted to deal with all these problems properly. No one knew, when he was going to take his last breath. It's not as if the Lord of Death trumpets His arrival. First, I'll let myself get better, he thought, then I'll deal with everyone else one by one. He lay down and wished for the list of things his wife had asked for. The items appeared as soon as the words had crossed his lips. As he smelled her warming the rich butter on the fire, he felt calmer.

The Brahmin's wife felt as if she had been given ten new lives. First she looked at the loaf of raw sugar, then at the pot of butter. In a home where even salt had been scarce, this was the greatest luxury imaginable. After some time she resurfaced from her pool of happiness.

She suddenly asked, 'Am I supposed to cook the things in my bare hands? I need a skillet and some nice bronze dishes. Then I'll have no problems.'

Surprisingly enough the Brahmin went along with it. The pots and dishes appeared before her in an instant. It would take her no time to cook up some *halwa*.

The Brahmin swallowed a mouthful of *halwa*. Then he turned to his wife and asked earnestly, 'I'm not dreaming, am I? Are my eyes open? Look at me carefully.'

'First you tell me. Are my eyes open?'

'Yes, they're wide open. You look awake to me.'

'And your eyes are open. You're wide awake. Really, today we made *halwa* on our own stove! Things I couldn't even dream about yesterday I'm seeing with my own eyes today.'

Soon they could think of nothing to ask for next. Before today, they had borne the worst hardships anyone could endure. Now they needed to bear the burden of happiness. They felt as if the world around them had suddenly vanished.

Twilight came and the star-studded night descended on earth with chirping, chattering birds like its jingling anklets. What a miracle the stars were to behold! What a soft, gentle breeze blew! How beautiful the world looked now that they were happy. This boon meant they could never again have to do without anything. The Brahmin's satisfaction twinkled amidst the stars. At the moment, he was blissfully unaware of anyone else's sorrow or joy.

He looked towards his wife and said, 'If we only had some cows and water buffaloes then we would really live life. The richest yoghurt and cream we could ever want would be ours!'

'If we don't even have a proper house to live in, what good are cows and buffaloes. Besides a nice meadow, we'd need a pen and a barn to store their fodder. Then we would be set.'

'With a boon like this, why just scrape by? We can live as we please!'

Suddenly, a thought flashed through the Brahmin's mind like a live spark. 'What do you say we use this boon to play a trick on the Goddess? Of course, she can go around bringing us all these petty little household things. But what if we wish for something really spectacular? She'd bow down before me begging to take back Her words. Let's see... when I was young, my grandmother used to tell about a legendary palace, a palace made of gold. If I wished for something like that, then She'd come grovelling before me wringing Her hands like a street beggar. Seven generations of goddesses couldn't grant a wish like that. And if She can't fulfill her promise, that would look pretty bad, wouldn't it? But what difference does that make to me?'

He made his wish as he lay there in bed, folding his hands in prayer. 'Hey Mother, oh Revered One,' he invoked, 'If you are good at your word, grant my wish to have a palace of gold, full of goldenware to match.'

As soon as the words left his mouth his Golden Palace sprung up around him. He felt as if he had suddenly risen up in the air as he lay there. The loose weave of his cot had become taut and rigid underneath his back. Even his cot had turned to gold! He sat up, flabbergasted. Instead of his crumbling walls plastered in cow-dung, there shone bright yellow walls. He rubbed his eyes and looked again. Had his impossible wish actually come true? His wife was standing nearby, gaping in astonishment. What magical stage fancy had they found themselves trapped in?

She lit a golden lamp. They both stood next to the walls, feeling them and admiring their lustre. How could the Goddess be capable of this? He told his wife, 'If only we had asked for this first off! If She can give everyone in our land a pair of Golden Palaces, then this is just a pinch of salt!'

The Brahmin's wife looked into some of their cupboards and found two or three of his pipes all turned to gold. Ah! Even the old clay *ganja* pot had turned to gold. The Brahmin filled his pipe and began to smoke. Then he had a coughing fit that lasted awhile. He really felt old now. If the Goddess had only come to her senses twenty years earlier, then his life would have been worth living. But now, how much longer did they have to enjoy such a palace? How many more nights, did they have to enjoy their pleasant nighttime dreams? The irony of receiving such a boon so late in life made it an agony rather than a pleasure. What was the use of a heavy monsoon shower when the crops had already withered and died?

The Brahmin looked into his wife's familiar face and said, 'You're getting too old, my dear. A person should be youthful and fit to live in such a palace.'

'Well, you look more decrepit than I do. Getting too old, you say. All I want is to leave this earth when you do. I ask for nothing more. I've seen the Golden Palace with my own eyes, so what more could I want? Hey, I have an idea. Can't the Goddess make us young again?'

'Hey, why not? We can at least ask. But why didn't I think of this before? What's happening to my mind? Well, never mind. Better late than never.'

The moment he asked the Mother to be young again, their youth was restored. It would have been difficult for a person to even think up the fantastic game they were living. As if anyone could have ever known such unbounded joy! They were so much out of their minds with happiness that they never even thought of enjoying the pleasures their youthful bodies were capable of. The blissful night passed in the wink of an eye.

The Brahmin got up at the first light of dawn and went outside. He said, 'I've got to see if the sun rises any differently on a day like today.'

He climbed his golden staircase to the roof. All around he could see nothing but Golden Palaces! It looked as if the earth were covered with countless rising suns. He squinted in the brilliant light. Everyone else had two Golden Palaces while he had only one! And it was all due to him. He could suffer whatever trouble came his way, but the thought that he was responsible for other people's happiness... this was more than he could take. What fate could be worse?

He felt trapped in a treacherous maze. The flames in his heart rose so high and strong that they would have scorched even the sun. The beasts in him that were his nature — the jackal, crow tiger and snake — caught fire. He began running around in circles, barking like a rabid dog. 'May one eye of mine go blind. May one eardrum of mine tear up. May a deep well be dug in front of my house!'

As soon as he had finished yelling his wishes, his wife shrieked, 'Oh, Lord, what's happening? Did your fabulous palace disappear? Has the rising sun descended back into the earth?'

He understood at once what this meant. His feet thudded down the stairs as he ran to her. His wife was feeling her way along the wall with her hand stretched out before her and was just at the doorway when he started shouting as loudly as he could. 'Stop! Stop right there! Don't take another step! There's a deep well right in front of you!'

But the Brahmin's wife couldn't hear a word of what he said. She tumbled down into a pit before he even reached the bottom step. He heard her splash at the very bottom. His life partner had met her end, just in the bloom of her youth.

He spent the day walking through every house in the area. In every village he reached, he looked around with his one good eye and saw people tumbling into their wells one by one. Before long every single person got finished off. He cackled like a demon. So pleased with their pair of Golden Palaces they had walked straight into Death's lap!

Now he was the sole proprietor of these Golden Palaces. There was no one left to dispute it. Each night he slept in a different palace. There was no one left to receive twice as much as he had. So the Goddess had wanted to teach him a lesson! Well, he had used his powers of human reasoning against Her! He jumped in the air, threw his arms around and admired his palaces with his one good eye. Was there anyone on earth happier than he?

If only there was someone left to see how happy he was!

Translated by **Christi Ann Merrill**

SINDHI

The Statement

Gobind Panjabi

If you are a resident of Bombay, you must have some time or the other seen the railway bridge at Kurla. The railway bridge, extending from Kurla West to Kurla East is gigantic. It is a big slum area where there are no hutments as such but where thousands of people live. Each has occupied his own area and built his hutment-like house there. They cook and eat there. They conduct their business also there. They produce their children there. Some take to begging. Some go out in search of some work throughout the day. Some sell cheap wares there. In short, every one, after loitering all day, comes back to one's abode in the night. If some stranger occupies someone else's place then there is a big quarrel. Between the two, one would be wounded, or even die and the other would go to prison.

India became independent forty years ago but still today, crores of people — homeless, unemployed and suffering from various contagious diseases are living a life of hell.

In the corner of that Kurla bridge, there lived a young, dark and ugly girl. Apart from her black colour and ugliness, she was young and youth is after all youth. Tall, young and full-bodied, she used to get up early in the morning and start collecting papers, plastic pieces, torn bags and rags lying on the roads and in the evening, having filled her garbage bag she would hawk her wares and earn around ten rupees every day. After the day's hard work she did not like to cook food. She would buy two small loaves of bread and a cup of tea. After satisfying her hunger, she would lie down comfortably. She had to get up again at four in the morning and hence, as soon as she lay down, she was so much overcome by sleep, that she would never be aware of the babbling noises of thousands of people around her. Born in one such hutment she had grown up there. She did not know anything about her parents. She only remembered that since childhood she had been doing some work and labouring hard—labour sometimes for others and sometimes for herself. All her life she had known only hard work. That is why, by evening she would be bone-tired and hence as soon as she finished her food, she would go off to sleep.

Quite late one night, she felt some one trying to molest her. First she felt some one's hands on her legs. She got up, startled and found that a stout person was trying to put her on the ground and rape her. There was no time to think. Mustering her courage, she kicked the man between his legs so powerfully that he let out a painful shriek and fell down. The girl's feet struck the genitals of the man with such force that he started bleeding.

As soon as the man fell down, the girl got up and started running in fright, dashing against some people sleeping soundly. In no time several people had woken up from their slumber.

Having noticed that a man was lying dead in a pool of blood, they started intuitively following the girl. The girl, having crossed the bridge from the West side, went into Nehru Nagar. She was tired after the run and began puffing heavily. At last she fell under a tree, exhausted. It was still dark. Having rested for a while she again started running. A policeman on night duty, thinking her to be a thief, caught hold of her.

Once a young girl comes into the hold of the police, what happens to her is left to one's imagination.

'Give your statement.' She was asked in the morning.

The girl remained quiet.

'Give your statement, otherwise we shall beat you.'

Even then the girl remained quiet.

The girl was brought before the magistrate on the charge that she had murdered a man on Kurla bridge.

The Magistrate also asked the girl to give her statement.

The girl, losing control over herself shouted: 'So many policemen have taken statements from my body. You also need a statement? I have no statement to make. You may do whatever you want.'

'But what have you done that the police has brought you here?" the Magistrate inquired with firmness.

'I collect rags on the roads. I am a destitute and live on Kurla bridge. That night when I was sleeping peacefully someone tried to rape me and in order to save myself I made that man invalid with my kicks. That is all. That is my fault.'

The Magistrate, considering the youth and age of the girl, took mercy on her and sent her to prison only for seven years.

❑❑❑

The Claim

Narain Bharati

'Brother, who gives claim here?' Joharmal asked of those standing in the veranda of the Camp No. 2 office.

'Uncle, no one gives claim; the claim is to be put in.' Smiling at the innocence of Joharmal, one of the men remarked.

'Uncle, come here.' Beckoning him, one of the persons sitting with the typist said, 'I am also putting in the claim. This officer is typing it out.'

'Brother, we don't even know how a claim is to be put in. My son studies in an English school. But here the officers have their own requirements. Later on they will say that this is not done, that is not done. That is why I said, when there are so many other expenses, writing charges of a rupee or two by this officer will not make us poorer.'

'Come and sit here,' one of the persons beckoned to Joharmal.

'Oh! God.' Sitting on the bench Joharmal said, 'Yesterday Manikamal was saying that the government will give compensation for the property left behind, that is why government is getting it in writing to assess how much is left. I thought, since we have forsaken so much property, why not give it in writing?' Taking out a *bidi* from his pocket Joharmal said. 'Brother! Do you think the government will count money and give cash? These are all only estimates; but every one is in a fix. If we don't give in writing and then by good luck, if the money is paid, then everyone will taunt and curse us. So let us remove this anxiety, then whatever is destined will happen. Even if we don't get anything we shall not be worse off than what we are now,' said one of the older men.

The typist continued typing and simultaneously kept on murmuring. 'The public road in the West, Khanmohomad's building towards East, the *caravansarai* of Seth Phagunmal. In the North — the area three thousand sq. feet, two storyed —.' Then he turned his eyes at the people sitting there. One by one, he typed the claim forms of all. Then, turning to Joharmal he asked, 'Yes Sir! Now you tell me.'

'Brother, whatever you ask me I shall answer. We have left our world, our honour, our friendships; everything of ours is left there. When will God have mercy on us that we shall again inhabit our homes?'

'Yes, uncle, what is your name?'

'Name? Sir, my name is Joharmal.'

The typist, making a sound of tick....tick on the typewriter repeated, 'Joharmal...Yes, uncle....Joharmal....son of?'

'Joharmal son of Bhai Wasiomal.' The typist again began typing and asked, 'What is your surname?'

'Nangdev.'

The typist typed it. 'Okay. Where did you stay in Pakistan? Which *taluka* and district?'

'All right. Village Halla, Taluka Kamber, District Larkana.' The typist kept on typing. 'Have you brought the details of your property?'

'What details?'

'Details, such as, how many acres of land, how many houses and their location, total area and the estimated value? Whether the land was leasehold or outright purchase? If it was purchased, for how much? For proof have you got any documents or receipts from the Revenue Officer for the payment of taxes? What was the total value of the land? All these details are required.'

Uncle Joharmal was stupefied. All these things were new for him. He thought, 'I have not brought anything. Manikmal was saying that whatever you say, he will go on writing, but here...! But I am after all a Sindhi. Is it not sufficient proof?'

Seeing uncle Joharmal immersed in thoughts, the typist again asked, 'How much property have you left in Pakistan? How many houses and other property?'

Reacting as if he were suddenly awakened from a dream, Joharmal said, 'Brother, say like that! My dear friend, you confused me. Okay, write. Joharmal son of Wasiomal, surname Nangdev. I have left all Sind in Pakistan. I am now putting in the claim that the whole Sind should be given back to him. The proof of it is that Joharmal is Sindhi, his language is Sindhi and his culture is Sindhi.'

'Uncle, how can that be written? How much belongs to you?'

'What have I left in Sind? I have left my Sind. If it is not my own, then whose is it? We Sindhis have left all comforts and have come here and still you are asking what I have left there? If you are thinking that I don't remember Sind or that I am forgetting it, then my dear Sir, you are wrong. Never entertain such ideas. Each nerve of ours is singing with memories of Sind. I am Sindhi and Sind is mine. I have a right to put in a claim for it. We hear that Punjabis got Punjab, Bengalees got Bengal, then what crime have we committed that we did not get our Sind?' Joharmal asked emotionally.

All those who were sitting there started laughing. Even the officer was smiling.

'But you be the judge,' turning to all, Joharmal said. 'You — we all have left our Sind. Is the officer asking you the same difficult questions? Or, taking me to be an old man, is he making fun of me?'

'No uncle. I am not joking. I am telling you honestly that it is a rule of the Government that any one who has left personal property, can put in a claim for it and not for anything else. See, everybody has put in a claim for his own houses and lands. Topanmal, son of Godumal Premchandani, of village Sajawal, *taluka* Mirokhan, district Larkana, two houses - one storeyed, area two thousand sq. feet, facing West; and land fifty acres — total property worth about Rs 15000/-. He has put in a claim for Rs 15000/-.'

Joharmal's face became pale. He had never even thought or dreamt that Sindhis would forget their Sind like this and each would go his own way. Then, turning to the officer he said, 'Are you not Sindhi? Were your forefathers not Sindhis? Did you not drink water from the river of Sukkur? Did you not bathe in Sindhu River? And still you say that I cannot put in a claim for Sind? Our ancestral Sind, where our forefathers lived their life; where we grew up. Have we no right over it? I shall not be able to meet again brothers Rajab, Ramzan and Mahboob the barber again. Can I get back their friendship?'

Joharmal once again became emotional. Tears came to his eyes and his face became flushed. 'But uncle.....'

Stopping the typist in the middle, Joharmal said, 'Let it go — Sir, let it go. I have not to put in any claim. Let it go to hell! For what else shall I put in my claim? What particulars can I give you? My friendship was greater than my fields. It was my native place. It is because my son-in-law forced me and the daughters cried bitterly that we migrated...otherwise I would never have left Sind!'

The typist realised that what uncle Joharmal had said was hundred percent correct. The true claim is that we get our Sind back. He too had many friends in Sind — Anwer, Hussain Ahmed—all with whom he used to go to Ramzan Garden for a stroll. He loved Nooran, the niece of the Head of the village-Haji Urs. When he was coming to India for the last time, Nooran had told him, 'Don't forget me. If Allah wills, you will soon come back and inherit these fields and buildings.' All this flashed through his mind. The whole map of Sind rose before his eyes...fields, friends and the whole community. He thought, Korea was also partitioned like this and even today the people are fighting for united Korea.

Suddenly the typist said, 'Yes, Uncle. We shall surely go back to Sind. Sind is ours, yours and of every Sindhi. Your claim is right. It is the true claim. It may be wrong in the eyes and books of the government, but it is a real and original claim. It is not only your claim, but mine also and of every Sindhi. Uncle, don't be disappointed. The time is not far off when all Sindhis will wake up from their slumber and put in their claim for Sind... the claim for *Sindhiyat*! When there will be true democracy in India and Pakistan, this artificial wall will be demolished and you — all of us, shall certainly get our claim.'

□□□

MARATHI

The Wan Moon

Gangadhar Gadgil

The train was speeding through a region all burnt up by the summer heat. People sat squeezed up in odd postures in the overcrowded coaches. They twisted and turned their bodies in various positions to rest their sore and aching limbs. Some had dozed off and were leaning awkwardly against other people's shoulders. Some were wiping off the sweat that streaked down their faces and necks with the hanging ends of their turbans. One of them was drinking water and the lump in his throat moved up and down uncomfortably. The faces of the menfolk were ash-coloured and sticky with grime. The women's faces were blanched and drooping. Their dry hair fluttered lifelessly in the dry breeze.

The sun beat down mercilessly upon them through the windows. Gusts of hot wind brought in clouds of dust.

She sat there humped and squeezed in a crowded compartment—a baby in her lap. She had covered it with the end of her *sari*, and only its rickety legs jutted out from underneath. It whimpered and kicked when it woke up spasmodically. Then she gently stroked its head until it lapsed into an uneasy sleep. Her two little daughters sat next to her on the edge of the bench. They were skinny and odd looking. Narrow strips of foreheads, flat noses that broadened awkwardly at the tips, uncouth lips, receding, almost non-existent chins—that about summed up their looks. One of them was slightly bigger than the other. She had a fairer skin and had more flesh on her. The dark one, however, was more lively and alert. The fair one blinked constantly. The girls had been almost pushed off their seats by other people who had asked them time and again "to move up a little".. But that did not really bother them. They were used to discomfort. Besides, they were lost in the tremendous excitement of travelling by train. Their eyes, bright with wonder, pecked at everything around them. They whispered their comments into each other's ears.

The father of the girls sat opposite, dozing, resting his head awkwardly on the back of the seat. His heavy face was glazed with sweat. His jaw had dropped and his half-open mouth made him look all the more querulous.

The luggage lay at their feet between the seats. There was a brass water-flask and two non-descript steel trunks. One of them, given to the woman by her mother, was in some sort of shape, but the other was battered and in a ramshackle condition. Its padlock had come off so that it had to be tied up with a clothesline. It was too big to be pushed under the seat. So it lay there between the seats, making it impossible for the woman to stretch her legs. This one had been given to the woman by her mother-in-law. A rolled up mattress lay on the steel box. The clothes bundled inside it hung out from its sides.

The woman was seated by the window. Less than twenty-five, she looked even younger. She had a stunted body that looked deceptively girlish. She was as simple-hearted as a child. She had never had the opportunity of experiencing the exuberance of youth and the fullness of maturity. Nor was she ever likely to have it.

She wore a faded *sari*.. After all, she was the mother of three children and nothing better was expected of her! She sat modestly with drooping shoulders. She was bending over the child to make it lie in a comfortable position. For years now she had been bending like this with children in her lap or over her work, so that sitting with a bent back had become her habitual posture. Her sagging breasts were a pitiful sight. She looked fragile and lifeless. Her hair was limp and dull. The child had pulled at it in one fit of ill temper and a strand of hair lay across her cheek like a scar.

Time and again the child sucked at her breast and drained away a few drops of milk.

Her daughters were pecking at everything with bright eager eyes. They whispered in each other's ears through cupped hands and giggled. The younger one espied the loose end of a man's turban, hanging oddly over his ear.

'Oh, mother!' she exclaimed, closing her mouth with her palm.

'What is it?' asked the elder sister shaking her by the shoulder.

The younger one jerked her finger at the man's turban. But the elder sister was clumsy and did not understand. So she kept on shaking the other girl by the shoulder. The younger sister giggled again and shook her head self-importantly. She would not tell the elder sister until she was close to tears. When at last she had enough fun out of teasing her, she relented.

'Do you really want me to tell?' she asked.

'Yes, yes,' pleaded the other girl.

So the younger sister told her about the loose end of the turban and then both of them started giggling. They put their palms across their mouths and giggled uncontrollably.

They laughed until they attracted their mother's attention and made her envious. That is really what they were looking forward to. The mother impatiently shook her elder daughter by the shoulder and asked, 'What is it? Tell me. What is it?'

'Shall I tell?' asked the girl, turning to her sister.

'Um, hum! No, indeed,' said the younger girl and emitted a malicious giggle. So the elder one giggled too and pushed her mother's hand off her shoulder.

The two girls treated their mother as if she were a younger and stupid sister of theirs. This added spice to their petty pleasures.

The mother looked downcast. She felt stupid and lonesome because she was not let into their secret. She shook them by the shoulder and pleaded with them. But the girls grew more and more coy. They just giggled. Rolled their eyes and giggled.

The woman lost her temper. She raised her girlish voice and shouted, 'What is this? Why don't you tell me?'

This disturbed her husband's sleep. He irately waved his hand across his nose. The woman froze with fright. So did the girls. They all eyed the man with fear. But luckily he dozed off again and they all celebrated their narrow escape from his anger with a secret exchange of smiles.

'Aha! Aha! That served her right,' exclaimed the girls when they had recovered from the fright, waving a pointed finger teasingly in front of their mother's face.

This annoyed her all the more and she pinched one of the girls. The girl squirmed with pain. She wanted to scream. But she paused and thought the better of it. The scream would have awakened their father and he would have shouted at her mother. He might very likely have slapped her too. A stinging slap across the cheek! She did not want to risk it. So she kept quiet. But she gave her mother an injured look and shook her little finger to indicate that she was no longer on speaking terms with her. The younger girl, too, did the same. They knew they could make their mother pretty miserable that way.

The woman puffed her cheeks angrily and looked away.

Nobody had ever treated her as a mature, grown-up woman. Her husband treated her sometimes like a child and sometimes like a maidservant. He was not really a wicked man. But he was obstinate and quite selfish. Her mother-in-law and other elderly women in the house used to order her about. Much of her time was spent with the children. She had to understand them and it was only to them that she could freely express her thoughts and feelings. No wonder she thought and behaved like a child!

The girls soon forgot this interlude and began to search for new excitement with eager eyes. Their eyes had a malignant glint like a lizard's, looking intently for prey.

Suddenly they noticed that their father's head was dropping forward. It kept on drooping before their eyes. This frightened them all. Involuntarily, they all clung together, digging their fingers into each other's arms. They kept on staring at the drooping head as if bewitched. Their heads too leaned forward in an oddly sympathetic movement.

The younger girl was bolder than the rest. She tried to touch her father's knee and call out to him to wake up. But her hand never touched the knee and the words died on her lips. The man's head drooped more and more.

Meanwhile the baby woke up. It stretched its body and started screaming and kicking. The frightened woman and the girls tried to quieten it. The woman pushed a nipple into his mouth. But the baby kept on screaming.

The man woke up with a start. The woman crouched over the baby like an animal expecting a blow. The girl's eyes fluttered. But they were lucky. The man did not lose his temper. He only said gruffly. 'Well! Why is the baby crying? You didn't beat him, did you?'

'Why would I beat him?' she mumbled.

'What did you say? When are you ever going to learn to talk loudly and distinctly? Eh!' He spoke in a gruff superior tone, which he adopted when making fun of one of his stupid students.

The girls could make out from his manner of speaking that he was in a jovial mood. So they smiled obediently and also from a sense of relief.

The woman was annoyed. Not with her husband but with the girls because they laughed. She, however, controlled herself and said in an even, respectful voice, 'It is very warm in here. That is why the baby is crying.'

'Well! Well! You are feeling warm, are you? What else could happen anyway if you are muffled up in a *sari* all the time?' said the father. He said this loudly and over and over again. He wanted his wife as well as everybody else to understand how very stupid she was.

But all this effort was really uncalled for. She had accepted long ago that she was a stupid person.

The man picked up the baby—his only son—fondly. He wiped the boy's perspiring face with one end of his *dhoti* and made him stand near the window. The fresh air and the passing scene made the child happy. It started playing with the window bars.

'Look now. See how happy he is,' said the father to drive his point home again.

The woman smiled weakly. After all she was stupid, wasn't she? Why then make so much fuss about it?

The proud father fondled the baby. He did it with a certain condescension but with evident pleasure. The girls and the mother looked on obediently and happily. They were all convinced for the time being that it was nice to fondle a baby although otherwise they found it very tiresome to humour a child. The girls too started playing with the little boy.

'Won't you come to me?' asked one of the girls, holding out her hands towards the baby. But the child showed resentment.

The other girl tried her own methods of persuasion. But again there were screams of protest. The father slapped the girl fondly and said, 'Why must you bother him?'

They all laughed. But the woman felt inexplicably jealous. She wished she had behaved foolishly and received that fond slap. It was a foolish thought and she knew it. After all that is not the way a husband behaves towards his wife. So she tried to forget about it and looked out of the window and for a moment experienced vividly the sense of speed. She was reminded of her childhood and how she, along with her friends used to ride high on the swing. They would sing in high-pitched voices and the rhythm of the swing used to be in the rhythm of their songs. She was reminded of a tune. She hummed it and it floated away on the breeze. It floated away carrying with it memories of a happiness so ecstatic that it hurt her to think about it.

For a moment she was riding high on a fair breeze that was happiness. Everything looked enchanted. She saw a little house—just the house she had built for herself in her childhood dreams.

'Look! What a lovely little house!' she cried.

Her gaiety surprised and disturbed her husband. He looked at the house and said in a superior, matter of fact tone, 'Well! What is so exciting about it? It is a house like any other house. It is not the Taj Mahal. It is just an ordinary house. What is so exciting about it?'

He said this loudly and sarcastically so that everybody might hear and appreciate his wisdom. Nobody took any notice of him. But he was not going to allow his thoughtful remarks to be ignored. So he looked at his daughters and asked, 'What do you think of that, girls?'

The girls laughed sheepishly. Rather too obediently for his liking. They evidently had not caught the point. So he repeated his words with enough stress to show off his own knowledge of existing monuments such as the Taj Mahal and the ignorance of his wife in matters beyond the household.

Why had he to do it? Why? The woman did not ask herself that question but just sat there helplessly like a tormented, captive bird. But her husband was not satisfied with that. He took a sadistic delight in making her unhappy and in erasing her personality.

He turned to his little son, 'Who is stupid, my darling? Who is stupid?'

He evidently wanted his son to point at his wife. But the child unpredictably turned round and pointed at him.

'You!' the man cried, passing it off as a joke. 'You!'

The little woman burst out into hysterical laughter. She utterly forgot herself and splashed around in a puddle of childish glee. Her husband was annoyed but he tried to continue smiling. The little woman however, kept on laughing. Peals upon peals of laughter. There was no stopping her.

This was too much for her husband.

'Stop it!' he shouted. 'What is there so funny about it? Why are you laughing like a donkey?'

His tone was menacing and her laughter died abruptly on her lips. The frothy merriment suddenly vanished. She was back in her cage. Once again she sat there with drooping shoulders. This reassured and pleased her husband and to clinch the matter, he growled; 'Now hold the baby, will you? And it is time the children had something to eat. Wipe the baby's face clean. Don't you see it is dirty?'

She obediently started doing all these chores. She poured a little water on a piece of cloth and wiped the baby's face with it. She cleaned the baby's nose very delicately so that it would not scream and give another opportunity to her husband to scold her. She then pleaded with the girls that they should hold the baby while she served them snacks. She opened a brass can and put the eatables on pieces of paper for the girls. She was careful to see that both the pieces of paper had pictures on them, for otherwise the girls would have started quarrelling over that. One of the girls was fond of *karanjis*. So she served her an extra *karanji*. The other one was fond of *chakalis*. So she gave her an extra *chakali*. She gave her husband a piece of paper and held the can to him so that he might help himself. For, however she served him and whatever she gave him he always found fault with her.

She thus tried hard to please everybody and when they needed her services no more, she put a few of the snacks on a piece of paper for herself and started eating with an appropriately guilty expression on her face. Her mother-in-law never used to give her enough of anything to eat, so that to eat less than what she wanted had now become a habit with her. While she ate, she had also to mind the baby. That made it impossible for her to eat with relish. But that didn't matter. For she knew her place and had accepted her role, and she could not make any demands on anyone.

While eating, she thought of the numerous other chores she would have to attend to later. They were to reach home late in the night. It would not be possible to get milk at that time. But the baby had to be fed. Otherwise it would whimper and cry and that would annoy her husband. It would not be possible to prepare anything more than a makeshift meal. And that was not likely to satisfy her husband or her daughters. Her husband would certainly refuse to eat if he was not served pickles. The younger daughter would not touch the food if she were not served a tasty curry. But what could she do about it?

These thoughts kept on revolving in her mind. The train sped on. The sun dipped in the western horizon and the evening breeze spread coolness all around. The passengers, dazed so long by the suffocating heat of noon, now came to life. They yawned and flexed their backs and started talking. She shared the general feeling of relief and tidied up her hair with a sweep of her hand.

The train stopped at a station. A vendor was selling ice candy on the platform. The girls pressed their noses against the window bars and stared at the vendor greedily. The woman too peered out of the window and looked hopefully at the vendor. They all looked at the head of the family out of the corners of their eyes.

The younger girl was bolder than the rest. She asked her mother with pretence of innocence, 'That man is selling ice candy. Isn't he?'

'I don't know. Why not ask your father?' said mother.

The mother and the daughter eyed each other slyly.

The girl's father was taken in by this stratagem.

'Yes. That man is selling ice candy all right. How about it, girls? Would you like to have some?' he asked.

The girls giggled with their noses pressed against the window bars. Their mother was forgotten. She kept on looking hopefully at the candy bars. The younger girl ignored that look in her eyes. But the elder girl took pity on her mother.

'Anna!' she said, 'do give one to mother.'

The man looked at his wife and asked. 'How about it? Do you want one?'

'Oh, no! What would I want candy for?' she protested.

'Don't you listen to her. She would like to have one. I know,' said the girl.

'Why then don't you say so?' growled the man and bought a bar of candy for her too.

The woman accepted it guiltily and sucked at it. It tasted sweet and cool. She paused to let that pleasant sensation sink in. She then opened her mouth to suck at it again. But the baby had been looking intently at the coloured object. It thrust forward its hand to snatch it. The candy bar slipped from her hand and fell down on the floor. It did not reach the expectantly open mouth of the woman this time.

That drove the woman mad with rage. She had had enough of her children and her miserable household. She wanted to thrust the baby in its father's arms and scream at him. 'Here are your children! You can do whatever you like with them! But I am through! Understand? I am through!'

She wanted to get off the train and walk away. She would walk on and on until she dropped dead. Nothing really mattered any more.

Of course, she did not do anything of that sort. The lid had blown off for a while. That was all. After a wild surge of animal fury she landed again in the dark damp hole of her existence.

Just then a woman entered the coach. She was about the same age as this mother of three children. But there was an air of ease and assurance about her. She ordered the *coolie* to put her luggage properly on the shelf and when he began to demand excessive payment she curtly ticked him off. Having disposed of the *coolie*, she looked around for a seat. Everybody was staring at her. But she coolly ignored them all.

The mother of three children looked at this woman and was fascinated by the way she bore herself. With an automatic movement, she tidied up her *sari* and her hair, and her expression became more stupid and guilty.

'It looks as if she is a doctor,' she said. To her mind a woman having a dispensary or running a maternity home of her own represented the pinnacle of feminine achievement. She glanced at her husband with a question in her eyes.

Her husband gave a start. She had caught him in the act of staring hungrily at that woman. So he tried to look unconcerned and said contemptuously, 'Nonsense! She couldn't be a doctor. I think she is just a nurse or a primary school teacher. She is giving herself airs. That is all. You know how things are these days.'

The elegant woman walked up to them and rather curtly asked the man to move aside and make room for her. He was occupying the space of two seats on a crowded train, and she showed her disapproval of his callous attitude towards others passengers' comforts by talking brusquely.

The man's wife was amazed. She was alarmed for the woman, for her husband was certainly going to snub her. She looked forward with bated breath to her husband's grand performance.

But things turned out differently. Her husband apologetically pulled himself together and said, 'Certainly! certainly! Do have a seat.'

The man's wife was disturbed and perplexed. The other woman had reduced her giant-sized husband to the stature of a timid little man. She stared at the woman with awe tinged with resentment.

But the respect was short-lived. She noticed that there was no *kumkum* mark on the elegant woman's forehead. She was a widow. A miserable, wretched widow!

She instantly drew for herself the conventional picture of a widow and eyed that woman. But soon she had her doubts. For there was not a trace of unhappiness on that woman's face. She did not look a cringing, forlorn person at all.

Her mind wove confused ideas for a while and then suddenly there was a dark suspicion in her mind. This elegant woman could be one of *those* women. She involuntarily put her arm protectively around her daughters and frowned at the woman with suspicion and contempt.

The elegant woman did not notice that look of hers. It could not have occurred to her that this miserable, insignificant-looking person could feel that way about her. Even had she noticed that look, she would not have cared.

After a while, the woman took out some biscuits from her handbag. When she saw the children, she offered them some. The girls stretched their hands timidly, watching their father for his reaction.

Their mother pushed aside their hands angrily. She wanted the woman to know what she thought of her. But to her amazement her husband reacted differently. He smiled profusely and said, 'Now, now girls! Take what the nice lady is offering you.'

The girls accepted the biscuits, while their mother watched them uneasily.

Her husband was all smiles and was trying to make conversation. The woman experienced a cramp of convulsive fright. For a moment she thought that the wily woman had cast a spell on her husband and was trying to snatch him away from her. But she could soon see that the elegant woman was not responding to her husband's attempts to break conversational ice. In fact she was curtly distant so that the man was snubbed into silence. This reassured the mother of three children but did not exactly please her. She was feeling very protective about her family now and she did not like that the elegant woman should snub her husband.

But she scarcely looked at anyone for long. She sat quiet for a while. Then she showed some interest in the girls. She smiled and then patted the one near to her.

'Do you go to school? Is it a nice school? Does your teacher use a cane to punish children? Well! My teacher used to do that.' So she went on talking pleasantly.

The girls' mother thawed a bit. This was the talk of a nice well-bred woman. Women of easy virtue certainly would not talk like that. She could not help being pleased with the way her younger daughter replied to these questions. She certainly was smart.

'Is that your little sister?' she now asked, pointing to the baby. She was talking to the girls but her question was aimed at the mother.

'He is their little brother,' replied the mother with obvious pride.

'Oh! Is that so? I would like to see the little darling.'

That wiped out the last trace of resentment in the woman's mind. She proudly handed over her baby to the other woman.

The elegant woman fondled the child and kissed it on the cheek although it was none too clean. That settled it finally. That certainly was the behaviour of a nice woman brought up in a good, old-fashioned family.

'I like children,' said the elegant woman. 'Why! I spent my holidays with my uncle. There are lots of children in his house and I certainly had a grand time with them.'

This naturally raised the question of who her uncle was. One question led to another, as always happens when women talk. Soon the mother of three children knew everything about the other. The elegant woman's husband had unfortunately died soon after their marriage. Her father did not like the idea that she should spend the rest of her life as a household drudge in the family. So he had asked her to take a course in nursing. This she had done. She had a nice job now and earned well. She did what she liked and had a good time. Her relatives were always nice to her and invited her to spend her holidays with them.

The elegant woman glanced at her watch.

'We shall be at the next station in a few minutes,' she said with a smile. She looked in her tiny mirror and tidied up her hair. She powdered her face and a delicate perfume floated in the air. Her eyes were bright and expectant.

The mother of three children lapsed into silence. She felt envious of the other woman. She seemed to have all the money and freedom and happiness she wanted. She was not saddled with children. Nor had she to cringe before a husband.

A horrible idea took possession of the mother of three children, if only for a moment. It certainly is nice to be a widow, she thought. One can have a lot of fun!

She suddenly realised how terrible and wicked the whole thought was. It offended everything she had been taught to revere and have faith in. It made nonsense of everything she had lived and slaved for. Is it not a cardinal sin for a devoted Hindu wife to think in that strain?

But try as she might to dismiss the thought, it kept coming back to her.

The train stopped at the next station. The elegant woman peered though the window. A tall, well-groomed youth waved his arm and called. 'Vimal!'

'Oh, Shyam!' she exclaimed and waved her little handkerchief to greet him.

The young man walked to the window and held her hand. He then jumped on to the train and they occupied the two seats near the window.

They were seated behind the mother of three children. She could not see them. But she could hear their pleasant chatter. She could almost see how their eyes danced and faces beamed. Their happiness hurt her somewhere deep down in her heart. It was a pain that made her numb and listless.

So this was what she had unknowingly longed for always in the midst of the drudgery that was her life? She had longed for it without knowing it and, now that she knew, everything else lost its meaning.

She looked at her husband with a forlorn hope. She looked at him imploringly. She wanted him to give her just this, a tiny bit of this—love. She was not a dreamy romantic. But her heart had always dreamt of having sweet nothings whispered into her ears. She had learnt all along to expect very little of life and she would not expect much from him. But if only he could give her a tiny bit of this happiness, it would make all the difference. She would then not mind all the drudgery and sickening poverty of her life. She would gratefully remain his slave. But of course, he could not understand the longing in her eyes. How could such things ever be put into words!

The train sped on. The sun sank below the horizon in a red glow. Lights brightened up the compartment. For an hour or so the carriage was full of pleasant chatter. Then gradually, people lapsed again into silence. Eyelids drooped and minds retired to their nests. People squirmed and tried to stretch their tired limbs and finally fell asleep. Then the moon tiptoed into the sky.

'Oh, the moon! So exquisitely beautiful today,' whispered the elegant woman.

'Yes, beautiful indeed,' the young man murmured.

The mother of three children heard them and anguish filled her heart. She wanted to lean on somebody's arm and watch the moon.

She looked at her husband hopefully and with yearning. But she realised immediately that her wish could never come true.

The child in her lap whimpered and kicked. She rocked it with an automatic movement of her legs and crooned.

'Uncle moon, uncle moon
What makes you so wan and tired'

Translated by the **Author**

The Debt

Gauri Deshpande

When Anita first met Sajan Singh, she had little information about India, and even less curiosity. She knew it only as a country that occupied a rather large area on the map of the world, was mentioned occasionally in newspapers for its floods and droughts, and was overpopulated by poor people. Never in her dreams had she thought that she would someday meet a man from that country, fall in love with him and actually end up marrying him. Yet that indeed was what had happened.

A girl from some obscure town in Texas, she had a chance to come to Berkeley thanks to her brains, and the very first day in her class she had come across Sajan, bearded and moustached, dark and foreign and dressed in strange clothes. She had been so taken aback by his strangeness that in the beginning she never thought about his personality. Later, she learned to ignore the strangeness of his turban, his dress, his hirsute face, and focus on the familiar: his fluency in English and his astounding scholarship. In fact he was the best student in her class of microbiology. Of course it helped that he was not given to talking about himself, that he preferred to stay in the background, that he was shy, reserved almost to the point of being mistaken for a misanthrope. The class was small. Although all of them were doing their own research, they would meet in the weekly seminars. The two came to know each other in course of time. At first their discussions were about their studies, the seminar topic, the professors, the other students; later they touched upon more personal matters.

Sometime in the second year Anita asked him about his home, his people. He told her very little: Mother died when he was young...three older sisters...father a doctor...home in a town north of Delhi...education all on scholarships...The tone of his reply was, 'What is there to tell? There are thousands like me in

India; it's the same story as everyone else, more or less.' She had no curiosity about the matter anyway, so the subject was dropped for good. The third year of their friendship and the last year of her doctorate she sensed that she felt something more for him. She was confused. But she thought about it with the typical thoroughness of American girls. She measured the nature, length and strength of her feelings, asked herself whether it was wrong to feel that way. She discussed it with her parents, her close friends, some of her professors, and the counsellor of the university who was also a psychologist. When she realized that it was the genuine, noble feeling of true love, although the focus of it was a strange foreigner, she went straight to Sajan and told him, 'I love you.'

He didn't hug her with joy as she expected, but instead asked her with a smile, 'So what do you suggest I do about it?' For a moment she wondered whether it would be wiser to step back right then since he was asking such a question. But she had considered everything so thoroughly before coming to her decision, that she couldn't just give the matter up. So she said with all sincerity, 'People who fall in love usually marry each other, don't they?' The smile lingered on his face although she thought that she saw a trace of pity, a little sorrow in it. He only said, 'Is everything that easy here?' She did not understand the question. But apart from that, she did have a reasonably good understanding of his nature. His three elder sisters had mostly brought him up. Rarely did he see his father, the doctor. So he must have acquired a habit of giving in to the demands of women.

After his doctorate he got a job in the same university, and then at last, he did marry her. He mentioned to her that his father was dead opposed to his marriage, but the letter that he received was in Punjabi. She didn't ask him for details, and he didn't give her any. After that he never received any letters from India, so she gathered that his family must have disowned him. Good riddance, she thought. Now he doesn't have any excuse not to settle down right here. She was a little puzzled though. All her friends and her family were so liberal that they were ready to accept him in spite of his being a dark foreigner, in spite of his strange religion, turban, beard and all, and his people should disown the daughter-in-law who is well-educated, pretty, well-to-do, blond, and American! What strange pride!

Their married life started like everybody else's. She found a job in a hospital. Her parents gave them a small apartment as their wedding gift. He even shaved off his beard and moustache and gave up the turban at her insistence. In short, apart from the fact that Sajan was not, in fact, a true-blue American, they were quite like the average young American couple of their age. Sometimes she would sense his foreignness in some small matter, but she learned to ignore it. In fact, she was quite happy that compared with other American husbands, he was so much more courteous, so obedient, so willing to help in the house. He was still a little shy. When Sara or Katie from the neighbourhood flirted a little at a party, he would blush and hide behind Anita.

She came to know how different he really was only when she became pregnant. She had no intention of having a baby. She was quite satisfied with her job and her research, and did not want to interrupt her career right then. It was by mistake that she had conceived, but she didn't make a great fuss about it. One day she casually mentioned it to him. For a moment Sajan's whole face lit up.

'Darling! How wonderful!' he said, getting up and gathering her in his arms. It must have been the first time he had spontaneously shown so much affection.

She pushed him away and said, 'I really don't want a baby you know, at least not right now. I have made an appointment at the hospital tomorrow.'

His face twisted in pain. He didn't want to understand what he had heard, so he asked, 'Appointment? What for?'

'To get rid of it, of course,' she said, rather brusquely. His eyes grew round. He said in an unusually loud voice, 'Anita, no!

Never!' And then realizing that she had stiffened at that, added piteously, 'Please please...'

When she saw all that entreaty, that begging on his face, she was startled. For a moment she thought it would have been easier had he thrown a tantrum. She turned to pick the coat off the hook, and going towards the door, said, 'Let's leave it. We'll talk about it later.'

But he came around and stopped her. For the first time she realized how big, how so very big he was, compared with her. She got really mad when she found she couldn't tear herself out of his hold. She remembered what she had once read somewhere: Indian men regard their wives as slaves and treat them as heir-producing machines.

She gave up her struggle and said in a tone of contempt, 'In your country they may think of women as just baby-making machines, but don't forget that I am an American. I don't want to live simply as a female animal, sacrificing my intellect, my personality. I will decide when to have a child if I decide to have a child at all. Understand?'

'How can you say that? Don't I have any right over this baby? Don't I have any share? Please Anita, have pity. Don't destroy our baby.'

'Stop being so melodramatic. Why say 'baby'? It's only a clump of few cells. I didn't think you were so old-fashioned, such a hidebound stick-in-the-mud.'

'What can I do to change your mind? I am begging you; shall I fall at your feet? Please grant me this, please!'

With every word of his, with every gesture she became more perplexed. She wondered how it was that although he was really so different, so strange, she had never noticed in all these five or six years. What she felt at the moment was a little dreary contempt for him. As he moved away from the door in his urgency, she quickly slipped through it and went away.

She never could understand or explain the malignancy of fate decreed that that very day, the bus that Sajan took every day to go to work should meet with an accident and he should be critically injured. He lay in a coma for four weeks in the hospital and then became a statistic along with the others who had died in that accident. She didn't even know the address of his father to cable him the news, but the university office supplied her with it. By the time everything was over and she recovered from the deathwatch, the funeral, the shock, it was too late to terminate the pregnancy. What Sajan could not have achieved while living, he had achieved by dying, she thought in her bitterness.

There were many who showed sympathy but no one could understand the confusion in her mind compounded of sorrow, bitterness, and a dry, grey hopelessness as well. She shut up her apartment, took leave of absence and went to live with her mother. Life in that little, sleepy, small, monotonous town made her mind go numb. Every day would pass with the same blankness while she would swing back and forth on the porch swing. She could not think of what she was to do now, nor of what was to happen to her child. Finally, it was the child that brought her back to life. It kicked her from inside. It insisted that it was alive. That 'clump of cells' changed her body, it made her awkward, heavy, sick. Finally it made her aware of its existence in spite of her numbed mind. Although intellectually she had realized that 'clump' was her baby and Sajan's, she only accepted it totally when the son was born and she saw that he looked exactly like Sajan. And she realized with a new, jolting certainty that there was no Sajan any longer. That was the first time she felt the pure pain of the unending loss of his nearness. That feeling had no bitterness in it, no grey dryness, just sorrow at the memory of Sajan. A deep sense of loss of all those qualities that were Sajan: his guilelessness, his shyness, and his intelligence.

When she talked to her parents about this, she realized that contrary to what she had earlier thought, nobody had really understood or accepted Sajan. In fact, although nobody said, 'good riddance,' she could nevertheless detect a general sense of relief that he was no longer around.

And so, she quietly returned to her own house and work. She found a live-in help and resumed work. There was relief in work. But there was sorrow in watching how much the growing boy resembled his father. Once, while she was giving him a bath, she wondered why she had named him after her own father and not Sajan's. And on that thought she got up and searched the whole house and found Sajan's old passport and looked for his father's name: Bishambhar Singh. She could not really get her tongue around the unfamiliar mix of consonants and vowels. But she thought it sounded sweeter than the strange sound of her son's neither-here-nor-there name: Peter Robert Singh. On the first page of his passport was also an address. Who knows on what impulse she sat down to write a letter?

The letter never got written. The phone rang. It was her lawyer calling to tell her that the mater of compensation for the heirs of the victims of the accident was finally settled. She could come next week to the office of the bus company. A letter was on the way to that effect, but her lawyer had called first with the news. That check adorned with a lot of zeros scorched her fingers in the bus company's office. She thought, 'While living, I rated his value at nil, but dead, he is worth so much to this bus company! She kept the check in the drawer of her desk and didn't think about it for a while. But one day on her way to work, she took a detour and ended up at a travel agent's office. After a little hesitation, she asked him about India. He scattered colorful advertisements and brochures on the desk. In front of her bewildered gaze sparkled the Taj Mahal, The Gateway, The President's residence, village beauties, tribal dancers, Kashmiri houseboats, snow covered peaks of the Himalayas, temples of Tirupati and Jagannath, Ajanta and Ellora.

With her Bankamericard she bought a ticket right away. It was the first time the agent had seen a customer wander into his office for a casual inquiry and go away with a ticket. He muttered something about it being quite warm there now and quickly rang up a few numbers to settle the matter. He took it upon himself to get her a visa and happily waved her goodbye.

Anita really felt the impact of her decision for the first time when she landed in Delhi. She was dead tired by the twenty-four hour long journey. Peter was screaming. She thought she had entered an oven. She was used to hot summers in Texas, but this was something else. Everywhere there was a sea of confusion, of noise, of people. Some dressed in suits and some looked just the way Sajan had in the beginning. There were airhostesses and other pretty women in saris, hippies in jeans and tunics, youngsters in mod clothes; it looked like a carnival. She wondered why everyone was shouting all at once.

The baggage conveyer had broken down, so her bags came in after two hours. Peter had cried himself to sleep. She held him somehow with one arm, shifting from foot to foot. It she could, right then and there she would have jumped onto a plane that would take her back. When finally her suitcases did arrive, she dragged them one by one to the customs counter. But people pushed and shoved her and rushed ahead of her. When Peter got up and started screaming again, an officer spotted her and brought her to the front of the queue. She had nothing to declare except Peter's clothes and hers, so she was let out at once, and when she came out, she just stood there petrified. She had just upped and left, and now she did not know where she was to stay, what she was to eat, or drink, or who to approach in need. Nor did she know how to get to Sajan's father. She simply stared in front of her, and rocking Peter, stood near her suitcases. A hippie came to ask her where she was going. She checked the address in the dairy from her purse. Roorkee. He shrugged his shoulders, said 'I don't know. Ask the cop. Do you have any money on you? Anita shook her head. The hippie finally took pity on her and led her to the policeman, but he could not understand her, so he took her to a table where a sign said, 'May I help you?'

The attendant at that desk advised her that the best thing would be to stay in a hotel overnight and go to Roorkee by taxi next morning. Without asking her permission, he rang up and booked her a room in a hotel. By the time she came back for her baggage, the suitcase with her clothes in it was missing. She felt so desperate, she even forgot to weep. Again the policeman. He still couldn't understand. Again the interpreter. Some documents were made, some signatures were necessary. An address was given where she could purchase a few clothes. Finally when the taxi brought her into the air-conditioned coolness of the five-star hotel, she felt the tension snap and tears flow. Poor Peter at last lay silent in the cool darkness of the room. His skin was already raw with prickly heat. 'At least this hotel is like any other American hotel,' she said with a sigh of relief and, after a shower, dropped into bed.

When she resumed her journey the next day, she felt that the nightmare had also resumed afresh. There was the larger oven outside and the smaller inner oven of the old taxi in which six people were stuffed to be baked and roasted. Everyone was sweating and gasping. It was as if they were incapable of doing anything else in this heat. The parched, dusty soil, dried up, leafless trees, skin-and-bone cattle, dark, stunted people, here and there a man looking like Sajan, tall and turbaned; everything passed unheeded before her hot and tired eyes. Peter was shrivelled up from the heat. He was not screaming any more, just whimpering. When Anita's mind started to revert to numbness as an escape from the horrible reality, she made a strenuous effort to shake it alive, and asked the man sitting next to her who was sticky, sweaty and smelly, 'Are you going to Roorkee?' He just grunted. She asked again, 'Do you know Doctor Bishambhar Singh in Roorkee?' He only stared at her. As it was, he had shrunk as much as he could so that he didn't have to sit jammed up against a strange woman, a foreigner at that. Yet, whenever the man on the other side pushed him, he would fall against her and apologetically try to move as far away as he could.

Anita was not much surprised to see six people stuffed in so small a car. She had seen the ocean of people everywhere around her, and could understand the shortage of space. But she had become wiser after paying an exorbitant bill for just one night's stay in the hotel that morning, and had inquired first the fare before getting into the taxi. Thirty rupees each. She saw that the driver charged the same fare to everyone. She thought it reasonable, and so had got in.

On the way she was dismayed to see only dusty, sun-parched industrial towns lining the road, with shabby, crummy little shops, dry, steaming hot lanes, and mud-brown houses with a lost, forgotten, godforsaken look. Where was that dream world of the Taj, snow-clad peaks, the swaying coconut palms, colourful village beauties? She began to think that perhaps the grand fountains, the broad roads, the tall buildings with air-conditioned rooms and gardens full of flowering trees and lush green lawns that she had left behind in Delhi had been a mirage in this desert. While crossing the bridge on the Jamuna, the driver had turned back and said for her benefit: 'Jamuna river.' But since she did not know what Jamuna was, nor why one should be curious about it, the information was wasted on her. All she felt at the sight of the small trickle of water in the middle of a broad, sandy bed was a little contempt.

When the taxi stopped at some place and people got down, she thought she had reached her destination and started getting her suitcases out, but the driver said, 'No no. Meerut. Tea.' God knew how they were drinking the steaming hot tea in this terrible heat. After drinking tea, of course, they all began to perspire more freely. The man who had sat next to Anita offered his seat to the gentleman next to him, perhaps thinking, 'If this woman starts to talk to me after just an hour's journey, heaven knows what she might get up to after three!' The other gentleman was not ready to give up his seat next to the window, but after a little persuasion, he came and sat next to Anita. Quickly he took out a piece of candy from his pocket and offered it to Peter. 'Sweet baby! Take sweet!' Peter resumed his crying at this overture by a total stranger. The gentleman shrank away hurriedly, saying, 'Sorry madam!' Embarrassed, Anita explained, 'He is a bit shy.' At that the gentleman broke into a lengthy speech about shy children and outgoing children. All his children and grandchildren apparently had no fear of strangers.

Then he asked, 'You are foreign, no?' Anita nodded. 'Where you are going?'

'To Roorkee.'

'You know someone there?'

'My father-in-law.'

'What name?'

'Doctor Bishambhar Singh.'

'Oh ho ho! So you are Doctor-*sahib's* daughter-in-law? Poor fellow, how may calamities can fall to one man's lot? Is this his grandson? Good, good. It seems you have come to look after him? At last now he might recover after seeing his grandson. And where is Doctor-*sahib's* son?'

Anita, staggering under the weight of all these questions, somehow managed to say, 'He died last year in an accident.'

'*Arre... re...re...re* ! So that's why Doctor-*sahib* is so sick! What a fate! Even the promising son had to die! And this poor child is now without a father!'

The gentleman then translated this conversation for the benefit of everyone else in the taxi. A flood of sympathy issued. Anita felt like crying. Their quaint English, and peculiar way of expressing themselves amused her, but she could also feel the genuineness of their feeling through it, which surprised her by its strength. So they all knew the 'Doctor-*sahib*'! Then how come they did not know of Sajan's death? And what was wrong with the Doctor's health? She asked them, but no one knew enough English to explain that to her. The gentleman next to her said, 'I shall show you his house. It is quite close to our *kothi*. His hospital is closed now, but people still go to him anyway. How unfortunate the Doctor is! Such a saintly fellow! Well, what can one do against God's will?'

Everyone said something similar and equally philosophical. God had not made a bed of roses for Anita either, but she wondered why there were so many exclamations of sorrow at the very mention of the Doctor's name.

Roorkee seemed no different from the other towns that they had passed by on the road, she thought, when she got out of the taxi. There were perhaps a few more trees, a few more open fields around it. There was a large canal just before entering the town. It must have been a famous one, since the driver had again pointed it out to her. The gentleman with her got her suitcase down and assisted her into a cycle-rickshaw. He haggled with the owner and then came and sat in it himself. When the poor, skinny rickshaw-*walla*, sweating under the blazing sun, started pedalling the rickshaw that pulled them and their luggage, Anita felt such shame that she wanted to jump out of it. After about fifteen minutes, they were on the outskirts of the town. More trees, a broad road and fast trucks on the road. The gentleman next to her pointed to a compound with tall, solid walls, and said, 'Jail. Very big. Very bad people here.' He seemed proud even of the jail in his town. As she was turning her gaze away from the jail, the rickshaw came to a halt. Five or six houses stood in a row, sharing a long outer wall. In front of that wall pierced with doors, in a little space between it and the road, under scrawny trees, stood a buffalo with her calf, some donkeys, some dogs, a couple of goats, and about a dozen naked children. On seeing the rickshaw stop there, the children made an uproar, and when they noticed a strange, white woman in a dress, they yelled for their mothers to come out. Some women peeped out with their *dupattas* pulled over their foreheads. The gentleman approached them and said, 'Doctor-*sahib's* daughter-in-law!' A woman came forward and beckoned to Anita to follow.

A slightly older boy pulled her suitcases out. Anita got down and was about to thank the gentleman but he had already climbed back into the rickshaw, which was on its way. When she saw him look back and wave and shout to her, 'See you, see you!' she too waved and followed the woman in through a door. Blinded by the sun, she could not see anything inside. But her nose took in the stench and she felt sick. She leaned against the wall waiting for her eyes to get used to the darkness inside. The woman went ahead a few paces towards the inner courtyard and waited for her. Peter hugged her neck and started crying again, perhaps frightened by the darkness and the stench. Someone from inside the room on the left asked something in a low, rough voice. The woman went in and answered hurriedly, and the same voice said something more. The woman returned to Anita and led her in, holding her hand, and then going to the other end, moved a curtain away from a hole-like window in the wall. A string-cot was visible in the light from that window, and on it a sack full of old clothes.

Or at least that's what Anita thought. When she moved closer, she saw that it was a man sleeping. Shaken by disgust, pity, amazement, and perhaps even fright, she realized that this was Sajan's father, her father-in-law, Bishambhar Singh. It was to meet this man that she had come thousands of miles as if pulled by a rope. She felt her legs give under her and she sank down on the soiled, dusty floor.

She said the first thing that came to her lips: 'Doctor Bishambhar Singh, I presume!'

Strange noises emanated from the sack on the cot and it started to shake. She realized that the man was actually laughing and then she too started to laugh. Very slowly, obviously making an effort to speak as clearly as possible, he said, 'Anita, welcome home.'

Anita's eyes filled with tears. She held Peter forth and said very quickly, 'This is Peter. Your grandson. I have named him after my father. When Sajan...When Peter...Oh...Peter was born after Sajan died. He is not a year old yet. Has just started to walk...' She stopped, at a loss for words.

Again Bishambhar said with an effort, 'Hello, Peter!' Then after a pause, 'You will get used to my speech. I cannot talk very clearly.'

Now Anita observed her father-in-law carefully for the first time. His beard was grey, his head quite bald, and his face was pulled to one side. A stroke, she realized. Was it the shock of Sajan's death? Or was it some other accident? Some other misfortune, talked about in hushed tones by her fellow travellers in the taxi? Who could tell?

Bishambhar must have said something in Punjabi. The woman, obviously used to his speech, went away.

Again slowly he said to Anita, 'It is dirty here. She will clean the other room for you. You can sleep there. There is water in the pot outside the door. The toilet is out there. She will show you.' He had trouble speaking.

Anita stood up and said hurriedly, 'Please, you don't have to talk. Doesn't anyone else speak English? I can ask someone else if I need anything.'

'Bahadur will come in the evening. He is my compounder. He will...everything...' He stopped and closed his eyes.

Hopelessly Anita stared at his grey face, grey bread, and the greyish dusty bedsheet which covered him. Again the woman came and beckoned to her. The other room was a bit brighter. Outside the door was the washroom—just a lean-to where there was a big pot filled with water. Inside the room were a bare string-cot and a frayed mat which had just been laid out on a hurriedly-swept floor. The dirt from it was piled up outside the door. When the woman once again beckoned, Anita put Peter down on the cot and went with her through the inner courtyard towards the entrance of the house. A strong stench that spread as the wooden door facing the road was opened, announced the primitive basket-toilet. Anita felt nauseated, but smiled at the woman and nodded. She was sure she could not use that toilet to save her life. What on earth was she going to do?

She came inside again and sat down near Bishambhar Singh's cot on the floor. He seemed asleep. Or maybe even unconscious, she thought in alarm. But he heard her, opened his eyes and said something.

Anita bent over him and said, 'Pardon me,' and he repeated it. With some trouble, she could make out one word, 'tea'. She looked around. No stove, no kettle. She asked, 'Would you like some tea?'

'No. For you.'

'No, thanks.'

On hearing this exchange, the woman came in again. He told her something. She went out and in about ten minutes brought in a plate and a glass. There was something like bread and a mess of vegetables on the plate. Anita did not know what it was, nor what she could give to Peter. Milk, maybe? She asked her father-in-law about milk. He called for some milk. When they brought it, he again said to Anita, one word at a time, 'Mix it with water. He won't be able to digest it otherwise.' Anita was going to ask where she could boil some water, but she gave up. So many people are drinking this water, she thought, so will Peter. She mixed milk and water together and gave it to him. Strange taste, strange place, and the terrible heat. Peter threw the bottle away. Anita had had enough. 'Suit yourself,' she said, and laying him back on the cot she came out and picked up her plate.

She found herself almost faint with hunger, but asked her father-in-law before beginning to eat, 'And what about you?' He said, 'I cannot eat that, I will get my rice soon,' and opened his mouth with an effort to show that there was not a single tooth in it. She broke a piece of the thick *roti* and put it in her mouth. It was tasty enough but rather dry, so, with the next piece she took a bite of the curry. She felt as if her mouth was on fire. She gasped and choked, tears starting in her eyes. Bishambhar opened his eyes and smiled. He said, 'Eat it now with water. I will ask for curd in the evening.' She was surprised that this time she could understand him so well.

Peter must have given up his protest and taken his bottle. He was silent in the next room. She took her empty plate and glass and came to the door, looking for a place to wash them. A girl saw her and called her mother, and the mother with a *dupatta* covering her face, came and took the plate from the hands. The stench near the door was unbearable, so Anita stepped outside. Under the dried-up tree the mother buffalo was chewing the cud. Anita went and stood near her, gazing at the trucks passing by on the road. Of course the children gathered around her, but now Anita was no longer surprised by their nakedness. If she could, she would have shed all her clothes too. The calf was asleep near its mother and so were the dogs and goats. Not a leaf moved. The only breeze was the dusty gust created by the passing trucks.

In front of her, the road with its heavy traffic; across the road, the huge compound wall of the jail; behind her, the wall enclosing the houses, pierced by their front doors and the low doors to the privies; some noise of the goings-on inside. The children were slightly shy of her but still clustered about.

What am I doing here? Who are these people? Who is the woman who brought me lunch? Could she be Sajan's sister? No. If she were Sajan's sister, she would have sat with me, she would have cuddled Peter.. Why do these strangers, these neighbours attend to Bishambhar Singh? Isn't there anyone else? If Sajan had returned without marrying me, his wife would have looked after the old man. Sajan would have been alive, working, earning, perhaps the father of a couple of naked children.

Mind engrossed in such strange musings, Anita's eyes were only vaguely aware that one of the donkeys from the motley group under the tree was dragging itself slowly away from the shade. God knew why. Gradually it left the patch of shady dust and started towards the road; inch by inch it hobbled until at last it was right on the road. Anita suddenly realized what was about to happen. Half-screaming, she jumped forward, out of circle of children around her, just as a huge, articulated trailer-truck hit the donkey and sent it sprawling to the asphalt. The truck then ran over its legs and sped on its thundering way without caring that it had hit something. Anita did not even realize that she was screaming. By the time she rushed to the donkey a couple of more trucks had gone over it. Steeling herself, she bent down to see it. Fortunately it was quite dead. The women inside the houses, shocked by her screams, came to see, and stood watching in amazement when they realized that all the screaming and crying was over a dead donkey. She was yelling, 'Pull the donkey away! Do something! Bury it!' The women stood gawking at her, and after a while, went away not knowing what to do or say. Anita could not pull herself to do anything either; she could not pull away the carcass herself, she was not up to it. She was so exhausted and spent by now, she simply turned back, and without stopping at the tree, went straight inside the house.

An older boy came running after her, and offered falteringly, wanting to help, 'Dead! Dead! Donkey dead!' She nodded and shut the door behind her. Without glancing at the bundle on the cot she went into the other room and lay down beside Peter, trying to sleep. She soon realized that it is impossible for more than one person to sleep on a string cot. Finally she lay down on the floor, on the mat and fell into an exhausted sleep in spite of the hardness of the floor and the humming and stinging of the insects, whatever they were. She did not really feel the tears trickling down her face.

The noise of people talking woke her up. Peter had started to cry because of the noise.

When she got up and lifted him, she realized how stiff and aching her own body was. She changed Peter's clothes after washing him and splashed her own face with a little water from the big pot before coming out. She left him on the cot with a new bottle and he seemed content. She saw that a group of people was sitting on the floor next to her father-in-law's cot. They fell silent as they saw her.

One of them came forward and said, 'I am Bahadur Singh. Doctor-*sahib's* compounder.
These are his patients.'

'Patients?'

'Yes. They still come to him. He still has the healing touch.'

Bishambhar Singh heard this, smiled crookedly and ironically tried to lift his now-useless right hand as much as he could. She only shook her head sadly, and not saying anything, sat down in a corner. He turned his attention back to his 'patients', resuming his interrupted questions. The people seemed to understand him quite well. Sometimes Bahadur would interpret. At first the people were a little shy because of her, but soon they began to speak up. One group left and another came in. Sometimes someone would give a few coins or a dirty bill, which he would accept, but if nothing were offered, he would not ask.

People kept coming in a steady stream until dusk. After talking to them Bishambhar would sometimes discuss the treatment with Bahadur in English. Anita could follow most of it, especially the medical terms. Once she even suggested something. It surprised Bahadur and he kept silent. Bishambhar said, 'You are right. But that sort or treatment is not available here. The poor folk can't go to Delhi or Bombay. Are you a doctor?'

'No. I am a microbiologist. But I work in a hospital, so I know some of these things.'

'And Sajan? What did Sajan do? Did he also work in the hospital?'

Without thinking she asked, 'Didn't you know?'

He only smiled with his crooked face. So she looked down and said, 'He used to teach at the university.'

Then she sat silent, not offering any suggestions, until all the people had left. Bishambhar was tired but when she too got to go, he said, 'Please sit down.' With his left hand he took out a small bundle of dirty rupee-notes and coins and handing it over to Bahadur, said, 'Half is yours, give the rest to Harjit's daughter-in-law as usual, for my expenses. Give her these ten more. For two days' milk for my grandson and dinner for my daughter-in-law. Tell her to send curd and plain boiled lentils or vegetables. Our food will be too hot for Anita.'

After Bahadur left, Bishambhar turned to Anita and asked abruptly, 'Why have you come here?

For a moment she thought of telling him that she too had been trying to find the answer since she landed. Instead she said, 'I cannot explain it.'

'I understand that, but there still must be some tangible reason that you can think of to tell me.'

She got up without a word and turned on the light. Brought out her purse from the other room and, talking out the zero-decorated check, put it into the half-open hand of her father-in-law.

'What is this?'

'It's the compensation for Sajan's accidental death.'

'How much?'

'—dollars.'

For a while he was silent. She wondered how she would persuade him to take it if he said 'no'.. How she could convince him that this was not a bribe offered to conscience. She had not committed any crime against anyone, knowingly, or unknowingly. Whether to return to India or not, whether to stay with his father or not, whether the father needed him or not — all those were Sajan's decisions. Not hers. If this father had taken the trouble to come close to his son in his childhood and youth, he would have come back in spite of her. But how often did a sense of duty prevail over an American life? Relationships based only on a sense of duty are no relationships at all.

As if he could hear the thoughts in her mind, Bishambhar said, 'Thank you. I can use this. It is the duty of children to look after their parents in their old age and you have fulfilled that obligation for Sajan by bringing this to me now. That is just as it should be.' He stopped to catch his breath.

Anita felt like asking, 'Why talk of duty? Did you take any trouble to be the sort of father a son would want to take care of?'

But she kept quiet.

Bishambhar again answered that unspoken question: 'You do not recognize such an obligation, such a debt. You put all the old folk together in a 'home' and pay strangers to care for them. Nothing wrong in that either; for, if a man's worth is measured only in terms of his utility, there is no other option but to relegate him to limbo. Unfortunately, even here, there is only one solution at present to that problem: to be a burden to your own children. It is my great good fortune that there is no one left any more to carry my burden. Strangers, in charity and for money too, care for me. Now I shall divide this money into five parts. One will go to Bahadur and one to Harjit as payment for looking after me; one will pay for my food and drink, and medicines, and maybe hospitalisation and funeral; one would cover my poor patients' medical expenses; and one you should take back for Peter. Sajan did not pay his debt as a son. He refused to do that; so it is right that you, as his wife, are now doing that for him. But he also died without fulfilling his duty as a father. So now I will compensate for that a little.'

'Peter does not need anything. What I earn is enough for him,' Anita flared up.

'If you don't need it, then give it to the orphans in America. Surely there are still orphans in America?'

Anita was shocked by the cutting roughness of his reply. She had expected praise from the old man for her own thoughtfulness. Perhaps even gratitude. Both were absent from his acceptance. He was merely apportioning what he thought was his due, in a matter-of-fact manner. She saw that he understood her unspoken thought again, and smiled a little at her before closing his eyes.

When Bahadur returned to the room, Bishambhar said to her, still with his eyes closed, 'You should go back tomorrow. Bahadur will see to that. You wouldn't last long in this misery. Thank you for coming. Take care of Peter.'

And then his head lolled back as if he was exhausted. When he made an inarticulate noise, waving his useless hand, Bahadur went to him and pried the cheque from it. He did manage to say, 'Bank...' clearly, but all his strength seemed to have left him.

Bahadur tidied his bed, gave him a shot and started to leave. By then Anita had checked on Peter in the other room and had come out. She said to him, 'Wait, I want to ask you something.'

He stopped, and then followed her out of the front door. He was short, she thought, much shorter than Sajan. Even with the turban he was just about her height.

'Where are the Doctor's daughters?

'They have passed away.'

'All?'

'Yes. One passed away during childbirth at about the time Sajan went to America. One had tuberculosis, she did not last much longer after that and the last one died last year of typhoid.'

'My God!'

He did not say anything.

'Did the Doctor disown his son for marrying me?'

'Not really. They did not write to each other a lot anyway. And when he decided to settle in America, the Doctor-sahib was disappointed. After that, what was the point in writing letters to him?'

'Why was he disappointed? Because Sajan did not come back to look after his father? But priorities shift, values change; why couldn't he understand that?'

'No, it's not that simple, and certainly not that selfish. I'd rather say it was because the son did not fulfil any of his obligations...to his family, to his country...Naturally, the Doctor-sahib was disappointed. Mrs Singh, all his life the Doctor-sahib has recognized the priority, the value only of the call of his duty; his duty to these people; he has rated his own life cheap before that, why should he try to understand any other values?'

Anita looked down. A line of ants was going somewhere in the dust. Her gaze followed it. Someone had finally pulled the carcass of the donkey away from the road into the bordering dust. Dogs, crows, ants, flies were raiding it. The vultures would come soon. No one could stand to live in its stench by tomorrow. But who knows, perhaps these people are used to stenches. Used to donkeys being crushed under trucks, used to people dying of disease, in accidents and floods and epidemics. It's all a question of how much one can get used to. She thought of Bishambhar on his cot. Even when he was so nearly dead, so incapacitated, when he could not even talk properly, his poor patients were still flocking to him, and he was still caring for them the best he could.

Sajan could not understand a father who would not put his children, his comfort, even his life ahead of paying his debt to these poor people; and his father could not understand Sajan who wanted to spend his short life in the warmth of a little love, a little luxury, paying his debt to himself in the world before leaving it. In the end there remained nothing between the two but this cheque...

'And Peter Robert Singh, of course!' Suddenly she felt as though she held in her hand a thread that would lead her to the very centre of the maze, if only she would persevere. She went in and ate the thick *roti* with some boiled lentils and lay her stiff and aching body on the mat, and before falling asleep, said to Peter Robert Singh sleeping beside her, 'Remember Peter, children must look after their old parents. That debt has to be paid. One way or another.'

Translated by **Vidyut Aklujkar** and the **author**

ASSAMESE

The Vulture

Manoj Kumar Goswami

A Motor Car!

It was Gonu who broke the news. He related how he had seen a motor car going by the road on the other side of the river. But Tutu, Rudra and Kon—no one believed him. Gonu was, after all, adept at playing an occasional prank. Then, some moments later Butu came gasping down—Yes, he also had seen a car moving by the other side of the river.

So, it must be true that a car was plying nearby. That meant another thing also—after several years a car had come near their village. For them the reality of seeing a car was something like a hazy dream. Once, at the time of the general elections a candidate had come down to their village on a motor car to canvass for votes. The car-borne men had resembled fat cows. Then also the car had stopped outside Butu's home. So there was no point disbelieving Butu this time.

It must be a car.

They did not intend to disclose the news to anyone else. Of course Lalu must be told. So a search was launched for Lalu. Gonu ultimately found him in the backyard devouring a few unripe guavas. Lalu listened to Butu with eyes bulging. When Butu had finished, he muttered a torrent of meaningless, obscene words. Lalu's effortless ability at uttering obscene words at this age won respect for him from the others. His manner of speaking was also like grown-ups.

'Well we will have to go. We should see the car,' Lalu declared with the green guava in his mouth. After contemplating over his own proposal for a few seconds, he uttered as if to himself. 'But where will the car go? The road is broken at the streamside.'

'Maybe the police is coming to Naharani' suggested Rudra.

'Yes, maybe they will come to estimate the number of those killed.'

'I was listening to my parents this morning. Father said that not a single soul was alive at Naharani.'

They all knew about the incident by now. Some four days ago they had been awakened in the middle of the night by cries of men and women. They had seen the fire light up the sky on the south bank of the river. On the following morning they had come to know that an entire village had been gutted. Again, yesterday morning they had heard that people from the south bank had come to Naharani and butchered all of them. But the news could not create any reaction in them. They were yet to comprehend the horrors of death. They had only noticed that their fathers were not going to the market anymore. Rudra's elder brother had not returned from the south bank. One or two corpses came floating down the river. Food ran short. They got something to eat only in the morning to quell the overnight hunger. Scraping whatever they could get as supper, all went inside and bolted their doors. The village resembled a graveyard.

'Was the car big, Butu?' Lalu inquired again and went on to exhort 'Let's proceed. If we cross the river by the banyan tree, we shall reach the broken part of the road very soon.'

To resist such a tempting proposal was hard for the others. But then, even grown-ups were not venturing out-side the village limit—let alone kids.

'Gonu must not go. If somehow the police chase us, can he outrun them?' Rudra tried to dissuade Gonu. In reply, Gonu made such a face that they were forced to include him, fearing that more trouble would brew otherwise. Gonu had just completed his fourth year of life.

They started their journey walking over the dry bamboo leaves through the serpentine alley of a labyrinthine bamboo jungle. They were all around ten years old. Gonu was stark naked. Lalu wore a tattered vest that would be impossible to wear again if it were pulled off.

The entire road was engulfed by an eerie silence. They considered themselves fortunate not to have encountered anyone on the way.

Snatches of *Bihu* song sung by cowherds, a whistle blown by someone from the other bank, the sound of a boat piercing the calm river water—all these familiar sounds were missing. Pregnant silence engulfed everything.

The winter river was shallow. It was around mid-day. The river *ghat* was deserted.

There had been a slight drizzle overnight. The clear prints made by car tyres on the road were easily discernible. They were delighted and began to discuss matters just like grown-ups. How big the car must be and at what speed it must be running!

After that there was an all-pervading silence and an ominous calm. The chirping of birds was missing. They must have gone somewhere else. Not a single soul was to be found anywhere. Besides the thick row of the wild cane by the river, there stood an up-turned bullock-cart.

'A man!' Kon cried aloud suddenly. They saw a man lying face-down at the end of the cane thickets. A spear lodged in his back had pinned him down to the ground. Blood stains were visible on his back and in the nearby grass. His hands were spread out wide. It looked as if his dying wish had been to touch the river.

Lalu and his compatriots halted in silence and shuddered. Lifting their eyes from the man, they saw macabre deeds of man's cruelty littered all around. There were houses reduced to ashes, half-burnt trees, a recoiling mud-smeared corpse of a naked woman, a youth with his head missing, a child pinned to a banana tree with a spear.

They moved forward dumbly, eyes full of astonishment. They could not comprehend why these people had been killed.

Probably those who were killed did not know why they had to die.

'That's the car there,' Tutu cried aloud in amazement. The broken road led to a small alley by the river, fit only for bullock-carts. A jeep was parked at an open space below. They approached the jeep at a trot. In the meantime—some people had disembarked from it.

In the front there was an open grassland and on it there lay some corpses of children. No serious injury could be noticed on their bodies.

'That is the boy who was always seen with his fishing rod,' exclaimed Butu. The boy's face was very familiar to them. They had seen him sitting on the other side of the bank with his fishing rod from morning to dusk. He did not come to search for mangoes like other boys, nor did he swim much. He could never hook a fish but he had remarkable concentration and purposefulness, strong determination and tenacity. Even now on his dead face he wore an impassioned look—as if he would rise up at any moment, collect his familiar fishing rod and stroll towards the riverbank.

'Hey—where from the blue sky have these appeared? Maybe they are kid ghosts', one of the men who got down from the jeep joked on seeing Gonu and his partners. A tall and lean young man was minutely observing the scattered corpses of children on the grass. Three cameras of different makes were strapped to his shoulder.

'Horrible business, isn't it, Raghuda?'

'I've seen much more than this', the man wearing glasses called Raghu said nonchalantly. 'Do you remember Sanjay, that time in Maldah? People all over India were later amazed at the photos taken by me. Haradhan Babu became so excited that he even presented us two bottles of champagne.'

The wheat-complexioned man called Sanjay nodded in reply. Incessant streams of sweat trickled down his forehead. Even the act of bringing out his hanky to wipe off his sweat at regular intervals seemed to tire him.

'My God, what heat and humidity! How do people live in such heat? Isn't there a cold drinks shop nearby?' Sanjay muttered in frustration.

'You are saying fine things. It's not your Boston city. You can write in *The New York Times* that there are still places on earth twenty miles off from motorable roads. The nearest station is forty miles way and to see an electric light one has to go another fifty miles,' said the lean and tall young man.

Looking at those jeep-borne men one could easily understand that they belonged to a different world. Their talks, behaviour, laughter were completely strange for Gonu and his lot.

They wore vibrantly shaded clothes. They had put on coloured glasses on their eyes. Cameras and tape recorders hung from their shoulders, and sunlight reflected up glossy metallic parts.

'Well, well, take the shots soon. Shadows of these trees will soon creep up. No photo can be bright without uniform light,' cautioned Raghuda.

The men got down to their business rapidly. The tall lean young man focussed his camera with deft hands. The costly cameras shone in the daylight.

'It's our luck that we have reached here early. By tomorrow the stench of the rotten corpses will become unbearable. What do you say, Lima?'

'I am lucky to have escaped the stench. I can't bear it. I could not have food for two days in cyclone-ravaged Andhra Pradesh. Do you remember, Hamen?'

'Hamen,' Raghuda inquired loudly, 'the man crying in front of the dead child—did you talk to him?'

'The child before him was his son. His wife had also died, he told me....'

'Arun, have you taken a snap of the man?'

'Yes, Raghuda,' the tall young man replied.

'Wait a bit, one cannot ascertain whether the boy is dead or alive. How did the kid die? There is no injury mark on his body. Do one thing Arun. Drag that man near to the child whose belly has been pierced by an arrow. Be quick! Mr Bhatta promised to wait for us at Nagaon. He is also arranging some drinks for us.

'Raghuda,' the woman called Lima said. 'An incident exactly like this involving Harijans occurred in Khansiram. Do you remember?'

'No, no friend, so many incidents have gone past before this very camera of Sharma's. How many of them can you remember?'

It seemed the tall young man was facing some difficulty. He was trying to take a picture covering all the scattered corpses of children. The wrinkles on his forehead indicated his frustration. He could not find the correct angle for the photograph.

'Hamenda, can't we lift some corpses from the middle and place them here, this way? Now, there remains a vast open space from every angle. The entire photo should be littered with corpses, to show how dreadful this scene is. Corpses must lie all across the photo. Am I right, Raghuda?'

'No, never,' the man called Sanjay protested vociferously at the suggestion. 'It will be unethical to lift from the middle. But if gaps between the bodies remain, the photograph will not be able to horrify people.'

All the men began mulling over the problem in silence. Even the veteran Raghuda slung off his camera in exasperation.

Suddenly the woman named Lima who was staring hard in the direction of Gonu and his partners said, 'Listen Hamenda. An idea has occurred to me, but...'

The Assamese-looking bald man and the others came close to her. Lima whispered something in their ears and their faces lit up, glowing in relief. Patting her back, Raghuda said something in her praise.

The man called Hamen suddenly turned towards Gonu and his friends.

'Hey kids, come here,' he spoke in Assamese. 'Don't be afraid boys, come here.'

Gonu grasped Lalu's hand hard. Their heartbeats increased. They became scared.

'The poor follows are scared. I think they will run away', the one called Arun said.

'They will have to come, they must come. Now, give me the bag of apples.' Hamenda brought down the bag containing apples from the jeep and pulled some out. The red ripe apples glowed in the sunshine as if tempting them.

'Come here, friends take these,' he prodded the boys in a persuasive, friendly voice.

Lalu went forward as if mesmerised. He was followed by Rudra, Butu, Gonu...Flames of fire from inside their stomachs leapt up, their eyes focussing only on the red ripe apples.

'Well, you all will get one apple each. But before that you will have to lie on the grass here like good boys.'

Gonu and the other boys were almost forced by Arun, Lima and Raghuda to lie prostrate on the grass and they meekly complied with their instructions. They lay beside the pulseless bodies of the fishing-rod-crazy, mango-searching boys who were gone forever. Skinny, terrified-faced, torn-clothed Gonu and Butu merged with the corpses easily.

Promptly, the camera froze this hair-raising scene.

'Once I went to see a movie of Godard. I think it was *The Lacrosse Players.* There was a scene exactly like this one. A school bus had met with an accident and the children had been thrown everywhere by the impact. One of them was still clinging to his school bag, text books and copybooks while lying in pools of blood. What a terrifying scene! After all Godard knew well how to create a scene,' said Raghuda. His aloof nonchalant face could still be warmed by this memory.

'Have you seen Godard's latest picture *All about Mrs. Kere....*'

Gonu and his friends stood up. Lalu was lying beside the corpse of the fishing-rod-crazy boy. Standing up, he stared hard at the pulseless body. Then he carefully looked at his own. Then at Gonu and Butu. Probably some equation was going on in his mind. The tall youth tossed away one apple each to the boys, in a dismissive gesture.

'You are, delaying, Arun. Mr Bhatta will get bored waiting for us at Nagaon,' the one called Ranjan was getting impatient. Moreover, if we are to visit Laarighat also....'

'Not Laarighat, Ranjanda. L-A-H-R-I-G-H-A-T.' Lima corrected him smilingly. 'The names are also a muddle. By the way, these people are fortunate. Otherwise the world would not have come to know the names of these villages. Now the names of the villages are in the headlines of each and every newspaper.'

Their jeep started.

The dumb eyes of Gonu and his friends saw how the engine of the jeep roared, how the smoke billowed out, how the wheel moved and how the machine sped away. The jeep disappeared out of sight, disturbing the innocent virgin dust of the village road....

The size of the apple on Gonu's palm dwindled gradually. They had never tasted an apple before. As soon as the jeep became lost to sight near the sharp turn of the river, the apples in their hands also disappeared.

The dreamy-eyed kids slowly returned home— a glorious taste on their tongues and the memory of a jeep on their simple minds.

Translated by **Jyotirmoy Chakravarte**

KASHMIRI

The Bride's Pyjamas

Akhtar Mohi-ud-din

Nabir Shalla, the darner, was already three score and ten. He owned a ramshackle, two-windowed wooden house on the banks of the Jhelum. He sat in the verandah of this house engaged in his work, his thick glasses mounted tight on his nose, and crooned his favourite rhymes with a child-like lisp:

She brought me a goblet of wine,
And took my breath away.

Nabir Shalla had passed most of his years sitting in the verandah and all this time had remembered only two songs, which he recited in season, and out. The second song was:

Her skin is smooth as a ripened peach,
Oh God! Keep her safe from the world's gaze.

From early childhood there had been a curious lisp in his speech. With the loss of teeth it had become more pronounced. The little swath of grey beard shone like snowflakes on his face as if small tufts of cotton scattered over the garment of Dame Shalla had been glued to his cheeks. In spite of a distinct tremor in his hands, he was able to make a living; indeed customers flocked to him for he has an expert at the job, many times better than most.

Nabir Shalla loved his ramshackle house and his wife Khotan Didi more than anything else in the world. Every evening she would gently press his back and caress away his day's fatigue, fetch him platefuls of hot rice, and fill his *hookah chilam*[1]. Whenever he sat in the verandah crooning his rhymes and running his darning needle through a patch of *rafal*[2] cloth, she

---

1 A clay receptable holding tobacco and live charcoal which is placed on the nozzle of the hookah.

2 A warm cloth of soft fibre, usually used by the well-to-do.

would sit in front of him, sifting cotton or spinning at her wheel. Nabir Shalla would make a sly comment, 'You be the 'prentice and I the master.'

Pricked by his remark Khotan Didi would retort, 'Why should I be the 'prentice? Why not you?'

Khotan Didi had only one tooth left in the front of her upper jaw; and since her lower lip had caved in, this tooth hung out like a nail. Her face was wrinkled like a shrunken turnip and her hair matted like dirty white cloth. It was twenty years now since she had her last child but in her life she had been confined about ten times. Unfortunately, none of her children had survived except her two daughters. Both of them were now settled in their homes and had relations of their own. In their wooden shack Nabir Shalla and his wife lived reasonably well without ever encountering a serious misfortune; they had run into debt to pay for their daughters' marriage but had gradually paid off the last penny. Khotan Didi had only one regret. None of her sons had lived long enough. It was rumoured that the Shallas possessed a large moneybag, worth a thousand or two. Heaven alone knew their real position; they lived off their meagre earnings and that was all.

His thick glasses mounted on his nose, Nabir Shalla worked on a piece of a *rafat* cloth today, crooning his favourite rhyme with the same child-like lisp:

> *She brought me a goblet of wine,*
> *And took my breath away.*

By his side sat Khotan Didi at her spinning wheel humming in tune to the music of the wheel. It had rained, though not for long, yet the waters of the Jhelum were muddy and the heat was oppressive. He would have preferred not to work in this heat but then he was the sole earner. Whether he liked it or not, work he must. He had begun to realise that it was his own sweat and blood that went into mending of other's clothes. He was all in a sweat and the *rafal* cloth on his bare knee gave him much trouble. But work he must, and in order to forget his discomfort he hummed his rhymes while he worked. He finished darning a patch, and in order to cut the cord, cast about in search of his scissors. But they were not to be found anywhere.

At last he asked his wife, 'Wherever have you put the scissors?'

'I put them on the shelf,' she replied.

'Bring them here. I need them.'

Khotan Didi had rheumatism in her legs. She could not move about and found it difficult to stand on her legs. If she had her own way she would not have moved about at all for the rest of her life. Yet she could not turn down her husband's request. She moved in considerable pain and began searching for the scissors. She looked on the shelf, looked into the small tin-box, but the scissors were nowhere to be found. Nabir Shalla grew impatient. He wanted to finish with his work and stretch his limbs and rest.

'Look sharp! Will you?' he cried.

Khotan Didi pulled a bag from the shelf; it was full of worn out children's garments and old clothes.

'How very sad!' thought Khotan Didi, 'The children all dead, but the clothes still intact.'

And one by one she remembered her children and the tears suddenly sprang to her eyes. Her flat breasts began to tingle. As she was throwing the old clothes about, she chanced upon a pair of rose red pyjamas. These were the pyjamas she had worn on her marriage day, a long, long time ago, But they were still there—the only thing left of her dowry. Her heart gave a sudden throb as she plunged into the memories of her youth.

Khotan Didi felt abashed. She tried to hide it away from her husband. But the glaring red colour of the garment screamed for attention. She blushed all over, her heart beating like that of a virgin's and tongues of flame licking her entire body. She was the newly wedded bride and Nabir Shalla her youthful groom. Images floated before her eyes of her godmother leaving her nuptial room and of Nabir Shalla approaching. For a moment

Nabir Shalla appeared before her once more as a young man. She looked sideways at her husband. He chuckled and hummed his usual melody:

Her skin is smooth as a ripened peach....

Nabir Shalla appeared really young in his *pheran*[1] and pashmina *chaddar*[2] while a turban of the finest brand of muslin crowned his head. Here was the groom fresh from the marriage ceremonial; here was the bride weaving a net of silly ideas and anticipating the advances of Nabir Shalla with trepidation.

With persuasive softness, Nabir Shalla cajoled her, 'Why don't you put on those pyjamas?'

Khotan Didi blushed again. She said nothing.

Nabir Shalla continued, 'Come on, why not?'

He let his patch of cloth drop and came near his wife, speaking with feeling, 'Why do you hesitate? Put on the pyjamas. You're a nice woman.'

'You're a big fool,' said his wife irritably.

'But why?' asked Nabir Shalla.

Khotan Didi sat quiet and motionless. It was not easy for her to make free movements with her body any more.

'All right,' growled Nabir Shalla, and went down the stairs. Khotan Didi felt relieved. She gathered up the clothes and tied them in a bundle. But she did have a last look at the rose-red pyjamas before hiding them under a pile of rags and tossing the bundle into the shelf. She looked around for her husband. Wherever could he have gone, she reflected. But in her heart she felt a twinge of regret. Why had he not forced her to wear the garment? She felt sad.

It was some time before Nabir Shalla came back humming his

---

1 A loose upper garment.

2 A kind of shawl.

rhymes. Khotan Didi now felt embarrassed, and she blushed every time she remembered her bridal pyjamas; it was difficult for her to live down the memories of her youth. But Nabir Shalla was in a gay mood. He ascended the stairs singing softly. Now he stood before her holding a pound of mutton in his hands and handing it over to her he asked, 'Did you put those pyjamas on?'

Then, after a pause, 'What an obstinate woman you are!'

'Aren't you ashamed of yourself? At your age, behaving like a monkey,' his wife remonstrated.

'Ashamed?' cried Shalla. 'Aren't we man and wife?'

Khotan Didi tried to change the conversation. 'What's this mutton for?' she asked.

'To cook, what else?'

Khotan Didi at once realised that she had a lone tooth and Nabir Shalla none, so who could do justice to the mutton? But Nabir Shalla was no fool.

He said, 'Boil it until it's soft. It won't be too hard to chew. But why have you still not put those pyjamas on?'

He tugged at her and pouted like a baby and would not let her go. At last she agreed that Nabir Shalla should leave her alone to change into the red pair of pyjamas.

Nabir Shalla left the room and went down the stairs holding the pound of mutton in his hand. Khotan Didi shut and bolted the door. She untied the bundle quietly, passed the string through the pyjamas and changed into them. She was all-aflutter. She forgot her rheumatism for the moment and went down, looking forward nervously to her encounter with her husband. Suppose some one saw them! O my God! Whatever was he up to at this age? Oh, God, what a prospect! With her thoughts all ajumble, she entered the kitchen noiselessly.

Nabir Shalla had mounted a pot on the hearth to boil the mutton and was sitting, now singing and now blowing into her fire.

Khotan Didi would have preferred to have sat down without her husband noticing her. But her foot caught on a mat string and down she came with a thud. Nabir Shalla gave a start. He saw Khotan Didi prostrated on the floor and uttered a long frightened cry. But in a moment Khotan Didi lifted her chin and smiled at her husband. Nabir Shalla held her arm and helped her to get up.

'You aren't hurt, I hope?' Nabir Shalla asked anxiously. Khotan Didi shook her head in reply, now thoroughly abashed.

'Well, get up then,' Nabir Shalla pleaded. Again the same shake of the head in reply. He insisted that Khotan Didi should stand up in her pyjamas. She tried to resist but he was on the warpath. He seized her and pulled her up like one possessed and began to tease her amorously like a newly wed. Khotan Didi forgot that she was an aged woman and had grandchildren; Nabir Shalla forgot that all his teeth had fallen out and that his son-in-law was already an old man. It was a marvellous sight to see Khotan Didi holding her ground and Nabir Shalla tugging at her sleeve, shoulder, or whatever he could lay his hands upon. Suddenly there was a knock on the door. Somebody coughed. Nabir Shalla hobbled back to his place and sat as if nothing had happened. Khotan Didi was bathed in sweat. The newcomer was none other than their elder son-in-law who had been watching their amorous antics with a puckered brow.

'*Salam-alaikum*,[1]' said Nabir Shalla. 'Please come in.'

But the son-in-law retraced his steps without saying a word, his face flushed like a red-hot flame. Khotan Didi felt drowned in shame like one caught red-handed.

She looked guiltily at her husband, but he suddenly got up saying, 'Why do you look so guilty? But why? Isn't this our home? And a man is a prince in his own home, isn't he?'

Translated by **Motilal Raina**

---

1 Muslim form of greeting.

The Enemy

A.G. Athar

I walked past the Indian picket. It was about noon. No one was in sight. Perhaps they were fast asleep or relaxing. They could not imagine that any mother's son would dare cross the border in broad daylight. Bathed in sweat, I raced like a train. My brother's face danced before my eyes. The messenger had said that his condition was critical. In that habitation on the Neelam River bank, he could call no one his own.

I lived on the other bank and bore the stamp of India on my brow while he, right across the narrow river, had Pakistan carved on his. The messenger's words were, 'He only mutters your name in delirium.' How could I check myself after such news? After all, it was a bond of blood.

I had reached the Athmuqam Bridge. His hut lay on the bank right ahead. It would take me just five minutes to get there. Like a thief, I stole a glance left and right, clenched my fists and darted across. Barely had I run a few steps when there was a loud shout — 'Halt!' I stood, paralysed. I looked up and saw them — two towering soldiers, rifles ready, straddling the bridge and heading my way.

They read the stamp on my brow and one of the two spoke, 'Indian!' The other pronounced, 'Arrest him.' 'No, no, sir, I am not an Indian. Neither am I a Pakistani. I am only a Kashmiri. Do you see sir, that log hut at Keran? That is my home. And you see that log hut on the other bank? That is where my brother lives. He is very ill and has no one but God to call his own over there. Please, sir, give me just half an hour — I need only to ask him how he is, get him some medicine, a drink of water, maybe.'

A rifle butt hit my neck and the earth shook under my feet. They dragged me to their bunker. More soldiers — they also read the tell-tale stamp and declared, 'Indian. An enemy spy.' And then began the torture. I was told that I must confess straightaway that I was an Indian spy and an enemy of Pakistan.

What was I supposed to confess? That I was my brother's enemy?

I was taken to the headquarter, adjacent to my brother's hut. Again I pleaded with them, 'Please sir, my brother is in a hut next door. He is seriously ill, sir. Please let me go to him, handcuffed as I am — just to ask him how he is.'

But they would not listen. They peeled off my nails, threw salt on the wounds and I fell unconscious. Next I found my brother lying alongside, gasping for breath, begging for water and I, manacled and bound in chains. No sign of water anywhere. The sharp point of a handcuff pierced my left arm and blood poured out. I cupped my right hand, collected the liquid and stretched it towards my brother to quench his thirst. The chains binding my hand did not let it reach his parched lips. At last, a desperate cry for water, a hiccup, and then the death rattle. I screamed — 'It is all over, finished, the human mind, its thinking — which breaks God's kingdom into fragments and calls a brother his own brother's enemy.'

I woke up with a start and saw tears flowing from the eyes of the mustachioed soldiers. They asked me to look out of the window and I saw it — my brother's shrouded body placed in a coffin.

'Let me go — let me see my brother's face — offer a last prayer for him — that's my brother, do you know?'

They said that they knew very well that the dead man was my brother but they could not let me participate in his burial rites. 'We are helpless,' they concluded.

'Seek permission from your officers, please,' I begged.

'They too are helpless,' they said.

'From the officers' officers then,' I pleaded.

'They too are helpless,' was the reply.

'Who is it that can help? Who has the power?' I asked.

'That is something we do not know.'

Translated by **Neerja Mattoo**

MALAYALAM

The Flight

Kamala Das

It was only last year that I decided to stop living in the big cities and settle down in Kerala. I had the occasional feeling that with my art products winning greater fame, my fingers were losing their skill. I feared that this might be due to my poverty of experience. Gradually, all my statues became mere repetitions. Art can imitate life. I don't complain about that. But what if art gets endlessly repetitive?

All those who came to model for me in the city seemed to have the spiritual poverty of city creatures. Their faces were pale and their hair appeared lustreless, with dust from the streets. Their muscles were slack like wet cotton. I noted with unease the boils on their bellies, the scars left by surgical operations, and their blue veins. During leisure time, they inserted cigarettes between burnt lips. They pecked at *pooris* and potatoes, brought in tins of candy, and urinated and defecated noisily in my bathroom. The briskness of their movements got on my nerves. They always showed the impatience of individuals disciplined by buses and electric trains.

I had always wanted to slow down time. I consciously cultivated in myself the patience of a seed lying dormant under the earth. My figures took shape slowly, like a plant growing luxuriantly into a tree.. I worked on verandahs without roofs. My statues, exposed to the scorching heat, wind and rain, underwent changes I never intended. Nature patted and stroked them and made them glitter. Perhaps on account of this, people said they were alive. The statues shone with a glow which should have been present in my models. The sale of my figures brought me wealth. But those without any love for art spread scandals about me, probably because my work involved looking at naked bodies. My husband once told me that those who spread scandals were like the sick with viscous liquid oozing from their lips. He taught me that the habit was nothing but a filthy sickness. After that the taunts of such people never brought tears to my eyes.

Then there came a time when my husband, at the age of forty-three, was laid up for three months with high blood pressure. His right leg and right hand became totally paralysed. For some time he even lost his power of speech. It was then that I took on the breadwinner's role and became a professional sculptor. Time went by. Gradually, he regained enough strength to speak and to walk about in the house with the aid of a stick. But by then he had lost his job. He would stand by my side, leaning on his walking stick, as I chiselled away uninterruptedly. He would say in the softest voice: 'Poor girl! How unfortunate you are! Fated to live as a total paralytic's wife!'

I did not deserve the sympathy in his words. Before getting transformed into the breadwinner I had just been a plaything in the hands of my oversexed husband. It was only through a sacrificial offering of my body that I could satisfy him. If I had been paralysed in his place he would not have put up with me for more than a year. He would not have fed and clothed a wife who did not perform her duties in bed. The priority he gave to sexual satisfaction had filled me with fear. Perhaps due to this I found a secret delight in supporting him. The belief that now he could not be unfaithful to me added to my health.

'You don't look into the mirror these days?' he asked me once.

'I am too busy. How can a working woman find time for amusing herself by looking in the mirror?' I answered.

'You should look in the mirror. You should see for yourself how beautiful you've grown these days. Even without applying beautifying liquids and paints, you are simply flaming.'

I used to feel immeasurably happy whenever he praised my beauty in the old days of idle comfort. Such praise is quite essential for a plaything. Such words will help one forget one's dependence on another. But, as I gradually realised, the one who is financially supporting one's husband and relatives and servants with a sense of responsibility never needs such praise. I did not have to make him happy by exposing him to visions of beauty. No such obligations remained any more. I thought with pride: I'm free. I'm not a slave. I've become free from traditional duties.

My friends advised me to take him to Kerala and give him Ayurvedic treatment. This advice became one of the reasons for our displacement. A broker showed me an old *naalu kettu* situated on the beach outside city limits. He said the rent would be very low, as it was an old house. The walls and the roof-tiles had gathered moss. The iron gate appeared rusty and corroded at many places. Beyond the gate and the wall there was a stretch of unused land with nettles growing on it. Beyond that there was the blue sea. The sky above the sea had a peculiar whiteness owing, perhaps, to the glitter caused by the sunlight on water. One look at the sea and the clouds and the sky and I told the broker: "I don't want to look at another house."

Opening the door of the house I entered into the darkness. The stench of the excrement of bats and rats hit us. Brushing away the dust on the doors and windows, the broker turned to me and said:

'Your never-do-well neighbours will tell you many lies. They're envious. They'll even tell you that someone was beaten to death in this house. These are just cooked-up stories to keep away the tenants.'

The windows were pretty small. From the central yard could be seen the courtyard paved with black stones and the cylindrical pillars. The house had passages through which air could move from south to north and from east to west.

I decided to place my statues in a row along the edge of the inner courtyard. I would get plenty of air and light when I worked on my statues there.

'This house will suit me.' I told the broker.

'You don't want to see the bathrooms?' asked my husband.

I shook my head. 'I don't want to see anything now,' I said.

The house became mine — the house that had waited alone for years, dreaming of me. Indeed, wasn't it this dream which had kept the old house alive? Otherwise, the wind and the rain would have brought down its roof beams and pillars long ago.

I had had a vision of such a house in my dreams for many years. Its rusty gate, the unused land covered over with brambles, the waves that dashed and rolled over, had all appeared in my dreams many times. The porch, the windows, the central courtyard, the pillars, the soft black floor, the mossy roof-tiles and the loft resounding with the beating of bats' wings — I had seen them all.

I engaged an old man to massage my husband with medicinal oils and to bathe him. An old woman joined us for cooking and for other household chores. The first few months were happy.

Then a rustic girl arrived to model for me. Sridevi. Hardly seventeen years old. Initially she was terrible shy and hesitant. Later, she started proudly displaying her nudity. I sculpted many figures, asking her to pose for me sitting, standing and lying down. By noon the girl used to collapse on the floor, exhausted. But my figures seemed to acquire a peculiar vitality, as though they had sucked her life-blood. As she collapsed like a lifeless doll, I watched with wonder the statues, merely her imitations, brimming over with a new vitality, as if they were showing off. Perhaps due to exposure to the sun, they had the warmth of human bodies too. The warmth remained in the stone and the wood until midnight.

One day my husband said, looking at the girl, 'Stop this sculpting! This girl is dead-beat.'

There was only anger on his face — anger directed at me. I was surprised. This man had never entered my studio, and he was now commanding me to stop making statues.

The girl was lying to her left on the black floor. Her eyes were closed.

'She's okay,' I said.

'Perhaps. But if this continues, she'll definitely die. You're like a vampire, sucking blood. Your statues will steal the life of your models.'

I looked at the girl's face again. Pale, beautiful face. Cheeks like water lilies. Eyes with long lashes.

'Do you think she's beautiful?' I asked my husband.

'My view has no relevance,' he muttered.

Sridevi. I learned to see through his eyes the beauty of that slim body from which you couldn't scrape out even a grain of flesh. Meticulously, I transferred to stone the little highs and lows and eddies of her body which looked like the peeled twig of a jack-fruit tree. Sridevi would collapse, exhausted, whenever I was about to complete a figure. It was the weariness of a wild beast. By the time I had completed six figures, she had started displaying the utter exhaustion of a woman who had given birth six times in quick succession.

Once she begged me with half-closed eyes, 'Ma, let me go. I'm quite tired.'

I gave her hot milk to drink and massaged her body with fragrant oils.

I loved Sridevi with all the love a sculptor was capable of feeling for her model. My husband asked me whether my love would fade abruptly once I was finished with her. I did not reply. Or, was it that I did not have the courage to reply? I did not have the heart to reveal my dearth of emotions. Perhaps I was afraid that I, who was regularly clothing and feeding him might lose part of the respect he had for me. As I was the breadwinner, I secretly despised his dependence and at the same time desired its permanence. I knew that he would need me only when he was living in luxury with no anxiety of the future, sucking my blood like a bug. He had not even pretended to adore me when he had his job.

How did I wake up on that accursed night? How did I wake up even though I did not hear the drizzle pattering against the window? An unnatural, pervasive stillness seemed to have enveloped everything. Could silence wake you up from sleep? Carrying an electric torch, I searched for my husband in every room. .... I found him in the corridor outside the kitchen. He was making love to Sridevi in the moonlight. They had the facial expressions and muscular spasms of creatures in agony as well as the tension which race-houses feel at the end of a race. I fled from the corridor. It was as if I had accidentally witnessed some primitive ritual.

After that I just fled from the house. Hadn't I become a stranger there? He might guess that I, who had always liked to walk along the edge of the sea must have been washed away by the high tide. I felt that the man who could not pay even the next month's rent might start hating the girl responsible for his misfortune. And then her beauty might suddenly turn into a deformity.

The beach was quite dark though streaks of light had appeared in the east. It was the darkness that had the colour of smouldering funeral ashes. Darkness that had the smell of clay which could be used for making statues. Did that house, one hundred and fifty years old, bid me a silent farewell when I walked away along the edge of the Arabian Sea with its countless mouths spewing froth and foam like rabid dogs? Except for the house, I did not feel any affection, at that moment, for any one sleeping in it.

I told myself: life so far has been just a dream. This flight alone is reality. This flight from the man I had loved once and from the respectable prison of marital life. Ignoring the grip of my fingers, the tip of the white *sari* I wore rose with arrogance against my onward rush, like the billowing sail of a boat. Solitude seemed to shroud me with the lightness of a cloud. I had known its touch from the days of my girlhood. My legs lost their balance each time the sea-wind blew. My feet sank into the wet sand which was full of crab holes. In those moments, the newly sprouted grief in my heart bound me to the world.

The cold sea froze my ankles. When the birds start crying in the yard, I thought, or when the sun reaches the central quadrangle, two persons, dead-alive, will rub their eyes, rise and look around in the house which I have left behind. With heavy footsteps, they will run to and fro and search for me in each one of those rooms.

The sun's rays will again fall on the statues along the edge of the central courtyard. And they will come alive. The man struck with old age and the seventeen-year-old girl will change into statues. They will be mere statues in the sex-act too. Statues, with the dilated nostrils of a race horse.

I suddenly felt that the sea had the smell of corpses. I ran forward like a kite about to take flight, swinging my arms so that my limbs would not freeze in the wind. Through the corner of my right eye, at that moment I saw the sun rising in the east.

Translated by **C.K. Mohammed Ummer**

The Flood

Thakazhi Sivasankaran Pillai

The temple occupied the highest spot in the countryside. But even there the deity now stood in water up to its neck. There was water everywhere. The people of the countryside had all gone to look for dry places. If a house owned a boat, one person stayed back to guard the possessions. In the three-roomed upper storey of the temple there were sixty-seven children, and three hundred and fifty-six older people, dogs, cats, goats and fowls huddled together in peaceful co-existence.

Chenna-*pariah* had been standing in water for one whole night and day. He had no boat-and his master had fled for his life three days ago. When the water first began to peep into the house, he had already built a loft with sticks and coconut leaves woven together. He spent two days on it hoping that the food would quickly subside. Also, there were four or five clusters of bananas and a hayrack. He feared that some smart chap would carry it off if he left the house. And so he remained.

Now there was knee-deep water above the floorboard of the loft. Two rows of the coconut leaf thatch on the roof were already under water. From inside, Chennan called out, but who was there to hear him? A pregnant *pariah* woman, four small children, a cat and dog—these were his dependents. He was sure that within twelve hours the water would flow over the roof, and that would be the end of them all. For three days there had been no end to the rain. He broke open one row of the thatched roof and looked in all directions. There was a large boat paddling northward. He called out to the boatman in the loudest voice he could summon. Luckily, they understood the situation and turned the boat towards the hut. One by one Chennan pulled his woman, his children, the cat and the dog out through the opening. By that time the boat had drawn close. The children were climbing into it when

Chennan heard a cry. 'Hai Chennacha...'— someone called out from the west, and Chennan turned towards the voice. It was Kunjeppan from Madiathara crying out from him housetop. Chennan hustled his wife into the boat. Taking the opportunity, the cat leapt in. Nobody remembered the dog. At the moment he was sniffing around on the west side of the house, examining things on his own. The boat moved forward and its distance from the hut widened.

The dog returned to the spot where he expected the family to be and saw the boat already far away. It seemed to be flying away. He began to howl in alarm. He produced a succession of sounds like a helpless human being in distress— but who was there to hear him? He ran on all four sides of the roof, and smelling it, howled on. A frog perched on the hut heard the cry. Frightened, it jumped with a plop into the water. The dog stood staring in fear at the spot in the water ruffled by the frog's jump.

He wanted food and went searching for it all round the hut. A frog urinated into his nostrils and slipped off into the water. The restless dog sneezed and coughed. With one of his front paws he cleaned his face. The rain started pouring again, and the dog crouched under its fury. Meanwhile, his master had landed safely at Ambalapuzha. It was night. A huge crocodile floated by slowly, almost brushing the hut. The dog howled in fear, tail down, but the crocodile passed along without noticing him.

The wretched animal sat on top of the hut. Looking up at the dark sky he howled. His sad cry must have been heard far and wide.

The kindly God of sound Vayu, bore the cry to other shores. Some people heard it and perhaps murmured to themselves, 'Ayyo, a dog is left desolate on the housetop-what a shame!' Perhaps his master was having a meal on the shore to which he had gone. Perhaps now the master must have remembered the animal as he ate. The dog's howl, long and whining, began to grow feeble. He heard a voice chanting verses from the *Ramayana,* pricked up his ears and became silent for sometime. Then, as if his heart would break, he started howling again.

In the deep silence of that dark night the chanting of the *Ramayana* filled the air. The dog again pricked up his ears and listened intently. He stood motionless. The sweet tones of the chanting mingled with the cold unabating wind. The only other sound that could be heard was that of the wind. He found his tender nose had become red and swollen.

In the afternoon two men passed along in a small boat. The dog barked and wagged its tail hopefully. He tried to make them understand his plight in as human a way as possible. He stood in the water, poised to jump into the boat.

'Hey, there stands a dog.' shouted one man. As if he understood the compassion in the voice the dog wagged its tail in gratitude.

'Let him be,' said the other man.

The dog prayed with his eyes and tried twice to jump into the boat; but the boat moved further and further away. As the dog started howling again, one boatman turned his head and looked back. '*Ayyo* -no that was not the boatman calling, it was the human groan of the dog.' The anguished, exhausted cry mingled with the shrieking of the wind and was heard once again above the ripple of the waves on the water.

The dog stood gazing at the boat till it was out of sight. As if hating the world and saying goodbye to it, he mounted the top of the hut. Perhaps he was saying to himself that he would never love man again. He lapped up some cold water. He looked at the birds flying overhead, and at a watersnake gambolling in the waves. Through the opening from which Channan had pulled out his family, the watersnake got in. The dog watched. Goaded by the fear of death and gnawing hunger he barked loudly. Anyone could have understood him now, for the language he uttered was universal.

Storm and rain started again. The roof was becoming unsteady because of the continuous lapping of the waves from somewhere nearby. The dog heard human voices again. 'From where is the dog crying? Haven't the owners abandoned the hut?' There, near the banana tree, the dog saw a boat moored. It was filled with bunches of bananas, straw, coconuts. He turned towards the boatmen and barked angrily, edging close to the water. One of the men in the boat reached up to the banana tree.

The other warned: 'Be careful; it looks as though that dog will jump.'

He did jump, so that the man let go his hold and fell into the water. The other man helped him back into the boat. Meanwhile, the dog swam out of the water and perched again on top of the hut. The robbers cut every single cluster of banana.

Hearing the dog's furious bark they said, 'Wait and we'll show you.'

They piled more straw into their boat. Finally, one man climbed on to the top of the hut. The dog fastened its teeth on the man's leg and bit off a mouthful of flesh. Crying in agony the man jumped back into the boat, while the other man administered a resounding blow on the dog's head with his oar. The dog cried in a faint voice-*myawoo, mayawoo*. Soon, even that sound could not be heard. The man who was bitten lay in the boat and cried out loud, the other bidding him be quiet lest they attracted notice. For a long time the dog kept on barking at the receding boat. By then it was midnight. A large dead cow came floating by and got caught near the hut. The dog came near it and looked at it, but did not dare climb down. Slowly the carcass grew disentangled and moved downstream. The dog sprang on to it. Tail wagging, he dug his teeth into the carcass and gorged himself on the plentiful flesh.

Abruptly, the dog disappeared as the carcass went under for a while. After that one could only hear the howl of the storm, the croaking of frogs, and the sound of the waves on the river. The dog was silent: his heart-rending cries and moans were no longer heard. Rotten carcasses floated down the river, crows pecking at them undisturbed. There was desolation everywhere and nothing to prevent thieves from plying their trade.

After a time the hut collapsed. There was nothing to be seen now in that endless expanse of water. Till his death the dog had guarded his master's possessions. The crocodiles had him now, and the hut also was finished.

The water began to recede. Chennan came swimming towards his hut to find out what had happened to his dog. Underneath a coconut palm he saw the dead body of a dog gently swayed by the ripples. With his fingers, Chennan turned the carcass over and looked at it. He wondered if it was his dog. The ear had been bitten off; the skin had rotted and that made it difficult to tell its colour.

Translated by **Samuel Mathai**

KANNADA

Kwate (The Fort)

Chaduranga

Sitting in front of the fire I pulled out a burning faggot, shaking out the embers and scraping them together mechanically. I placed on them a brass dish filled with castor-oil. In the boiling oil I seemed to see Ayya's face dancing and shaking...(a hide and seek vision).

Every Monday it was his habit to sit for his oil-massage and hot bath. Indeed, Ayya's oil-bath was famous in the neighbourhood. When they saw him erect and strong in spite of the grey in his thick moustache and in the hair on the chest, they used to say that this oil-bath was what kept him strong and erect.

My arms used to nearly drop of exhaustion when I gave Ayya his elaborate oil-massage. He would say 'My bodyaches just vanish when your hands rub me.' He would look at me in a very special way through oil-filled eyes and say, 'Our Awwa's arms were not strong.' I used to stop him saying, 'Why should we discuss a dead woman.' It had always struck me that it was no joke for a weak woman like my mother to have lived with this hefty mountain of a man for over twenty years.

My hands felt as if they were rubbing a stone when I rubbed him. The water had to be steaming hot and as I poured it on him-shoulder, thigh,head-my hands would be steaming. He would then lie down covered with four *kalkunke* blankets. I had to keep the blankets pressed on him for at least half an hour. When he rose, the bed would be wringing wet...

The castor berries put out to dry in the yard began popping in the sun and I woke up from my reverie. Even as I took the oil dish off the cinders, memories of Ayya troubled me. Pulling out a faggot from the roof beam, I walked out. The castor berries were slowly opening out as I squatted in the yard and pounded them with the acrca strip.

When Ayya was alive she used to say , 'The daughter has grown up chest-high. Should you not get her married?' Ayya would answer lightly 'Yes...yes...let the right bridegroom come.' So many prospective grooms were suggested, including Ayya's brother but Ayya did not approve. Why, Ayya was sturdy even now and if he wanted to marry, who could refuse?... No, Ayya would not hear of it. He fell that to ask for another woman was to lost all respect; and if any one hinted at another marriage he would stare at them and ask them gruffly to shut up. They would fall silent in fear. Even I felt afraid of him except at the time of his oil-bath. Sometimes, when he sat with a *beedi* in his mouth, staring at the wall in heavy silence, I would wonder 'Is this really my Ayya?'.... I had studied his nature well. If he wanted something of me, he would be a pretty parrot babbling innocently. At other times he would be a silent brooding ascetic.

Getting up and going into the kitchen I brought out a wooden plank. Placing the pounded castor berries on it she put all her weight on the plank and ground them. As the skin of the berries was being rubbed out, she felt something was being rubbed out within...

Sankranti came. It was a day of great joy for my Ayya. He would get up as dawn was breaking. He could drive his cattle to the pond, scrub them clean,bring them back,spread hay in front of them and tie them up in the cattle shed. He would mix colours-red,blue,yellow-in oil or milk and paint the horns of his cattle. He would then stick pretty buntings and decorate the horns as well as the silver caps on the horn ends. My work on that day would be to apply turmeric and *kumkum* on the foreheads of all the cows and bullocks and garland them, do *arathi* to them and light *agarbathies.* Later I could feed every cow and bullock with morsels of *kichadi* mixed with *payasa* and then bananas. In the evening, the cattle were made to jump through the flames. At that time Ayya would be like a man inspired, moving here and there, as if possessed. A hundred times would he ask me 'Is the decoration all right?' (But why was he not equally anxious to see his daughter beautifully dressed and decorated, I wondered. Everybody should admire his decorated cattle, but if any one as much as even looked at me, why did cinders come out from his eyes?) In the evening they spread bundles of hay and dry grass near the Doddakere lane and lit the fire. The flames rose waist high. All the other cattle took fright and ran away, Ayya's thousand rupee pair jumped over the flames. And how Ayya cried out: 'Ho...Ho...Besh...Besh...' Ayya's joy on that day was to be seen in order to be believed.

Sankranti reminds me of one particular day when I was about eleven or twelve. I was taking out the cows from the shed to tie them up in the back-yard. A calf was being a little difficult. I gave it a tap with a stick. As I turned away, it butted me. I screamed and fell. Awwa came running out of the kitchen. By the time she had thrashed and tied up the calf, I was standing up crying. I had bruised my knee. She took some mud, cleaned it carefully, pouring it from one palm to the other, blowing gently several times and patted the mud on to my wound. 'You must always be careful, child, with a naughty calf. Come, don't cry.' She kissed me on the cheek and went in. I wiped my eyes. Just as I was limping out of the cow-shed, I felt squelching wetness on my thighs, as if something was pouring out of my thighs. Alarmed, I thought that I had been wounded inside, and lifting up my skirt, peeped in. There seemed to be a wound between my thighs from which blood was oozing out. I cried out aloud for my mother. She came rushing out, crying anxiously, 'What is it again, my child?'

With her there was another woman who must have come to borrow chillies or salt. Awwa hugged me saying 'Don't be frightened, nothing will happen. The injury on your knees will heal in a day or two.' The other woman said, 'Why does this lass fuss so much over a little thing?... Wait let me get some *dathai* twig and squeeze the juice on the wound.' And she went away to look for the plant. I did not stop crying and told Awwa amidst sobs, 'It is not from the knee, it is in the thigh.' Anxiously she lifted up my skirt to examine. When she saw what had happened she smiled and said... 'This is not an injury... you have started getting your periods, that's all.' She pinched my cheek, when the other woman came and Awwa whispered the news. The woman opened her mouth wide and cried out. 'Must you cry over this? You should be happy.' Then turning towards Awwa she asked her to get me ready for the ceremony. So this wasn't a wound, but the onset of periods. Shouldn't Awwa have told me what 'periods' really meant? And that other friend who had her periods just three months before, shouldn't she at least have told me instead of merely giggling when I asked her? Bringing a *mora* from inside she began winnowing the seeds to clear the husk...

Work at home and work in the field. Eighty years had passed thus. Onkaramma had once kissed me- 'You brat, your used to be a skinny lizard. How you have filled out prettily like a ripe fruit! I want to take a bite and cat you.' How I had tried to rub the spot where she had kissed and she had teased, 'Yes, yes, my kiss is dirty but if a young man had given it...? Onkaramma had winked at me and smiled. This Onkaramma was of a special kind. She must have come out smiling even from her mother's womb. Even when she wasn't smiling her eyes kept laughing. Only in Ayya's presence her smile would vanish. Sometimes she would breeze into our place in high spirits, but seeing Ayya, the laugh would vanish-her face a quenched torch. Onkaramma didn't belong to our area. She was from some place near Dharwar. Only Goddess Pattaladamma knew what caste she belonged to. She wore a huge three-striped vibhuti-mark on her large forehead. Some said she was Lingayat, others said she must be a Jangama. Yet other said she might be a Basavi. It seems she had came to our village before I was born. No one really spoke much about her. To do so they would say 'Oh, that woman!' and smile. Only mother used to swear-'That bitch!' I didn't understand much, but sometimes as she came sporting that playful smile of hers, I felt like hugging and kissing her. By then she had passed her youth. Still, when she oiled and tied her hair into a knot it looked beautiful. The neighbours would stare curiously, whenever she came to out home. As for Ayya, he would behave as if he were sitting on a *Kare* thorn.

After soaking the clean seeds in water, I went to light the fire in the oven in the yard. I saw Kariya sprawling on the old ash. Since I couldn't drive him away I carried him out. It came back and began licking my leg again. I poured kerosene on the faggots and lit them. The sudden flame would keep telling me, 'How much longer will you continue to lead this lonely life?' I kept a vessel of soaked castor seeds on the fire, and blew the flame high. When I drew back from the smoke I saw the dish of castor-oil near the oven. Deciding it was too late for an oil-bath, I kept the dish of oil on the wooden *chadi* in the kitchen and came back to the fire and blew at it. In the dancing flame I felt I was seeing many things that had happened in the past...

As was the custom, *Akka* and *Bawa* came home for this year's *Deevalige* (festival of lights) also. Their children had come too, one of five and the other hardly a year and a half old. When their cart came and stood in front of our home I was lighting the tiny earthen-lamps in the small niches in the front wall of out house. The boy-child had come running to me and embraced me and I had kissed and fondled him. Turning towards Akka, Bawa had said, 'See how fond your sister is of children. We must quickly look for a husband of her,' and made me blush. 'Bawa was always like this. Under some pretext or the other, he would keep chatting with me. How he used to tease me when I was a small girl! He would pull my plait, pinch my cheeks, kiss me and say he would surely have married me instead of Akka, had he seen me earlier! Now that I was grown up, he couldn't do all that but itched to talk to me and follow me around. Akka didn't like this at all and would ask him to keep off, but he didn't bother.

Sitting with Ayya after the festive lunch, and munching betel, Bawa had broached the subject of my marriage. Standing nearby, Akka had added a word here and there. Somewhat reticent in the beginning, Ayya had said clearly, as if he were snapping a twig-

'I am simply against this match. I do not like giving both my daughters into the same household. Have I not told you so before?'

I had liked Ayya's answer-Bawa's younger brother was a loafer, addicted to gambling and cards. My sister had said in an unguarded moment- 'I would rather stay single than wed such a fellow!'

After a heavy *Obbatoo* meal at night everybody went to bed. After finishing the kitchen chores I too went to bed and slept. Sometime later I felt something heavy pressing on my chest. Frightened to death I couldn't even scream. When I did manage to scream 'Akka, Akka,' it must have been a gurgle in the throat. Suddenly the pressure lifted and I sensed someone moving away. Unable even to open my eyes, I just lay where I was. A little later Akka also gave a shriek. Bawa struck a match and asked what was wrong. Akka stammered 'I felt as if someone fell on my body.' He smiled and said 'Should you get alarmed over this small thing? Can't you see tnat black cat, going there?'

'Where? I cannot see any cat at all,' she said doubtfully.

'Look, it is crossing the mud-wall of the middle room and going into the kitchen.' Akka now insisted, 'I cannot see any cat.'

And Bawa scolded her, 'You seem to have all kinds of nightmares these days. If you are so frightened, I myself will come and lie down next to you.'

I heard him going towards her. Then snatches of their talk... 'Shame on them both *Thoo... Thoo*...not caring for my presence! Even as I am sleeping here!... surely, whatever fell on me now fell on Akka'...

How could one be sure it was Gourakka's black cat? If it was really a cat, then Akka should have seen it. Or was someone telling a lie? I began to suspect Bawa. Could it not be he who had tried to sleep with me and, finding me unwilling, gone and pressed on Akka also? Could he be lying about having seen a black cat? Why should he have come to me when he had Akka to sleep with? She was not very old... May be five years older than me, that's all... I couldn't understand anything... My mind swayed and lurched till day-break.

When the seeds dried out fully over four days in the sun, I ground and pounded them, winnowed and put them to boil again...

That Tuesday, in spite of my entreating him not to go, Ayya insisted on going to Kadahalli to purchase a pair of bullocks. The trip became fatal for our home. There was plague at Kadahalli, but the villagers there had hidden the news from outsiders. Like others, Ayya too was deceived. When the returned home, he was running a high temperature. I gave him gruel to drink. That night he squirmed and tossed about like a rat dying of plague. He couldn't lie on his back or his sides, nor could he sit up. He was burning with fever. By the next morning he had a small boil on his left armpit. He couldn't lift the arm any more. I went out and brought the Pandit who lived in our village outside the Fort in which we lived. When he came and examined him he said:

'This is not any ordinary boil; it seems to be a plague boil. Let us see and wait till tomorrow. Meanwhile, let me go and get some medicine.'

He brought some dry roots and rubbed it into a paste on our round stone-disc used for grinding sandal-paste. 'Apply this paste every hour. Maybe the boil will melt.' I did as he said. Next morning the boil became bigger and more painful. Pandita came again. He was now certain that it was plague. I felt as if the skies had come down on me. I fell at his feet and pleaded with him to save Ayya. Stroking my head, he said kindly:

'Don't worry. I shall do my very best.' He went and brought a different root and sat grinding it and I sat near him weeping.

'Don't cry. Have faith in God.'

When he came to wipe my tears with his cloth I felt shy and turned away. But at that moment I felt consoled somewhere deep within me. In that anxious hour he had appeared like God to me.

'Take this paste and smear it on his boil.'

I took it in a dish and went to Ayya. He wouldn't allow me to touch him. I would not leave him alone. Ayya was always like that. A man strong enough to stop a charging bull in its tracks, but one who would fuss like a child over little ailments like cough, cold or headache. He would not allow me to touch his boil and started of screaming. It was only after Pandita himself coaxed him that he allowed me to apply the paste on his boil.

The boil got worse day by day. Even though Pandita laboured hard day and night there was no sign of the boil either opening or shrinking. On the eighth day, Pandita brought a bundle of a variety of medicinal roots. He made me apply the pastes, one every hour.

That night, even as the whole village slept, the light in our house continued to burn. Clouds gathered in the dark sky and it began to rain. I took the paste near Ayya and called out gently to him. He didn't wake up. He was groaning in his sleep. He didn't seen to be conscious. I withdrew silently step by step. Pandita sat dozing against the wall.

'Sir, you shouldn't lose more sleep. By now I have come to know roots to grind and when they must be applied. Please go home.' And I yawned.

'Even you have not slept the last three nights. So you sleep first. I shall remain here. Please go.'

He looked at me strangely and repeated the word 'Go' like a caress. I started wondering about everything he did and said. While his mouth uttered 'Daughter, Daughter,' his eyes, seemed to be saying something else altogether.

'Go, I myself will wake you up when it's necessary.' The words were smooth. I had always felt that people living within the Fort were different from those outside it, and their behaviour always seemed odd.

I stumbled in the darkness towards the room. I was groping for a mat and pillow when, sensing a light behind me, I became frightened and screamed. On the threshold, holding a burning torch was Pandita.

'Don't get frightened, it's me.'His face seemed very broad and his nose was like that of a hawk's. I felt him entering the room, and my heart hammered. In the yard it rained. I saw him going out slowly into the darkness. Reassured, I stretched myself on the mat and closed my eyes. The drumming of the rain increased and somehow Ayya's mournful illness seemed to have become a little distant. I could not sleep in spite of having kept awake for the past few nights. I saw the burning torch near the yard-pillar being quenched; the dark filled my eyes. The moist air seemed to seep through my Kalkunke blanket and I shivered with the cold. I bunched myself up, too tired to take the trouble of getting myself another blanket...

Sleep must have come I don't know when In my dream I saw myself as the princess of the story Awwa used to tell me. Dressed in my rich silk sari, wearing my diamond ear-rings and gold bangles I was wandering in my garden. Ah... the Prince arrived on his white horse!... He got down from the horse!... He was coming near me... He came and embraced me.

'It's me, it's me. Don't be afraid.'

Pandita whispered smoothly as he slipped his hand in, unbuttoning my blouse. Wide awake now, I felt as if I was in another world. I had lost all control. Outside, the rain poured, rushing from all the four outlets into the yard. When I stammered 'Ayya,' Pandita said 'I have just applied the paste.' The pungent smell of the paste assailed my nostrils. And then it vanished, and I was the dream princess again. Riding the magic horse...

When Pandita slipped out of the house, the rain had thinned into a drizzle. When he disappeared into the darkness just four steps beyond the yard, I giggled. Even though I hadn't eaten well for the past weeks, I felt full and happy. I seemed to have forgotten Ayya's plague boil and Pandita's paste. I was happy as I used to be when in the past I would stand in the sun, after an oil-bath. Forgetting that it was night, I went out and stood in the rain. I felt like dancing when the spray fell on my face. Sticking my tongue out, I tried to drink the drops of rain.

I stumbled against Kariya as I came back into the house. The rain had stopped. Ayya's paste had dried up. After gazing at his face for a long time, I went to grind some more fresh paste.

Though he was lying like a log, Ayya seemed disturbed within. As I was applying the paste, he was mumbling. His lips trembled as if the word came struggling out from within and shuddered to a stop on the lips. Sensing the moment of death, memories of the past must have troubled Ayya's mind.

I remembered what Awwa used to say:

Ayya was really young then but had he thumped the earth with his toe, then water would have surely sprung out of it: He was that strong. His wife was a sick woman.

'I was like a touch-me-not plant. If I slept with him one night, it would take three months before I recovered...' Awwa used to say.

Ayya groaned.

Even before the wedding, everybody in the village said: 'What,such a frail bride for our hefty young man?'

Ayya's father, had been won over by the gold offered and had agreed to the match—Ayya himself had told me this. He had been glad when she had given him two chubby daughters. He would always curse his father and say that the pleasures of the bed were not destined for him.

It was during this time that Onkaramma had come from Dharwar and set up a small shop in our village. She was hefty like a buffalo. She would giggle for no reason whenever Ayya went to buy *beedies* at her place.

One night Ayya lingered on in her shop after all the customers had gone away, and she called him in for a cup of tea. When he had finished, she spread the bed,laughing all the time... ('Your Ayya told me all this himself shamelessly,' Awwa had said).

Ayya opened his eyes suddenly, like a dish opening suddenly when the lid is removed. He gazed at me as I applied the paste on his boil... I looked at him,and when I thought of how strong he had been and how weak he was now, my eyes filled with tears. Pandita's medicine had only made the boil bigger. I felt sick in the stomach.

Ayya was staring at me... His gaze troubled me... Was he thinking about what would happen to me after he went away? Was he feeling guilty hat he hadn't got me married, but had kept me at home to look after him,after Awwa's death?

I saw tears in Ayya's eyes and dabbed them even as I was applying the paste to the boil. Tears brimmed over in his own eyes. As I went on staring, I felt that Ayya was no more there. I was all alone at home. Darkness filled my eyes and I shuddered...

Though Swami was high in the heavens, Pandita had not turned up. So I began grinding the paste myself. Ayya's face looked more wan and thin today than yesterday; the eyes were becoming glassy. By night it became difficult for him to swallow water. Another day and night passed. Ayya was struggling for breath. Towards day-break, just when out cockerel was crowing. Ayya's big soul flew away. Six others in out village caught plague, and two of them died. It didn't fortunately kill more.

Akka, Bawa and other relations and friends came over. All of them went away one by one, after ceremonies.

Only Akka stayed on for a while. When I missed my periods that month, she was alarmed. I told her everything. She wailed that I had brought shame to our home. She asked Onkaramma to give me medicines to get it out. The thing inside did not budge. She tried every conceivable remedy. Nothing happened. Her husband started writing to her frequently. 'There is no one to cook at home. The younger child is ill, come soon.' The people of the village began to get suspicious and Pandita fled one night. Akka embraced me as she was about to leave.

'I am going most unwillingly, leaving you in this condition. What can I do? I shall tell Onkaramma. She will look after you. I shall come without fail for the delivery. Don't worry. Let people say whatever they like.'

Akka was weeping as she got into the cart...

I stirred the thickening mixture with a ladle. When all the water had dried up the mixture started oozing oil. I poured out the oil into another dish, leaving the sludge behind. I kept the oil again on the fire. I was perspiring profusely in the heat.

'If it's male, I shall bring him up, even if I have to wear myself out...'

I must have said this aloud, for Onkaramma, who had come in just at that minute lisped, 'If it's female, give her to me... I shall bring her up…'

The oil thickened further. Stirring it vigorously, I put a drop into the fire. The oil flamed out immediately. 'It is the right consistency', said Onkaramma. After kicking aside Kariya, who was licking my feet I peered down. Even as the odour stung my nostrils, I poured the oil onto a pot.

Translated by **Dr Rajeev Taranath**

Amasa

Devanoor Mahadeva

Amasa is Amasa's name. Maybe because he is dark, maybe because he was born on a new moon day (amavasya), the name Amasa has stuck to him. If his parents had been alive, we could have found out why he came to be called Amasa. But by the time he could walk around on his own, the mother who bore him and the father who begot him had been claimed by their separate fates. Since then the Mari temple has meant Amasa, and Amasa has meant the Mari temple. But just because he lives in the Mari temple, it doesn't mean that he is an orphan. The Mari temple has offered shelter to many like him. Especially in the summer, the little temple becomes a regular camping ground for people seeking shelter from the heat.

Now, apart from Amasa, there is also an old man living there. He's really ancient. So old that every hair on him, on his head, body and limbs, has gone grey. Nobody so far has seen him get up from where he usually sits. In a corner of the temple is spread a tattered, black blanket, nobody knows how old. He's always sitting on it, feet stretched before him, or leaning on a pillar, with his hands behind him. Apart from these three or four postures, he doesn't seem to know any other. It has somehow become his habit to sit like this, his eyes half-closed. He never sits any other way. Sitting like this, he looks as though he were lost in thought. Maybe it is his face, all wrinkled, that makes him look so thoughtful. Or perhaps it is his white moustache, thick as an arm, which comes all the way down to his neck from his side. There is always a man-sized bamboo stick. It doesn't have much use though, since Amasa is always around whenever he wants to move about. But it comes in handy to chase away the hens, the sheep and the young goats that wander nearby.

We've talked of all this, but we haven't told you his name.

Everyone in the village, from the youngest to the oldest, calls him Kuriyayya (Sheep man). Was he named so at birth? That concerns neither you nor us. But this much is certain; from the day he could stand on his own feet to the day his feet could no longer walk, he has herded the sheep of the village headman. Even now when he sits with his eyes half-closed, he counts the sheep, one by one, on his fingers, to himself. This goes on, six or seven times each day. And he hasn't missed a single day. Amasa began to grow up right in front of his eyes. He is now around ten or eleven. Whenever Kuriyayya calls, Amasa answers. Every evening as the night descends on the village, Amasa and Kuriyayya wait eagerly for the monastery bell to ring. The moment it strikes, Amasa grabs the plate and glass kept by Kuriyayya's side and runs. As the night has already fallen by then, you can't see Amasa running in the dark. But if you skin your eyes and peer into the inky night, you can see the darkness stir at his flight. One doesn't know for how long he has gone. It's only when his call 'Ayya' shakes the night that you know he has returned. Kuriyayya sits up if he's lying down. As always they eat the gruel from the monastery in the dark. Amasa then goes to sleep. Though the village too has by then gone to sleep, the silence of the night is broken now and then by the barking of dogs and the hooting of owls. The old man, unable to sleep, stares into the night. He mutters things to himself, calls out to Amasa a few times and, getting no reply, finally falls asleep.

Mari festival comes to all the neighbouring villages once a year. It came to Amasa's village too. It was only then that Kuriyayya had to shift himself to another place, for the villagers scrubbed the temple, painted it with white-lime and red-earth, and made it stand out. When it was done and all sides freshly painted with stripes of white-lime and red-earth, the morning sun fell on it and the Mari temple shone with an added brilliance. Only Kuriyayya's corner, surrounded by all this brightness, looked even gloomier. In the hall, a dozen men milled around, busily running back and forth, getting the torch ready, cutting paper of different colours for decorating the yard and doing a hundred other jobs. And since almost everyone there wore new white clothes, the Mari temple sparkled in whiteness.

One of those present—Basanna, was a short dark man sporting a French moustache. He too wore new white clothes and in them he shone darker still. His big yellow teeth protruded through his closed mouth and reflected the lustre of his clothes. In his hand he held a broom. Basanna stomped over to Kuriyayya's corner and shouted 'Ayya'.. Since Kuriyayya would respond only after he'd been spoken to a few times, everyone, spoke loudly to him. Kuriyayya slowly opened his eyes and looked up. He stared at the white figures that kept coming and going in front of his eyes. As he watched, old memories stirred and began to form in front of his eyes. The Mari festival meant the Tiger Dance. That meant him. The Tiger danced in front of his eyes. The drumbeat in his ears. Those were the days of the elder village headman. Kuriyayya had just been a boy then, about as high as Amasa. The vigour of Kuriyayya's dance had impressed the elder.

Giving him a gift of clothes, he had said, 'You must stay in my house till the end of your days. You'll have your food and clothes. Just look after the sheep, that's all.'

His shrivelled face blossomed; the brightness of the Mari temple and the people around glinted in every wrinkle of his face. Basanna shouted 'Ayya' in his cars, this time even louder. He turned his head and looked up. Seeing Basanna, he grasped the reason for his presence. He held the bamboo stick in his right hand and stretched out the other. When Basanna held the outstretched hand, he pulled himself up and slowly walked over to the other corner. Leaning on the stick he sat down once again. Basanna shook the blanket a couple of times and spread it out in the corner where Kuriyayya was now sitting. The dust, shaken out from the blanket swam in the morning sun. Where the blanket had been before, there now lay a thick layer of reddish dust and dirt. But as the morning sun fell on it, it too seemed to turn white.

❀ ❀ ❀

It was noon by the time Amasa returned from his playful ramblings. He couldn't believe what he saw. All kinds of things were going on there. The smell of white-lime, of raw earth, and freshly smeared cow dung around the Mari temple crowded into his nostrils.

Kuriyayya had been moved from one corner to the other. In the hall, some men had crowded around in a circle and were jumping up on their toes to look at something—at a man in the middle who was doing something. Amasa too, hopped over and peeped. He saw diadems, two headed birds and other such things being crafted out of coloured silver paper. Everything that had been made there seemed wonderful to his eyes.

As the man in the middle crafted these things the crowd alternately offered instructions and uttered appreciation, 'It should be like that... It should be like this... Besh! Ha!' and so on.

A long while later, after his eyes had soaked in all that they could, Amasa went over to Kuriyayya and sat by his side. In a row on the other side and leaning against the wall were several large red and white parasols and whisks for the deity which had been put out in the sun to dry. In a nearby corner was a tall coconut tree, gently swaying against the sky. Amasa's eyes ran up to the top of the tree. Seven or eight large bunches of coconuts had weighed it down. When he ran his eyes down the tree he noticed that someone had painted the stem of the tree in stripes of white-lime and red earth.

He slid closer to Kuriyayya and said, 'Ayya!' Karuyayya looked at him askance. Amasa said excitedly, 'Look Ayya! Look! Someone's painted your tree with white-lime and colour.' Kuriyayya peered closely. He could see only a short distance, and then everything was lost in a haze. But what he saw was this; someone had used a coconut for sorcery and had buried it in the cremation ground. It had sprouted, cleft the earth and sprung up.

He had plucked it from there and planted it in the corner of the Mari temple, saying, 'Let it be here; at least as mine.' It had grown in front of his eyes; sprouting leaves and shedding them, bearing scars on its body where it had once borne leaves. It had grown taller and taller, and now stood fully-grown.

❀ ❀ ❀

As the festival days went by, relatives and friends from all around started descending one by one on the village. As usual they would first visit the Mari temple and then go about their business. Some would forget everything and settle down there to gossip. All the old scandals from the various villages would be dug up and updated. While all this was going on, in the yard Basanna was warming up the drum over a straw fire and turning it. A bunch of kids was jumping around him like an army of monkeys. Amasa was one among them. As Basanna raised the drum to his chest and beat it, its sound rang through *chad, chad, nakuna nakuna nakuna,* like a gong to the four corners of the village. Unable to resist, the kids around him started to dance. Basanna was inspired too and started to dance, beating his drum *dangu dangu dangu chuki.* The kids danced, Basanna kept step, all of them falling over each other and the passers by.

Heaven only knows who had taught Amasa to dance. He was easily the best of all. Everyone watched him in amazement. By then the women too had gathered around to watch. Bangari just couldn't take her eyes off Amasa. As she watched him, she once again felt a deep desire to have a child of her own in her arms. It had been six or seven years since she had been married; but so far nothing had come to fruit. Raging at people's taunts, she had even slept around a bit. Yet nothing had borne fruit. She couldn't afford medicine men and things like that; she and her husband were too poor for that. While women like her were already old by their thirties, she was one who could pass off for a new bride. Men who saw her couldn't help wanting her, even if for a moment— such was her bearing. And yet, nothing had come to fruit. Things couldn't go on like this forever. For a long time, as the night set in stones would start falling on her house, one after the other. Her husband would raise welts on her back, and hide himself in the house. The stones had since stopped falling, and the people had begun to forget. Now, in her eyes, Amasa continued to dance.

❀ ❀ ❀

While all this was going on, two landlords dragged in two fattened goats. The crowd instantly split into two. Children ran about this way and that. The goats panicked at the beating drum and started to pull away frantically. As the men holding them faltered, two more men joined in and holding on tight, stood them in front of the Mari temple. The frenzied drumbeat continued. The goats stood frozen, only their eyes rolled round and round. The temple stood in front, the silver deity shining through the open door. From within, billows of incense smoke wafted out. A man, wearing only a piece of cloth between his waist and knees, came out with holy water and a garland of flowers in his hands. He stood in front of the goats, closed his eyes and started to mumble. His dark body was covered with veins. They seemed to throb in time to his mumbling. He then cut the garland into two and tied them around the goats' neck.

Then he placed the loose flowers on their foreheads, sprinkled the holy water on their bodies and, joining his hands in prayer, said, 'If we've done anything wrong please swallow it, Mother, and accept this.'

His shrill voice resounded throughout the temple. But for the distant din, everyone around the temple stood with bated breaths. For a while everything stood still, except for the eyes of the goats, which were rolling round, and round. All of a sudden the goats quivered. The drumbeat rose again and drowned all other noise. The group moved on. A bunch of kids, including Amasa, ran behind it. The elders drove them away, but the kids returned the moment their backs were turned. The procession reached an open field. There, a well-built man stood casually by a tree stump, a knife in his hand. As two men held the goats by their fore and hind legs and stretched out their necks on the stump, the man brought down the waiting knife and severed the heads from the bodies in one stroke. Someone poured holy water into the mouths of the severed heads. They gulped a couple of times and then closed shut. On the other side the bodies were writhing. By now the heads lay still, eyes turned upwards. Blood spurted from the writhing bodies as they thrashed around drenching the earth red.

An adventurous on-looker shot into the middle and pulled from the goats' necks the garlands of flowers dripping with blood. Not satisfied with that, he draped them around Amasa's neck and instructed: 'Dance!' As the blood drenched his throat and started to drip down, Amasa panicked and ran. A few others followed. Even in his sleep Amasa saw only this sight. Several times that night Amasa sat up, frightened. They kept the lamps burning all through the night. The outsiders slept all around the temple, curled up in their white shawls. That night the Mari temple was lit up enchantingly.

That was also the night the railway gangman Siddappa had one too many. He had come with his belly full of spirits. It wasn't actually his fault. It was the spirit in him that played around with him that night. If he closed his eyes a storm raged within him. So he staggered around leaning on his stick, weaving aimlessly through the streets. When he came to a lamp-post he flew into a rage. He lashed out at it kicking and flogging it with his stick. The fury of it shook the entire neighbourhood.

Not content, he made it take on the role of the local politician, the contractor, his railway boss or the moneylender Madappa, and yelled at it; 'Bastard!' You think you are a big shot just because you go around in white clothes? You hide your face when you see me. Forget us, we are loafers. We hang out on any street corner. He let out a long wail and wept.

And then he continued with renewed vigour. 'Don't vent your anger on me. Look at him laugh at my words... Laugh, laugh away. It's your time to laugh. What else would you do but laugh? You are, after all, the one who uplifts the poor. Laugh... let the communists come. They'll put an end to your laughter. Till then you can laugh, so laugh, laugh....' His laughter and shouts rose and fell as he stumbled down the village street and whined through the cold, dark night. Unable to sleep through all this Amasa woke up with a start every now and then. This must have gone on for a long while. Nobody quite knows when or where Siddappa finally fell. His laughter, his shouts, simply died out.

It was dawn again. The village spent the morning yawning. Every verandah was filled with people. But still there were many who hadn't woken up. For instance, Siddappa. At noon, the Tiger dancers arrived at the Mari temple.

The headman's bond-servant came and said, 'The headman's house needs coconuts.' and before Kuriyayya could say yes, he had climbed the tree, plucked the coconuts, and was gone. Back at the houses, the women had oiled and combed their hair, decked it with flowers and were running in and out. The young men teased the passing girls and were chided in turn. The drumbeat of the Tiger Dance drew everyone to the Mari temple. Everyone was eagerly awaiting the arrival of the Tiger dancers. All of a sudden the Tiger's cage flew open. All eyes fell on it. A huge Tiger leapt out, holding a lemon in its teeth. The startled crowd moved back and formed a circle around him. A few more Tigers, a Hyena and a Clown emerged one after the other. Among them was a Tiger Cub too. After all of them had come out, they stood in a row, joined their hands in prayer to the deity and accepted the holy water. The dance began immediately after. The Hyena was the best of all, and his costume fitted him perfectly. Remember the man who had sported the knife so casually at the sacrifice yesterday? It was he. The crowds would run away when he strode towards them, keeping step with the drumbeat. When the dance came down the street, women and children clambered up the parapets and watched it, with their lives in their hands. The dancers had only to turn towards them, and they would dash into their houses and bolt the doors. The dancer continued, entered the landlord's street and danced in front of the village-hall. All the worthies, even the upper-caste ones, like the headman and the priest, had gathered there to watch the dance. They presented gifts to the dancers according to their status and expressed their appreciation.

Long after night had fallen and the dance was over, everyone in the village continued to see the dance and hear the drumbeats. Those who fell asleep and closed their eyes, as well as the men as they undressed their wives, saw only the Tiger Dance along with the drumbeat *dangu dangu dangu chuki*. The village headman, unable to sleep, came out for a stroll. The bondservant, who was awake, saw him and stood up. The headman put a *beedi* between his lips and struck a match. For a moment his face glowed red in the dark and flickered out. He gulped the smoke in silence for a while and then turned to the servant.

'The one who played the Tiger Cub. Whose boy is it?'

'That's Amasa,' came the reply.

'Who's Amasa?' enquired the headman.

'That's him. The orphan boy who lives there with Kuriyayya. That's him.'

The headman was astonished. 'My, when did he grow up so?'

Before his eyes, Amasa's Tiger Dance came dancing in its many and wondrous forms.

Translated by **A.K. Ramanujan** and **Manu Shetty**

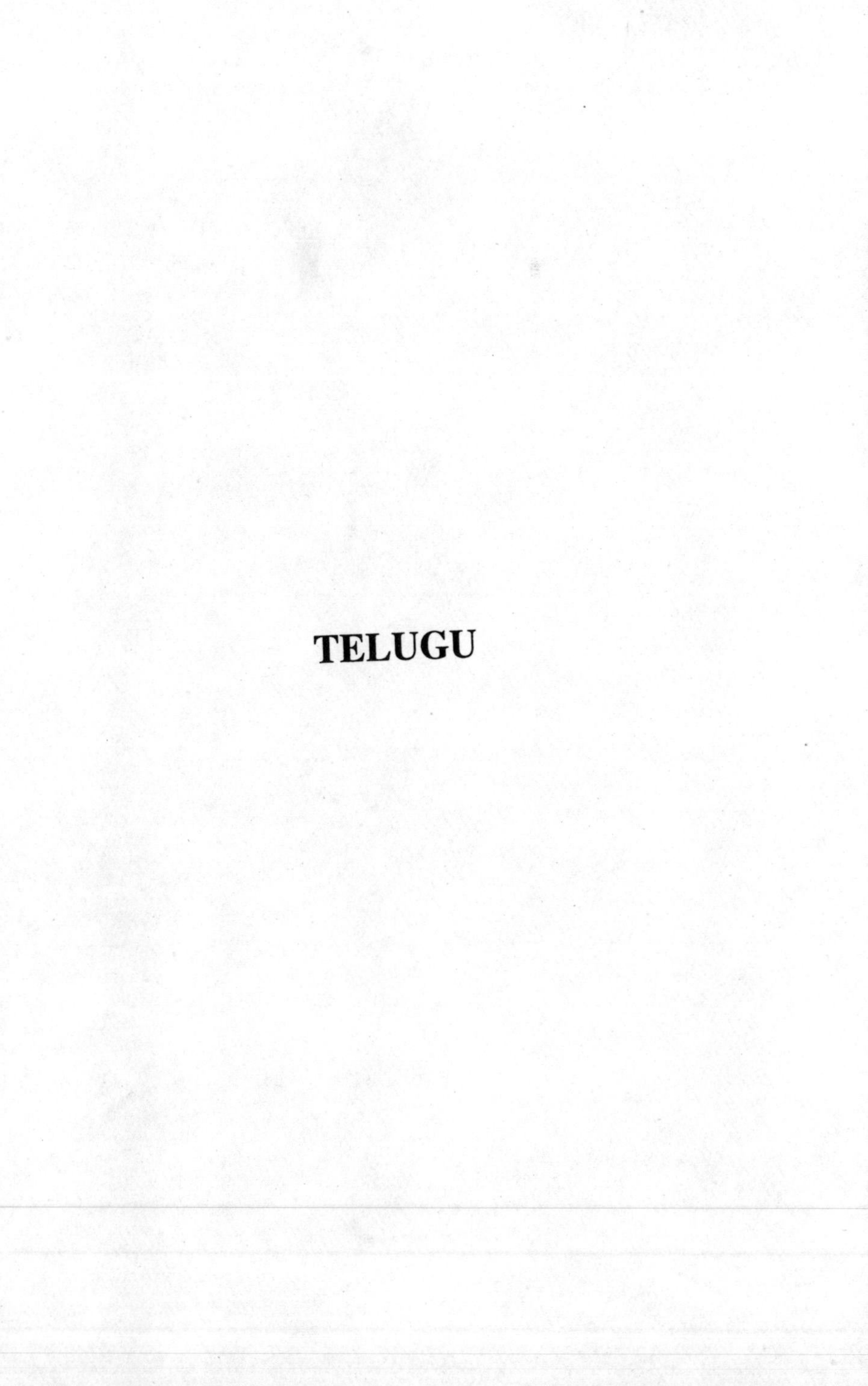

TELUGU

On The Boat

P. Padmaraju

After sundown the world was enveloped in a melancholy haze. The boat glided softly on the still river.

The water lapped against the sides of the boat in soft ripples. No life stirred as far as the eye could see, and the dead world hummed soundlessly. The hum was inaudible but the body felt it and it filled the mind with its reverberations. A feeling of life coming to an end, of peace inexorable and devoid of all hope, crept over one's consciousness. The vague, mysterious figures of distant trees moved along with the boat motionlessly. The trees, which were nearer, moved backwards, like devils with dishevelled hair. The boat did not move. The canal bank moved backwards.

My eyes looked deep into the still waters penetrating the darkness. The stars relaxed on the bed of water swinging dreamily on the slow ripples and slept with eyes wide open.

There was no stir in the air. The rope by which the boatman pulled the boat sagged and tautened rhythmically and the bells on the guide-stick in the hand of the leader tinkled at each step. At one end of the boat, there was the red glare of a fire in the oven, alternately glowing into a flame and subsiding. With a small bucket, a boy baled out the water percolating into the boat through small leaks. Sacks filled with paddy, jaggery, tamarind and other produce of the land were stacked in the boat.

I lay down on the top of the boat, staring at the sky. From inside the boat, tobacco smoke mingled with soft inaudible voices, spread in all directions. In the small room where the clerk sat, there was a tiny oil lamp, blinking in the darkness. The boat moved on.

A voice hailed us from the distance, 'Please bring the boat to this bank-this bank!'

As the boat drew near the bank, two figures jumped on the footboard. The boat tilted slightly to that side.

'Please do not mind us. We'll sit here on the top,' said a woman's voice.

The man at the rudder asked her, 'Where were you all these days, Rangi? I have not seen you for a long time.'

'My man took me to many places-Vijayanagaram, Visakhapatnam and we climbed together the Hill of Appanna.'

'Where are you going now?'

'Mandapaka. How are you, brother? Do you still have the same clerk?'

'Yes.'

The male figure fell down in a heap and his lighted cheroot, slipped from his mouth. The woman put it out.

'Sit down properly,' she said.

'Shut up, you bitch. Do you think I am drunk? I'll break your ribs if you disturb me.'

He rolled over from one side to the other. The woman covered him with the sheet of cloth which had slipped to one side when he had rolled over. She lighted a cheroot herself. When the match caught the flame, I saw her face for a brief moment. The dark face glowed red.

There was a hint of bass in her voice. When she talked, you felt she was artlessly confiding to you her innermost secrets. She was not beautiful; her hair was dishevelled. And yet there was an air of dignity about her. The black blouse she was wearing gave the impression that she was not wearing any. In the darkness her eyes sparkled as if they were very much alive. When she lighted the match, she noticed me lying nearby.

'There is some one sleeping here,' she said trying to wake up the man.

'Lie down, you slut. I'll break your neck if you disturb me again.'

With an effort he moved away from me.

The clerk stood on the footboard with the oil lamp in his hand. He asked, 'Who is that fellow, Rangi?'

'He is my man, Paddalu. Please do not charge us, sir, for the journey.'

'Is it Paddalu? Get him out! He is a rogue and a thief. Have you no sense? He's dead drunk and you have brought him on to this boat!'

'Why says I am drunk?' complained Paddalu.

'You fools. Throw the fellow out. Why did you allow him to step on the boat? He is dead drunk,' the clerk shouted to the boatmen.

'I'm not dead drunk. I have merely quenched a little of my thirst,' protested Paddalu.

'Why don't you keep mum?' admonished the woman.

'Please, sir, I beg of you. May God bless you, sir. We'll get down at Mandapaka,' she pleaded.

The man joined in the pleading, 'I'm not drunk, sir. Please be kind and allow us to go to Mandapaka.'

'If you make any row I'll have you thrown into the canal. Be careful.' The clerk went back to his room. Paddalu sat up. He was not really drunk.

'He will have me thrown into the canal—the son of a bitch!' he said in a low voice.

'Keep quiet. If he hears what you said, then we will be finished.'

'Let him look around the boat tomorrow morning. He puts on airs, the son of a bitch.'

'S..s..s. Someone is sleeping there.'

Paddalu lighted a cheroot. He had a very thick moustache. His face was oval. His spine curved like a bow drawn by a string. He was lean and sinewy and there was an air of nonchalance about him.

The boat was gliding along softly again. The boatmen were washing the utensils after dinner, talking among themselves.

It was not cool, but I covered myself with a sheet. I felt a little afraid of leaving my body exposed helplessly to the darkness. The breeze was sharp-the boat glided softly on the water like the touch of a woman. The night was wrapped with tenderness-as in the caress of an unseen woman. I felt lost in that embrace and many memories of my past as well as tales tinged with melancholy about woman tending man and bringing him happiness flitted across my consciousness.

At a little distance from me two cheroots were glowing red in the darkness. It appeared as though Life was sitting there heavily, smoking, and thinking about itself.

'Which is the next village on our way?' asked Paddalu.

'Kaldari,' said Rangi.

'We have a long distance to go.'

'Don't do it today. You ought to be careful. Not today. We will try some other time when it is safer. Will you not listen to me?' pleaded Rangi.

'You are afraid—you slut,' said Paddalu. He tickled her side with a dig of his finger.

'Oh!' she said and looked skyward as if she wished the feeling this gave her would last forever.

Gradually, I fell asleep. The boat moved downstream as if also in sleep. The two figures not far from me were talking in whispers to each other for some time. Though I was sleeping, a part of me was awake. I knew that the boat was moving, that the water was lapping its sides, that the trees on the banks were moving backwards. Inside the boat every one was asleep. Rangi moved from my side to the rudder and sat beside the man who was handling it.

'How are you, brother?' she asked.

'How are you?' asked the man at the rudder.

'Oh!' what wonders we have seen, my man and I! We went to a cinema. We saw a ship. What a ship it was! Brother, it was as big as our village. I do not know where its rudder was.'

She told him of a hundred things and her voice caressed me in my sleep.

'Oh girl! I am feeling sleepy,' said the man at the rudder.

'I'll hold it, you lie down there,' said Rangi.

The boat moved on silently-slowly. Without disturbing the silence, Rangi raised her voice in a song:

Where is he! Oh where is he, my man!
I put the food in the plate and
Sit there awaiting his return.
Like a shadow the night deepens,
But no sleep comes to my eyes-Where is he, my man?
The cold wind stings me like a scorpion
And my nerves contract and ache,
Unless you press me with your warm body
I may die...Where is he?—my man!

Rangi's voice had music in it. It seemed as though all living creatures heard the song in their sleep. Age-old tales of love reverberated sadly and mysteriously in that song. It spread like a sheet of water and the world was afloat in it like a small boat. Human life, with its love and longing, seemed heavy, inevitable and strange.

A little distance from me, Paddalu sat with his head covered with a sheet. But a gulf seemed to separate him from Rangi.

After some time Paddalu went inside the boat. I shook off sleep and lay looking at the stars. Rangi was singing.

You thought there was a girl in the lane behind the hut
And sneaked there silently.
But who is the girl, my dear man?
Is she not I in my bloom?

Rangi's song travelled through the worlds; then returned and touched me somewhere in my heart. I felt drowsy. In my sleep, the elemental longing of man and woman for one another danced before me like rustic lovers playing hide and seek. A dream world entirely new to me, spread before me in my sleep. Rangi and Paddalu moved about in a myriad forms. The song slipped away from my consciousness, and the doors of my mind were gradually closed even to dreams.

Some confusion in the boat woke me and I sat up. The boat was tied to a peg on the bank. The boatmen were moving about hurriedly in the boat and on the bank, with lanterns. On the bank two men stood on either side of Rangi holding her by her arms. One of them was the clerk. He had a piece of rope folded in one of his hands. It looked as if Rangi was going to receive a thrashing. I jumped on to the bank and asked them what was wrong.

The clerk's face flushed with anger. He said, 'The rogue has run away with some of our things. This daughter of a bitch must have got the boat to a bank while everybody was asleep. She was holding the rudder, the slut." There was a note of despair and helplessness in his tone.

'What were the goods stolen?' I asked

'Two baskets of jaggery and three bags of tamarind. That was why I said I would not allow them on the boat. I will have to make up the loss.' Then he asked Rangi, 'Where did he unload the goods?'

'Near Kaldari, my good sir!'

'You liar! All of us were awake at Kaldari.'

'Then it must have been at Nidadavolu.'

'No, she will never tell us. We will hand her over to the police at Attili. Get on to the boat!'

'Kind sir, please allow me to go.'

'Get on the boat,' he ordered pushing her towards the boat

Two boatmen dragged her into the boat.

'Sleepy beggars! Careless idiots! Have you no sense of responsibility? Why should you put the rudder in her hands?' The clerk was very angry. He went back to his room.

Rangi resumed her former seat. One boatman sat beside her to guard her. The boat moved again. I lighted a cheroot.

'Kind sir, spare me one too,' she asked me in a tone which suggested intimacy.

I gave her a cheroot and a box of matches. She lighted it.

'Dear brother! What can you gain by handing me over to the police?'

'The clerk will not let you go,' said the boatman.

'Is Paddalu your husband?' I asked her.

'He is my man,' she replied.

The boatman said, 'He seduced her when she was a young girl. He did not marry her. Now he has another girl.'

'Where is she, Rangi?'

'In Kovvur. Now she is in her bloom. When she has endured as many blows as I have, she will look worse than I do. The dirty bitch!'

'Then why do you have anything to do with him?' I asked.

'He is mine, sir!' she replied, as if that explained everything.

'But he has another woman.'

'What can he do without me? It does not matter how many women a man has. I tell you sir, he is a king among men. There is not another like him.'

The boatman said, 'Sir, you cannot imagine what this fellow really is, without knowing him. She was just bubbling with life and youth when she got entangled with him. One night he locked her up in her hut and set fire to it. She was almost burnt to death. It was only her good fortune that saved her.'

'I felt like strangling him with my bare hands. If I could have only got at him. A red-hot bamboo fell across my back from the roof of the hut.' She lifted her blouse a little. Even in that darkness I could see a white scar on her back.

'Why are you still with him after all this cruelty?' I asked.

'I cannot help it, sir. When he is with me, I simply cling to him. He can talk so well and my sense of pity wells up like a spring. This evening we started from Kovvur. On the way, he begged me on his knees to help him in this affair. He said he was completely broke.. We reached the Nidadavoli channel by a short cut across the fields...'

'Where did he land the goods?'

'How should I know?'

'Oh! she will never tell the truth, the rogue!' said the boatman laughing.

There was a sudden impulse of curiosity in me to have a close look at her face. But in that darkness, she remained hazy and inscrutable.

The boat crawled slowly on the smooth sheet of water. As midnight passed, the breeze developed a colder sting. There was a slight rustle of leaves on the trees. I did not sleep again that night. Rangi's guard tried ineffectually to fight his overpowering desire to sleep and finally yielded to it. But Rangi sat there listlessly smoking her cheroot, reconciled to her position.

'You were not married at all?' I asked her.

'No. I was very young when Paddalu took me away.'

'Which is your native village?'

'Indrapalem...Then I did not know he was a drunkard...Now, of course, I have caught it from him. There is nothing wrong if one drinks. But sometimes when he is drunk, he is wild.'

'You could have left him and gone back to your parents.'

'That is what I feel like when he becomes wild. But then there is no one else like him. You do not know him. When he is not drunk he is as meek as a lamb. He might take a hundred women, but he comes back to me. What can he do without me?'

The woman's attitude struck me as strange, and I could not divine what held those two together. Rangi said again. 'No job suited either of us. So we had to take to thieving. When my mother was alive, she used to scold me for making a fool of myself. One night he brought that girl to my hut.'

'Which girl?'

'The one he is now living with. He put her on my bed and lay down beside her. Before my very eyes! Both of them were drunk. The slut! I pounced upon her and scratched her violently. He intervened and beat me out of my breath. About midnight he went away with her somewhere. He returned again. I called him names and refused to admit him into the house. He collapsed on the doorstep and began to weep like a child. I was touched. I sat beside him. He took me into his lap and asked me to give him my necklace. What for? I asked him. He said it was for the other girl. I was beside myself with anger and heaped on him torrents of abuse. He told me, weeping that he could not live without that girl. My anger knew no bounds. I pushed him out and bolted the door from inside. He pulled at it for a while and went away. I lay with my eyes wide open and could not sleep for a long time. But after I fell asleep, the house caught fire. He had locked the hut on the outside and set fire to it. I tried the door desperately and at that time of the night my shouts for help did not reach my neighbours. My body was being fried alive. I fell unconscious. My neigbours must have rescued me in that state. The police arrested him the next day. But I told them categorically that he could not have been the author of the crime. That evening he came to me and wept for hours. Sometimes, when he is drunk he weeps like that. But when he is not drunk, he is such a jolly fellow. I gave him that necklace.'

'Why do you still assist him in these crimes?'

'What am I do when he comes and begs me as if his whole life depends on it?'

'Did he really take you to all those places, Vijayanagaram, Visakhapatnam and what not?'

'No. I wanted to gain the confidence of the boatmen. On two former occasions, this very boat was robbed.'

'What will you do if the police arrest you?'

'Why should I do anything? What can they do? I have no stolen goods in my possessions. Who knows who was responsible for the robbery? They might beat me. But ultimately they will have to set me free.'

'Supposing Paddalu is caught with these goods?'

'No, he would have disposed of them by now. I remained in the boat to give him enough time to effect his escape.'

She heaved a sigh and then said *sotto voce,* 'All this goes to that damned bitch. He will not leave her till her freshness fades away. I have to suffer all this for the sake of that slut.'

There was not a trace of emotion in her voice, nor was there any reproach. She accepted him as he was and was prepared to do anything for him. It was not sacrifice, not devotion, not even love. It was simply the heart of a woman, with a strange complex of feelings, tinged with love as well as with jealousy. There was only one outward expression for this medley of feelings and that was the longing she felt for her man. Every fibre of her heart thirsted for that man. But she had no demands to make of him, ethical or moral. She did not mind if he was not true to her, even if he was cruel to her. She loved him as he was, with all his vagaries and pettiness and with his wild and untamed spirit. What did she derive from such a life with the dice so loaded against her? What was her compensation? Was not such a life unhappy and burdensome? But then what was happiness except the lack of a consciousness of the unhappiness? Was I happy judging by that standard?

The wind rose gradually. The boat moved faster. There were signs of the world waking up slowly from its rejuvenating slumber. Here and there peasants could be seen going to their fields. The morning star had not yet risen. Rangi drew her knees closer, folded her arms around them and sat looking into the fading night.

'He is my man. Wherever he goes, he is bound to return to me,' she said slowly, not particularly addressing me. These words summarised the one hope, the one strength, the one faith that kept her irrevocably linked with life. Her whole life revolved around that one point. There was pity, fear and above all reverence in my heart for that woman. How confusing, grotesque, terrifying, even insane, are the affairs of the human heart!

I sat looking at her till the day broke. Before I got off the boat, I put a rupee into her hand without being observed, and went away without waiting to see her reaction. I never met her again.

Translated by the **Author**

Cloud Stealing

Malati Chendur

For three years the soil had not tasted a drop of rain. It was a town — a taluk headquarter renamed as *Mandala Kendra.* There are a lot of habitations in India where the land is not fortunate enough to receive even a drop of rain. There are several villages in Rajasthan where it does not rain for three to four years at a stretch. Scarcity of water is not a surprise and a small town not experiencing a shower is no rare phenomenon.

The inhabitants of this particular small town performed *Varuna Yagya* in the fond hope that the Rain-God would heed their repeated requests. And they fervently prayed to the local goddess to have pity on them. They even invited talented singers from a neighbouring town to sing *Amruta Varshini Raga.* One devout musician in wet clothes played on the violin non-stop for forty-eight hours. As tradition would have it, they performed the marriage of frogs, fetching water from a distant place, as all the wells had become dry. Even the groundwater disappeared and the municipality, which looked after the civic needs of the people was in utter distress.

'Frogs would be countless if the tanks were full' — sang Poet Vemana. But the water-tanks in that town had become waterless long back. Even the mud at the bottom had become dry. Frog marriage was performed in all its ceremonial pomp with *nadaswaram* and drums, but everything turned out to be futile. The God of Rain showed no consideration to these well-meaning townsfolk.

When will rain-water bless us? How long are we to depend upon water-tankers from the adjoining State?

These were the questions, tormenting all. How could they leave their ancestral houses, landed property, office and high school to migrate to a new place? It was impractical and impossible.

All the *Poojas, vratas,* festivities, frog-marriages had come to a meaningless end. When the entire population of the town was in a hopeless mess, there suddenly loomed on the horizon—rain-clouds. With deep concern they watched the clouds moving in the sky, entertaining fond hopes of the black clouds blessing them with a few showers. Every evening, people would come out into the open and watch the sky for a pleasant look at the racing black clouds. On the first day, they did not notice any airplanes but on the second, they did spot one, flying along with the clouds.

'Not one, but two.' said Chalapati, from his bridge table at the local Club.

'Could be some young pilots practising,' said Samba Murti, sitting calmly at the bridge table.

'It is no motor driving with an 'L' Board,' retorted Chalapati, making a dig at his friend.

Samba Murti, an Insurance Man, was in the mood of picking up a quarrel with Advocate Chalapati. He said, 'It could be a test-flight.'

'They do not allow test flights in inhabited places,' retorted Chalapati, after which both settled down to cards.

For about a week every evening, the people watched those black clouds along with the airplanes that constantly encircled them. The boys in the town spread the story that the 'planes were carrying passengers and the Pilots were waving coloured kerchieves to the people on the ground. One schoolgirl said it was green and the other swore it was red.

'I noticed very clearly the red kerchief,' said Parimala.

'Oh, that's why you are in a red border sari and a red blouse today. Maybe you expect the Pilot to lift you up from your backyard,' said Rekha.

'You are insolent. This is my normal dress,' said Parimala. Her secret had become public! In her heart there was a lurking desire to marry a Pilot who would make her fly like a bird. In uniform, a Pilot appeared to be a charming Prince to her.

'The sky has been full of dark clouds but there has been not a single drop of rain.' said Chalapati's wife Vandana that night to her husband.

'No thunder-no lighting. Clouds simply continue to chart the sky.' Chalapati responded to his wife's observation.

'You are always deeply engrossed in cards at the table. I wonder if you care to listen to thunder or see flashes of lightning. Cards hold your complete attention.' Vandana was quick to reply.

'Maybe they are supplying water through airplanes. There was no thunder, Dad, just the noise of airplanes,' said Rekha, Chalapati's daughter.

'Who said this?' Chalapati asked.

'Meenakshi's daughter-in-law Subhadra says, 'When water is being carried by shiploads to needy places, why can't this be done by air? Every evening they have been sending drinking water from Orissa to some place not far off from here.'

He never questioned the wisdom of the city girl, Subhadra. Who had spread this gossip? That night after dinner, he asked Rekha to fetch for him the entire bundle of newspapers of the month and arrange them date wise. He glanced through all the sheets carefully. When water could be transported by ship, there was nothing incongruous in its being carried by air.

After all, trains had carried water when the metropolis had faced acute shortage. Subhadra's statement could not totally be dismissed, he thought. That night he had a disturbed sleep. It was certainly quite unusual and unbelievable for airplanes to carry drinking water. Nowhere had it happened, as far as he knew. But his legal acumen could smell a rat. Every evening the airplanes drew the attention of the young and the old. Even the schoolboys and schoolgirls were observing them in anticipation. That particular morning on two occasions, he noticed those 'planes flying with the clouds. What was this mystery all about?

Around that time, Jagannath, his brother-in-law from the city visited them. Suddenly it dawned upon Chalapati that there was a border town of two neighbouring States.

'Chalapati, people in your town are no innocents. They have waylaid the train carrying water and have emptied all the tankers.'

'What is wrong in that? Some daredevils have looted the train— not for money or goods— just for drinking water.'

'We first thought of getting water by ship from Orissa but the Estimates Committee said that the price of doing so would be exorbitant. Then we thought of getting it by railway wagons but your townsfolk robbed us of the water intended for us. Now that transporting water by railway track has been ruled out and we wanted to avoid a law and order problem, we have devised a new method,' said Jagannath.

'What new method?'

Chalapati was taken aback for a moment but kept quiet, as restraint was the lesson he had learnt after joining the legal profession. That night he patiently heard his brother-in-law's narration of the new scientific method of driving clouds. The method adopted was similar to driving cattle. The clouds were made to obey the orders of the customers. Chalapati carefully assimilated all that his brother-in-law had said with enthusiasm. Next morning, he closely observed the two 'planes and the black clouds. That very afternoon he left for the State Capital.

Within a fortnight, Chalapati could successfully persuade the State Government to file a suit against the neighbouring State, alleging that they had been wrongfully stealing their lawful clouds in a crafty manner. By doing so, they had been reaping the benefits of rain water by depriving the aggrieved State of its natural right of getting water from the clouds which gathered within their territory and within the boundaries of their own State. The neighbouring State was forcibly robbing their clouds to enjoy the benefit of rainwater. This was outrageous, atrocious and highly immoral behaviour on the part of a responsible government. He prayed to Their Lordships to restrain the neighbouring State government from this gross violation of their natural rights. With misconduct and misuse of scientific knowledge they had been depriving their town and their people of the natural enjoyment of God's Rainfall.

'The Offender is a neighbouring State and if the case is filed in that State, we may not be able to get an impartial judgement due to pressure of public opinion' was one of the points mentioned in the plaint.

The respondent pointed out: 'This case cannot be tried outside our State's jurisdication as an accusing finger has been shown towards us. The neighbouring State is hurling a lot of allegations against us. In modern times, adopting scientific methods is no offence. We plead `Not Guilty'.'

This line of argument was advanced by both the States and argued to its logical end. After patiently listening to a series of arguments quoting several precedents, both the High Courts thought it fit to refer the matter to an Apex Court at New Delhi. Thus, the two High Courts washed their hands off the ticklish problem of deciding the rightful owner of the clouds in the sky. To whom did they belong? Clouds are not stationary; they do not flow like rivers within a geographical boundary. They appear in the sky in a particular season, taking on different shapes and simply gallop off on their way. They do not obey any man-made laws.

We have border disputes, river-water disputes, boundary disputes between countries, maritime rights of the sea and navigable rights of air space. These are all well defined. Disputes go to the International Court at Hague or to the United Nations at New York. There is a clear understanding about the utilisation of Outer Space as well. The Sun, the Moon, the Stars, the Milky

Way, Air, Water, Earth, Sky — to whom do they belong? The Sun God and Rain-God are the most ancient of gods. Clouds are said to be the Chariots of Rain-God. The rivers and the waterways belong to a country or a region. But what about rain — the gift of clouds?

Law became helpless in the matter. There were simply no precedents for the advocates to quote. When people in a particular border-town were experiencing water scarcity and purchasing water from nearby places to make both ends meet, was it justifiable on the part of a neighbouring State to spill carbonised crystals on the driven clouds to make them pour out rain water?

'Nothing wrong in Cloud Seeding. We have spent a lot of money in inviting the scientists and making this experiment a success. We have evidence of the huge amount spent on this project. It is no offence. We are within our rights to give the benefit of scientific advancement to our people. The allegation that we stole the clouds is baseless. Clouds never stay at a particular place — they drift perpetually.' That was the defense of the respondent.

The learned Judges of the Apex Court were in a fix. No national or international law could enlighten them on this particular case. They were not unaware that the aggrieved town had natural justice on its side and the arguments advanced by the defense had their own merit. They had spent a lot of money for Cloud Seeding. Enterprise, enthusiasm, excellence and scientific advancement were on their side. They did not hide any basic facts. Nor did they admit the allegation of theft.

'If scientific advancement is to be labelled as stealing, then we admit our guilt,' was their gallant admission.

The judgement had to be delivered and the entire nation was anxious about what the verdict would be.

'What a pity that Man has come to this pathetic plight of stealing rain clouds! What is the reason and what are the circumstances for such a steep downfall? Continents, countries

and States within States—these are all at the mercy of Mother Earth.

Mother Earth is one and indivisible. The seas, the rivers, the mountains, the forests, the air, water, sky, light, sun, moon and stars — all these belong to mankind and to all living species. Let not Man think all this is intended only for him. In his pride and pettiness, how often does he think that there is none to beat him? The fruits of Mother Earth are for one and all.

Who is responsible for this water scarcity and drought? Man. He cuts trees unashamedly for private gains and then experiments with artificial rain. Why doesn't he allow the natural phenomenon to benefit him in its own way? Stop deforestation! Grow more and more trees, instead of working as slaves in concrete jungles. If we look at Mother Earth with understanding, compassion and love, within a decade we will have plenty, instead of scarcity.

We find both the States to be culprits. We order them to plant a few thousand trees in the border area of the two States and report to us periodically of the progress made.'

❑❑❑

TAMIL

The Journey

Indira Parthasarathy

The sound of the newspaper landing on the *verandah* woke up Babu. It was daybreak and the golden sunlight was streaming in through the curtains.

Was it all right to read the newspaper, he wondered? What had happened in the Calcutta Test?… Couldn't listen to the commentary at all yesterday! Why didn't they have a radio in each ward in the hospital? Why did grandmother's condition have to worsen yesterday when the Test was at its most interesting stage! Does that thought mean I was not attached to her? If I had been, why wouldn't the tears come yesterday evening when she died?

This had been my first encounter with death. It was the machines that had kept her alive.... The oxygen cylinder, the iron lung... She was quite cheerful till the day before, but the whole situation had changed yesterday.

She couldn't speak but her eyes were eloquent. The doctors were amazed that she had not lost consciousness...

But then she had always been a stubborn person. Had she not refused to come and live with father until last month when she had relented? Was that why I couldn't cry?

When grandmother drew a deep breath and closed her eyes for the last time, father left the room abruptly, his handkerchief covering his face. It was much later that father could shed tears.

Mother just stood there, looking at father. Her problem appeared to be the same as mine. The tears would not come, however hard she tried....

What was funny was that mother's aunt, Periyamma, instantly set up a howl. No doubt she had been one of our family for years, but how could granny's death have affected her so deeply?

It is indeed an extraordinary feat to be able to demonstrate strong feelings one moment, to recover the next and become matter-of-fact immediately after.

Periyamma said in a low voice, 'It is our misfortune, Lakshmi, that she couldn't live to see Babu married.... Hmmm. It was God's will.... Now, how do we remove her bangle?... Thanks to those horrible doctors and their injections, her wrists are puffed up.'

Father's friend Venu, the Income Tax Officer suggested, 'Do you have a pair of scissors? We can cut it.'

'Ask the nurse,' said Periyamma.

With brisk professional efficiency, the nurse was removing the oxygen cylinder and covering the body with a white cloth. It was then that she noticed the wrist. 'This bangle...'

'Looks like we cannot take it off.... Do you have scissors?' asked Periyamma in Tamil. The nurse was a Malayalee, but knew Tamil.

'That won't be necessary.... You take hold of her hand.... It is easy...'

Periyamma took firm hold of the hand and the nurse pulled the bangle off.

'It is not the modern 16-carat stuff. It is solid old gold,' said Periyamma.

Venu weighed it in his hand.... 'Must be six sovereigns.'

'Babu, tie this bangle up carefully in your handkerchief,' said Periyamma.

'Are you taking the body home? Have you talked to the doctor?' asked the nurse.

'You keep it yourself,' I told Periyamma and gave the bangle to her. Tying it up in the *pallav* of her *sari*, Periyamma answered the nurse. 'How can we take the body home? We have a rented house... And an upstairs flat at that.... Can't they keep it here? We can take it from here tomorrow morning straight for cremation.'

'That is right.... I shall arrange with Dr. Satyanathan for it to be kept in the deep freeze,' said Venu.

'It will be difficult to secure room in the deep freeze,' said the nurse.

'Let me see,' said Venu.

'Shouldn't we consult Babu's father?'...asked mother. 'I shall tell Gopal. He will understand,' said Venu and went in search of father.

Father said nothing. He signed wherever he was directed to do so.

His eyes were red and his face appeared swollen.

On our way home, Venn said, 'It was not easy. Finally they threw out a post-mortem case and put the old lady in the deep freeze.... It became possible only because of my friend Dr. Satyanathan...'

'Granny was lucky'... I wanted to say. Perhaps I would have, if father had not been with us in the car... That seemed the only possible reply to Venu.

Father looked as if he had not slept at all last night. There he was now, sitting on his bed. He got up, walked to the window and remained there....

Gopal came back in, and drew the curtains. How different, he thought, was today's daybreak from yesterday's. I had a mother yesterday... Today she is gone. No, not gone.... Safe in the hospital deep freeze... How on earth did I acquire a philistine like Venu for a friend? He must have mentioned the old lady's deep freeze luxury at least a hundred times yesterday... But what would I have done without him yesterday? Preparing a list of those to be informed, sending off telegrams, arranging for the priest.... I couldn't have managed all that. For Lakshmi's aunt the whole event was routine. She had been married at the age of eight, widowed at ten.... had lost her parents before she was twenty... She was the first to appear whenever there was a death in the house of any relative.... A tear or two, then free advice on whatever was to be done... Babu told me that she had sent for the priest yesterday afternoon 'just in case'... Babu is a curious chap.... Assisting with the same enthusiasm at a marriage as well as a funeral. No ceremony, auspicious or otherwise took place in Delhi without Babu. And here I was, thinking of all sorts of things when trying to think of mother.

I do not have mother's grit. She said she would never come to Delhi and finally came only to be cremated on the banks of the Jamuna — died within a month of coming — she must have known. How many books she had read in this one month! I could not supply them fast enough for her — Four books a day — She never used to devour books like this — Why didn't I realise the meaning of her hurry?

Is there an appointed age for the loss of one's mother? The umbilical cord is cut at birth — Does the mother-son attachment come to an end with this physical severance? Can any pair of scissors cut the chain of memories that is one's heritage? That look mother gave me before she died.... What a history was contained in that look...a history that only she and I could understand.... That one moment was to me a glimpse of eternity.... I could not stay in the room after that.... My tears were the only answer I could give to that look of mother's. When my tears stopped, she was gone.

'I am sorry Gopal.... How sudden!' It was Raghavan's voice and Gopal turned.

Raghavan's mother had died last month. I was not able to manage the natural voice he used now. I have always been self-conscious.

'What was wrong with her?' asked Raghavan.

'Did he expect a reply?' Babu started to answer him. Lakshmi was wiping her eyes now and then to keep up appearances. But not Babu. He was probably upset that this grandmother had passed away during the Test match. He did ask his mother whether he could bring the transistor to the hospital but I had glared at him... Perhaps I need not have done so.... Why doesn't it occur to people that it is the decent thing to show respect to death even if they do not grieve for an old woman?

But then, it is only when the human being is respected as an individual that one can expect respect for the fundamental decencies of life... This is a democratic world. We function in groups. We kill each other in groups.... The achievement of the human intelligence is the power to destroy a whole city with one bomb — What a joke then to talk of respectability in the presence of death? Where's the individual man? We kill him in the name of democracy. So what if the man dies, democracy must survive!

'Mr Gopal, I am so sorry,' it was Bhardwaj, trying to look grief-stricken.

'She was all right last week.... '

Babu was perhaps tired of repeating the sequence of things. He went out of the room....

Babu picked up the paper from the *verandah* and went into another room. India had lost the Test. He was angry. He threw the paper away.

'Babu,' it was Periyamma. 'The priest has not turned up. Will you go and see if he is coming?'

'He is sure to come. It is only half past seven,' said Balu, who came in just then.

'Is he coming here or did he say he was coming to the hospital?'

'He said he would come to the house at eight.... If he is not able to make it, he said he would go straight there to make the arrangements and then come back to the hospital.'

'That is right. Why should be come here?'

Balu sat down and placed his bag on the floor. He took five or six packets tied up in handkerchiefs.

'I have brought change in four anna, eight anna, twenty paise and ten paise denominations,' he said.

'You have put yourself to a lot of trouble,' said Periyamma.

'Oh, no! This is nothing.... It is getting colder, isn't it? Particularly in the mornings?'

'Yes, we felt the cold last evening while coming back from the hospital. Thank God the old lady didn't die in mid-winter. Think of having a dip in the Jamuna in December...'

'Gopal bathes with cold water in winter also. He would have had no problem.'

'That is a bath under the tap at home. It is different bathing in the Jamuna.... Will this change be enough today?'

'More than enough.'

What did that mean, thought Babu. Enough for one more death? Balu had covered his head with a muffler. His bare torso was covered with a thick towel. He was smiling when he said, 'More than enough.' Perhaps he was admiring his own feat in securing so much loose change. As he counted the change, he looked up at Babu.

'Is he going to ask me also to count? Perhaps I had better leave the room!'

The hall was full. There were a number of father's friends. Venu was telling Rajagopalan about the deep freeze. Was it his regret that he had not been able to manage it for his mother who had died when he was ten? Poor thing, she had not been able to derive any benefit from her son's friendship with Dr. Satyanathan.

There was a sudden silence. Each looked at the other.

'Gopal!' called Balu from the next room. Father went in.

'The priest has fixed his time for reaching the hospital — after eleven,' informed Venu.

'It will be very warm after eleven,' said Vedagiri.

'Have you arranged for the van?' asked Krishnamurthi, looking out of the window. Perhaps he was making sure his scooter was safe.

'Oh yes.... From the hospital.'

'The hospital van is better than the N.D.M.C, van. All the vans in the municipality are rickety and old,' said Rajagopalan.

'But they go on increasing the taxes.... The water tax was 75 paise per 1000 gallons. Now it is three rupees.... Who shall we complain about this to?' grumbled Chakravarti.

'It is not the N.D.M.C. that levies the water tax. It is the Corporation. You are all mixed up,' Vedagiri corrected.

'Also, Rajagopalan was wrong in saying that the N.D.M.C. vans are old and rickety.... They are first class, new vehicles,' clarified Krishnamurthi.

'Are they better than the public transport buses?' asked Chakravarti.

'After all, it is a long distance journey. So it better be a better vehicle,' said Vedagiri.

Babu could not help smiling. Venu saw this and said, 'Babu, please call your father.'

In came a gentleman in a black suit. He was holding a walking stick and looked about sixty. Babu had never seen him before. Sitting down hesitatingly, he said to Chakravarti, 'I am sorry Gopal...How old was your mother?'

Chakravarti grew red in the face. 'I am sorry. I am not Gopal.'

'You are not Gopal? Who is Gopal here...'

What was this and why had he come if he did not even know who Gopal was?

Babu went inside and told his father about this stranger. Periyamma peeped into the other room, came back and explained,

'It is Vaikuntam Iyengar.... Lakshmi's mother's cousin. I sent word to him since I knew he was here.'

Babu explained about Chakravarti's embarrassment. Gopal said nothing but walked into the next room with his hands behind his head. He was sick of nodding his head in response to the words of condolence from perfect strangers. Why should Chakravarti not be Gopal for a short while? He was just a money making machine — no sense of humour whatsoever! Why couldn't this Periyamma mind her own business? Who on earth had heard of Lakshmi's cousin?

'This is Gopal,' declared Venu.

'I am sorry Gopal,' said the black suit. 'How old was your mother?'

Chakravarti got up and went towards the *verandah*. His face looked as though he was perpetually grieving over the loss of someone. I wondered how many times he had been asked this kind of question before? He seemed to have come to a halt near the balcony. Was he going to jump? They talk of transplanting all kinds of organs. Is it possible to transplant the face? Why, even the *Puranas* have stories of transplants! What about the *Puru-Yayati* story? That was a case of transplantation of the whole body! When I grow older, my face too will look like mother's did yesterday. I have to consign that body to the flames today...What a cruel joke...I do not remember father's death.... Why shouldn't we bury the dead? That would not be so heartless. But it is our belief that only if the body is sanctified by fire can the soul go to heaven. *Agni* is the purifier.... That is all the value attached to the body...Is it this body that was my conception of my mother? Or is it the chain of permanent memories that pervade my mind like the soft fragrance of joss sticks?

I must have been about ten or twelve. I was down with small pox. Burning pain racked my body. I could not sleep. I was very seriously ill that night. I was twisting and turning in bed. Suddenly, I looked at mother's face. She had been by my bedside day and night. That night her face appeared uncommonly effulgent, blood red by the light of the chimney-lamp. She was staring hard at me. The tears were flowing freely from her eyes and she made no attempt to wipe them away. I was suddenly beset by a doubt. Was it mother there or someone else? The next day the pain in my body disappeared. My mind could not understand this experience. There were many more, similar experiences...

'We should leave at nine for the hospital if we are to be in time,' announced Balu, coming in.

'We must pay the dues at the cashier's counter and hand over the receipt in the mortuary for the body to be released,' said Venu. 'Let us start.'

'There will be queues both at the cash counter as well as the mortuary,' warned Balu.

Will there be as long a queue at the mortuary as at the maternity ward? My worry is that I am also one of those in the mortuary queue.... After me, it will be Babu in the queue.... After Babu, his son.... I am waiting to become part of history. Each generation is a memorial to the previous one. The present is a reflection of the past.... Then, which is the real, and which is the copy? My head is reeling.

Babu came in. 'Periyamma says we should start.' Gopal took off his vest and covered himself with a towel.

Those assembled left one by one. Some, recalling their wives' injunctions regarding the proper practice on such occasions, moved away without a formal leave- taking.

The old gentleman in the black suit came to Babu and asked him, 'Are you Gopal's son?'

'Yes.'

'How old was your grandmother?'

Apparently he had not got an answer to this question from father. Why was he so interested in grandmother's age? Was it selfish interest in finding out, now that he had become an old man, at what age other old people were passing away?

'Sixty-five.'

The gentleman tapped his stick twice on the ground—lifted up his head and looked down. 'So I go,' he said with a smile. What did he mean?

The old gentleman left.

When everyone was out of the house, ready to start, Periyamma asked Balu, 'Have you got the sandalwood?'

'Of course I have it.'

'If you trust a job to Balu, you don't have to worry about it,' said Venu.

'Then I don't have to worry,' said Periyamma.

When she found that no one had understood her, she laughed and said, 'I do not know if my lot will be the Cauvery or the Jamuna.... What I meant was that, if it is the Jamuna, I do not have to worry.'

Babu couldn't help thinking of how Periyamma had tied the bangle to the hem of her *saree* the previous day.

The priest was waiting at the hospital. There were two others with him.

'There is a gate at the back. All the things are there. If you bring the body there from the mortuary, we can go directly. You do have mortuary receipt, of course,' said the priest.

'We have to make payment at the cash counter,' said Balu.

'If you go to the left, you will find a small building next to a big one. It will be open now. Make the payment there and bring the receipt to the mortuary...Right...shall we go now?' The priest sounded as if he was a daily visitor to the hospital.

The mortuary was behind the hospital. There was a big crowd

there. Black vans moved away from there one by one like laden lorries at a wholesale market.

'What did I tell you, it is quite warm at this time of the year,' said Rajagopalan.

'Do you remember when Santhanam died...Santhanam of the D.G.S. & D. in June.... My God! It was hot and we had a hell of a time,' said Krishnamurthy.

'Gopal is lucky that his mother died now...It is neither too hot nor too cold,' said Vedagiri.

'Have you arranged for the van from the hospital?' asked Rajagopalan.

'Yes...thirty-two rupees,' said Venu who had joined them just then.

'Thirty-two? It was only twenty-four or so two years back' said Krishnamurthy.

'Living is costly enough. Why should dying also be expensive?' complained Vedagiri.

'It is costlier to die than to live in our religion. That is why people used to live to be a hundred,' said father...Everyone looked at him in surprise. Babu too had not expected this remark from him.

'Apparently, you have paid an advance and the receipt is in your mother's name. The clerk said that for clearance of the dues, the balance would have to be paid by the person on whose name the receipt stands. When I told him that the lady was dead, he wanted a Succession Certificate. I had a job persuading him to issue the clearance,' said Balu.

'Who has gone to the mortuary?' asked Vedagiri.

'Venu. Come on, let us also go. Two more people would be useful.'

They brought out grandmother's body covered in a white sheet.

When they took off the cloth covering the face, father stared at it. His face remained wooden. It wore no expression.

The priest then, helped by two others, placed grandmother's body on the bier.

'The ladies can stop here. They don't have to go there,' said the priest.

'That is correct' said Venu. The priest chanted some *mantrams* and distributed the sacred turmeric-coated rice.

At last mother triumphed. There were two teardrops at the corner of her eyes. Periyamma wailed. 'I am only two years younger. I shall join you soon!'

She wiped her eyes and said to Babu in a low voice. 'Be careful when you get into the Jamuna. You are not used to it.'

'There is no water in the Jamuna at this time of the year,' said Balu. Though Periyamma had meant to whisper the words he had heard her.

'Why can't I also come along then?' asked Periyamma.

'That spot is not very convenient for ladies,' explained the priest.

Periyamma started to wail again. 'You are going all alone, leaving all of us behind!'

'We all have to go alone one day...Balu Sir, do you have the change?' asked the priest.

'Don't worry,' said Balu.

The black van now drew up close.

'Is this for us?' asked the priest.

Balu inquired of the driver and said, 'Yes, let us start.'

'Gaadi ke andar chaar admi baith sakte hein,(Only four people can sit inside)' said the conductor.

'Myself, Gopal, Venu, Balu, Babu...' counted the Priest.

'I am also coming,' insisted Vedagiri.

'He says that only four people can go,' said Periyamma.

'If you press two rupees into his palm, he will agree to more,' said the priest.

'You tell him that yourself' said Venu.

The priest muttered something under his breath to the conductor. The conductor looked at the ground, drew some figures with his nail and said something in reply.

'Right...all of you get in..... He has agreed.'

'Trust our priest,' said Balu.

The priest acknowledged the tribute with a silent smile.

Grandmother's last journey began. After passing *Purana Qila*, the van turned right into a small lane.

'Why is he turning into this? Is this a good road?' asked Vedagiri worriedly.

'First class road...It is new...It goes straight to Rajghat after crossing the bridge' assured the priest.

'Whatever its other lapses, the Corporation has been laying good roads atleast,' said Venu.

'What more do you want them to do?' asked the priest.

'Here, we have reached Shantivan,' said Balu.

'Yes, Rajghat, Shantivan, Vijayghat...' reeled off Venu.

'Look what a lot of advertisement for Gandhi Darshan,' said the priest.

'Is it advertisement for Gandhi Darshan or for telling the people, 'Look at what we have done to Gandhi,' asked Vedagiri.

'Both...looks as though Gandhi is the biggest industry now,' said Venu.

Gopal did not join in the conversation. Babu felt as if he were in the middle of a coffee house debate. It was only the firepot in his father's hand that drew one's attention to the body on the floor of the van.

'Here we are,' informed the priest.

The van stopped. The place did not look like a Hindu cremation ground. There was a lovely garden with a piece of modern art on the wall near the gate. There was a cool breeze blowing inside.

'There is a counter over there. Pay the usual fee and arrange for some firewood. I shall arrange for the formalities in this pavilion here,' said the priest. Balu and Venu went to the Counter.

'Gopal Iyengar, Babu...come with me. You can have your bath there,' said the priest leading the way.

'Do they provide firewood here?' asked Babu.

'First class firewood. It is used for *yagnas*. No bargaining as in our part of the country,' said the priest.

'This place does not look like a cremation ground.'

'Of course not. The crematorium in these parts is holy ground. Even the attendant here has to be addressed as *Panditji*... Grand-mother was lucky to have died here.'

'Will you please stop jabbering and shut up!' burst out Gopal, suddenly.

For the life of him the priest could not understand why he had shouted.

Translated by **K.V. Ramanathan**

Brahma-Vriksha

Prapanchan

We moved into our newly built house. Surprisingly enough there was a patch of vacant space in front of the house. It looked as though a four-cubit cloth was spread out there. We discussed endlessly about how to use it. In accordance with the custom of giving respect to the elders in the house, we first asked granny about it.

She advised that we could purchase a cow, tie it there and rear it — the traditional view. That would bring grace to the house. The arrival of a cow was something like the arrival of Lakshmi herself. The cow would yield milk. From the milk we could get buttermilk, curd, butter, ghee and other goodies. Those days every house had a cow. People have changed for the worse now, said she. Mother turned down granny's suggestion.

She said, 'All my life I have slaved for this family and have lost all the strength I had. As if that were not enough, should I now collect cow dung too?'

From the day she had come to the house as a young bride, she had been noticing things. Her sister-in-law had given her a rough time. She had to get up at four o'clock in the morning and was allowed to go to bed only at two o'clock the next morning. Even her husband could not be with her. She was not given silk *saris* on auspicious occasions. When all sorts of people were adorning themselves with diamonds, she was not able to wear even gold ornaments. On occasions of marriage she would feel ashamed because of all this. Thus she mused and finally came back to the world of reality.

She said, 'We can have a vegetable garden, plant lady's fingers, brinjal, tomato and other plants. These would be useful for making curry. We could even plant coriander.'

My younger sister Soundara opposed this suggestion vehemently. She was a student of Home Science. A friend of hers had jasmine, *kanakambaram* and rose in her garden. If these flowering plants were cultivated she could gather the flowers and adorn her hair with them. That would be a pleasant sight for all, she said. Flowers are wonderful. One should, after all, know how to enjoy beauty. Brinjal and lady's fingers were useful only for eating. Man did not live on food alone. Soundara lived on dreams.

The assembly dispersed without coming to any decision. All of us had many things to think about and do.

It was evening. Two days later, father called us and told us that we could plant a *murungai* branch in the vacant space. He gave us convincing arguments for his decision. Among trees, the *murungai* was the best. Its roots would not snake all over and pull down the compound wall or the foundation of the house. It would not fill up the entire space. Among greens, the *murungai* leaves were the best in quality. They were a very good expectorant. They also contained calcium. She could prepare *sambhar* with the fruit. Its aroma would enchant the entire village. You could make tamarind sauce too. Also, curry with coconut gratings. The tree would add beauty to the front of the house and provide a good canopy of shade. The heat of the sun would not come anywhere near the room by the roadside. The room would always remain cool. Father really likes *murungai*. I do too. Mother however, has no preferences.

Next morning, the son of my father's friend brought over a *murungai* branch. He woke up father and gave it to him. By that time we were already up and were taking coffee. It was a Friday.

Mother had taken her bath and had tied a towel to the end of her hair to drain the water out. Her face held a faint smile. She looked all the more charming.

Coffee was served to the boy who had brought the *murungai* branch. Father went in to take his bath. He usually took 30 or even 45 minutes to finish his bath. But that day he finished it very soon. He came out, water dripping and a towel wrapped around his middle.

Father had a silk *dhoti* and a silk towel. He used to wear these on occasions such as our grandfather's death anniversary and other auspicious occasions. Its colour was neither yellow nor brown but somewhere in between the two. The border was green and a span in width. When the rays of the sun fell on it, it sparkled. The *dhoti* and the towel would be used only on ten or twelve days a year. The rest of the year they would be folded and kept away in the almirah. They had a special smell. Whenever they were taken out of the almirah, the scent of camphor would permeate the entire place. When father was surrounded by that scent I used to like him very much. As though that day was special, father had the *dhoti* around his waist and the towel thrown over his shoulder.

The *murungai* branch had been cut only a few minutes earlier. Sap was surging from it. The fresh smell of a green tree emanated from it. The thin outer skin had been crushed and I could see the green inside. Father dug a hole and set the branch firmly at the centre of the vacant space. Mother helped him in planting it. When she bent down to hold the branch, the back of her shoulder became wet because of the towel tied around the coil of her hair. I was watching the fun of all this. Soundara ran, brought a bucketful of water and poured it all around the branch. Mother went to the neighbour's house, brought some cow dung and placed it on top of the branch. All through the morning the *murungai* remained the subject of our talks. Father and I went to our offices late that day, as did Soundara to her college.

For the next few days we completely forgot about the *murungai* branch. None of us felt as if the *murungai* had come into our lives.

One morning, Soundara woke me up from my deep sleep. She was agog with excitement.
'You devil, why do you pester me at this early hour?'

'Anna, come and have a look. The *murungai* branch has sprouted!'

Instantly I sat up. Both of us rushed to the wondorous spot. The entire household collected around the *murungai.*

The *murungai* branch looked stark and thin but on its bark at many places, there were green dots—dots like green grams stuck to the branch. I was thrilled to see the spirit of life throbbing and pushing its way up. Unaware of what I was doing I stretched my fingers to touch it. 'Shh, don't touch,' warned grandmother. 'You shouldn't point fingers at children, flowers and leaf buds. Shouldn't touch them either. Touching harms them.'

From that day onwards, the first thing we did as soon as the day dawned was to peep regularly at the *murungai*. Before our fascinated eyes, every node on its branch seemed to grow—the leaf buds, the tender nerves of the branches, the green pea-like leaves, the new leaf buds — everything unfolded before our enchanted eyes. One day, secretly, I plucked one—its only leaf, put it into my mouth and tasted it. It was delicious.

The first day when we used the *murungai* remains etched on my heart indelibly. Mother had to melt butter. Grandmother advised that if butter were clarified with *murungai* leaves it would have an excellent aroma. Mother followed her instructions. We used the freshly made *ghee* for lunch. Was it the peculiar quality of the *murungai* tree or the state of our minds? The *ghee* had a special taste that day. The leaves in the *ghee* were delicious. The tender leaves of the *murungai*! But the thought that mother should have plucked them thus and used them, disturbed me.

The *murungai* branch reminded me of Soundara because of the manner in which the sapling had grown into a full-size tree. Mother had given birth to Soundara at a time when the best part of her life had been nearly over. There is a difference of fifteen years between Soundara and me.

I had seen Soundara from the days of her childhood. I had seen the green tree from the very day it sprouted up. As a child, Soundara would turn on the mat and, seeing only a portion of my leg would cry. This was her signal to me that she wanted to be lifted. The tree swayed its small twigs in the breeze and drew me towards itself. A new skirt and blouse were stitched for Soundara on the day she went to school for the first time.

Time passed. In the dry, desiccated branches there appeared bunches of green fruit. Soundara matured. One day she was seated and garlanded in the middle of the hall. Her smile expressed her shyness. She ate *puttu* and *kali* and the usual rituals were performed. All these scenes of Soundara and the *murungai* passed through my mind one after the other.

When I took the cycle and started to go to office the *murungai* would wave its arms at me. It always appeared as though it was about to talk. Our conversation needed no words. Feelings were enough. Our eyelids became lips.

When Soundara occupied the chair in the middle of the hall, so did the *murungai*. Between its legs shadows gathered. Father and I decided to lean our cycles against the tree. In the noon day heat I would place my easy chair below the *murungai* and lounge on it. In the soft breeze and the delight of the shade I lost all track of time. It had become a matter of routine for me to read and write under the tree. Until darkness set in, my reading and writing would continue under it. Away from it, I just couldn't perform these simple tasks.

My college days were spent on the banks of the Kaveri. It was an ancient tiled house. I learnt Sanskrit here. Like the people of those days the houses too were big. There was a broad verandah and a courtyard in the middle. Inside the house, our teacher had a *murungai* tree. It was under this beautiful tree that I had my schooling. I always thought that if the tree had a tongue it would have recited *Ramasabdam* and *Godastuti* in a mellower tone and with a deeper devotion than I did. Sitting under its shade, countless students had been initiated into the world of learning.

One day, our teacher told us that the *murungai* was actually a *brahmavriksha*. Its bark, roots, leaves and other parts add to man's potency— the vital force that has perpetrated the human race. Brahma is the Lord of Creation; so also is the tree. Hence, it is known as *brahma-vriksha*.. From that day onwards, whenever I looked at the tree I saw in it the four-headed *Brahma*.. The teacher and all the children grew in the shade of the *brahma-vriksha*

A bridegroom was chosen for Soundara. She too liked him. The marriage was celebrated soon after. When she left the house with her husband she wept, as did father, mother, grandmother and I. Separation from relatives is always painful. I knew that among the loved ones Soundara would miss, the *murungai* tree would occupy the pride of place.

As days passed, women began to frequent our house. They were women of mother's age—women from the opposite house, the next house, and the third and fourth houses. They were a varied flock. They would be mostly stout or very thin because of their age. When I entered the house they would pass me by in a hurry. Their body odour would hit me right in the nose. The pungent smell of chilly powder, the smell of coriander, the odour of dirt, the stink of unwashed bodies—the stench would assail my nostrils. Unfailingly, each of them would clasp in their hands either a bunch of leaves or a few fruit. Pretending that they had come for something else they would appear highly elated, laugh and chitchat until mother plucked the fruit and gave them some. Mother was not the type to go to neighbouring houses to gossip. She was not interested in that. Therefore, women had slighted her earlier. But now they came to her because of the *murungai*.

All those who used the leaves of our tree told us that they tasted like honey and that the fruit was sweet. Mother would take it as a compliment to herself.

The tree's aim appeared to be to touch the sky. It had neither a thick growth nor was it stout and strong. Even though its top now touched the sky, to me my *murungai* appeared to be a toddler.

One day, several men, their hideous teeth popping out, came to cut down all the trees in our area. They put up stones one over the other and built houses and crematoriums there. As a result, all kinds of birds left their nests and flew over the sky. Our *murungai* tree became an abode for crows and sparrows.

The sound of human beings and the roar of machines began to offend our ears. But that passed too and the chatter of birds became music once again for us. We could see the top of the *murungai* tree through the window of my room upstairs. I could see it even while lying in my bed. I become addicted to opening my eyes only after hearing the songs of birds.

I loved seeing the first pale streaks of dawn when the rays of the sun had not yet touched the earth. I enjoyed hearing the chirping of a house sparrow, the cawing of a crow or the rare twitter of a *mynah* and the sound of a *karuvaattuvali.* We felt surprised at how people lived by themselves in their houses. It was the world of birds which welcomed our dawns with eagerness and joy. Their enthusiasm and playfulness would remind us of the romping of children in the *maidan.* They would spread their wings and hop from one branch to another. They would brush their chests with their beaks. In the evenings, they would appear to be different and call out in different notes. In their tones could be felt their contentment. Also, the peace and the anguish that the day had come to an end.

When we looked at the *murungai* tree filled with birds and loaded with fruit. We felt that it resembled a grandfather jumping up and down with his grandchildren on his shoulders. All of a sudden it would heave a sigh as though it had completed a thousand years. That would be a sad sight. But immediately it would dance up in joy like a youngster.

Not a day would pass in our house without a dish being cooked with some part of the *murungai*. We had *murungai* fry; *murungai kootu, murungai sambar*. The *sambar* had its own mouth-watering taste. I liked it very much. The fruit would be used to make a tangy sauce or fried. One such dish always adorned our dining table. We loved every produce of our tree.

One day, a headmaster came and occupied the third house from ours. He was the senior most teacher in a very big school. He ignored us. It was as if we were insignificant creatures for him. On seeing us, he would walk straight ahead, looking up at the sky. One day, the man in the opposite house tied his cow to the pillar in the verandah of the headmaster's house and started milking it. The headmaster came out and began hopping up and down in a fit of temper. His hair was dishevelled and his cloth and towel fluttered around him. People of the entire street heard the grating in his voice.

Another day he came to see me. He was in his official dress. We chatted about the declining standards of everything—from modern education, to cinema, to flour-machines, to family planning—all in Elizabethan English. No, that is wrong. He alone talked.

Finally he exclaimed, 'Hey.. a *murungai* tree...' There seemed no need for me to confirm his statement. I plucked some fruit and leaves and gave them to him. He had a fine set of teeth.

Monsoon arrived. It had now become impossible to sit under the *murungai* tree in the evenings. There would be a sudden downpour of rain. Nature did not fail in her duties. There was a chill in the air and it was more pleasant to sit inside the room. The mud road became wet and marshy. One had to be careful while walking. Often, the wind would roar and lash about, hindering daily life. Wild winds swept past our village.

One day, as I was leaving for office, it started to rain. A strong whirlwind swept past. Windows rattled violently, making us afraid. And then, just as suddenly as it had erupted, the whirlwind stopped. There was perfect calm as I returned home for lunch.

In front of our house I saw a huge crowd of children and old people. The *murungai* tree lay stretched across the entire street. Its twigs appeared like slender fingers, beseeching help.

People flocked around it, tearing out as much as they could of the leaves, fruit and branches. Even while we were watching all this, the place where the tree stood was tidiness itself.

Mother, father and grandmother were standing a little further away, their faces distraught. I took the cycle and stood it at its usual place— a habit I had acquired since the tree had come into our lives. The tree appeared as though its waist had got broken. Half of it was sunk under the ground and the other half was dirt-streaked.

Only the next morning did I feel the impact of its absence. Yesterday it was there. Today it was not. Only the stump remained.

More days passed.

One day, I came down from upstairs for my morning coffee and as usual stood by the *murungai* tree. A miracle was waiting for me there.

From the stump of my ravaged tree, a small sprout peeped out.

It was life.

Translated by **M.S. Ramaswami**

DOGRI

The Farm

Chaman Arora

It took me four days to take over charge of my new job. The beauty of the valley captivated me. What a lovely place! It seemed a far cry from our *kandi* where even a blade of grass did not grow, and which many rainy seasons skipped without shedding a single drop of water. Here I could see green fields and water everywhere—a rivulet here, a stream there and springs all around. No berry trees or *brainkhads* here—only tall pine trees and high rising deodars. No hot *Loo* here—only an invigorating coolness. The valley's beauty seemed opposite of what its name—*Karsog* (literally meaning, 'condole'), suggested.

It was evening. But an evening in the hills is very different from that in the plains. Here the sun disappears behind the hills much before the birds stop twittering. In our parts, it is not evening till the sun, looking like a ball of fire has rolled down somewhere below the earth's rim and until flights of sparrows and crows have taken shelter in the leaves of banyan and berry trees. I noticed that in the hills the sun did not set; it just disappeared.

Putting my signature on the charge-sheet forms, I looked at the *babu* whom I had just relieved. Suddenly, I remembered something and inquired, 'There are only three gardeners for an area of twenty acres. How is the work managed here? Is it easy to hire labour?'

He hesitated awhile and then began to laugh. I noticed that when he laughed his eyes narrowed. He was also squint-eyed. 'There may be problems on other farms. But not here. Here we can always get labour and good labour at that. Otherwise these hill people would not care to even pee at a bleeding finger.'

I was relieved, even pleased to hear that. Next morning I asked Milakhi Ram, the gardener, to get some labourers for weeding the rice field. Fifteen to twenty workers turned up. I noticed that there were more girls and women among them, their ages ranging between sixteen and fifty-five. I had never before employed women. I asked the gardener whether there was any problem in getting men. He assured me that if the women did not work properly he could throw them out. But they had been working in this farm ever since its establishment. He explained to me that otherwise too, in these hills women did most of the work on the farm and in the fields, except ploughing.

'Sir, all of them are dependent on the farm for their livelihood and with them around we have never felt any labour shortage. That is why this farm is famous in the whole of the district. Every *babu* who has left this farm has now become an officer.'

I nodded my approval. Milakhi Ram started assigning work to the labourers and I went across to my quarters. After breakfast, lighting a cigarette I looked out. Green fields stretched right up to the foothills of Kailodhar. Beyond them lay forests of pine and deodar and kail, and still higher, white snow rested on the tops of mountains and hills. What a lovely landscape! Then I turned my eyes to the fields. Red, blue and yellow scarves tied on the heads of the girls and women seemed to bob up and down. *Shalwars* tucked above their calves and hands busy weeding grass, the women presented an enchanting picture. The only sound came from the rising and falling of *bhakhs.* I felt light and pleased with myself. After watching this scene for many days I started feeling that the women were indeed indispensable to the farm.

There were the older ones—Bilmoo, Seti, Malati, and the middle-aged ones—Murtu, Durgi and Papalu, who never missed a day's work. Then there were Bishno, Savitri and Kamalo who worked less but were more lively and full of fun. They were young and pretty and laughed uninhibitedly. In movement, their red, blue and yellow scarves looked like butterflies in flight. I felt like *Kahna* among *gopies*.. I would keep standing at the boundary on pretext of supervising their work. My eyes would sometimes wander to the collars of their shirts and at other times catch the beauty bursting out of their torn clothes. I would pull up one and get blessed by another. Thus my days passed. B*hakhs* livened the weeding of rice fields and the digging of maize fields.

One day Milakhi Ram said to me hesitantly, 'Sahib, you are still alone. Days pass somehow. I wonder how you pass the nights. If you wish, shall I make some arrangement?'

I gave him the go-ahead signal but on condition that no one should get to know of it. The same night Savitri came to me. What I had considered as the most difficult act till my age of twenty-one turned out to be such a simple matter!

That night I grew up from an awkward boy of twenty-one into a man. After that it was sometimes Bishno and sometimes Kamalo who continued to help me become a full-fledged man. In order to please them I would always give them something—sometimes hay, sometimes corn and sometimes money. It did not cost me anything. I was surprised that nobody talked about this matter. Savitri was the prettiest of the lot and it was she who kept me company on most of the nights.

The rainy season had just got over. Crops started changing colour. They turned from green to red and then donned a golden coat until the plants started dancing in the wind. Their beauty was too much for them to hold on their own: it called to be reaped.

That night it was Savitri. Somewhere near, a drum was beating; *bhakhs* were being sung and perhaps *nati* was being danced. Just then Savitri told me that a 'little babu' was on its way. The sounds coming from outside turned into a pandemonium. Each beat of the drum was like a hammer blow on my head.

The crops were good that year. Therefore, every night there would be drum beating and *bhakh* singing, sometimes on one side, sometimes on the other. It always seemed to me as if a crowd was coming to my quarter, raising their voices and brandishing their arms. And then the pounding inside my head would begin.

The paddy was harvested, but the hammer blows inside my head. I ceased to listen to the music of the mountain hills or enjoy the beauty of Nature spread out in front of me. The mountains now appeared to be like walls. I felt encircled by tall pines and *deodars* with no way to get out. The encirclement seemed to be zeroing in on me. I felt the noose rolling down from the tops of hill ranges, passing over the pines and *deodars*, coming down, stepping over the barbed wires around our farm, and closing in on my quarters. Sometimes, lying in bed I felt as though somebody had clutched at my heart. There was no respite from the hammering in my head and chest.

I thought of my mother and of my younger sister. What would they think when they came to know of this? Why had I done it? How would I get out of it? Sometimes I consoled myself with the thought that Savitri was not involved with me alone, but must be having other lovers too. Yet what seemed strange was that nobody had said anything to me so far.

Milakhi Ram seemed to have sensed what I was going through, as I had not sent for any girl for many days. It was an off day perhaps. I was reading the newspaper seated in a chair in the courtyard of my quarters when Milakhi Ram came in. He had with him three or four small boys. A handsome one— about five or six years old struck me. The little boy looked at me and smiled. When he laughed, his eyes narrowed a bit. I noticed that he was squint eyed. I beckoned to him to come closer but he didn't and continued to laugh from afar.

Milakhi Ram said, 'Sir, can you guess whose son he is?'

I remembered that I had seen someone who resembled him. Who was it? I could not recollect. Suddenly my predecessor's face flashed before my eyes. The same hesitant smile, the same squint eyes. The hammering in my head started again and my face became flushed.

I looked towards Milakhi Ram. He was smiling. The blue gums over his yellow teeth gave me a strange feeling of revulsion. His upper lip was raised like a dog's.

I turned white and blurted out. 'The previous *babu*?'

The hunter was quick to grab its victim. 'Yes, sir! the previous babu. . .You have got it right. But why are you alarmed? You are not going to remain here forever. A year, or at the most two or three years. Then a new *babu* will come. This Murata and Durgi and Papalu,Kamalo, Bishno, Savitri, they are all products of this very farm. And they are all here to render services at the farm, whatever the form of service. This arrangement must continue, otherwise there will be a dearth of labour here also. After all, *Sahibs* must leave behind some memento!'

Wheat began to be harvested but Savitri did not come. I learnt that she had given birth to a daughter.

I could clearly see what Savitri's daughter was going to undergo fifteen- sixteen years hence.

I wished I could get myself transferred to another place before seeing the face of the infant at Savitri's breast.

❑❑❑

Dislodged Brick

Om Goswami

A *koel* was cooing. But Kalo was silent. The bunch of boys was laughing. Kalo was quiet. Amman's corpse was empty but Kalo's eyes were full. Memories had become congealed like ice at a spot beyond thought — a wordless realm. There was a certain void in the mind which rankled somewhere inside.

She cast a glance towards the park. Bapu was digging in the dahlia flower beds behind the *saintha* and *mehndi* plants. How thin he had become in a single day! Eyes swollen and a deep red — like the red petals of *malwa*. Hair dishevelled like the grass in the lawn.

She wondered and kept wondering for a while how they would live without Amman. Amman, whom she had seen and lived with ever since she remembered. Amman would be sweeping the lawn with a broom and she would be holding the end of her *dupatta* which trailed along. She would watch the children playing in the park timorously. She felt like playing with them. Seeing her looking at the children thus, Amman would say, '*Kaffanus!* the day has just begun and they've come to spoil the place.' Amman had got a tiny broom made for her, just like a toy, with a red handle and sticks of different colours tied together. She would sweep with great enthusiasm the interior of her little hut.

Both she and Amman assisted Pheenu in his work but still he had so much to do that he became tired. How difficult it was to complete all this work and keep the long park spread on both sides of the canal tidy! It was too much for a single man — picking up leaf plates, fallen leaves, empty matchboxes, cigarettes stubs, bits of papers. It could drive a man out of his wits.

People simply came, spread a lot of litter and left. Pheenu would survey the whole thing in the morning, get annoyed and then start cleaning up.

'What do these bastards thinks? They spread offal and go,' Amman would start swearing in a quivering voice.

The flow of water in the canal was closed during the winter months. The canal looked like the bed of a dry drain. The number of visitors had also dwindled. Only in the afternoons and evenings some people came, ate what they brought along, played cards or just lazed around. They would pick the leaves of flower plants or split canna-leaves and crush them with their fingertips. Amman hated these people, 'Why can't they eat and drink at home?' she would say. 'The trees are without leaves. It is not spring and there are no flowers. These rotten people come here only to spoil the garden.'

'Fun lovers revel even in cremation grounds, Amman! What do they have to do with spring or autumn?' Pheenu had tried to make her see the point every now and then during these ten years.

Amman would offer thanks-giving when the dry grey season ended. She wished that *saabs* from the city would come with their families and spend their afternoons in the park, and children would chase butterflies. In summer, when there was a rush of people, the number of those who came to the park to drink, decreased. All told, summer suited all the three of them when the whole park turned into a fair. They had to work till late in the night. It would sometimes be daylight while they were still sweeping the litter. Sometimes they would find some small treasures in the heap of sweeping — spoons, cigarettes; notes, small coins. The canal flowed with snow water from the Chenab, Amman took her bath thrice a day or sat on the square stone slab placed under a *sheesham* tree on the water's edge, with her feet dipped in the cold water. A branch was bent over the stone slab and thick leaves spread a sort of umbrella overhead. In the scorching heat, when some wandering whiff of breeze shook the tender leaves, Amman would start humming some *Pahadi* folk-song. Kalo wondered how Amman's voice became so sweet at such moments. If one were to hear her shouting abuses, one would close one's ears and jump into the canal. That slab was Amman's throne on which she sat like a Mughal queen, surveying the *meena-bazaar* of the fair.

In winter, work was less but there were no gains. At best, they would find some half a quarter liquor bottle among the cypress bushes, which could be sold for a few *annas*.

Amman waited impatiently for the onset of summer but when it came, she started feeling fed up. Hearing the interminable noise of people, she longed for winter. While waiting for winter, she had encounters with several men and women. Those who tasted these encounters did not dare to talk to her again.

'The old hag looks every inch a witch.'

'She can fly in the air and gobble up a sparrow's liver.'

'She changes herself into a witch at night. Then her eyes burn like lights and her hair is let loose.'

Gossip of this kind was indulged in by the children of clerks who would go to the park to pass their afternoons. These children repeated what they heard from their mothers, like parrots. Then such talk would travel to the children of petty vendors who played truant from school and came for a cold bath. The gossip then gathered more floss. Some children rubbed sandy soil over their bodies, seated themselves under the shades of trees and narrated stories heard from their uncles and those concocted by themselves. As the lips of the raconteurs moved slowly, those of the listeners trembled, their eyes widened as though ghosts had really descended around them. Vendor Sharma's little son said, 'If you see a ghost or a witch, you should repeat the Hanuman *mantra.*'

'Will the ghost allow you to do all this?'

'Be quick with it, mentally. Hanuman is so powerful!'

All the boys had their faces shadowed by dread. The whole

group looked up to the young Sharma. He knew more than the others. But Kaku bucked all of them up. 'If you have a piece of iron in your hand, no evil spirit or ghost can come near you. Or you should have fire in your hand. It can be a lighted cigarette also. The ghost will simply flee.'

That day other boys were surprised to see a steel bangle in Dayal's wrist and a lighted cigarette between his lips.

'One should have all one's weapons ready. One never knows which weapon will work against the ghost.' said Dayal.

The next evening all boys except young Sharma came equipped with steel bangles and cigarettes as soon as it was dark. Sharma looked odd without the bangle and the cigarette. He begged Dayal to give him his bangle.

'You get another. I've spent full four *annas* for it.'

'Is this how you value friendship? I'll tell your brother that you smoke stealthily.'

This strategy worked. Dayal removed the bangle from the wrist and gave it to him, saying. 'There is one condition, however. You should teach us the entire Hanuman *mantra*.'

'Yes, Yes,' shouted all of them: some of them threw up their cigarette packets in the air to catch them falling. It was decided that like the school prayer, Sharma would pronounce the *mantra* first and others would repeat it after him, like a song. In order to purify themselves before singing the Hanuman *aarati*, they jumped into the canal. Then, coming out of the water, they sat in a circle under a mango tree and began singing: "*Aarati keeje Hanuman Lalaki.*" But when they saw the old woman coming towards them with a twig in her hand, they started shivering with fright. They showed their steel bangles, lighted their cigarettes and puffed at them singing — "*Aarati Keeje Hanuman Lalaki, dushta-dalan Raghunath Kalaki.*" On the one hand, the cigarette puffs made them hiccup, and on the other they were seized with a fear of the old witch. They were shivering. Singing the *Aarati* loudly, they began to take to their heels. If only one of them would take the lead!

They looked at each other for support. Suddenly the old woman turned back, and they heaved a sigh of relief.

'See how powerful the *Mantra* is! The witch had come so close and yet she turned back,' they told each other.

They would come to the canal for a cold bath and repeat the *mantra* over and over again. And when they started this topic, a sensation of fear would run through them. That is why, even these stale stories tasted fresh.

'If you come across a puny ghost, catch him by his hair and lift him into the air. Never allow him to touch the ground. Then you can have control over him and make him do things for you." Sharma would tell them. Then they would talk of how a *jogi* conjures up a ghost, how *a jogan* takes *jadian* by becoming stark naked and putting her hands behind her. And if she does not transfer them to another for six months, they start troubling her inside. How a *duala* makes a ghost dance, how people master ghosts on moonlit nights, sitting in cattle pens.

Then all the boys would imagine themselves to be master *dualas* whom no ghost, no *dakinis* could harm. Sometimes, they would shed all fear and walk up to the old woman's slab. One day the old woman asked little Sharma, 'Why do you smoke?'

Nobody replied. It were as if they had been stunned into silence. Suddenly, an unripe mango dropped on the bank opposite. The boys looked in that direction. The old woman said. 'Go take it.' Dayal was crazy about unripe mangoes. As he made to move towards the fallen mango, Sharma caught him by the shoulder and took him aside. 'Nobody should touch the mango. The old woman must've used her *mantra* on it. Didn't you see that even the crow dropped it?'

'Oh, yes! Maybe the same crow is the keeper of her life breath. How cleverly she asked you why you smoked. The cigarette has fire at the burning tip and because of this she can do us no harm.'

Meanwhile, Dayal took out his *gulel* and aimed it at the crow sitting on the mango tree across the canal. The stone flew and there was the sound of *chhar-chhar* among the leaves. Some crows shrieked *caw caw* and flew off. Another unripe mango fell on the ground.

'Don't touch it. It's all the old woman's *chhala-vidya*.'

'Why does she keep her feet submerged in the water, *yaar?*'

'Her feet are facing backwards, she does not want to show them.'

It was decided that an effort should be made to see her feet, by repeating the Hanuman *Mantra.* And the crow that kept her life breath should be shot down. The next day each one of them came armed with *gulel*.. They shot at several crows but could not hit any. A stone or two hit some passerby and Dayal had to take a few slaps.

Seeing the falling leaves, Kalo told the boys, 'If you need unripe mangoes, I shall get them down for you.'

Sharma was the commander of the corps of boys. He shouted at Kalo. 'We don't want any mangoes. Who are you to give them to us?'

'If not unripe mangoes, then is it the leaves that you want?'

'We want that which keeps the life-breath of the witch.'

'I see.'

'We shall finish it. We have *Hanuman Shakti* with us.'

'But all the crows have flown away. You are throwing stones on branches of the tree.'

'Then what should we do?'

'I shall call the crows.' Saying this, Kalo imitated the call of crows. The crows flapped their wings on the trees at some distance and started floating in the sky. The boys broke into a dance of joy. The crows responded to the call of *caw-caw* and returned. The boys shouted. *"Pawan-Sut, Hanuman Ki Jai"* and filled the sky with stones.

Just then Amman arrived on the scene tapping the ground with her staff, looking for Kalo. Seeing the boys shooting at the crows, she cried, 'You should go to hell.'

'The witch, the witch has come!' shouted the boys and ran off. Kalo kept standing, crestfallen and sad. What was all this? Kalo felt her blood freeze in her veins. The witch could tear her up and gobble up her heart. But this was Amman. Her own Amman. Even so, Kalo said in fright, 'They were saying that you are a witch, and your life breath is imprisoned in a crow. They are out to kill that crow.'

'What?' cried the old woman, 'they called me a witch! I shall teach them a lesson that they will remember all their lives.' Her words reached the fleeing boys. 'See, how the old woman senses human presence. She rushed for the smell of human flesh.'

The boys were convinced that day that the old woman was surely a witch. There were consultations and it was decided to espy her feet. Dayal said that he would dive into the water, go near her quietly and thrust a *babul* thorn into her feet. And when startled thus, she would take her feet out, everyone would get a look at them. He filled his lungs with air, sang the *Hanuman aarati* in his mind and entered the water at the bend. His other companions hid themselves and waited to see the old woman's feet which rested in the sand-tinted waters of the canal.

All of a sudden, the old woman shrieked, scared out of her wits. She thought that some water-snake had bitten her. Old age and light body. As she pushed her legs, she slipped from the slab and fell into the water. There was a rumbling sound in the water. Kalo shouted for help but all those who collected around just looked on. No one wanted to pull out the sharp-tongued old woman. At last, Pheenu jumped in and rescued his mother from the jaws of icy death.

None of the boys had been able to see the old woman's feet. All of them had fled as she fell in to the water.

For a few days, Amman's stone slab seat remained unoccupied.

There was not the slightest change in the old woman's nature. 'Let the scoundrels come. I'll teach them a lesson!' Amman was showering abuses on their airy existence. Pheenu thought she was annoyed with those who had spread litter. Kalo knew she was referring to those boys.

Amman sat muttering something to herself. One moment her face would be overcast by a frightful shadow of death and at another it would start flushing with anger. Kalo felt as though she was talking to ghosts. Seeing Amman's eyes turn towards her, she became scared. She took the broom from her father's hands and said 'Bapu, I'll do the sweeping, You make the flower beds.' What Amman was going to say remained unsaid, 'Why are you staring aimlessly like that? Eating all the time and becoming fat! You have no concern for your ageing father?'

Pheenu took the *khurpi* in his hand, tied a rope between two sticks on two ends of the flower bed and began to straighten out the side. She joined bricks thus, forming a jagged line. Somebody would come along and casually kick a few of them out of place. Pheenu would put them patiently back again. Somebody would again dislodge them. It would go on like this.

'Bapu, why don't you pull the ears of those who break the line?'

Pheenu just smiled back. She had grown tall, like the sunflower plant, but she continued to be innocent.

'If I were you, I would catch them and push them into the canal and shut out all those who spoil the park.'

'Yes, you are very brave. But, daughter, the government has employed me to make these beds.'

'The government has also hung up the notice on the poplar tree. PLUCKING OF FLOWERS PROHIBITED. Then why should we allow them to pluck?'

'The pluckers are also government servants, daughter.'

A *koel* cooed in the canopy of the green leaves and Kalo's attention was drawn in that direction. She mimicked the *koel's* voice.

A group, of men drinking near the hedge became excited at this childish prank. Pheenu thought to himself, 'She will never grow up.'

The red-streaked eyes of the fat drunkard had become frightening. The group had been having its sessions there for a number of days. Pheenu knew the contractor. Young boys from the villages who had not yet grown moustaches worked for him. Many years ago when Pheenu had first come to town, he too had worked for a couple of days with this man but his destiny had made him a gardener.

He feared white-collared men. Fear teaches respect for others.

'O Chaudhari, come here,' one among the group called out to Pheenu, 'This stuff...'

'Shut up...' the fat contractor quickly put his hand over the man's mouth and laughed loudly, like a querulous cat.

'Who are you going to vote for, Pheenu?'

For the last few days, election propaganda had been in full swing. Pheenu did not understand the meaning of all this noise and claptrap. People said that a vote could decide governments. If the government got changed, what would happen to them? They got their daily bread from the government. He pondered, but nothing seemed clear. If he voted against the government, it would amount to betrayal of someone whose salt he ate, and if he voted in favour of the government, he would be breaching the unity of his community as well as exposing himself to excommunication. I shouldn't vote at all. Why get into all this trouble, he brought. But to the government contractor, he replied:

'We'll vote for the government, sir.'
'Good, come, sit down, and smoke this cigarette.'
'No, sir, I've too much work to complete.'
'Come on, friend, work never finishes as long as one lives.'

The contractor handed over the darkish cigarette he had in his hand to him. Pheenu had always wanted to smoke a sweet-smelling cigarette. He had tasted the stubs of such cigarettes which he had found in the sweepings. But they did not taste like this. Pheenu squatted and started pulling at the cigarette. The long-faced one opened the packet of sweets and placed it in front of him. 'Come, have some,' Pheenu wanted to refuse but couldn't. His mouth had started watering and the words of offer floated with the seeping saliva down his throat. When all of them began to pick up pieces to eat, Pheenu also wiped his hand over his dirty shirt and picked up a few pieces. He wanted to hide one sweet for Kalo secretly . Why couldn't this be done? As a child when he had sat down for meals, he would get the maximum quantity of rice in his plate. Amman would say. 'Take only as much as you can hold in your belly. If you leave some uneaten, you'll get slapped.' The belly got filled but the eyes? He would tell Amman. 'See Amman, there is a lizard behind you.' When Amman looked behind, he would quickly push handfuls of left-over rice into her plate.

'Where is it?' asked Amman.

'It was there on the wall, Amman.' And she failed to catch his trick. Remembering his childhood, he said, 'See, what is floating in the canal.' All of them looked in the direction of the canal. He put some pieces of sweets in his pocket. There was nothing in the water. They broke into guffaws. They thought perhaps that a few puffs had made the gardener have hallucinations. They knew what to do when and decided accordingly, as if they had perfect rapport with the moments. They started filling their glasses with liquor. Pheenu felt the compulsion to leave.

'Sit down, friend. Saab (the contractor) has got the payment of his bill today,' said the long-faced one, 'This was for the work of your canal only ....'

❀ ❀ ❀

Then Kalo passed by that way again, frisking and prancing. The contractor looked at her open-mouthed. He was about to say something which was left incomplete and his arm was raised as if he was about to shout some slogan. It remained hanging in the air. Glasses were refilled, emptied again and the cycle went on. In between, Pheenu kept saying, 'You are very kind, sir.' In reply, the contractor said, 'Your days of hardship are going to end. Please know that a new age is going to dawn. All that is necessary is the use of the vote.'

'You are very good people, Bapuji,' repeated Pheenu. He felt that he was losing control over himself. His head felt like a leaf in the wind. And his legs and feet felt as if they were not there at all.

For quite some time they kept jabbering and singing songs. Pheenu got up and started walking towards his shack. Faint light from an earthen lamp was filtering through it outside.

He entered and the door was shut behind him. Kalo became scared. Pheenu fell unconscious on his broken cot. Amman was muttering. 'May you lose all, may you become paupers. You, who spoil others' homes. May your children die. May you die intestate.'

Away from the lawn, some distance near the hedges, in the dark, strains of singing could still be heard. The impetuosity in Amman's nature made her intolerant of this sort of interference in her domain. She thought of going out and giving them a piece of her mind. What foulness they were mouthing! Don't you have mothers and daughters at home, you bastards? Kalo's eyes were getting heavy with sleep. The shadows in the shack, dancing to the tune of the moving candle light looked very frightening. Bapu lying unconscious was like a ghost and Amman a sorceress incarnate. How deep are the wrinkles on her face! The upper two front teeth are missing! Was she the grand-daughter of this sorceress? Kalo broke into a cold sweat. She hastened to hide herself in the quilt.

Amman was too annoyed to get any sleep. The indecent voices of the drunkards outside were coming closer, "*Mali! Mali!*" inflamed by anger, Amman picked up the lamp and came out. The drunkards, rolling on the grass sat up holding their breath when they saw the light coming in their direction. Amman was confused with rage. Even in the light of the lamp she could not see anything. Suddenly, she stumbled upon a brick at the edge of the flower bed. The tin lamp flew out of her hand. Everything was drowned in darkness. She could not even hold herself up. The hands of darkness seemed to catch her in their grip. A hand gagged her mouth tight. She could neither shriek nor cry. In the darkness, different voices whispered the same sentence, one after another, 'How she warbles, like a *Koel!*' Then the darkness and stillness thickened. Amman dipped into the well of unconsciousness, down and down, to the bottom!

❀ ❀ ❀

Next morning when Pheenu emerged from sleep, he rubbed his eyes for sometime. His insides seemed to be on fire. He gulped some water to calm himself. Picking up a broom he made a move towards the park. He was surprised to notice that the water in the canal had come down to knee level. The canal was muddy. In the lawn lay some torn clothes, empty bottles and tins strewn around. Seeing a naked woman lying in their midst, he mouthed a terribly foul invective. Coming closer and seeing the clothes in shreds, he remembered the contractor. I wonder whom they had brought here to commit sin! Was this a park or a whorehouse? If the police came to know, he would be the first to be harassed. *Chh...* he covered his eyes with his arm and spat.

Getting still closer, he was struck speechless. He felt as if a big hole had sprung in the earth under his feet. Underneath, was a bottomless ocean. In the ocean were waves dragging him into dark caves full of algae. He did not know how to get out of the hole.

Moving up, he saw Amman's body. It had turned stiff like a log of wood: it bore marks of injury at different places. A dog was going around her body. Nose to ground, it was sniffing at the parts of her body covered with blood. Pheenu clenched his teeth and threw a stone at the dog. It ran away. The stone had hit the tin lamp lying near the dislodged brick. All of a sudden, Pheenu seemed to catch the thread of all that had passed before he had become unconscious and all that must have happened thereafter.

But these threads were unconnected, without any link. To link them and come to some conclusion was beyond him. After the sweets and rounds of glasses full of liquor, he wondered what had been said.

The pieces of sweets he had kept in his pocket last night, were still there. What should he do? He was at his wit's end. Can a brick that breaks be put together again? What should he do with the brick of his house which was now broken? Without it the entire roof would come down!. A straw structure with weak foundations would not be able to withstand a single shower of rain. What would become of Kalo? He put his hands on his head and squatted on the ground.

It was daylight. At the temple of Hanuman, bells were ringing. He gathered the corpse, put it on his shoulders and took it inside the hut. Kalo was fast asleep. Pheenu's wail startled her and she sat up. Then she fixed her eyes on her father. He was wailing. 'Amman, don't leave me, Don't go. You should have at least thought of your Kalo.' Kalo got up and went to the corpse. She lifted the sheet of cloth to see her face and pulled back in fright. 'So, they have killed the crow?' She murmured. She felt that Amman was actually a sorceress. How dreadful she looked! Pheenu kept striking his head against Amman's chest, crying all the while 'Hai Amman. Hai Amman.' Kalo looked on, petrified.

It appeared to be noisier outside than inside. Had something worse happened outside? She got up and came out. She heard shouts outside the gate of the park—

Vota da kun haqdar? (Who deserves to get the vote?)
Duloram Thekedar! (Duloram the Contractor!)
Jittega bhai jittega (He will win, surely he will win!)
Ghode ala jittega! (The one whose symbol is the horse will win!)

She saw that the boys were dancing a *bhangra* on the stone slab where Amman used to sit. She flared up, picked up a broom and ran towards them. Before she could get to the slab, the boys had jumped into the water.

'Kalo, we hear that a vampire has chewed up your Amman?'

'Outside the park, there is also a crow lying dead.'

'Your Amman's soul has found release?'

She picked up some clods and began throwing them at the boys who swam across to the bank on the other side.

She kept looking at them with burning eyes. Then, as she moved to retreat, one of them said, 'Wonder if the old woman's soul has entered Kalo now?'

❀ ❀ ❀

Kalo had covered some distance when her eyes fell on a dislodged brick. This reminded her of Amman. How much care she used to take of these flowerbeds! She glanced towards the slab where the canopy of leaves was swaying in the wind. It was absolutely empty. It was a scene of complete desolation. Even though the sun shone, raindrops kept falling. Across the canal, on the other bank, the boys were rejoicing. 'Hey! ah! *buddhi da byah..*'

(See, see, the old woman's wedding!)

Eyes full of tears, Kalo dug at the ground to put back the brick. Bapu's wailing became loud and relentless.

Translated by **Shivnath**

KONKANI

Hippie Girl

Chandrakant Keni

Sunday

It was five in the evening and raining heavily. One look at the looming black sky told me it wasn't going to stop soon. It was already getting dark. I was driving home quite slowly when I saw this girl thumbing a lift. She had no umbrella or raincoat and was completely soaked. I stopped my car and invited her in.

'Thank you,' she said.

'Where are you going?'

'Anywhere under a shelter.'

I took her home with me. My wife was astonished to see me with this hippie girl.

She was wet and shivering. I told my wife to take her inside and give her a change of clothes.

Half an hour later she emerged in a sari, her hair tied in a bun. She had put *kumkum* on her forehead. She came into the sitting room and posed before me.

'How do I look?'

Sexy, was the word that came to my mind, but since my wife was standing behind me, I only murmured:

'You look like the typical Indian woman.'

She laughed and settled comfortably in a chair. We chatted for a while, sipping hot tea and eating the savouries my wife had fried for us.

Her name was Cinderella. She came from France. She had been in India for the last six months. Before that she had studied science at a college in France. She was twenty years old but looked nearly thirty. She lived in Colva along with several other hippies.

'What made you go out in this rain without even a raincoat or an umbrella?'

'I don't buy such things. That's the only way to know the joys of getting wet in the rain. Have you ever tried doing that?'

'Very romantic, I'm sure, but frankly, getting wet is not my idea of fun.'

'How can you sit here cooped up inside this prison while all Nature is dancing at your doorsteps? If you want to know what true happiness really means get out of the four walls of this room.'

I appreciated her point of view, but I knew it wouldn't have suited me at all.

'Why do you wander about like this? Why have you abandoned your home and your education?'

'For a new wisdom, for a new way of life, here in the lap of Mother Nature!'

'But how did your parents allow you to go?'

Cinderella laughed. For a while neither of us spoke. Then she said: 'Do this — come and spend a few days with us.'

I accepted the invitation without batting an eyelid, and asked her, 'But won't your people make me feel out of place among you?'

'We don't usually like strangers poking and prying around us, but you're different. You're an intelligent, responsible person. Having you for a few days isn't going to hurt us.'

'Suppose I find your way of life so enticing that I desert my family for you?'

'I'll consider that an achievement on my part!'

Cinderella had dinner with us that evening. After that my wife and I dropped her at Colva. She had put on her own clothes before leaving, but she hadn't wiped off the *kumkum*.

Sunday

I ran into Cinderella again when I visited Colva today. It wasn't pouring this time. She was on her way to the beach. Alone. She asked me to join her. We went and sat on the wet sand. Her loose, long hair billowed in the sea breeze. She wore a flimsy shirt that fluttered over her chest. The top two buttons of her shirt weren't fastened and every now and then my eyes strayed there.

'Cinderella, tell me. Why do people wear clothes?'

My question made her a little self-conscious and she put on one of the buttons.

She said, 'To cover one's body, I suppose...'

'From whom?'

'Not from the view of others. But from the cold, the rain, the sun.'

'So that's your sartorial philosophy, is it?'

'What's yours?'

'Human beings can't live outside society; so they should behave decently if only for the sake of others. Birds and animals don't dress but humans do. If they do, they should do it properly.'

'What about your *sadhus* and *sanyasis*?'

'They have renounced the world.'

'So have we!'

'But there is no vice in their world; I'm not sure about yours.'

'I know what you're trying to suggest about us hippies, and you're wrong! By your line of thinking all our males should be rapists, considering the number of naked women they see every day. The truth is quite the opposite, if anything.'

'You must be accustomed to this. But what about our boys and girls who are not?'

'We don't intrude into their world; they shouldn't in ours.'

'How can we avoid that? You wander about on the beach, in the city...'

'In what way are we indecent?'

'When our adolescent boys see young women with not a stitch on, they might get the wrong ideas about sex.'

'What you're saying is you repress Nature in the name of Morality. Let your boys and girls live in freedom. Then they won't have any trouble with immoral thoughts.'

'That's only half-true. Total freedom will only lead them to lust after one another's bodies.'

'Let them. Provided the boy and the girl agree.'

'And what if they have children?'

'They should bring them up. Children are the responsibility of their parents. When they grow up God and the Government can solve their problems.'

But if we do this won't the family institutions itself collapse?

'What institution! Despotism is the right world.'

Our ideas were so diametrically opposed to each other, I realised we would get nowhere with this argument. I got up to leave.

'Are you leaving?

'It's late. My wife will be worried.'

Why didn't you bring her with you?'

'I got to the beach today only because I happened to be passing this way. And as chance would have it there you were...'

Cinderella took a bottle of *kumkum* from her bag and said, 'Please put a dot on me.'

'Why don't you do it yourself?'

'I don't have a mirror. For a woman the mirror is another tyrant.' Opening the bottle of red liquid, I dipped a matchstick into it. But then a disturbing thought rose in my mind. I wiped the red colour off the matchstick.

'What is the matter?'

'In our land only a husband may put *kumkum* on a woman. It signifies an intimate relationship between husband and wife.'

Cinderella giggled.

'Then you can make love to me.'

'We're followers of Lord Rama - we're monogamous.'

'Your traditions are very repressive, aren't they? Now what would happen if I were to fall in love with you?'

'Our lives would be ruined.'

'Why should that be so? If you love me does that mean that your love for your wife should diminish?'

I was confused. To end this inquisition, I put the *kumkum* on her forehead. She clasped my right hand with both her hands and taking it to her lips, kissed it. My body quivered as though a streak of lightning had passed through me.

I got up and walked towards my car. Cinderella walked beside me.

Abruptly she asked, 'When shall we meet again?'

'Next Sunday.'

'No. Sunday is a long way off. Come tomorrow.'

'Let's see. But I can't promise anything.'

Meanwhile another hippie came towards us. Cinderella raised her arm in greeting. The moment he drew close, she slipped into his embrace. He rested his chin on her head and hugged her tightly with one arm while his left hand caressed her breasts. Cinderella introduced me to him.

'Meet my friend Paul.'

I greeted him politely, but my heart seethed with envy. I wondered if it showed on my face.

Tuesday

Cinderella came to our house this evening. I wasn't at home. My wife can't speak English but perhaps she understood a little of what Cinderella said. Apparently she wanted to know how to make curry, but since we make enough of it in the afternoon to last us for supper she didn't get to see how it was done. But she seemed to like my wife's dry mackerel salad and ate quite a bit of it even while it was being made.

At dinner we tried to convince her to spend the night at our house.

'And become a barrier between you and your beloved wife? Oh no!'

'There's a room you can have all to yourself.'

'Won't that be a terrible punishment for you?'

I felt like laughing. My wife couldn't follow the conversation and Cinderella didn't venture to explain anything to her.

'So you won't stay, after all.'

'Yes, I will. But on one condition — all three of us should sleep in one place.'

'That's not possible. I'll take you home.'

'Why don't you stay with us instead?'

'And leave my wife alone at home?'

'Don't you ever go out leaving her alone?'

'I do, but what do you think she'd feel if under her very nose I go away to spend the night with you?'

'That's true. You can drop me and come back home.

It was quite dark when I drove the car with Cinderella sitting beside me.

'You surprise me. Why do you consider me a stranger?' asked Cinderella.

'Is that what you feel?'

'Yes. The other day you put the dot on me, but even now, if my hand so much as brushes against you, you seem to shudder.'

'That's because of the way I've been brought up.'

'Can you honestly say that you look upon every other woman, besides your wife, as a mother or a sister?'

'Frankly no. But in my culture that's how it ought to be.'

'Which means you do have desires but you repress them.'

'That's true. But to do otherwise is immoral...'

'There you go again with your morality. Tell me, are all these *sanyasis* and *brahmacharis* and *yogis* really like what you said?'

'Yes. Their minds are devoid of passion.'

'How can that be?'

'What else are their terrible sacrifices for? If someone moves his finger over the sole of somebody else's foot, it tickles. But move a finger over your own sole. Does it tickle? It doesn't. Why not?'

'You tell me.'

'Because the mind is aware that what is moving is one's own finger. In the same way it's not easy for a mind to believe that just any woman is a mother or a sister. It has to be conditioned to achieve this state.'

'So it's possible to conquer one's desires!'

'Yes.'

'But why should your suppress your desires?'

'If I didn't I would be being unfair to my wife!'

'What if another man was on your wife's mind?

'I wouldn't like that.'

'Doesn't this mean you are against her being a free person?'

'How can I help it?'

'You can. You can free your mind by snapping the chains of tradition. The more you suppress your passions, the more it increases, but once you satisfy them, that's the end of it.'

We had arrived at Colva by then. Cinderella exclaimed, 'See how quickly we got here. Let's go and sit on the beach.'

'But my wife is alone at home.'

'Just for a little while. Let's finish this discussion. Before coming to India I had visited Iran and I want to tell you about an incident there.'

'About the satisfaction of desire, isn't it?

'What else?'

Both of us laughed.

When we settled down on the beach, Cinderella said, 'Why does society expect only women to cover their bodies?'

'That stops people from lusting after them.'

'You mean it stops men.'

'Yes.'

'Don't you think women get aroused when they see men bare their chests?'

'How should I know?'

'All these standards of morality that women have to abide by have been imposed on them by men.'

I was silent.

Then, self consciously, Cinderella peeled off her blouse. Embarrassed, I turned my head away.

'Don't blush like that. Once you grow accustomed to this, you won't feel ashamed.'

'How can I control my feelings?'

'Don't control anything.'

Trying to behave as naturally as I could I turned towards her, while Cinderella talked away without the least trace of embarrassment.

She narrated an incident about Mazook, an Iranian *sanyasi*. He had left home with the intention of relieving the miseries of mankind. After having traversed the entire country, he came to the conclusion that when man's desires remain unsatisfied he becomes unhappy. Man suffers from two kinds of hunger, hunger for food and hunger for pleasure. If these hungers are placated he is at peace.

One day Mazook saw a young man singing a melancholic song by the bank of a river. Mazook felt that what issued from his lips was no song, but a shower of misery. He approached the youth and asked him why he was so miserable.

The young man replied, 'I love a girl but she does not return my love.'

'Why?'

'I don't know.'

'In that case the girl's at fault. One who gives rise to sorrow in a fellow creature commits wrong. Come, let's go to her.'

They went to the girl.

'Why have you made him miserable?'

'I have done nothing to him. But I cannot give him what he demands.'

Mazook turned to the young man:

'What have you asked of her?'

'I long for her embrace.... I want all the pleasures that man expects of a woman.'

'Young lady, why do you deny him this?'

'Should I lose my purity just for the sake of his whims?'

'Purity? The Kingdom of God has no place for such concepts. Out of such pretty words as Purity are made the chains that bind you. Have nothing to do with them! The hungry should be fed; the passionate should be gratified.'

'Then won't we turn into beasts?'

'Let it be so. Only thus one can achieve happiness. Which man has Morality ever made happy?'

I laughed.

'What's so funny?' asked Cinderella.

'So this is your way of life?'

'Yes.'

'But why should the one who seeks gratification impose his will on another?'

'That's true. There should be no compulsion. Suppose I wanted you to make love to me now and you were willing, then...'

I looked away.

Cinderella snuggled close to me. The cloak of morality in which I had shielded myself till now succumbed to her charms at last. I held her in my arms and kissed her fiercely.

'Are you satisfied?'

'No. This is only the beginning,' she replied.

God alone knows for how long we remained locked in each

other's arms. Suddenly the thought of my wife came to me and my grasp loosened.

'What happened?' she asked.

'I have to go home. It's late.'

'Aren't you being unjust to me?'

'I shall repent for it,' I replied, kissing her again.

Sunday

I don't smoke cigarettes. But I wanted to experience that state of transcendence they say one could achieve after smoking marijuana. We were sitting in a room of a hippie's house. Everyone had arrived in some state of undress, but no one felt self-conscious about this. Cinderella was completely naked.

She ripped open a cigarette, mixed the tobacco with some hashish, rolled it in new cigarette paper and lit it.

She took a deep drag at the cigarette, savouring the sweet aroma of its fumes before holding it at my lips.

I sucked at it greedily. The smoke streaked to my brain. I coughed and gasped frantically. Cinderella slapped my back and cautioned soothingly, 'Slowly, slowly.'

For the first time in my life I experienced the world revolving around me.

'Enough,' I said.

'You haven't seen anything yet. Have another drag.'

'Stop!'

The beast in me was aroused. Her naked torso stood before me. From it jutted out breasts and thighs to taunt me. There and then I satisfied my lust for her like a beast and afterwards continued to smoke till I passed out.

When I returned to my senses I discovered that I had been sleeping with my head on Cinderella's bare midriff. Shaking my head, I got up and sat down. Cinderella was still asleep. I glanced at her naked body and shuddered. I could not believe that the lure of this flesh could have made me so blind. I looked at my own body. There was no cloak of morality there anymore. I felt ashamed of myself and, getting up put my clothes on.

Cinderella was still unconscious. I could not bear to see her in that state any more. I found a bedsheet and covered her with it. I searched my pockets for a piece of paper but couldn't find any and there didn't seem any in the room either. Finally, I found a bill somewhere. On the back of it I wrote:

Cinderella,

Thank you very much. My urges have been satisfied. You are always welcome at my home. But please do not invite me to this place again. Your philosophy may be true and it also may be good but I am not accustomed to such a purely hedonistic existence. Neither do I wish to get accustomed to it.

Yours

I returned home that night but I didn't have the courage to look my wife in the face. Women intuitively understand such things. But if she did realise what was going on, she didn't utter a word.

Sunday

Cinderella didn't turn up after that. I kept thinking about her again and again. I was mortally afraid that she would drop in my absence and in her usual frank manner explain all that had happened between us to my wife. But she didn't come at all. When one evening I asked my wife if she'd like to come for a stroll on the beach at Colva, she replied, 'You want to meet Cinderella, isn't it? Why do you want me along? I wouldn't want to get in your way.'

She had hit me where it hurt most. But I just laughed lightly and teased her, 'Are you jealous?'

'I am not jealous. But the moment I saw that bitch step into the house I knew she was up to no good.'

'All right, madam. Now get ready.'

'There's work to be done. Who'll do that?'

'Let's enjoy ourselves while we have the chance. In future who knows if we'll have the same opportunity, when we have children...'

'If you want to go, go! Don't bother me.'

Having said this, my wife went inside.

I didn't move from that chair for a long time. On the one hand I was constantly reminded of Cinderella and on the other I didn't want to offend my wife. Feeling guilty as I was, I didn't have the courage to meet Cinderella without my wife.

Eventually I did go to Colva alone.

I met Paul the moment I stopped my car. He told me that Cinderella was sitting in a restaurant.

Two couples were seated at a table drinking beer. 'Hi! Cinderella called me over.

I pulled a chair and sat with them.

'What'll you have?'

'A Coke.'

'Have some beer,' someone said. 'We're celebrating.'

I wondered why and looked at Cinderella. She certainly wasn't the shy type but to my surprise she actually blushed.

Before I could say anything somebody thrust a glass of beer into my hands.

'Cheers,' I said.

'Cheers to Cinderella and her baby in the womb!' said the other girl.

My hand shook in agitation and beer spilled all over my clothes.

'What happened?' the other girl inquired.

'He's thrilled!'

Taking a handkerchief from my pocket, I wiped the beer off my clothes and the cold sweat from my face. While I did this one of the hippies kissed Cinderella on the lips and caressed her belly with his left hand. Guiltily I hung my head down and began to sip the beer.

Quietly, the others slipped away leaving only Cinderella and me at the table.

'Cinderella, is this true?' I demanded, my voice hoarse.

'I win. You lose,' Cinderella replied.

'What do you mean, Cinderella?'

'The other day you left a note for me and disappeared, didn't you? But I was sure that you would return. And here you are - I win.'

I heaved a sigh of relief and asked her, 'Is it true?'

'All the angels and saints will swear to it!'

'Who is he?'

'How should I know?'

'It's not me, is it?'

'I really can't tell... But you needn't look so worried. I'm going to bring it up as my very own illegitimate child.'

'But why should the child suffer so?'

'If the father has no guts what else can be done?'

'But what about you, afterwards?'

'Me? I'll become a mother!'

'Without being married.'

'What's wrong with that? My dear man, do you know you haven't congratulated me yet?'

'Congratulations. May I leave?

'Go! But don't forget me. Come here once in a while... Or should I come to your place?

'Cinderella, I find it very difficult to say this, but please do not come to my house. Please, as a favour.'

'But you know, I didn't mean I'd come to your house for my delivery.'

'I know that. But my wife...'

'I won't say a word about what happened. I promise.'

'No, Cinderella, it's not that.... We've been married for eight years and till today she has not conceived.

Cinderella laughed. She said, 'In that case it's not yours!' and left.

Translated by **Augusto Pinto**

A Cup of Hot Coffee

Edwin J.F. D'Souza

The mere thought of going into the kitchen sent a chill down her spine. There was no one in the house but she really needed that glass of hot coffee. Her son would have preferred to say a "cup of hot coffee," she chuckled to herself inspite of her old bones creaking and the pit of her stomach demanding the warmth of caffeine.

A cup of hot coffee! Modern house and modern terms had to be used. It was a well-equipped kitchen. 'It's nothing Mother,' he had said. 'Just the flick of a switch and the turn of a knob.' Now she had to do it all by herself.

The rains! They had come, at last. The downpour was torrential, the sky being perpetually overcast. The air was chilly. She had known rain before but this was her first in the house her son had built. It had happened suddenly. She had found herself drawn out of her cocoon unawares.

'Mother, this is our new home,' he had said proudly. His words had choked her. Home, he had said. Why not a house? This concrete giant which came alive at the flick of a switch and turn of a knob?

Another chuckle was in order. She had glasses of coffee on an afternoon like this. Her man had been alive then. Her husband. Quite a man, quite a man. The warmth around the crackling firewood stove would be cosy. The coffee would be bubbling through a decoction of jaggery, providing the background music, and the warmth of aluminium tumblers would be in their hands. Quite a man, who had given her three sons. The first drank himself to death; the second was pulped in a bus accident. These two deaths took her man away leaving her the mud-walled house and the third son.

And then she had taken up the reins herself. She had had to. The pace was so fast that only on the day her third one came and told her he was leaving for some place in the Gulf could she stop and look around.

'No more mud-walls Mother,' he had said. 'No more milking cows, goats and rearing pigs. We are going to have a home of our dreams.' But she had never had any dreams.

And he left; the firewood stove and the mud-walled house remained with her. He had written regularly and she had sent her replies through a nun whose convent received generous charity from her son. Even the Vicar was suddenly kind to her when she had dropped a hundred rupees in the mite box. She was gaining ground!

And then came the daughter-in-law. Quite a doll. A working girl, smart and beautiful. She had twisted her lips when she had first entered the mud house. She had said, 'And once our home is up we will pull down these mud-walls and all the past with it.'

She had said nothing. She had nothing to say.

And then it had happened. A concrete giant had slowly risen next to her mud house. When the noise, dust and the hammering of steel had finally died down there had remained a brief silence only to be followed by a few more weak, floppy sounds. Her mud house no more stood there, even its dust had settled down so quickly! She saw her son standing amidst the rubble, his hands folded on his breast, looking way beyond the sky. Triumph was written all over his face. She too had looked up years ago when her husband's coffin had been lifted up on the shoulders of hired pallbearers. She had cried out in raging silence to her Creator — now, let the rest be upon me...

How she needed that coffee!

The kitchen was spotlessly clean. All she had to put together was some boiling water, a teaspoon of instant coffee, a dash of milk and sugar. She found a pan and filled it with water. It wasn't the firewood stove anymore; a shimmering, new cooking range stood in its place. And all the firepower was in that little red cylinder. She placed the pan on the cooking range and turned the knob. Hadn't he said, just the flick of a switch and the turn of a knob?

Where were the matches?

In her mud house everything was within her arms' reach. She looked around and searched for it. 'Oh damn you,' she screamed within herself, 'You and your home! You and your money! Where was it when your brothers died and your old man slowly wasted himself in grief? The bile rising in her throat choked her and she coughed briefly. There was a fishy smell in the kitchen and a faint hiss.

'Everything has a place in here' her daughter-in-law had said. 'And everything should be in its place.'

So where is the matchbox, she smiled to herself rather wickedly. Ah yes, her college-going grandchild... that chirpy, bubbly thing who was left behind with the grandmother…she had seen her puffing away to glory. She was supposed to be in her care. She wobbled her way up to her grandchild's bedroom and a brief search revealed not only the matchbox but also an ashtray filled to the brim with cigarette butts. It wasn't her concern anyway. All she needed was that coffee.

Her joints creaking, she reached the kitchen once again. What was that obnoxious smell? New homes stink too? Should she twist her lips now? Everything has its own place, the words pounded in her ears. What is my place, she heard herself ask. Did I ask for all this? The firewood stove, the three deaths and the demolition of her house loomed large in front of her. Each scene distinctly carving her descent, bringing her down to a state with which she could not compromise.

'What the hell,' she screamed, 'What the bloody hell!'

And then she struck the match.

❑❑❑

ENGLISH

The Portrait of A Lady

Khushwant Singh

My grandmother, like everybody's grandmother, was an old woman. She had been old and wrinkled for the twenty years that I had known her. People said that she had once been young and pretty and had even had a husband, but that was hard to believe. My grandfather's portrait hung above the mantelpiece in the drawing room. He wore a big turban and loose-fitting clothes. His long white beard covered the best part of his chest and he looked at least a hundred years old. He did not look the sort of person who would have a wife or children. He looked as if he could only have lots and lots of grandchildren. As for my grandmother being young and pretty, the thought was almost revolting. She often told us of the games she used to play as a child. That seemed quite absurd and undignified on her part and we treated it like the tales of the prophets she used to tell us.

She had always been short and fat and slightly bent. Her face was a crisscross of wrinkles running from everywhere to everywhere. No, we were certain she had always been as we had known her. Old, so terribly old that she could not have grown older, and had stayed at the same age for twenty years. She could never have been pretty; but she was always beautiful. She hobbled about the house in spotless white with one hand resting on her waist to balance her stoop and the other telling the beads of her rosary. Her silver locks were scattered untidily over her pale, puckered face, and her lips constantly moved in inaudible prayer. Yes, she was beautiful. She was like the winter landscape in the mountains, an expanse of pure white serenity breathing peace and contentment.

My grandmother and I were good friends. My parents left me with her when they went to live in the city and we were constantly together. She used to wake me up in the morning and get me ready for school. She said her morning prayer in a monotonous sing-song while she bathed and dressed me in the hope that I would listen and get to know it by heart. I listened because I loved her voice but never bothered to learn it. Then she would fetch my wooden slate which she had already washed and plastered with yellow chalk, a tiny earthen ink pot and a reed pen, tie them all in a bundle and hand it to me. After a breakfast of a thick, stale *chapatti* with a little butter and sugar spread on it, we went to school. She carried several stale *chapattis* with her for the village dogs.

My grandmother always went to school with me because the school was attached to the temple. The priest taught us the alphabet and the morning prayer. While the children sat in rows on either side of the veranda singing the alphabet or the prayer in a chorus, my grandmother sat inside reading the scriptures. When we had both finished, we would walk back together. This time the village dogs would meet us at the temple door. They followed us to our home growling and fighting each other for the chapattis we threw to them.

When my parents were comfortably settled in the city, they sent for us. That was a turning point in our friendship. Although we shared the same room, my grandmother no longer came to school with me. I used to go to an English school in a motor bus. There were no dogs in the streets and she took to feeding sparrows in the courtyard of our city house.

As the years rolled by we saw less of each other. For some time she continued to wake me up and get me ready for school. When I came back she would ask me what the teacher had taught me. I would tell her English words and little things of western science and learning, the law of gravity, Archimedes' principle, the world being round etc. This made her unhappy. She could not help me with my lessons. She did not believe in the things they taught at the English school and was distressed that there was no teaching about God and the scriptures. One day I announced that we were being given music lessons. She was very disturbed. To her, music had lewd associations. It was the monopoly of harlots and beggars and not meant for gentle folk. She rarely talked to me after that.

When I went up to University, I was given a room of my own. The common link of friendship was snapped. My grandmother accepted her seclusion with resignation. She rarely left her spinning wheel to talk to anyone. From sunrise to sunset she sat by her wheel spinning and reciting prayers. Only in the afternoon she relaxed for a while to feed the sparrows. While she sat in the veranda breaking the bread into little bits, hundreds of little birds collected around her creating a veritable bedlam of chirrupings. Some came and perched on her legs, others on her shoulders. Some even sat on her head. She smiled but never shoo'd them away. It used to be the happiest half-hour of the day for her.

When I decided to go abroad for further studies, I was sure my grandmother would be upset. I would be away for five years, and at her age one could never tell. But my grandmother could. She was not even sentimental. She came to see me off at the railway station but did not talk or show any emotion. Her lips moved in prayer, her mind was lost in prayer. Her fingers were busy telling the beads of her rosary. Silently she kissed my forehead, and when I left I cherished the moist imprint as perhaps the last sign of physical contact between us.

But that was not so. After five years I came back home and was met by her at the station. She did not look a day older. She still had no time for words, and while she clasped me in her arms I could hear her reciting her prayer. Even on the first day of my arrival, her happiest moments were with her sparrows whom she fed longer and with frivolous rebukes.

In the evening a change came over her. She did not pray. She collected the women of the neighbourhood, got an old drum and started to sing. For several hours she thumped the sagging skins of the dilapidated drum and sang of the homecoming of warriors. We had to persuade her to stop, to avoid overstraining. That was the first time since I had known her that she did not pray.

The next morning she was taken ill. It was a mild fever and the doctor told us that it would go. But my grandmother thought differently. She told us that her end was near. She said that since only a few hours before the close of the last chapter of her life she had omitted to pray, she was not going to waste any more time talking to us.

We protested. But she ignored our protests. She lay peacefully in bed praying and telling her beads. Even before we could suspect, her lips stopped moving and the rosary fell from her lifeless fingers. A peaceful pallor spread on her face and we knew that she was dead.

We lifted her off the bed and, as is customary, laid her on the ground and covered her with a red shroud. After a few hours of mourning we left her alone to make arrangements for her funeral.

In the evening we went to her room with a crude stretcher to take her to be cremated. The sun was setting and had lit her room and veranda with a blaze of golden light. We stopped halfway in the courtyard. All over the veranda and in her room right up to where she lay dead and stiff wrapped in the red shroud, thousands of sparrows sat scattered on the floor. There was no chirping. We felt sorry for the birds and my mother fetched some bread for them. She broke it into little crumbs, the way my grandmother used to, and threw it to them. The sparrows took no notice of the bread. When we carried my grandmother's corpse off, they flew away quietly. Next morning the sweeper swept the bread crumbs into the dustbin.

❑❑❑

BIRTH

Mulk Raj Anand

The Earth seemed to groan as Parvati heaved away from the *busti* in the hollow of the hills and her throat tightened in the breathless dark. The *kikar* trees on the road loomed like *Jinns* before her eyes, while the tremors in her belly drugged her with a dull pain as sweet as the scent of the Queen-of-the Night. Her father-in-law, who had been keeping a respectable distance from her, was almost lost to view, except that she could hear his short, angry voice, now and then, beckoning her to hurry. And, in order to assure him that she was following, as also to assure herself against the frightening trees, she answered that she was following. But her feet were getting heavier and heavier this morning while her torso, in spite of the bundle on her head, pushed forward like the prow of a stately ship.

As she had started off in the early hours of the morning from the cluster of huts near Karole Bagh towards Ridge Road, where her husband had already gone to work, road mending, she had felt the child stirring in her belly. Perhaps it was turning over to take another, more comfortable position as he had seemed to be doing all night. And she had put her hand on her belly ever so tenderly, as though to reassure the babe. And she had smiled the slightest wisp of a smile to think of what Ramu had done during the night and throughout the middle months of her pregnancy whenever she told him that the baby was stirring in her: he had put his ears on her stomach and listened and, then playfully tapping with his fingers, he would intone a crazy, humorous sing-song:

Patience, son, patience,
You must learn to be patient,
You must learn to cultivate the long-breasted-sense of your ancestors.

Now as she felt another stirring in her belly she superstitiously thought that it was probably Ramu's tricks which were responsible for the disturbance in her womb. For, not only had her husband been teasing her all the way from Ambala in the train, but he had had her until only a month ago in spurts of wild desire while her father-in-law was asleep in the hut.

She paused for a moment, balanced the bundle of food on her head with her left hand, while she stroked her belly with her right hand. The growing life in her swirled from side to side, so that her heart throbbed violently with fear and her head was dizzy with weakness. She gritted her teeth and clenched her hands to avoid fainting and, mercifully, the griping pain passed. She breathed hard and proceeded on her way.

The feeble echo of her father-in-law's voice fell on her ears: 'Oh hurry.'

She lifted her voice and answered back: 'I am following, Baba, I am following.'

And, all aquiver at the momentary passing of pain, she was now anxious for the old man, sorry to be a burden on him who had really broken under the burden of responsibilities, specially when he had to mortgage his land and buy the fare to Delhi. And yet, throughout, he had been solicitous for her welfare, and that had always moved her. Actually, of course his concern was more for the son's son that she might bear for him than for her. But, nevertheless, his consideration was more touching because he was so child-like in his anxiety and so warm-hearted, in spite of the bad luck that had been pursuing him like a malevolent spirit all these years. For instance, he had refused to believe her mother-in-law when, lingering on her death-bed, she had maliciously attributed the decline of the whole family to the day when, five-years ago, Parvati had come to their house as Ramu's wedded wife. No, he had not believed the old woman and had scoffed at her even when the price of his disbelief in his wife's obsession was a protracted sulking on her part which hastened her death from cancer. And she, Parvati, had felt ever since that she must justify the old man's faith in her and give him a grandson, if only as a compensation for the loss of his wife and as the only happiness that might compensate him for the slow agony of his ruin through the debt and the drought.

Another tremor of pain, and the sickness of bile in the mouth...

But she gritted her teeth again and felt that she must hold out if only for the sake of appearances, because, earthy and natural as the old man was, he might be embarrassed if she gave birth to the child on the way to work. She must wait till her husband was near at hand and could fetch a woman from among the other stone-breakers to deliver her.

She hurried along, the tension in her nerves heightening under the layers of heat that oozed from the shadows of the lingering night. And beads of perspiration covered her nose and her forehead, and she felt as if she were choking for lack of breath. But she did not relax her hold on herself and, keeping her belly uplifted before her even as a drummer keeps a drum, her head held high, she strode along majestically forward.

For moments she could see herself walking along, almost as though she were the spectator of her own acts. Perhaps, it was from the nodal point of a strange apathy, which comes on to a pregnant woman, that she could see her soft advance, proud like that of a she-peacock, feeling upon feeling in her body spending itself into a silence which was somewhat like the death from which all life begins. Over her tendons spread the morasses of inertness, from which came the echoes of pain, dull thuds of the sound of her babe stirring, struggling, reaching out through the sheaths of liquid held up by the trauma of birth. And through this pent-up race between the elements in her belly, the vision of the dull whites of her eyes played havoc with the black points, so that each branch of a tree became the intricate coil of serpents from which hung the skulls of donkeys, stags, lions, elephants, monkeys side by side with the bodies of the damned humans in the orchards of hell.

There was the slightest whirr of fear at the back of her head as this image of an early legend about the trees in hell crept up behind the film of grit in her eyes. The sight of a white-washed grave, with a green flag on top of it, increased the fear and she shook a little. This caused a rumbling in her belly and sent sparks of shooting pain charging the quagmire of her mind, stirring the memories of terror built up through the talk of her mother. She was in the panic of a confusion and began to run, trying to hold her head erect and her torso suspended before her, as though she were guarding both the beauty of her gait as well as her unborn child against the shadows of the trees, against all the grisly populations which confronted her. The films on her startled eyes became thicker in the blind rush forward and her nostrils dilated like those of a young bay mare pursued by the devil. She opened her mouth to shout for her father-in-law, but though her lips were agape no sound came out of them.

And now she tried to control herself, to banish the fear of the haunting shadows by an extroversion of will. And for a moment, she paused, her breasts heaving, her breath coming and going quickly, and the whole of her body bathed in a sweat. But now a spiral wave of weakness rose to her head and she felt giddy. Through her half-closed eyes, she could see her father-in-law like a speck of dust against the huge boulders of the Birla Temple on Ridge Road, outside which was the pitch where she was to go to break stones. If only she could survive this faint, she could make it and be out of the reach of these graves!... The opiate of heat and fatigue was on her numb body now, however, and, while she clenched her hands in readiness to advance, the pain in her abdomen became a growl like the noisy motion of the wheel on the road-making engine and she receded back into the arms of the *doots* of hell.

She stamped the earth, as though to beckon it, as Sita had done asking it to open up and swallow her hour of peril. The earth did not open up, but she steadied a little. The pain in her belly was swirling in wild waves, round and round, up and down, the *aus* stirring in the cauldron of her belly, sizzling and boiling over.

Shaking her head in defiance of the demons both inside and outside her, holding her stomach in her left hand, the corners of her tightly closed mouth twitching in a frenzy of desperation, her face wrinkled, she moved with a deliberate calm towards the hollow ditch which stretched by the road. And lowering the basket off her head, she fell back with a thud on to the humb of the ditch. Fortunately, she had landed on her yielding bottom.

For a while she lay back and tried to rest herself, hoping that the spell of pain would pass. But as soon as she closed her eyes she felt the moisture between her loins and knew that her baby had started.

Slow aches of yearning, like the bursting desire for her man, blended with the rich smell of *aus*, and she felt as though she was in a drugged stupor, involved in a kind of ennui in which the nerves of her body seemed to relax. Her brows knitted into a frown, the corners of her lips tightened and her eyes contracted. There were pinpoints of sweat on her nose and a scowl on her face. She felt afraid that she might evaporate into nothingness, just pass out, a sagging heap of flesh dissolving under the pressure of the child in her belly.

She wanted to harden her mind so that she could save herself, but the mind is the body and the body mind, so that the will to power over her soul only rigidified her flesh; and she lay in a tense, unbending pose.

In moments, however, her ego dissolved under the impact of further waves of pain. And now she was gasping for breath, a helpless, grey bird, smothered by the overwhelming forces that rose from her belly, the powerful music of her distended entrails drowning her resistances through a series of involuntary shrieks.

'Oh god, oh my god!' she cried out.

And then, as though the invocation of the Deity had put her in touch with heaven from the drugged stupor of her brain, there arose glimpses of random visions, configurations formed by the specks of cloud on the blue sky. Beyond the haze of delirium in her eyes, there stood the picture of an enormous woman lying down flat. And it seemed to her as though this woman in the clouds was also in the travail of childbirth.

Suppressing her groans, urged by deep curiosity and the superstitious belief that heavenly powers often appear to help human beings in their time of trouble, she stared hard at the hulking form. The image seemed to change and get fixed before her in the shape of the Goddess Kali, recumbent in her benevolent mood by the side of the crouching God, Shiva. And she felt a sudden wave of resentment that her husband was not by her side, seated there, helping her. He had known that she was nearing her time. In fact, he had known it this morning because she had tossed about from side to side restlessly all night. And yet he had rushed off to work, leaving her to bear the pain all alone... Oh, if only, only... if she could touch a sympathetic hand, or limb - oh anything, if only she could clutch a straw to help while the excruciating pain gnawed at her entrails and twisted her from hip to hip...

But she turned her face away from the clouds in the sky and cursed herself for thinking ill of her husband, the lord and master whom her parents had married her off to and whom they expected her to worship. And then she thought of the joy she had had when he had come to her on the night that she conceived his child.

Senses emerging from indifference and the fatigue of the day's work like a rich perfume drugging her body into excitement. Aroused vitals urging her strong buttocks against the pressure of his body. Surging of warmth in her belly and under her breasts, even as there was this heat inside her now, melting of mouth to mouth... And then the soporific faintness in the head, not unlike the giddiness that possessed her in this childbirth. Sighing, eyes half closed, limbs taut, enraptured at the swirling of his maddening strokes, smothered...

She could recall the feelings of those moments with a strange clarity on the curve of her present pleasure and pain, she could sense in the spell of writhings in her haunches the swelling and unswelling of passion. Only, the pain was gradually reducing her to pulp till her eyes were closing against her will and she was shrieking...

'Oh mother! Oh my mother!' she cried, panting for breath as though she was suspended between life and death. And, for a moment she lay back exhausted as though she could not go on with it.

Then, with clenched teeth and a deliberate intent to control the spreading panic in her limbs, she raised her head and sat up in a crouching position.

Daggers of shooting pain seemed to plunge into her sides as though each nerve had sharpened into steel. Crushing weight of centuries of anguish seemed to press on her belly. And there was the endless grain-grind of a churning of the oceans inside her, the crushing of worlds over her head and the struggle of random enelements, each shooting pain emerging out of the source of energy in her belly into a storm-tossed outer universe. Perspiration simply poured down her face now and blended with the pressure of the elements that dug pinpoints of heat into her flesh.

'Oh, come come, child come,' she cried out aloud almost like an incantation. 'Come, come my babe,' she whispered even as she had breathed love words on the night that the seed was sown.

And she hardened her body so that the tenderness in her could be released, whipping her buttocks with her hands, striking the sides of waist, swaying to and fro, gritting her teeth and hissing till she felt her haunches sagging and her bones twisting, till she could see her frame being pulled by elemental forces which seemed to have come and taken possession of her, the opposite tensions arising from nothingness and swaying like a strange and heavy rhythm of the earth's primitive energies.

With a smile on her face, a grim smile, she held her head in her hands and lay back in the position in which she had first fallen. And, beckoning all the resources of her will, collecting the tension of her nerves in her clenched fists, she strained and heaved in a series of protracted efforts. The heavy smell of an extraordinary drowsiness sustained her as involuntary tears rolled down her cheeks and she groaned. The twistings and turnings of her waist contorted her body into a strange amorphous shape. And, above the protuberance of her churning stomach, her heart beat like the echo of all the throbbings of previous months...

At last after an hour of torment as she lay drenched in a pool of blood and *aus,* she felt a boundless surging overwhelm her.

And, with a twitch of horror which faded into a mute triumph, the child came with a thin little cry, a dark bundle of tender, wrinkled flesh, a boy breathing softly but tingling with warm life.

Clutching him with eager, deft hands, she performed the services of the midwife on herself with the cool, assured touch which only the old *dai*, Kesari, in her native village, was known to bring to her task. And, what was most surprising, even to her, was the fact that having cut the naval strings which united her child to her with the rough end of the silver *hansli* round her neck, she emptied the basket in which she carried the food, donated the *roti* to the birds as a gift-offering, put her baby in it and strode forth towards the Ridge to go and break stones.

The darkness of the twilight sky was crumbling and the early morning sun had brightened the sky. But, as Parvati approached the pitch where she worked, the other stone breakers could not recognise her, because she looked different with the basket in her arms rather than on her head as she usually carried it. When, however, she came and laid the whining child at their feet, they were breathless with wonder. 'A witch this Parvati!' an old woman said, 'To be sure, a demon!' a man remarked.

'To be sure!' added Ramu, her husband coming towards the basket to have a look at his child.

'The Goddess helped me in my travail,' whispered Parvati. 'I saw her in the clouds....'

The women left their work and rushed towards her, some open mouthed, some with prayers and incantations on her lips.

'Stop all this *cain cain,*' shouted her father-in-law as he came up from where he had been tarring the road to look at his grandchild. 'Get away', he said with a bluff of rudeness. 'It is no wonder that she had the little one all by herself. She is a peasant woman with strong loins like many other peasant women of our parts, who have given birth to sons all by themselves, so that our race can be perpetuated and our land tilled for grain...' And he picked up the whining baby from the basket like a practised hand and put the little shrieking one to his shoulder, saying with a gruff tenderness: 'Come, come, my lion, my stalwart, don't weep... come, it won't be so bad. Come, my son, perhaps with your coming, our luck will turn...'

❑❑❑

Of Cows and Love

Atul Chandra

The day seemed to be preparing for a sundowner. A small herd of cows grazed leisurely along the thin strips of green on the other side of the road adjacent to my house. My neighbours had not stirred out. Nor was there any passer-by in sight to break the monotonous stillness.

I do not know how long I stood there before realising that I had been watching cows. What a moronic pastime, I told myself. Yet I stood there, arms resting on the cold iron of the gate, watching cows.

I felt lonely and miserable. Involuntarily I searched for the line of happiness on my palm. What have I done to deserve this fate, I mumbled? This was not the first time that I had put this question to myself. Like always, there was no answer. I looked skyward for the bluebird of happiness to fly by. It was nowhere to be seen.

Suddenly, a cow's frantic cry startled me. My eyes turned in the direction of the cow tottering towards my house, tail up, eyes popping and froth at the mouth. I caught a glimpse of a swift, slithering movement in the grass. Before I could say "snake" the cow fell right in front of me, sprawled across my gate.

'Oh Saba, what has happened?' I suddenly heard a shocked voice. It was Preeti's, who seemed to have just come out of the neighbouring house. 'What is wrong with this cow? Looks like it's dying,' she continued almost in the same breath.

'But how did it happen?' chimed in Prabha, the fat middle-aged woman popular in the colony as aunty, covering her nose and mouth with her *pallu* as if the fallen cow was stinking already and the germs would invade her nostrils.

I could see a glint of suspicion in her eyes as she gave me one of those penetrating looks of hers. I could immediately guess what was going on in her mind. It has become so easy to read people's mind these days. She must be thinking I had killed the cow. Just imagine!

I hate to use the word, but Prabha aunty is a bitch.

'It seems a snake has bitten her,' I explained, a little concerned about the cow and what I could do to save it. I knew I should drop some water on the thick, dark, protruding tongue. It would not have saved the animal but perhaps it could have reduced its suffering a wee bit... and brought salvation for these neighbours of mine. But their attitude forbade me from doing anything.

I could feel a silent, impotent rage rise within me. All that these women could think and whisper within earshot was how the cow had come to die in front of my house. As if the animal had a choice!

It was appalling. Despite the incidents of 1992, I never believed that religion could make people so inhuman and insensitive. Listening to their barbs made me feel sick.

'I think she must have poisoned it...' murmured Prabha aunty.

'These people are fanatics... all of them, even the women,' whispered Suneeta, who had studied with me in the university. In those days I had found her not only tolerant but also warm and friendly. She used to argue for amity between our two religions and talk of Lucknow's composite culture.

Today it was a different Suneeta. Perhaps this was the real Suneeta. The transformation was indeed hard to believe.

'*Chhi, chhi*, how could a cow die in front of her house,' said Sadhvi incredulously. She did not seem to care about my hurt feeling or sad reaction. These women did not even bother to consider how rabid their thoughts and utterances were.

The irony was that I belonged to the place. I was not new to them nor they to me. I had lived there for thirty years, growing up with some of them, sharing meals and friendly embraces on *Holi* and *Id*.. Yet at the moment they all seemed bent on making me feel like an alien.

In our teens when we would discuss boys, we would never talk of religion. Looks and intelligence were the traits which some of us *mohalla* girls found attractive in the boys we knew and pined for.

That was then... years ago. It's different now. The heart really has its reasons. And the mind is where the fallen angel often finds refuge.

By now I was seething with anger and could hold it no more.

'So what if it has died in front my house?' I burst out. 'I have not touched it to make it untouchable for you all. Don't you worship it?... Can't you pour a few drops of Ganga *jal* or just tap water?... You all have warped minds to be thinking like this...' I thought I would go on and make a spectacle of myself.

Since they had known me for so long, they were also familiar with my temper. Of course I was certain that my losing cool would not spark off riots... just as the death of this cow outside my gate would not. And it didn't. They simply made a face, gave me angry, piercing stares and walked off.

Their turning their backs on me did not work like a coolant. My blood pressure was still high and another incident flashed through my mind.

Prabha aunty had come over to my house one evening about three months ago. She had a bad cold and my mother asked me to make *tulsi ki chai*, the age-old prescription for common cold.

Thinking that I would have to go to someone's house to get *tulsi* leaves, Prabha aunty asked me not to bother. I told her, 'Aunty it will be no trouble at all as we have a *tulsi* plant in our house.'

In total disbelief and with her usual sarcasm she said, '*Haan bhai, kalyug hai na*.' It took me some time to figure out what was so strange about a *tulsi* plant prospering in my house.

I took her to a corner of my lawn where stood a bushy, green *tulsi* plant. Prabha aunty was both disappointed and jealous. What is a *tulsi* plant doing in the house of a non-Hindu? As if plants and animals were classified on religious lines!

'Saba,' she blurted out crudely, 'why don't you give this plant to me... it should be in my house and not yours, don't you think so? I don't know what is wrong but *tulsi* plants don't survive in my house,' she added rather dejectedly.

'That's precisely the reason why you shouldn't ask for it,' I said. 'Besides, aunty, it is a medicinal plant and for that reason anybody can grow it,' I quietly told her while plucking a few leaves.

After this, whenever she came to our house, Prabha aunty would find an excuse to go to the lawn and look at the *tulsi* plant with envy. Each time she would unabashedly repeat what she had said on first seeing the plant, 'This should not have been in your house.'

It was irritating. I offered to get her another plant but she wouldn't agree. I decided not to let her go anywhere near the lawn. Finally, she took the sensible decision of not coming to my house at all. It made me happy and I did not bother to find out if she also felt the same.

The cow had by now turned into a carcass. What should I do? These people who are ready to shed blood over a cow are not even concerned about it when it is dying. Their annoyance was over the animal dying in front of my house. That had deeply hurt their religious sentiments. I know they would not have touched it anyway.

The problem was getting the carcass removed. It was blocking the way to my house and I had to find a scavenger before it was too late. There was no other way but to go looking for one.

I locked my house and went to see if Radheyshyam, my rickshaw-man, was around. Fortunately, he was. I told him about my problem. He said he knew somebody and agreed to take me to him. At this time of the day he would charge a lot of money, Radheshyam warned as I sat on the rickshaw.

I was not worried about money. My only worry was what if the man refused? Radheshyam took me to a narrow lane where pigs lolled in filth in one corner. Some children sat in a row, defecating. A short distance away men and women sat on *charpoys.* It was a world that had barely changed even as we entered another century with much fanfare.

The rickshaw stopped near a man in striped underwear, smoking a *bidi*. 'Kallu, *bahanji* wants to get a carcass removed.'

'Please remove it today as it is blocking the passage to my house. I am ready to pay you extra for it,' I pleaded.

'I will charge five hundred rupees,' he said without batting an eyelid. I was quiet for a while. Five hundred was a lot of money. But I had no choice. 'Okay,' I said feebly and Kallu did not waste any time in picking up a rope and hopping on to his bicycle.

Once there, Kallu parked his bicycle against a wall. He then tied the legs of the carcass with the rope and laboured hard to drag it to a vacant piece of land away from my house. 'I will do the rest tomorrow,' he assured me.

After paying Kallu and Radheshyam, I decided to take a shower.

The day's events had drained me physically and emotionally and I wanted to forget everything. Yet, as I lay in bed the rewind and play buttons in the mind's video got automatically pressed. I could see and hear those women talk in audible whispers.

Memories of the days when I was still young, and in love, came galloping. He and I had spent a good part of our lives together, walking across the rainbow into a world of prismatic beauty. My family had left the search of a suitable boy to me and I thought I had found one.

I realised my naivete when he told me that his family would not accept me as a daughter-in-law. I had woven all my dreams around him but he chose to hurl me from rainbow heights to the depths of loneliness. He awakened mental and bodily stirrings but left at the point where I could experience ecstasy. He did not marry me because I was from a different community. Our thoughts did not reflect religion. Nor did our breaths and emotions. I was shattered. But I accepted his verdict as *fait accompli* and set him free.

Even now his memory fills my mind and body with an indescribable emotional amalgam of pleasure and pain. I don't long for him. Yet, in some remote corner of my heart he is still there. Wrapped in folds of love. And I knew why I could not hate my neighbours.

The Road to Tikratoli

Shoy Lall

Somebody once told me that I live on one of the most beautiful roads in the world. Yet the road to Tikratoli, not unlike the events in my life that led me to it, is full of ups and downs. You drive through a variety of countryside once you leave the road of Ranchi and, starting with an outcrop of twisted and tortured rocks, which bear a striking resemblance to a deserted landscape on some alien planet, you roll down to a narrow bridge which spans a dry rivulet. Then you climb steeply to a single clump of bamboo, and to a solitary Jackfruit tree which look strangely out of place in the barren countryside.

From there, the road slopes downwards again to a brick kiln on your right, and then climbs steadily once more to a coppice of trees on a wooded hillock. Under the Sal and Eucalyptus trees, at this spot, you will pass a tribal graveyard, and a little mud hut where you can always get the local brew, and will then come into flat, open country with many thousands of small, square fields, crowded one upon another, as far as the eye can see. I call this "The Rice Bowl" for, during the monsoons, it is a vast, seemingly endless plain of tender green blades of rice. There are a couple of tanks, by the side of the road here, in which there is usually some water, but they have more weeds and lotus flowers in them than fish. There are no trees on this stretch of the road, save for a single, massive *Kusum*, which has an old, partly hollow gnarled trunk and twisted branches that seem to be forever reaching for the sky.

Every summer, this tree comes into bloom, and when it dons its cloak of brilliant red, it can be seen for miles. And you drive along the flat, straight road until you are suddenly among the hillocks again, and you branch off left, and begin the final gentle climb. You turn sharply right into the gates of Tikratoli, and you are at once in the midst of tall, cool pines, the leafy Cassias, the Gul Mohars, ever green Acacias, Jacarandas, Firs and Silver Birches. And you forget the world outside, the harsh eroded land, the dirt, the overcrowding, and the poverty in the neighbouring town.

The story of my farm, and the life I have chosen for myself in this quiet rural setting, is a very personal one; and the road which brought me to Tikratoli was, and still is, a long and varied one. It was a road which I struggled along, despite temptations to turn back and abandon for more lucrative offers from a crowded and smoke ridden city. It was a road I was compelled to take after a long, trying and expensive illness in Switzerland. And when I first stepped upon it, I took a journey into the unknown for, almost twenty years ago, I hadn't the faintest idea what starting a farm in India, from scratch, particularly on a shoestring budget, would entail.

If anyone had told me at the time, that it would involve converting myself into something of an architect, engineer and builder, accountant, entomologist, vet and animal husbandry man, agronomist, botanist, horticulturist and forester, all rolled into one, I would have felt deeply discouraged and dismayed, to say the least. Yet today, when I look back down that road, it seldom bothers me that, after so many years of farming and, more recently a few years in commerce and industry, I have gradually learned to be a jack of most trades while actually being master of none. Nor would I now ever dream of altogether forsaking my rural interests for urban ones, of leaving this quiet corner of the country, or of setting foot on any other road which might take me away from Tikratoli, or the simple village folk who live around me here. Admittedly, there have been times when I have been discouraged; when I have felt that this is a road without an end; when I have found the way strewn with boulders, with obstacles which have seemed insurmountable. But equally, there have been other moments when my road has unexpectedly skirted these, when I have found that it is sometimes better and more satisfying to journey down a road which has indeed no end.

And the people I have met all along the route have been helpful and kind. They have taught me that if the road rises, it also falls; that an outcrop of curiously twisted rocks at one spot, does not necessarily mean that there are boulders all along the way; that barren countryside can suddenly, unexpectedly, be replaced by cool, wooded knolls; that even adjacent to a quiet cemetery it is possible to find love and life and laughter; that in a parched and unyielding land, the lotus blooms in stagnant pools, even in the midst of burning summer; that at some stage of the journey, when you are hungry, and wonder where your next meal is coming from, there will always be a full rice bowl awaiting you; that a single flowering tree, however old, can provide you the cool, welcome shade you need; that if you should stumble and fall, there is always a pair of eager hands to help you to your feet, and that, sooner or later, after a hard day, you will climb that last hillock and come home to a well earned rest.

They have taught me to work with my hands, to smile calmly in the face of famine, to conserve water in almost every possible form, to sleep under a clear, starry sky, and to husband and respect the soil, even when it fails to yield. They have taught me to tell from the direction of the prevailing winds whether it is going to rain or remain dry, and to gauge from the chatter of the birds, the incessant drumming of the cicadas, exactly how many days away the monsoons are. They have taught me not to discard entirely, old beliefs, old values for new ones in a fast changing rural environment, but to successfully blend together the two so as to get, in the end, the best of both worlds. They have also shown me, through their tribal culture, through traditional custom and usage, how simple it is to take pride in a profession and a way of life, which is still largely looked down upon and regarded as a poor and an illiterate man's occupation in this country.

Twenty years ago when I first came to Tikratoli and started building my home, I was very much a bachelor. At that time, with my finances and my horizons rather limited, it did not seem even remotely possible to me that I would one day marry and acquire a ready made family. Yet, something of a sixth sense, if you can call it that, kept prompting me throughout the long years I spent building, to construct a house in which there would be room to breathe; a home which could be the pride of my family which might, one day, come after me to Tikratoli.

So I built myself something of a country mansion in these sylvan surroundings, never for a moment thinking that I would actually be thankful one day for having done so and spread myself out over the years and made myself quite comfortable. I had plenty of room and I encouraged friends to come and stay with me every so often in order to relieve the tedium and the monotony of a lonely life in the country.

During these years, while I was building Tikratoli, I also tried my hand at Journalism and, thanks to the encouragement and help I received from friends and colleagues, (in particular, the very valuable advice and assistance I received from one of the Editors of *The Statesman*) I was able to travel fairly widely and see something of farming in different parts of India, Australia and the UK.

Just when I thought my building days were over, (I have since built a complete home nearby for my sister and set up an entire Rubber Factory in Ranchi), fate played an unexpected part in my life and brought into it a young widow, already the mother of three children, whose family and mine had known each other for a great many years. Of the three children, the eldest was a girl of thirteen years, and the younger two twins, a boy and a girl, twelve year old at the time.

So I made a few structural alterations inside the house to give them each a little nook of their own, and we soon settled down to the joy of living together as a family. If Tikratoli was a nice, spacious and attractive bachelor's den, when I got married and acquired my family, it soon became a beautiful and a complete home. My wife and children filled it, bringing into it light and music and laughter, where before there had only been the sounds of silence, and the vacuum of many quiet summers—years of wasted hours.

Today, combining as I do my industrial and my agricultural pursuits, I race the Sun from east to west each day and view distantly, even more gratefully, all my yesterdays with a growing sense of tranquillity and fulfillment. Today, I watch the colours spring to life in my quiet garden, sit in the sanctuary of my restful home, far from the smoking chimneys and the smothering smog of industry, and see my children grow in salubrious surroundings, able to distinguish for themselves, proper values of life in both the city and the country. On all the winding roads that lead to Tikratoli, their myriad tracks and pathways, there are visible signs of movement and transformation. A stirring and an awakening.

And, despite the present economic crisis, the continuous famine of goods and services, the growing drain of rural youth to urban areas, the fact that the cost of living has almost quadrupled itself since I first came to settle in this quiet corner of the earth, the stars still come down like rain every night. And, at the end of each full day, I am still able to see through the settling haze of dust, count my innumerable blessings, give thanks, and stretch out my hands and touch the Face of God.

❑❑❑

A New Tomorrow

Neelam Kumar

Humming softly, Parvati picked up the last white jasmine from her slender lap and guided her needle through its delicate green stalk. Though her eyes had stood her in good stead these 59 years, they had now started watering and, something she was too vain to admit, had dimmed a bit despite the pink-rimmed glasses her son had bought for her from New York. The fragrant flower threaded perfectly into place with the others, transforming her garland into a work of art. The moment of completion never failed to stir her. When she twisted the crown of blossoms around her hair as she had been doing for over four decades now, it reminded her of the moon in full bloom.

Each morning, Parvati would wake up with the birds to follow her self-imposed routine of bathing, praying and decorating the entrance of her house with a well-practiced intricate pattern made from pounded, colour-soaked rice powder. Each morning, she plucked the scented blossoms to weave around her long plait. And each day she examined her work critically, resting only after she could detect no flaws. Thus it had been for the last 41 years of her married life. And thus it would be, she hoped, for as long as she lived.

Once done with all this, she then entered the kitchen to brew coffee just the way Shivaswamy liked it and begin the day's cooking - a routine she enjoyed immensely. This morning, she had packed her husband's lunch with special care - taking pains to make the curry appetizing without adding too much oil (in reverence to his rising cholesterol) and his favourite dessert delicious without adding too much sugar (with deference to his diabetes). Despite herself, a smile trembled on the edges of her lips. Perhaps this was the last time she would pack his tiffin. All day, as she went about her chores, the imp of a smile would suddenly jump out of her heart and make its way resolutely upwards until it lit up the shores of her lips before she sent it down forcibly within the confines of her heart.

Outside her two-roomed Madras house, evening was silently creeping in. She refused to call Madras by its new name - Chennai, just as she refused to call Calcutta *Kolkata* or Bombay, *Mumbai.* What would they re-name next, she wondered with indignation? The moon and sun above each city? The roll of the new names on her tongue felt unfamiliar and, in her routined existence, everything unfamiliar and unexpected was to be shunned. Defiantly, she created her own realities - of an era when love was spoken through the eyes and not through pelvic gyrations she saw on TV nowadays... when truth was an unchangeable value, not a commodity that changed colour, texture and meaning depending on whose hands it was in - a politician's or a policeman's.

The approach of evening always made her heart pound expectantly. She could hear the muted sounds of whispering waves nibbling on the shores of Adyar beach. The evening breeze wafted in the tinkling sounds of bells from the *Ashtalakshmi* temple nearby. On cue, she lit the gleaming ornamental brass oil-lamp in the prayer room. In the flickering lights, the divine faces of her familiar gods glowed back conspiratorially at her.

Today was an important day. The day when her husband Shivaswamy would retire as Construction Engineer from the city's reputed firm. How happy he had been when the age of retirement had been extended to 60! As if he had been granted a new lease of life and would remain king of his kingdom forever. She had smiled to see him so happy. But those two years, like all the others before them had also flown by. And today...

The front door unclicked open. He was back. This time she allowed that irrepressible smile of hers to have its will. She hurried forward to greet him. But this time, the unborn smile was speared back firmly into place by a frown. He seemed unusually disturbed.

Shivaswamy slumped down tiredly into the big brown armchair with its frayed yellow cloth cover and wobbly front leg. He had never found the time to get it repaired - even after she had once, during her pregnancy, fallen right over. Today, he felt truly defeated. Today, he felt truly lost. All these years he had considered his work to be his mainstay, his pride and his identity in life. As if driven by inner ghosts, he had relentlessly nourished his work with his heart and soul, concentrating only on getting his firm a big profit each time. His dedication had turned him into a legend. Stories abounded about how he had continued attending the crucial meeting even after receiving the news that his wife had gone into labour; of how he had stepped into the waiting train to go to the important Conference even after being informed of his son's fracture.

Shivaswamy's climb up the executive ladder had been strewn with numerous obstacles, more than his share of treacheries and the occasional successes. It was the treacheries that had given him unbearable pain. Men he had helped get a professional footing, colleagues he had granted personal favours to—it was their backstabbing that had hurt him immensely. Some had cleanly blanked him out when he had needed their support most. Others had trampled on him to move further ahead.

But hadn't he always known it was a ruthless world out there? Why then was he feeling so cynical? Perhaps because in their own discreetly cruel manner, they had succeeded in making him feel OLD. Old enough to have outlived his usefulness. Especially today - on his last working day, his heart had ached at their impatience about seeing him out quickly so that they could claim his table, chair and room. Oh yes, there had been a few pretty speeches made but now, confident in the knowledge that he could take no official action against anyone, they had spoken laughingly of his Hitlerian ways and his strangely obsessive workaholic character. Why did he feel a stab in his heart when they greeted the new incumbent - a youngster he had painstakingly groomed but finally given up on, after discovering that he was just a dishonest fast-buck making wheeler-dealer? All the same, he joined in their thunderous applause made in the new man's honour - even smiled when they said he would 'usher in a new era full of much-needed vitality and dynamism which would be a welcome change from the constricted, outdated values the firm had been forced to follow until today.'

Somewhere along the years, he had forgotten that nobody was indispensable. He had forgotten that the new and the glittering always swept away the old and the fading. Yet, why did he not feel retired? Wasn't his mind supposed to have stopped ticking the moment his superannuation orders came? Weren't his fingers expected to forget the way he signed his name with a flourish and rubber-stamped it with a decisive thud the moment the clock struck 5 p.m.? Why did his fingers still itch to ring the call bell to beckon the peon to arrange the files systematically or call out to his colleague for a last-minute advice nobody wanted? The treachery of his body disgusted him. He felt like a high-speed sprinter suddenly forced to confine himself to a wheelchair all his life. Before him stretched the bleak prospect of interminably idle, inactive days. He knew he would never start a 'consultancy'—a front for crumbs of charity - like his other retired colleagues had ventured into and given up after becoming unwanted, shrivelled up, bitter old men.

Parvati watched him silently, as he sipped the steaming hot coffee she handed him, absorbed in his thoughts. With a start she realised he had turned 60 and she, 59! Where had time flown? Was it not only yesterday that she had been a radiant young bride on the brink of life? Had she really once been that sprightly, vivacious young girl who had jumped at the prospect of a job in a reputed Bank? The job had been necessary to tide over the financial constraints they found themselves faced with at the beginning of their marriage. But she had laughingly given it up when their son Kartik and daughter Puja had been born. The pain of that decision had jabbed at her heart but had never escaped her lips.

Since then, she had been sucked into the vortex of family responsibilities, incessantly feeding, clothing, coaxing, cajoling. It was only sometimes, when her husband had been away on tours and the children away at school, and later college, that she had felt her soul light up with a secret fire. Wistfully, she would think of what she could have been had she not let her brains go down the kitchen sink. Like a cool misty monsoon shower, the thought of Vinay would envelop her. Vinay, who decades back had looked deep into her twinkling eyes and had said, 'I can see the rainbow colours of your soul, Paro. These are the colours I want to make mine.' But instantly, with a twinge of guilt at her own disloyal thoughts, she would push the memory away and focus her mind on making the spotless white shirt a shade more spotless and the well scrubbed floor a trifle shinier. She had discovered that there was nothing like routine to keep your mind away from wayward thoughts.

In the ensuing years, she had loved her husband with a fierce loyalty - even though he had been so work-absorbed and so far away emotionally. To her, love was not the heady emotion of youth that depended on the freshness or the tautness of the flesh. It was the serene emotion that remained with you after the youthful fires had been quenched and the roller-coaster hungers of younger days had been dealt with. It was the joy you felt at the familiarity of the morning sounds of your partner's inevitable sneezing (six to start the day!) and the familiar irritation you felt with his neighbourhood-shaking yawns (four to end the day!). It was the concern you felt when his eyes looked puffier (indicating that the blood pressure was higher that morning) and the fear that gripped you when his hands trembled (indicating that Parkinson's could be just a diagnosis away). Even their occasional 'coming together' were affectionate trips across well-travelled terrain. It was this familiar routine which she clutched on lovingly to and supposed was what people called love.

Both her children had been married — Kartik in New York and Puja in California. On their invitation, she had gone to stay with them, to 'play with her grandchildren' - the flesh of her flesh. But to be honest, these spells away from home had saddened her. For she longed to be in her own house with her husband, even if in the rush of everyday living, they found little time for each other. Little time to share the simple joys of life. To express their caring and concern.

If she were really honest with herself, she would have admitted that she had been reduced to a mere cook and housekeeper in her children's home. How could she explain the difference in cooking in her own house and theirs, under the guise of being 'on vacation'? On weekends, ofcourse, they would make an effort to take her along the sea-coast and 'for a spin around town to see the lights' but deep down she knew that they were ashamed to show her to their friends because of 'this peculiar length of cloth you insist on wrapping yourself with' and 'the quaintly accented English you insist on speaking in.' If truth were to be told, she was also upset at their change of names to Ken from Kartik and Patty from Puja.

But it was just not their fault, she always told herself. One had to move with the times. So when her children's letters did not arrive during her illness or his, and when they conveniently forgot their parent's birthdays and anniversary, she always rationalised about how busy they were. Ofcourse they loved their parents, but where was the time? Nowadays everyone was so wrapped up in his own family problems that it was just not possible to care in the old world manner of caring. They were wonderful, loving children, but if anyone was to be blamed, it was these crazy times, certainly not they.

The truth was that at the end of life's journey, it was just you and your partner, if you were lucky to still have him or her by your side. Parvati looked tenderly at hers. Today he looked dreadfully weary. Tremulously, she reached out a furrowed hand and put it gently on his bony shoulder. Their eyes met and she smiled lovingly, the missing side tooth lending the smile a luminous warmth.

Her silent gesture of understanding moved him. He looked at the work-worn, aged hands, stamped with the complicated network of time. Yes, the rigours of housework and the years of penny-pinching had made her age quickly. Would anyone imagine that these hands had once been delicate saplings he had longed to touch? And that face! Why had he never noticed the rivulets of wrinkles that criss-crossed it? Would anyone believe that this was the enchanted golden cup he had once so eagerly caressed and drunk deeply from? With a start he realised that time had tricked them.

'My God! in all these years, we have hardly been together,' he realised with a start.

She had been busy raising their children, getting them married and then raising the grandchildren. And the stark pall of old age had quietly descended on her. As it had on him.

It had been a proud day for them when Kartik had landed himself a job in New York and had asked his mother over, to look after the youngest one for a while. Shivaswamy suspected that Parvati had been really hurt by her daughter-in-law's impatient admonitions during her stay there. No, she had said nothing. But the hurt swam in her big, black expressive eyes. Like directionless lotus flowers in a pond, snapped off their stems.

He felt a great rush of tenderness for her. Though her once plump skin was collapsing on itself and the exciting curves were giving in to the pull of gravity, he was still amazed at how gracefully she had aged. The narrow waist, which he used to cover with loving kisses, now lay hidden beneath layers of flab, but from its mysterious folds she had borne him two wonderful children. Those long legs that once seemed to go on forever, now creaked with arthritis, but had stood by his side solidly through life's upheavals. 'How beautiful she looks,' he thought! This is the woman who had been there for him always. Even now, when others had deserted him. Strong and silent. Always giving. Demanding nothing. Not even his time.

Impulsively, he said, 'Let us walk to the beach.' In the distance, the sun was dipping into the horizon — a red orb of fire. It reminded him of the luminous red sun on his woman's forehead. They stopped awhile, hypnotized by the majestic beauty Nature was unfolding before them. Soon the western horizon would be painted in various hues of orange before surrendering to the spangled freckles of the night sky.

Never before had he philosophised on love. Why was he doing so today on the day of his retirement? There was something about the crispness of sea breeze that made you feel younger, he thought...and, if he dared to give the new emotion words - in love once again. But the love he was feeling now was not the hormone-induced madness of yesteryears. It was the comradeship of questions such as 'Do you remember when...?' or 'I wonder what happened to...?' popped at the person by your side who you could trust would dip into the common treasure trove of shared memories and say something long-forgotten or long-loved. Yes, true love was the pure essence of a thousand roses distilled in the receptacle of a lifetime's chaos, anxiety, pain, hope, dream and fulfillment. Nothing dramatic, it was just the sharing of the daily adventures of life. It was this cumulated *ordinariness* of shared events that transformed the concoction into a heady cocktail which could only be termed *extraordinary*. It was the glow of golden memories shared by two ageing bodies.

Standing by the water's edge, she gave in momentarily to the tickling of the waves on her feet and their insistent tug on her *sari*.. Instantly it brought back treasured memories of youth. It was strange how, when youngsters saw an aged couple they dismissed them as 'old geezers' who would not understand what love was all about. Little did they know that love was love in every season, every clime, and every age. Yet each succeeding generation continued to feel that they had exclusive monopoly on it. The truth was that even when the husk became withered, its kernel - the heart never really aged. In America, she had missed his gentle laughter, his familiar smell, the way she could look into his eyes and see the reflection of the desirable woman she once was. Age and Nature merely slowed one down, compelling one to give love another form. Wasn't love the pure music that rose from the depths of one's soul after the body had been spent?

To Parvati, true love was when the partners shifted from feeling *spousal* to feeling *parental* about each other. She now loved him as a mother loves her child - with a fierce sense of proprietorship and a tender sense of indulgence. Love was a gradual shifting from an obsession with the body parts to their sudden packing up. It was all about worrying whether the morning's medicine for various ailments had been taken or not. It was about wondering whether the tiring walk or the coolness of the air could induce another attack of asthma.

Where once you dwelled on thoughts of your lover's rose-bud lips (hers) and the strength of your lover's manliness (his), you now dwelled on the gaps in one's teeth, memory and hearing. Love was about noisy expulsions of the breath and the erratic ticking of the heart. It was about age-induced paunches and hunches. It was about the gentle popping out of your teeth and the loud disappearance of your acquaintances. And it was all about the increasing intensity of love despite all these....

The cool evening breeze played wantonly with her salt and pepper hair. Her daughter Puja had sent her a letter, inviting her to America. The newest arrival was on its way and she wanted her mother to look after the baby. 'House-help here is frightfully expensive, Ma' she had written. She was even sending a ticket, she wrote-but only for her mother. 'It's really expensive, Ma, I'm sure you'll understand' she had explained.

With a sigh, Parvati wondered whether she should discuss the matter with her husband. Kartik's infrequent letters home had proved that she had outlived her usefulness for him at least. How long would it be till her daughter felt that way too? No, this time she would not go at their bidding. For once she would live life on her own terms.

The children, being young, would find a way. They would chart their own paths. It was her man who needed her now. How could she explain her attachment to this 60 - year old retired man? To the world he was just another grey, bespectacled, balding old man. For her he was the very meaning of her existence.

With a sigh she came to a decision. No, she could not leave him now. Not even for a day.. He was as helpless as a child without her to cook for him and lay out his clothes. Surely his need for her was greater than theirs. No, I will not go this time, decided Parvati, coming to a final decision.

Beyond, at the *Ashtalakshmi* temple, myriads of oil-lamps glowed. Around them, the sea breeze whispered longings. Above, the stars rained down endearments. Tenderly, Shivaswamy reached over and picked up the ends of her blue silk *sari* which the breeze had playfully pulled down from her frail shoulders. In a forgotten gesture of youth, he bought a sweet-scented rose and fixed it lovingly on Parvati's hair. Sun, sea and sand merged into one. Time stood still.

The Eternal Man and the Ageless Woman. Shiva and Parvati. Everyman and Everywoman. They had been together since the beginning of Creation. They lived on in the hearts of each couple who grew old together.

The sun had dipped into the spacious expanse of water, transforming it to liquid gold. Tomorrow, it would rise again to unfold a new, glorious day.

Shyly, Parvati took her husband's proffered hand. The gentle hands which now looked like twisted oak branches, weathered and gnarled. In the gathering dusk, they walked together in silent companionship. Yes, their life together had just begun.

❑❑❑